N LEPP

'ST

THE FIELD

ARCHAIA™

RUST VOLUME ONE: VISITOR IN THE FIELD, October
2016. Published by Archaia, a division of Boom
Entertainment, Inc. Rust is ™ and © 2016 Royden Lepp.
All Rights Reserved. Archaia™ and the Archaia logo are
trademarks of Boom Entertainment, Inc., registered
in various countries and categories. All characters,
events, and institutions depicted herein are fictional.
Any similarity between any of the names, characters,
persons, events, and/or institutions in this publication
to actual names, characters, and persons, whether living
or dead, events, and/or institutions is unintended and
purely coincidental.

BOOM! Studios, 5670 Wilshire Boulevard, Suite 450, Los
Angeles, CA 90036-5679. Printed in China. First Printing.

ISBN: 978-1-60886-894-0, eISBN: 978-1-61398-565-6

Written & Illustrated by
Royden Lepp

Flatted by
VShane
Joanna Estep

Logo Designed by
Fawn Lau

Designer
Scott Newman

Original Series Editor
Rebecca Taylor

Collection Assistant Editor
Cameron Chittock

Collection Editor
Sierra Hahn

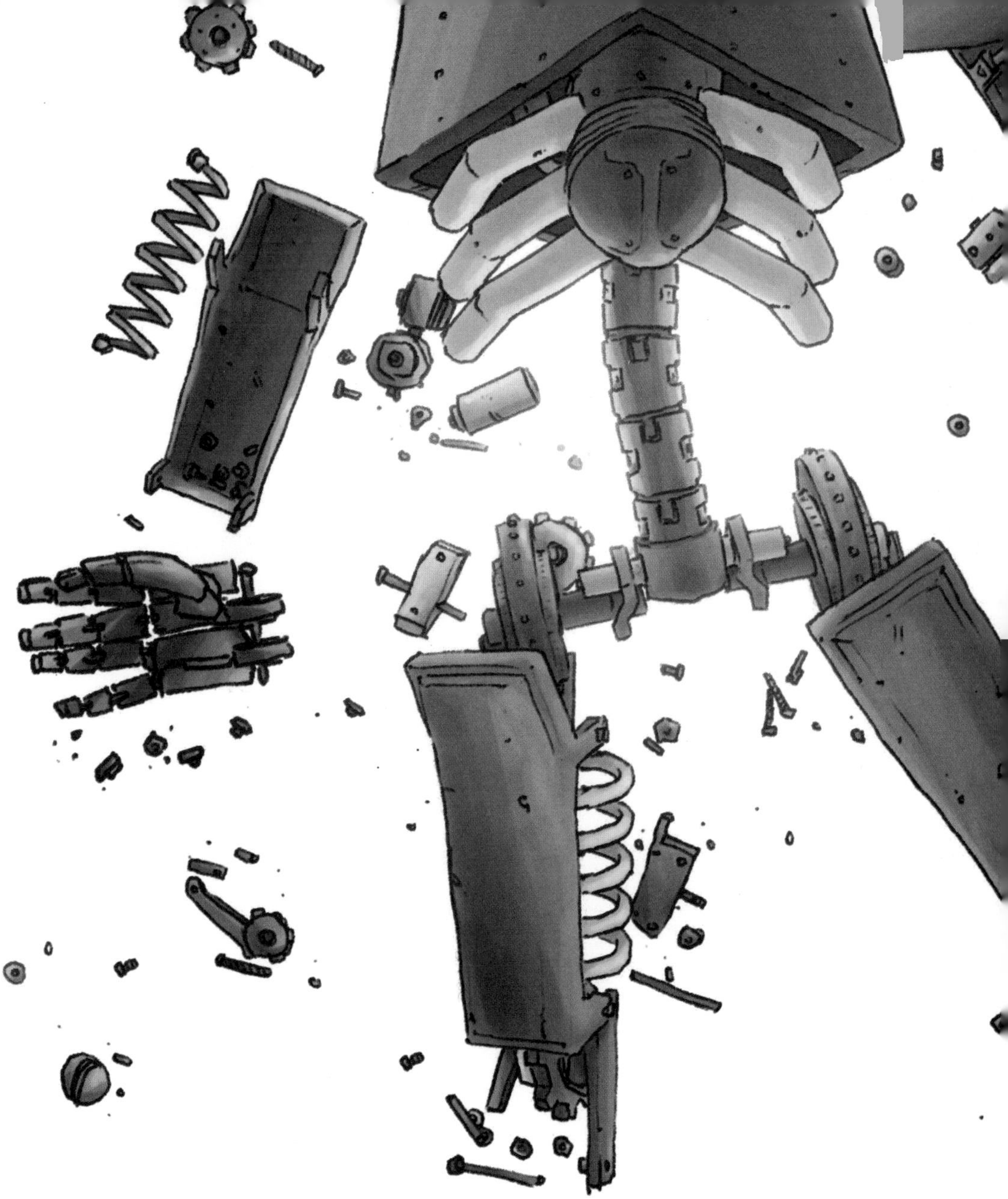

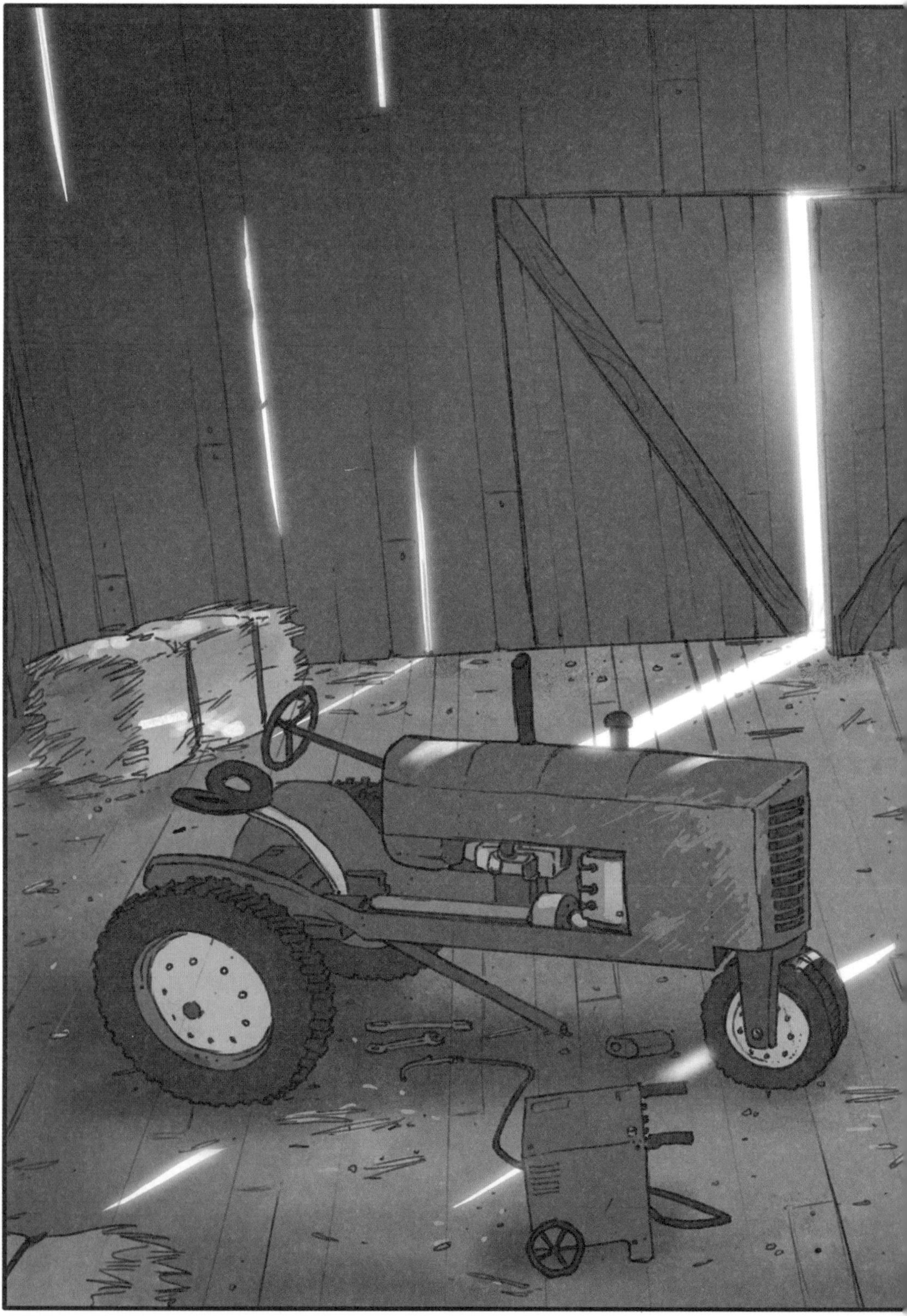

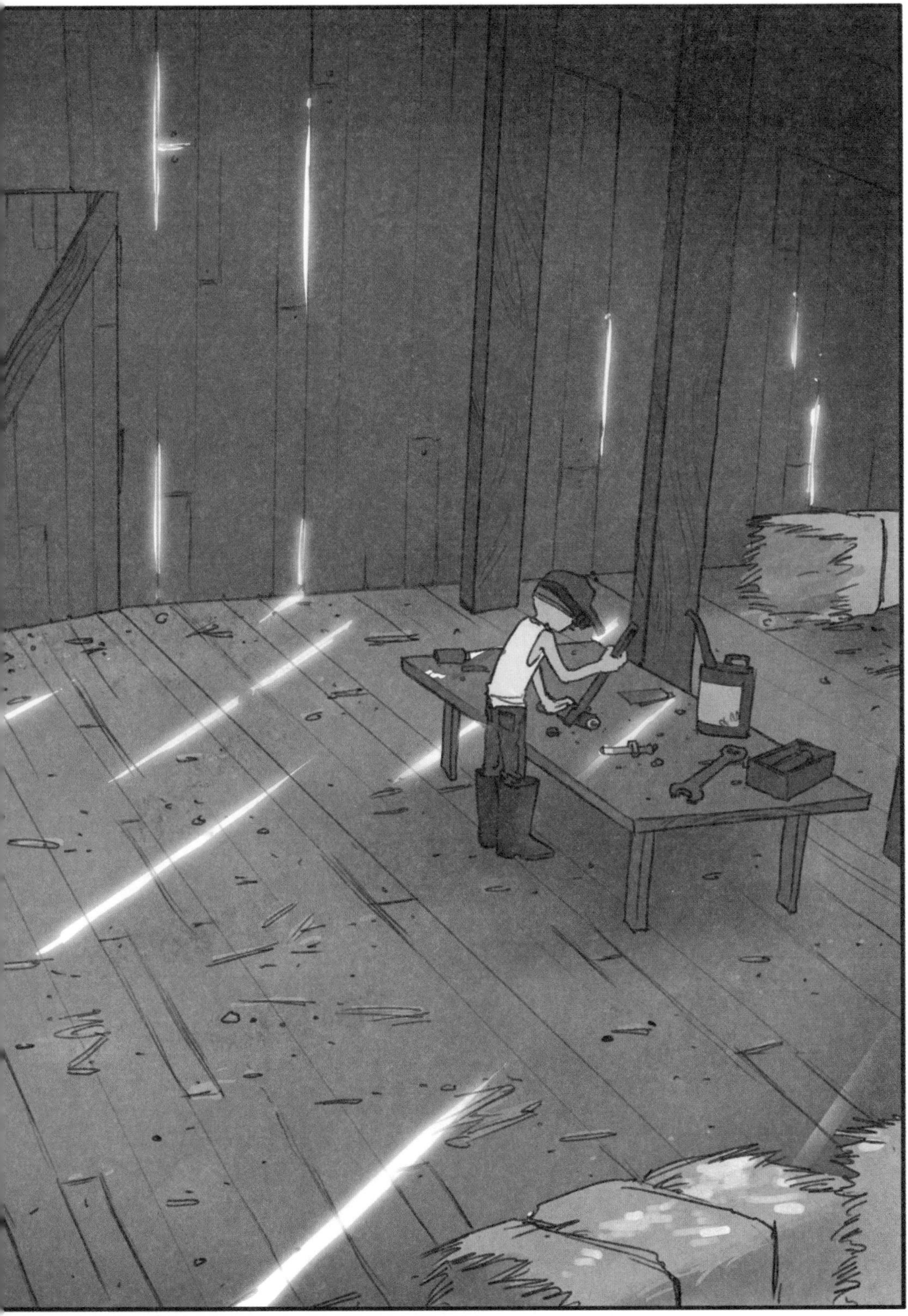

PRESENT. TAYLOR FARM.

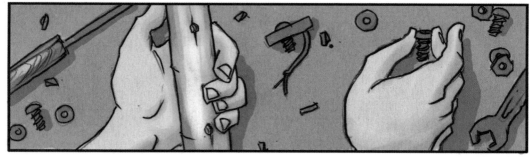

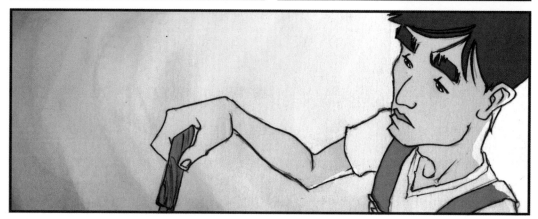

Dear Dad,

How are you?

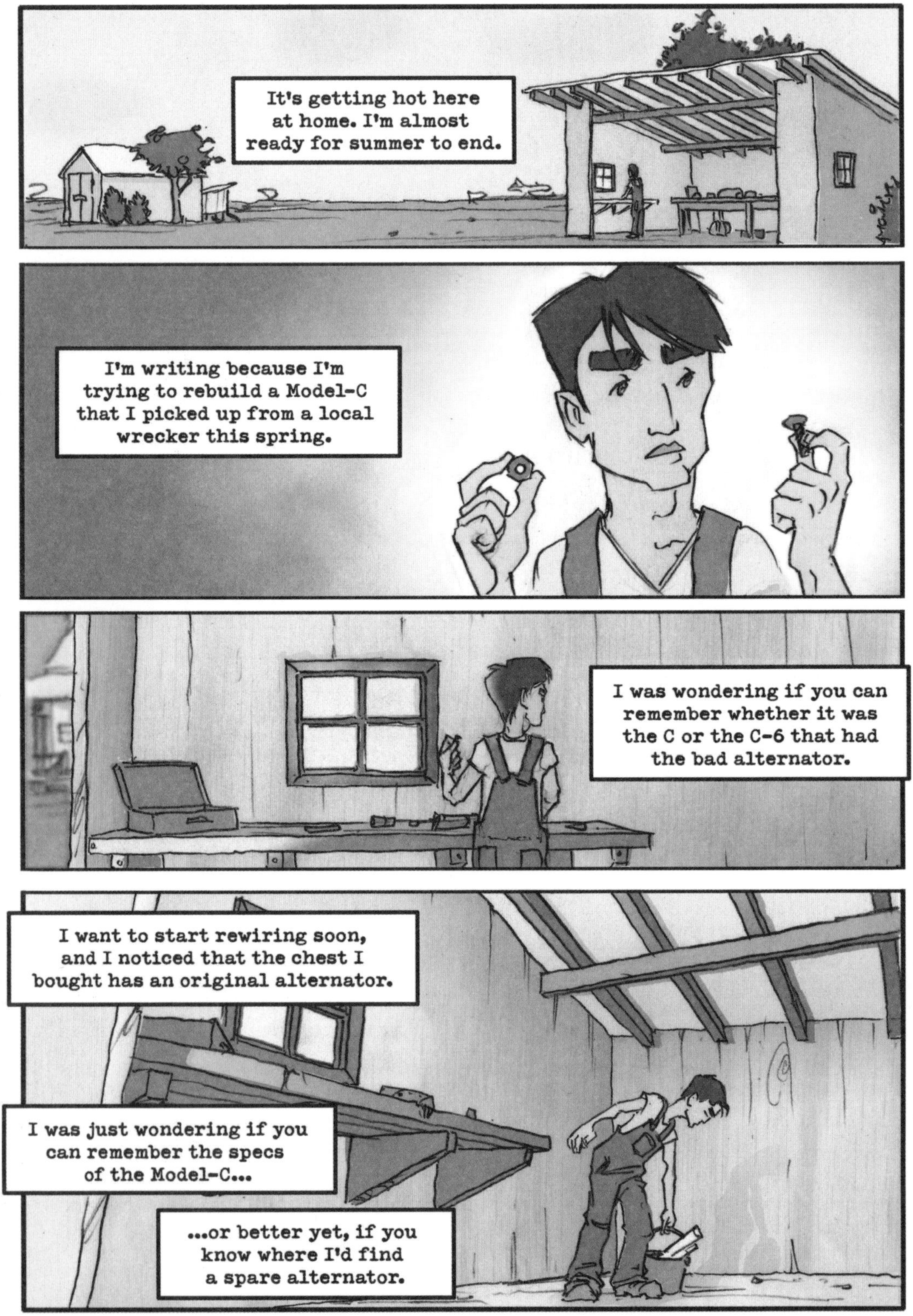
It's getting hot here at home. I'm almost ready for summer to end.
I'm writing because I'm trying to rebuild a Model-C that I picked up from a local wrecker this spring.
I was wondering if you can remember whether it was the C or the C-6 that had the bad alternator.
I want to start rewiring soon, and I noticed that the chest I bought has an original alternator.
I was just wondering if you can remember the specs of the Model-C...
...or better yet, if you know where I'd find a spare alternator.

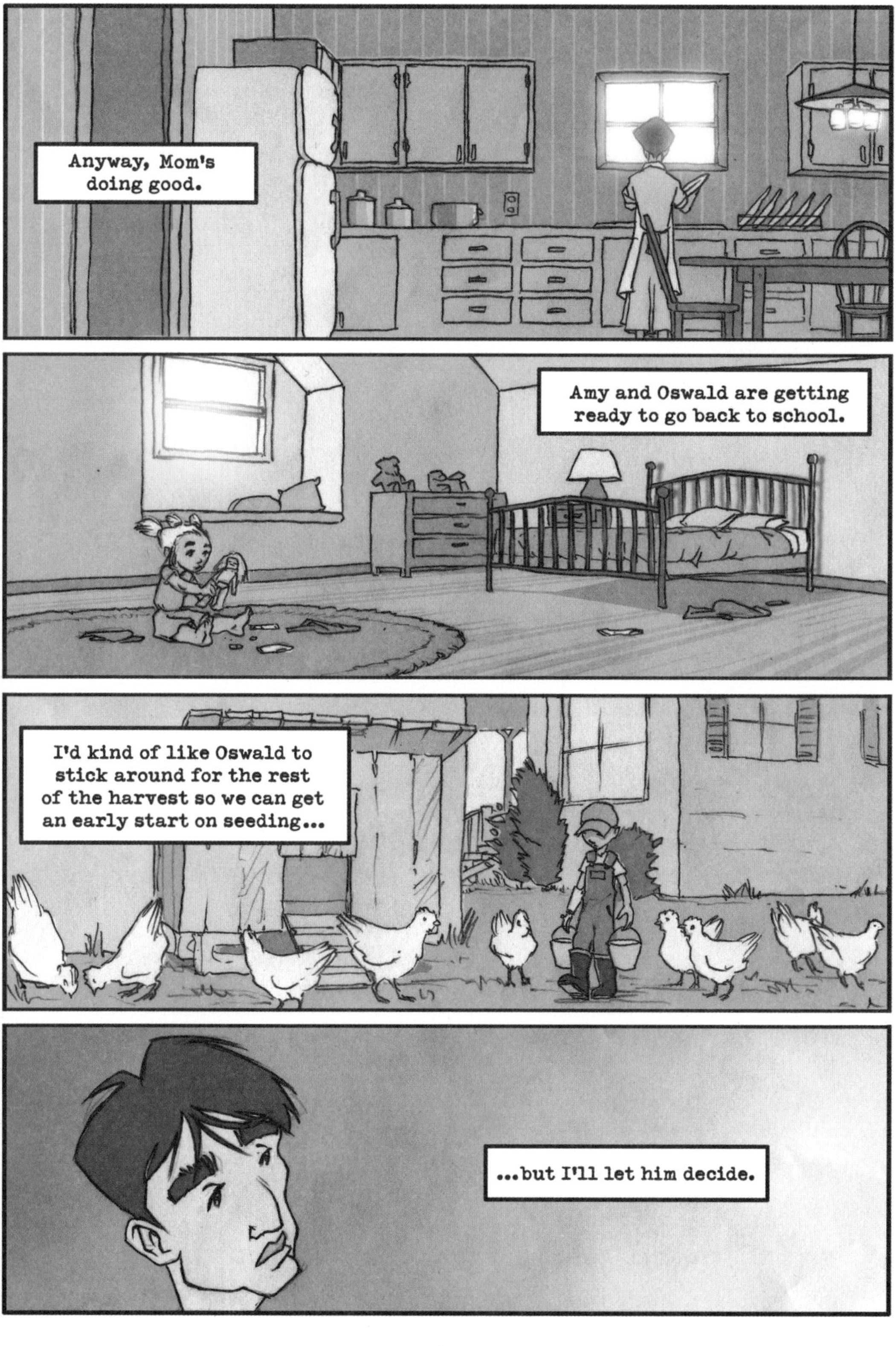
Anyway, Mom's doing good.
Amy and Oswald are getting ready to go back to school.
I'd kind of like Oswald to stick around for the rest of the harvest so we can get an early start on seeding...
...but I'll let him decide.

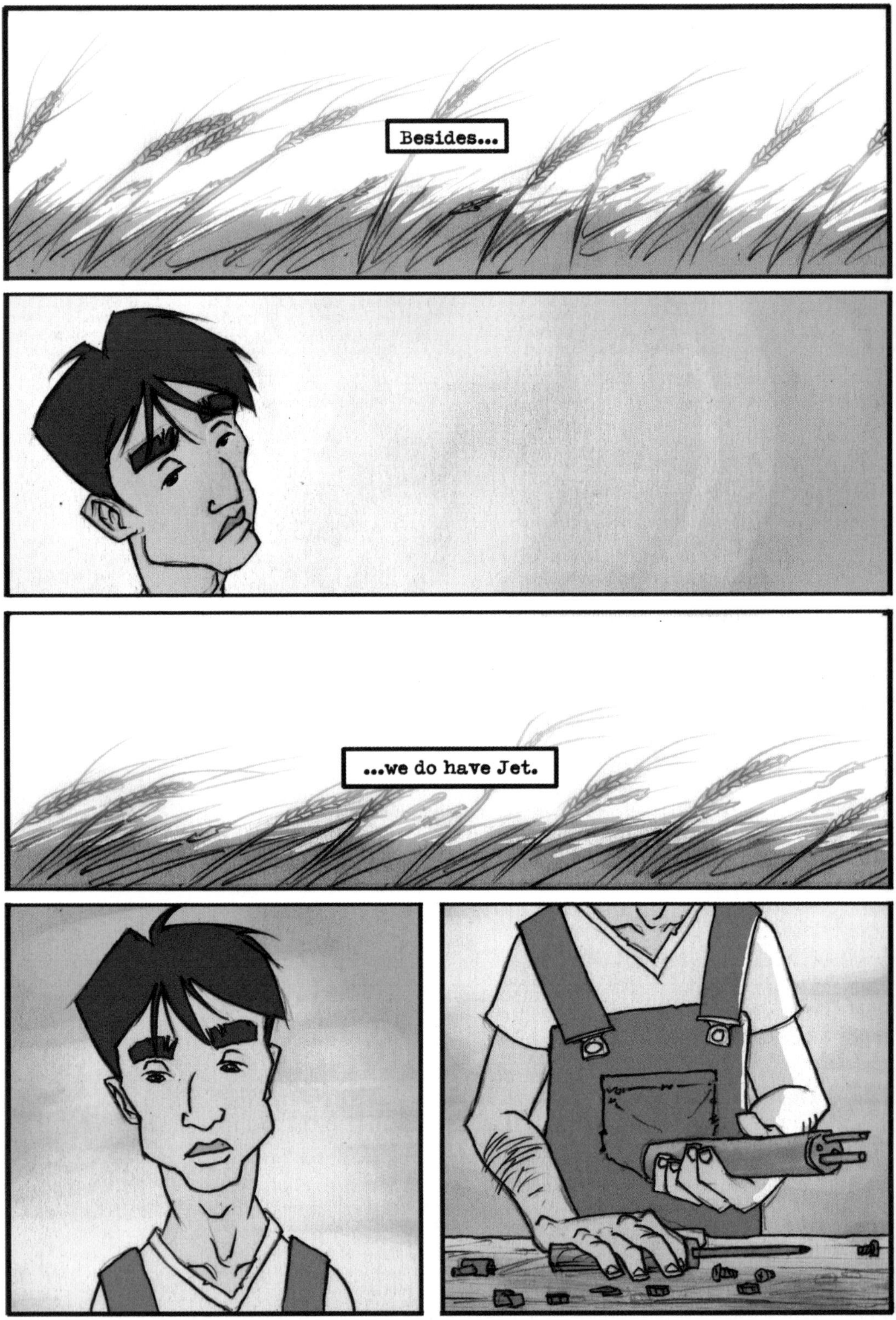
Besides...
...we do have Jet.

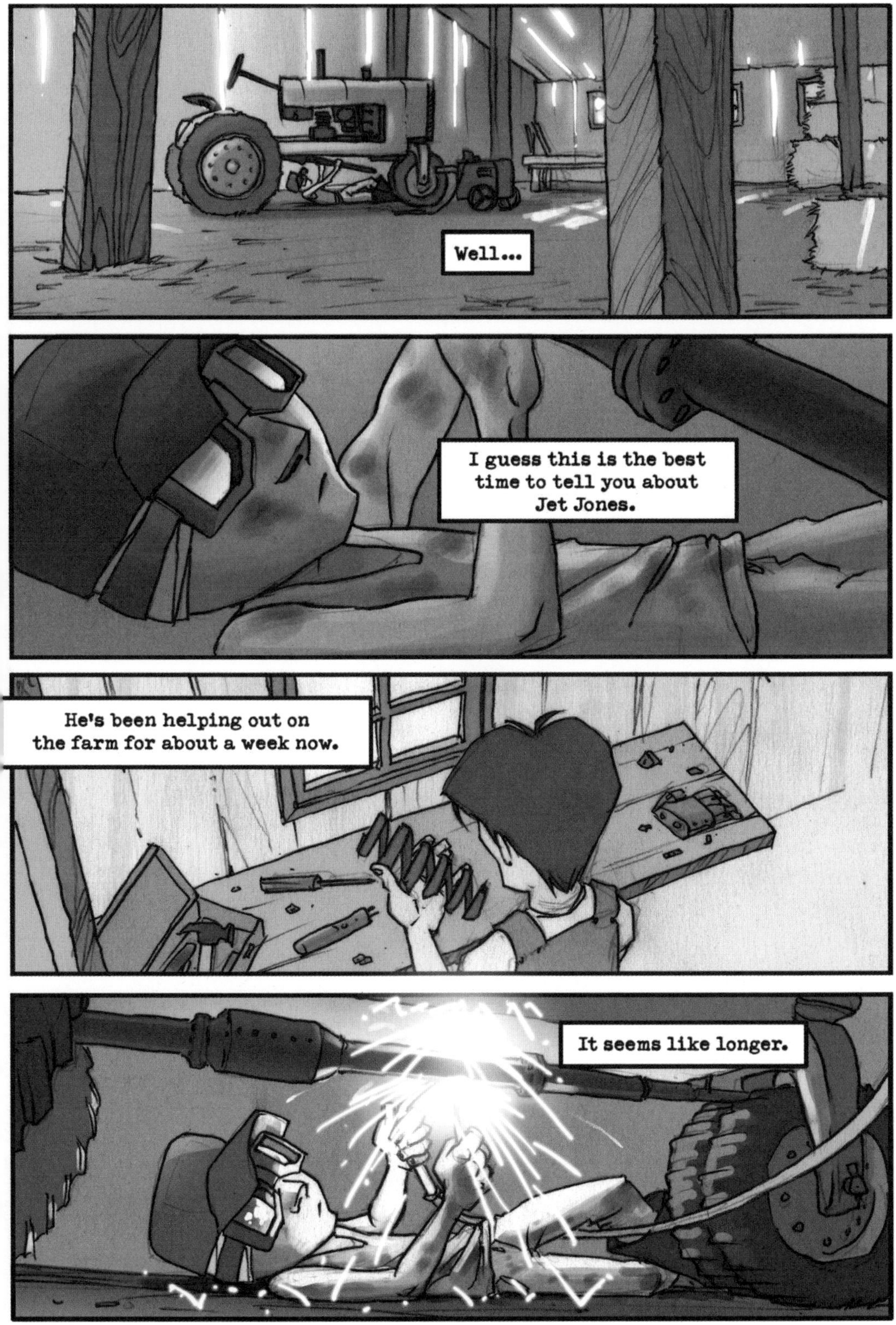
Well...
I guess this is the best time to tell you about Jet Jones.
He's been helping out on the farm for about a week now.
It seems like longer.

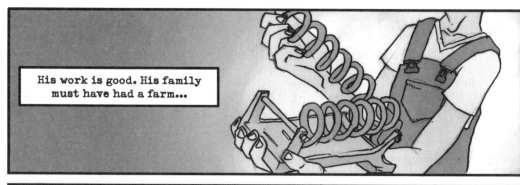

His work is good. His family must have had a farm...

...but I don't know for sure.

He never talks about where he came from. He never talks about where he's going.

He's trying to fix the tractor.

We had an accident.

He thinks he owes me.

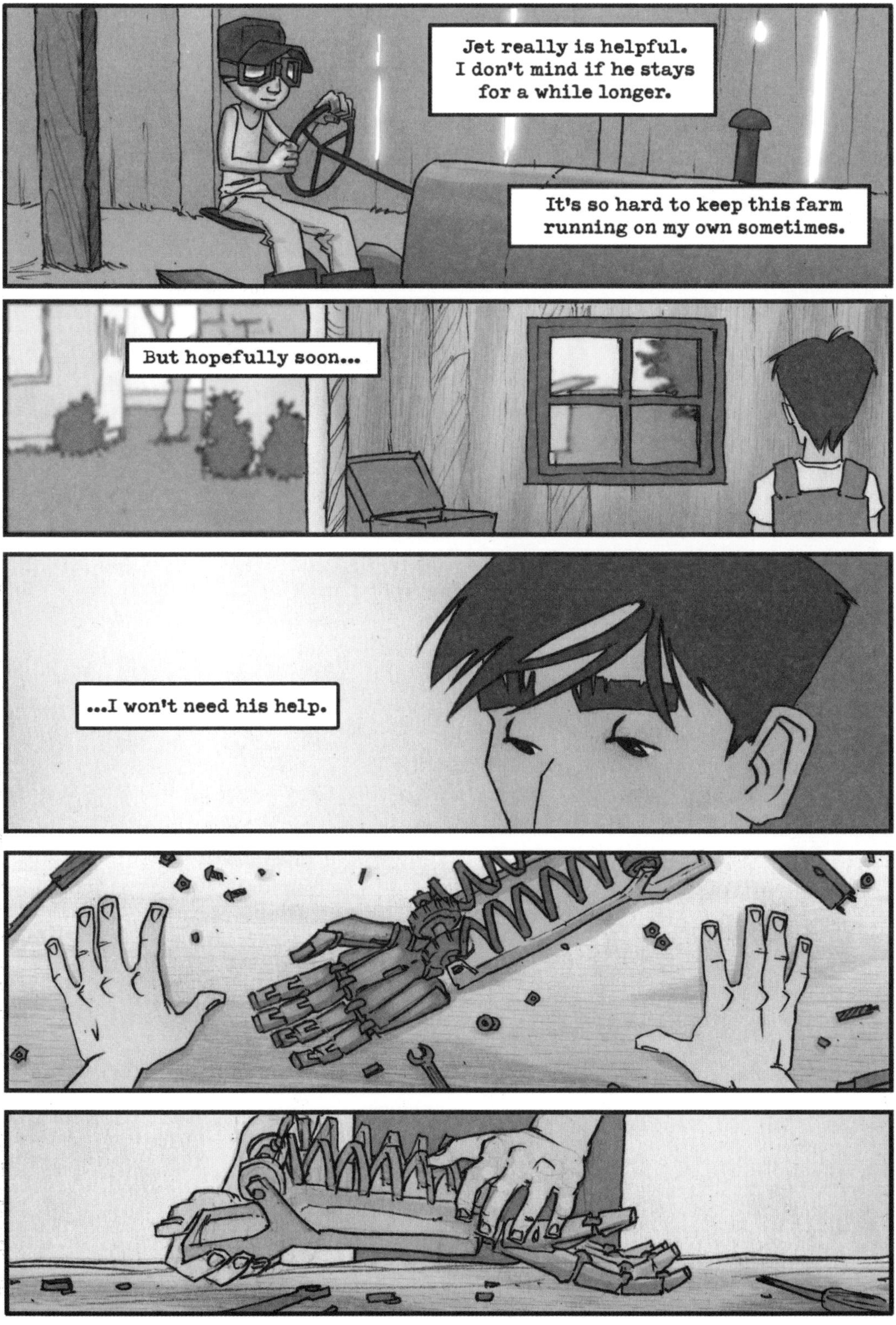
Jet really is helpful.
I don't mind if he stays
for a while longer.
It's so hard to keep this farm
running on my own sometimes.
But hopefully soon...
...I won't need his help.

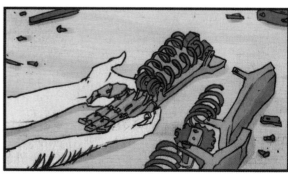

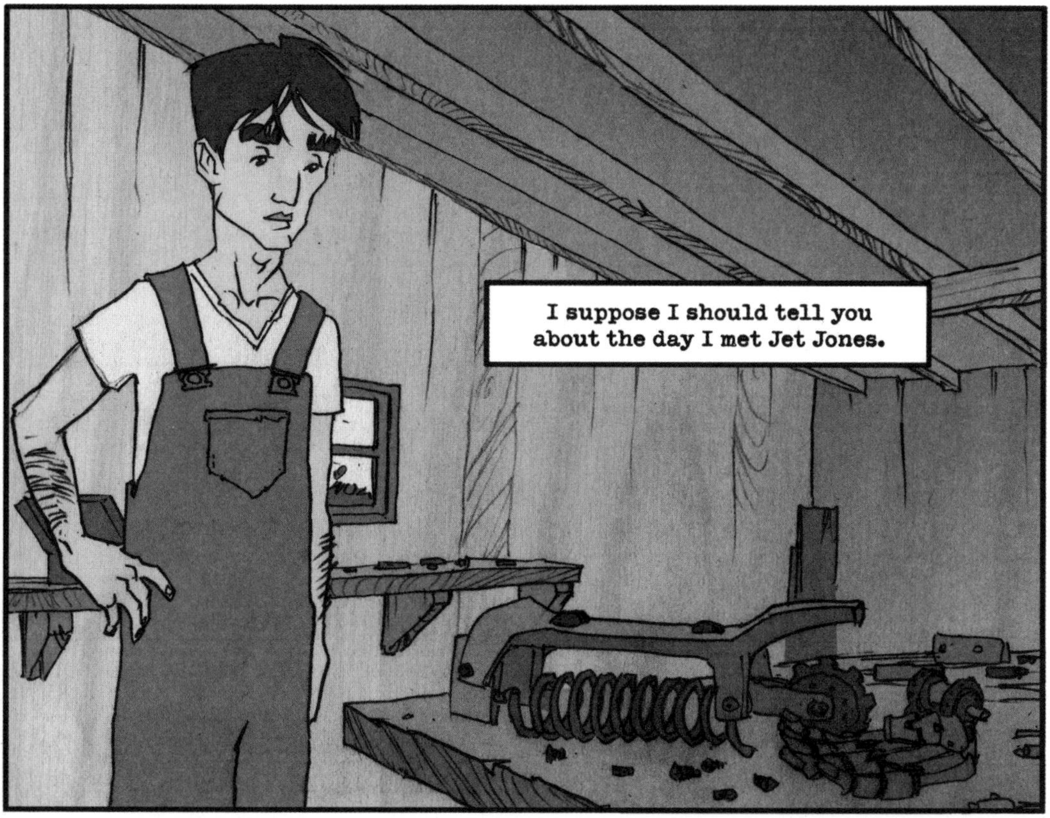
I suppose I should tell you about the day I met Jet Jones.

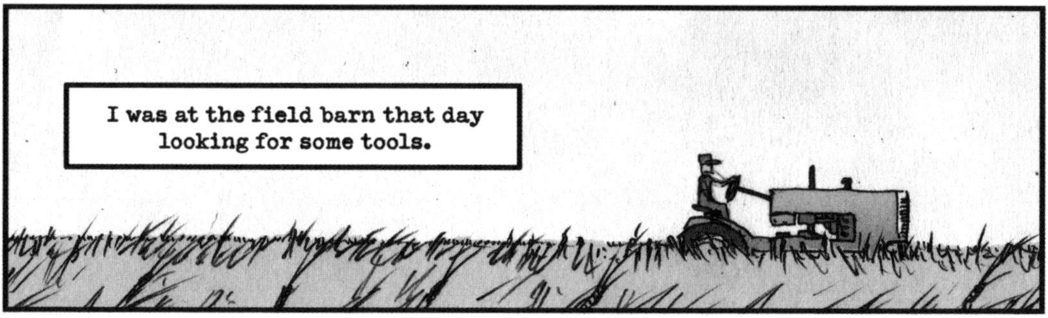
I was at the field barn that day looking for some tools.

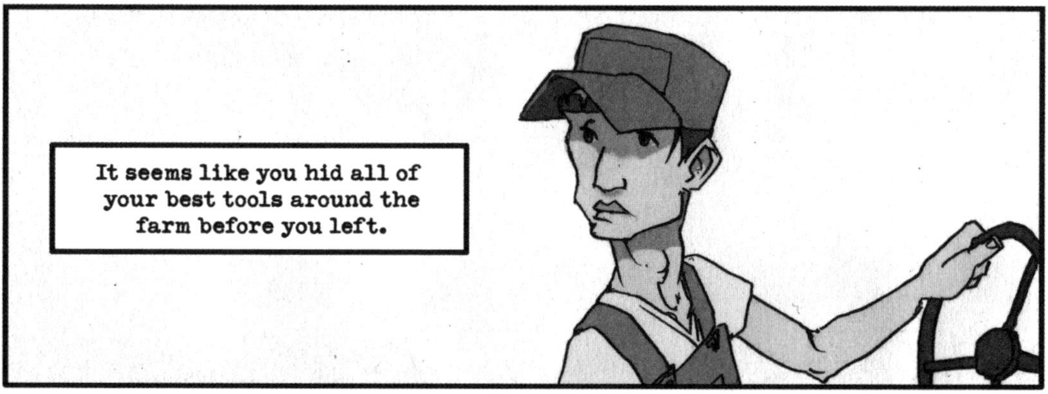
It seems like you hid all of your best tools around the farm before you left.

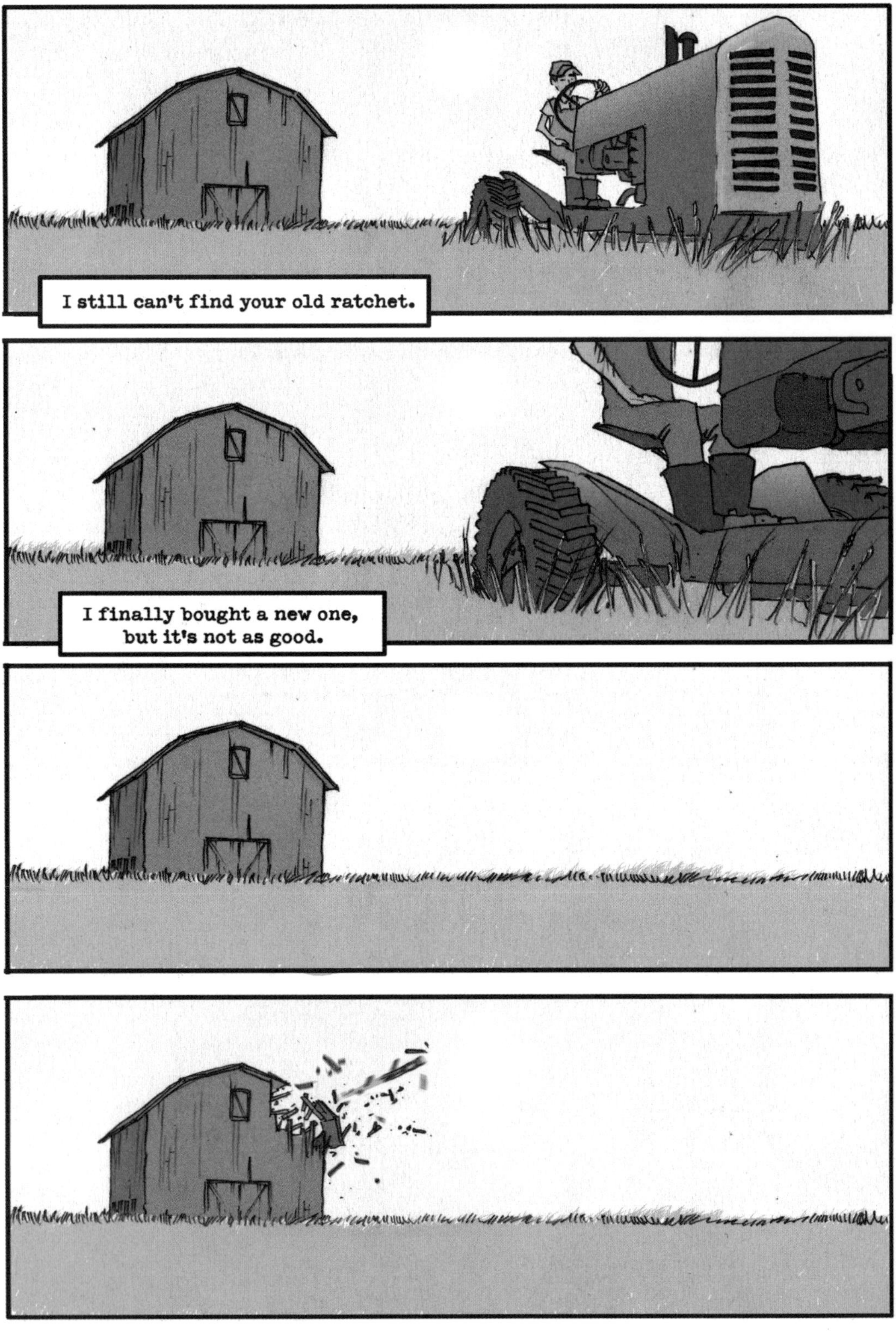
I still can't find your old ratchet.
I finally bought a new one, but it's not as good.

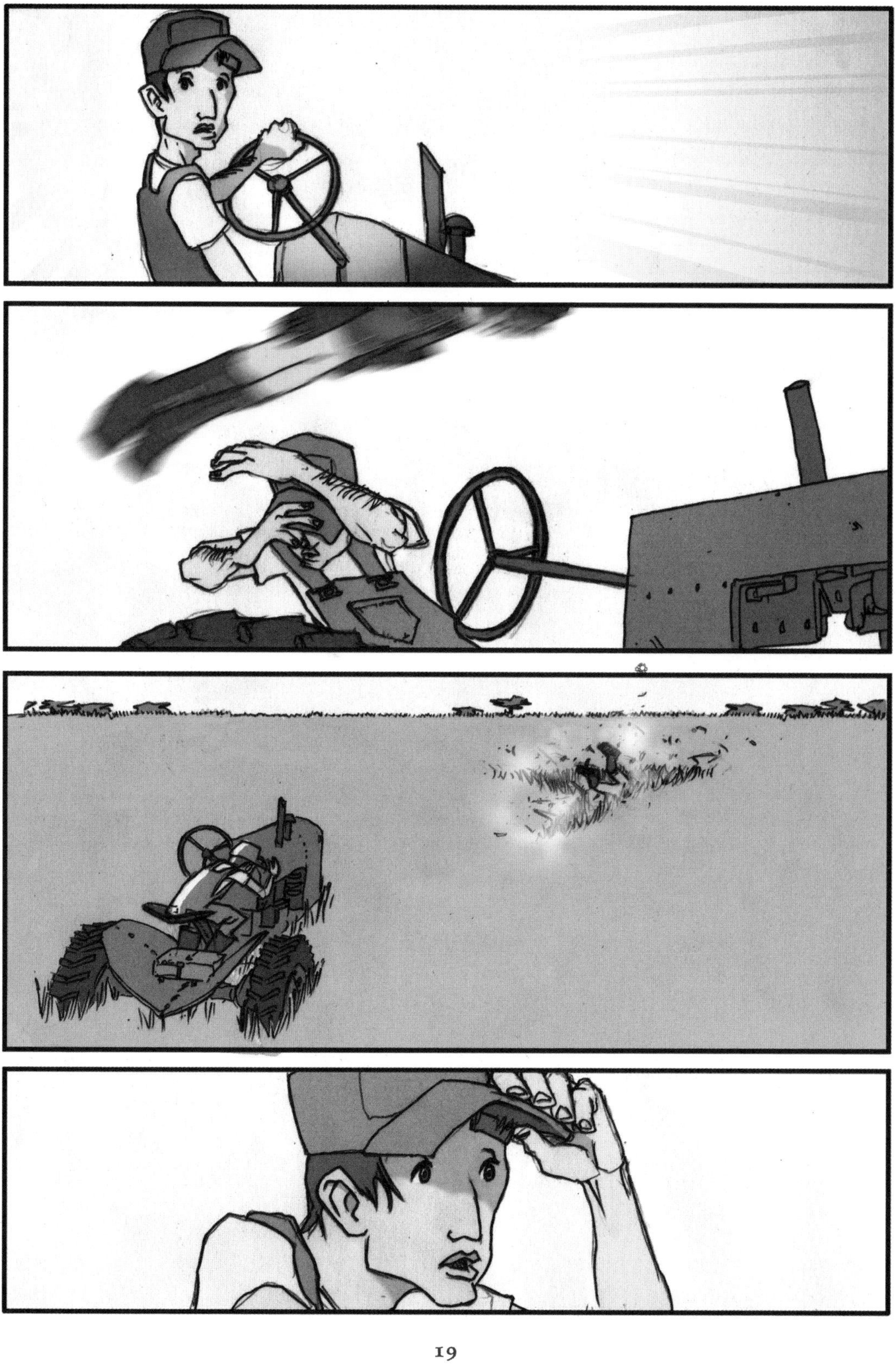

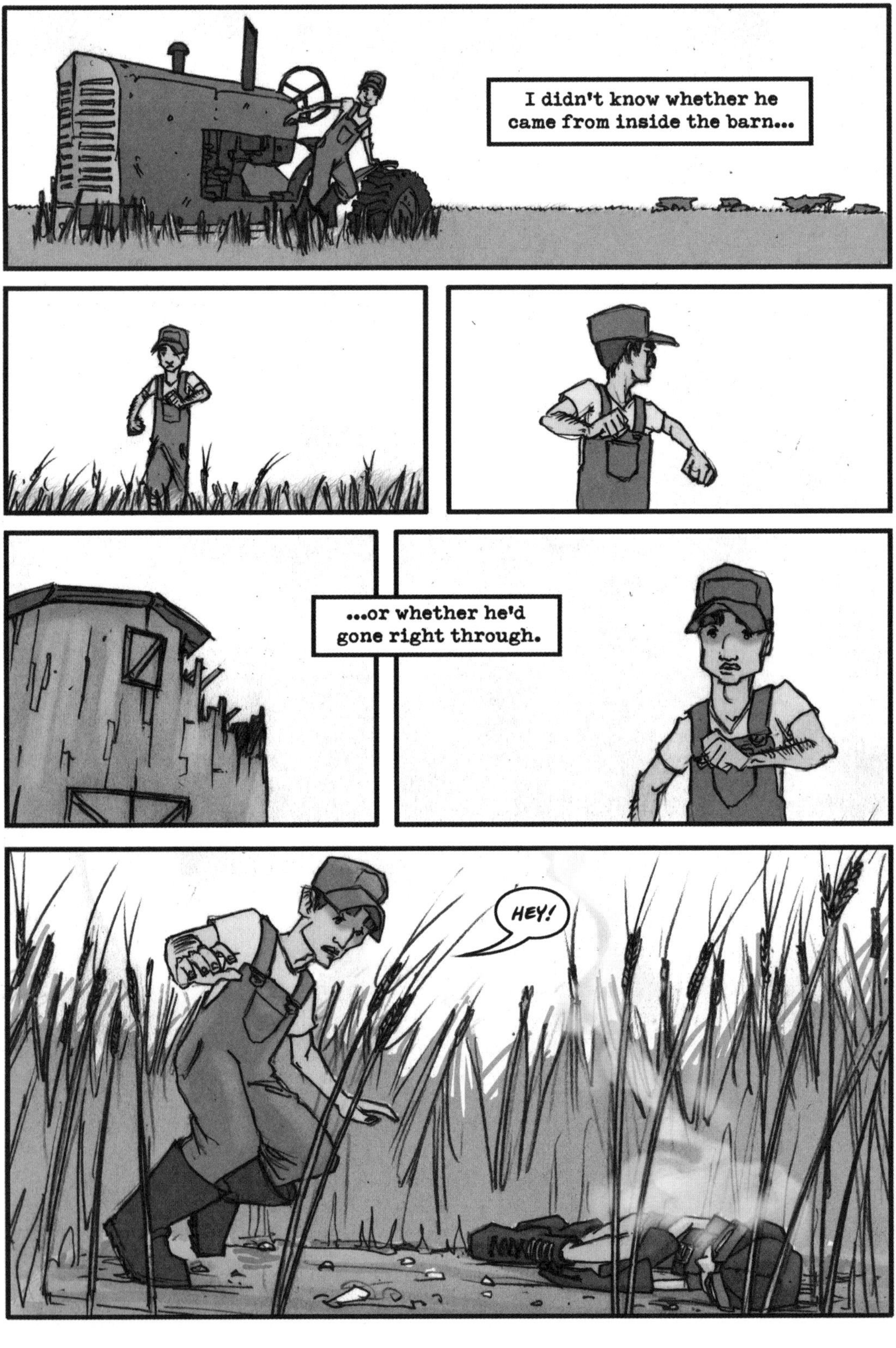
I didn't know whether he came from inside the barn...
...or whether he'd gone right through.
HEY!

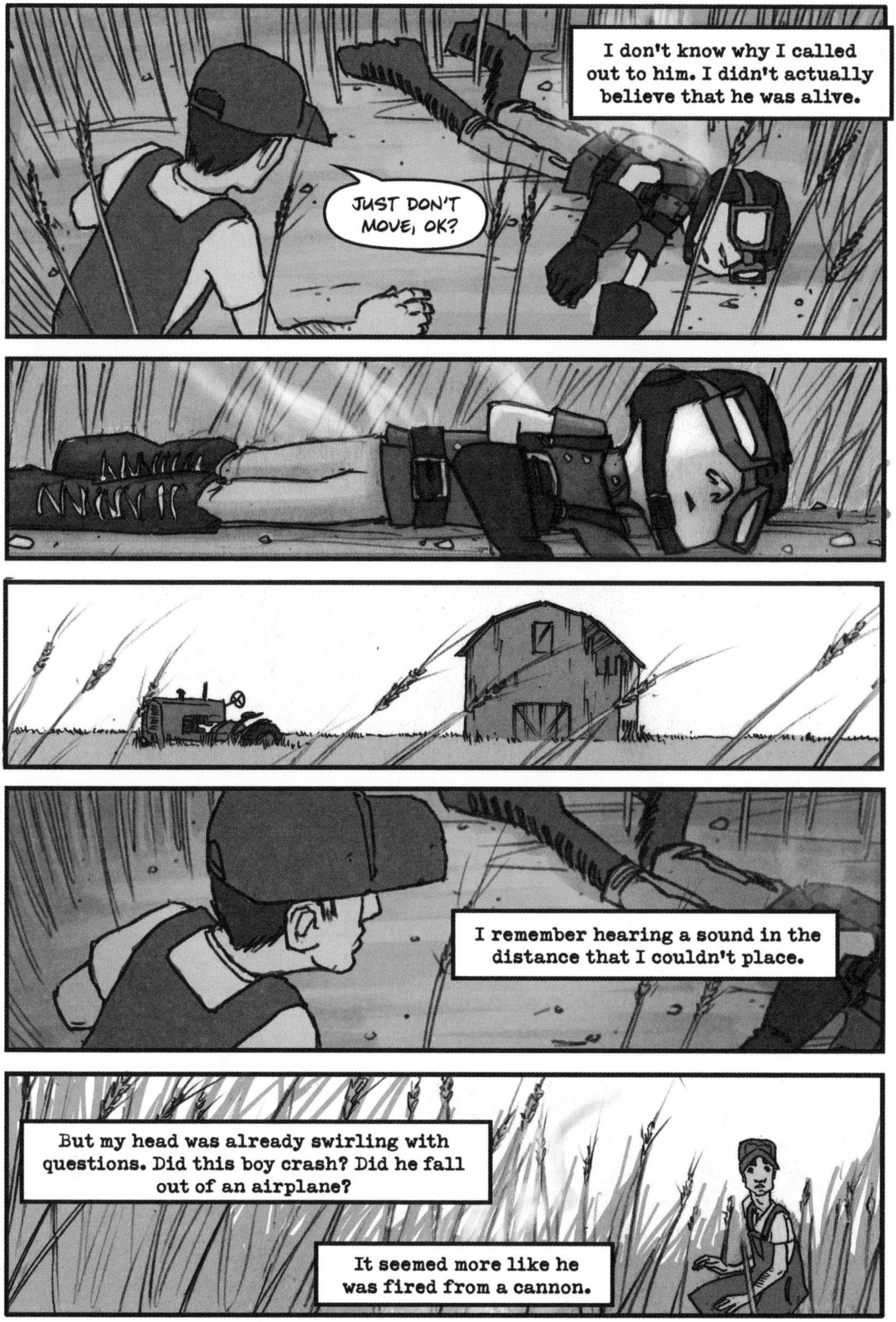
I don't know why I called out to him. I didn't actually believe that he was alive.
JUST DON'T MOVE, OK?
I remember hearing a sound in the distance that I couldn't place.
But my head was already swirling with questions. Did this boy crash? Did he fall out of an airplane?
It seemed more like he was fired from a cannon.

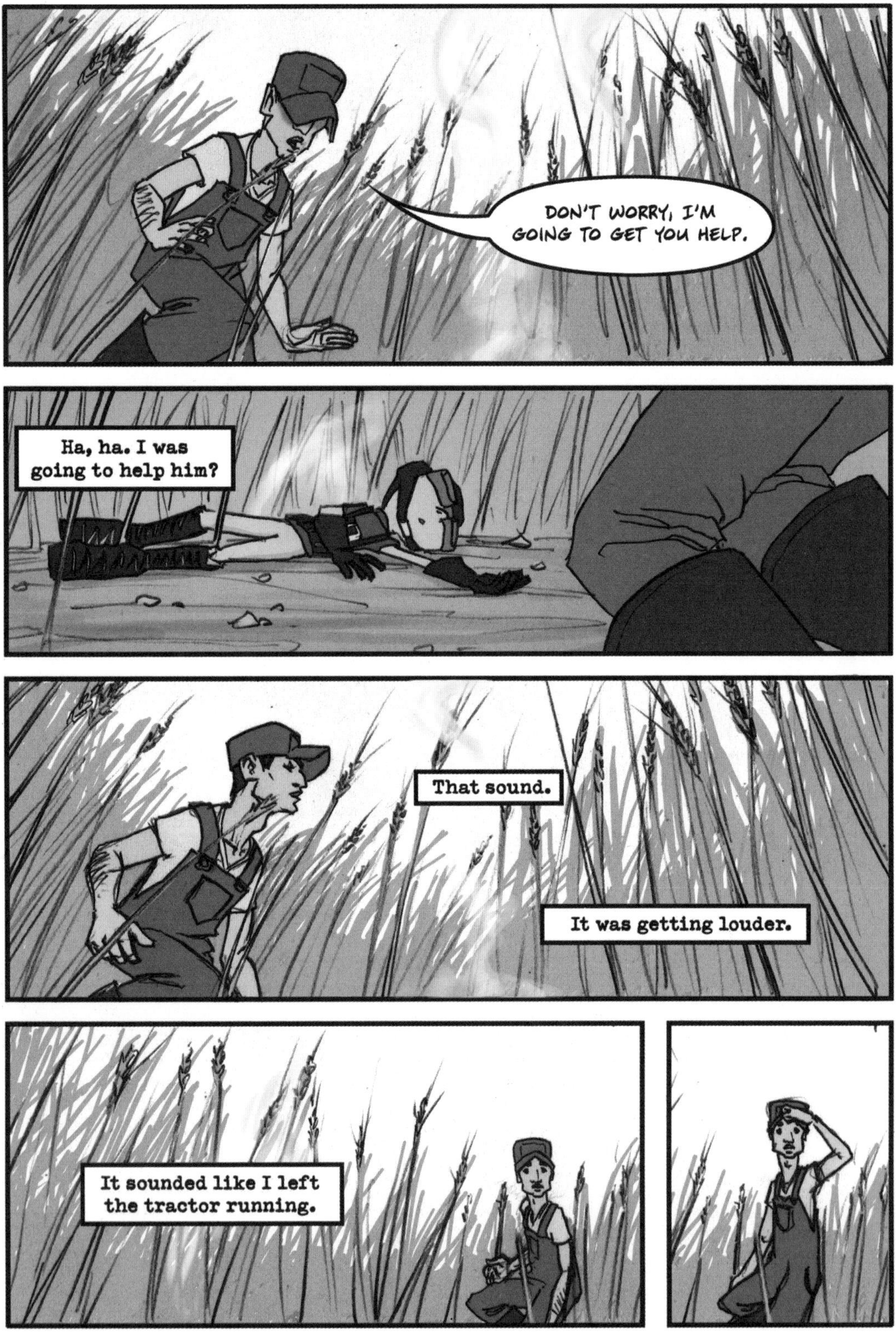
DON'T WORRY, I'M GOING TO GET YOU HELP.
Ha, ha. I was going to help him?
That sound.
It was getting louder.
It sounded like I left the tractor running.

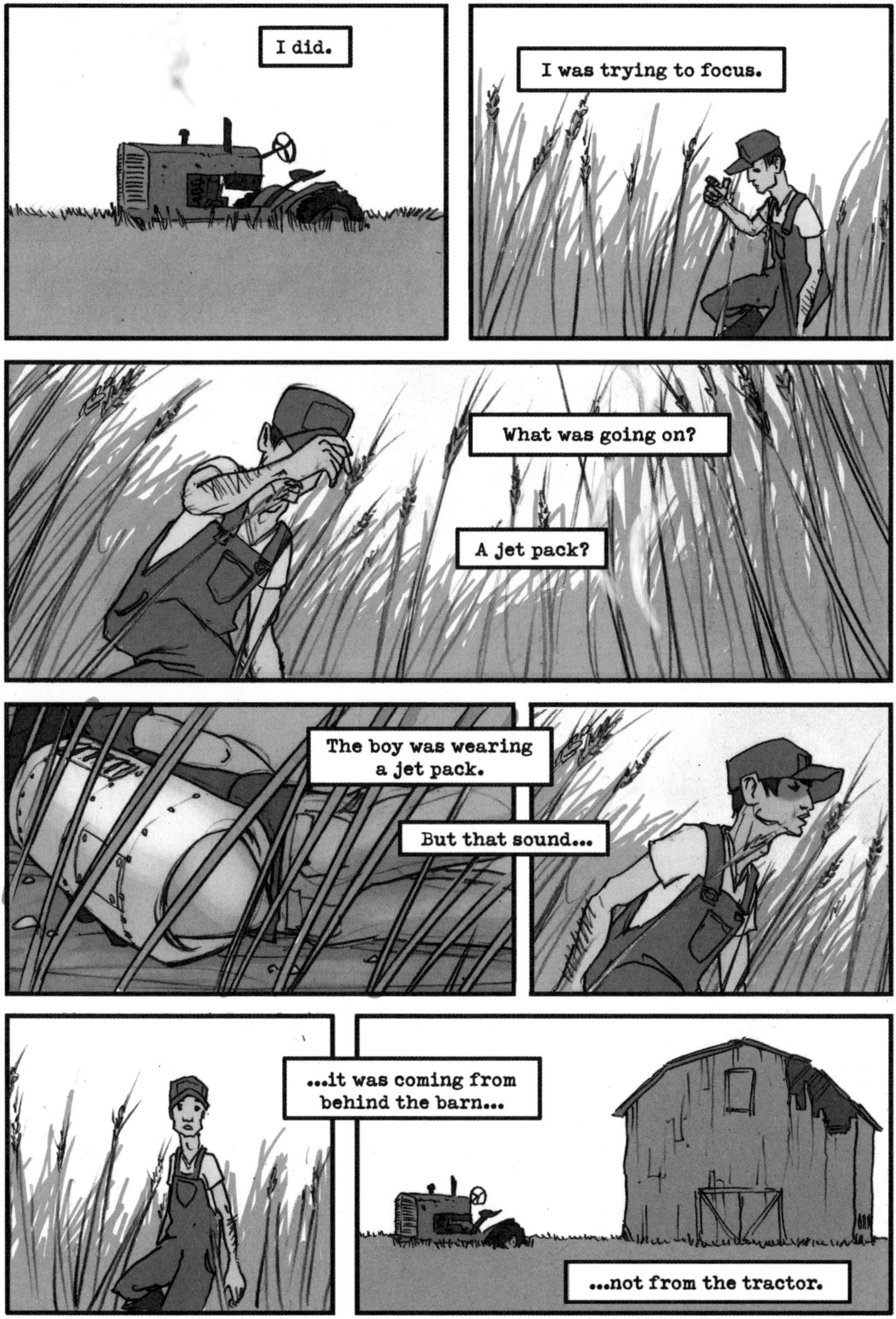
I did.
I was trying to focus.
What was going on?
A jet pack?
The boy was wearing a jet pack.
But that sound...
...it was coming from behind the barn...
...not from the tractor.

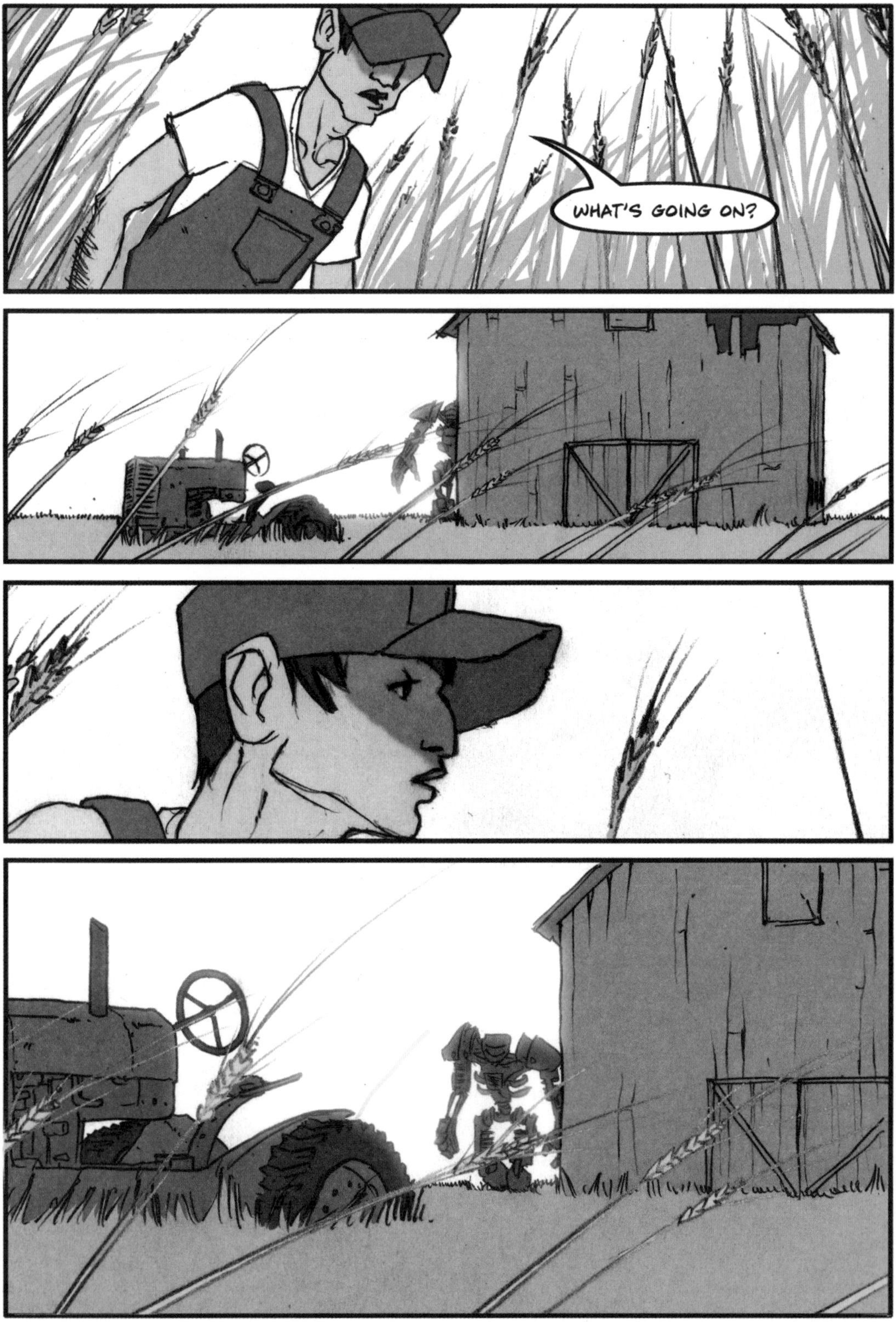
WHAT'S GOING ON?

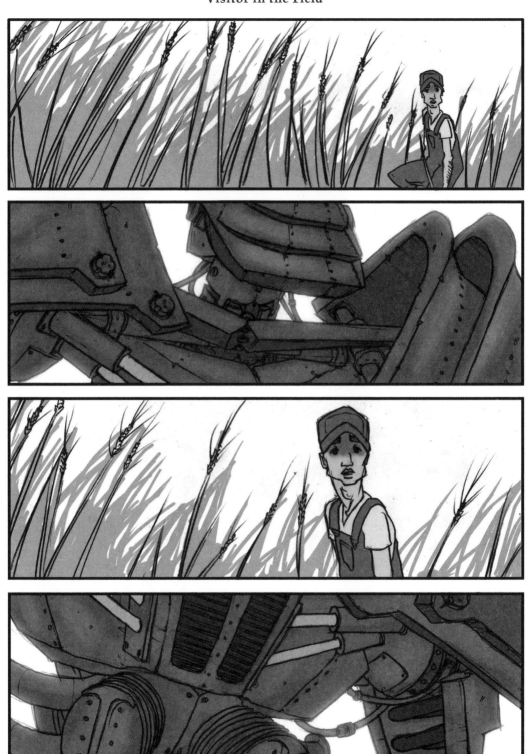

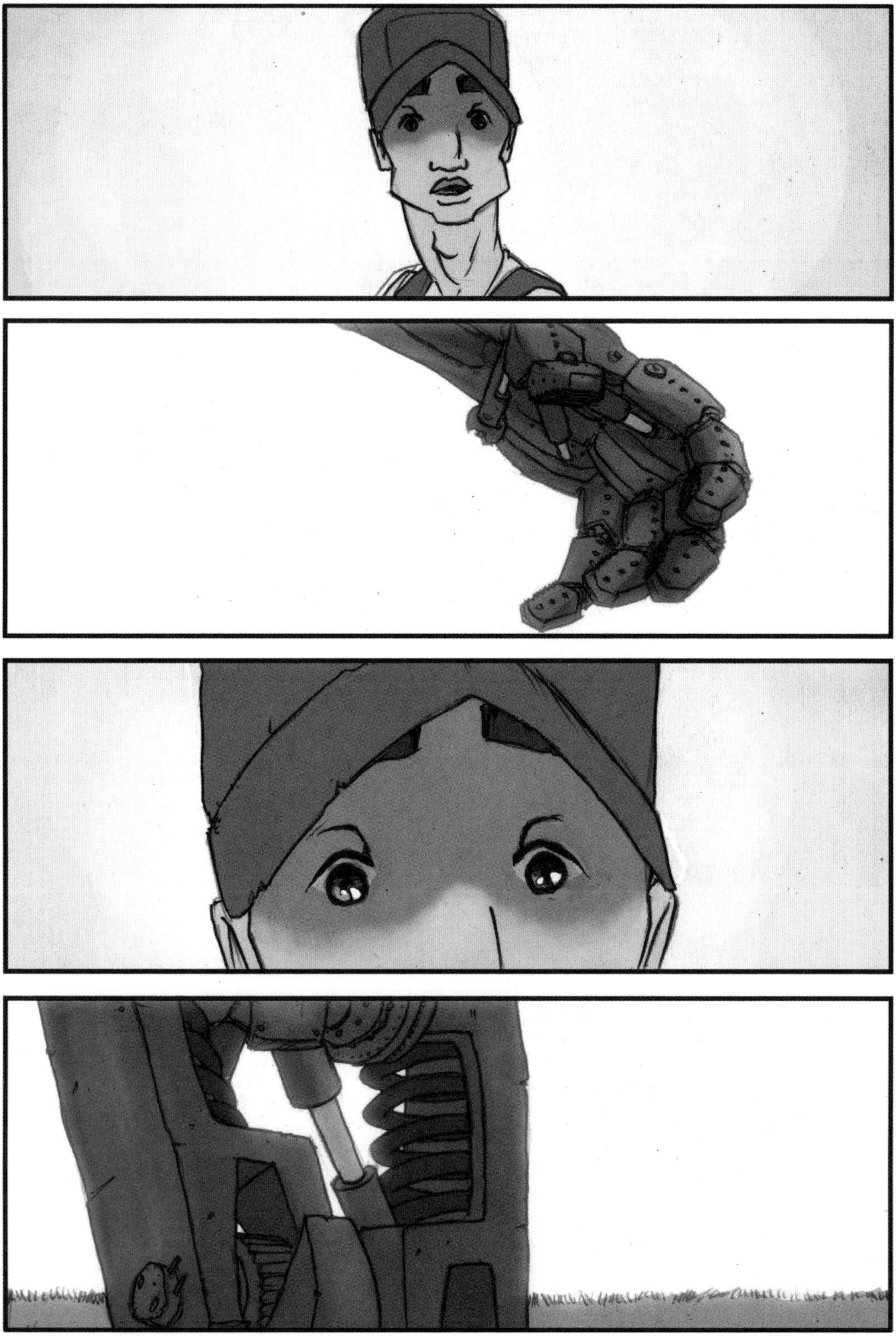

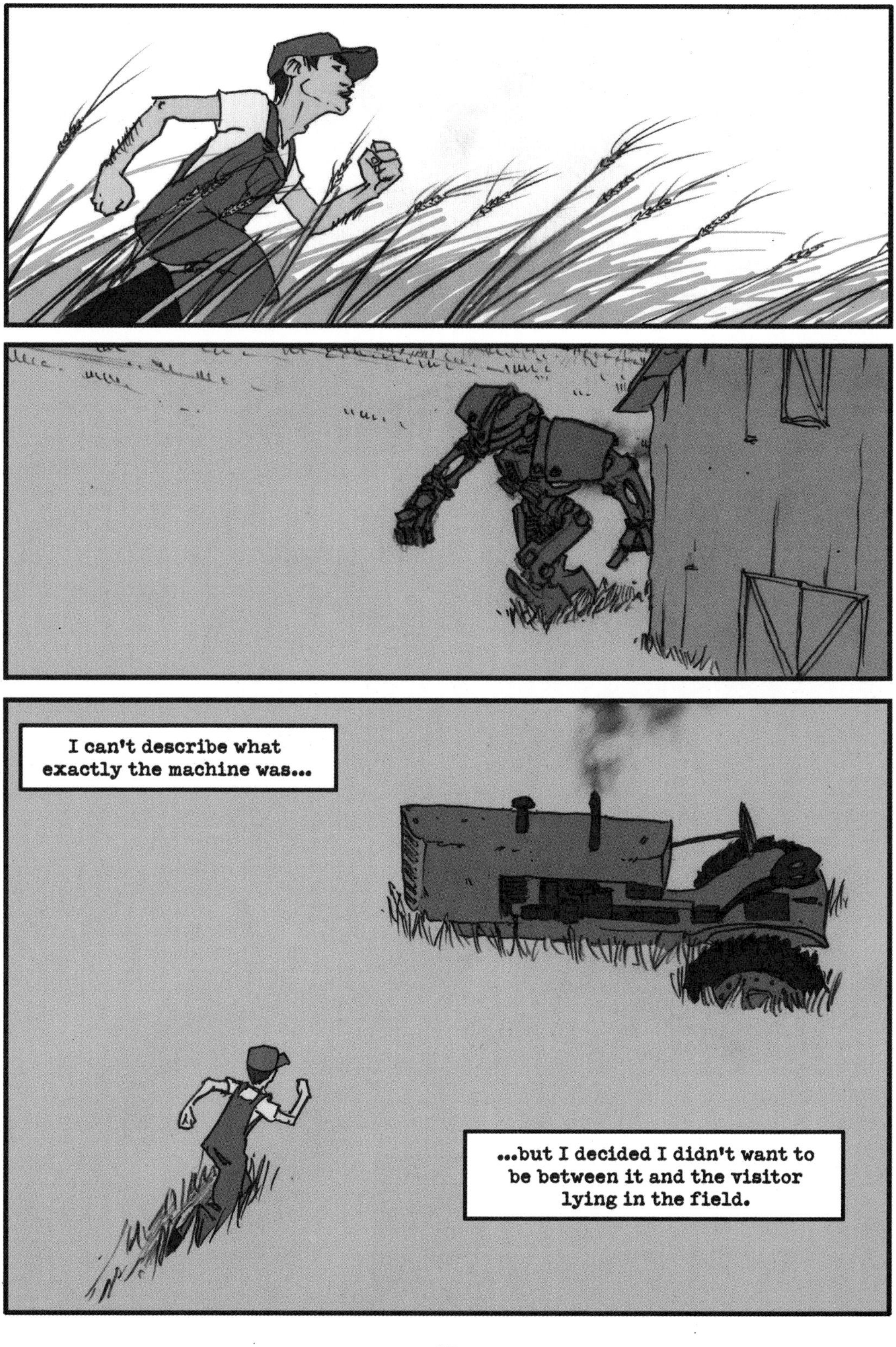
I can't describe what exactly the machine was...
...but I decided I didn't want to be between it and the visitor lying in the field.

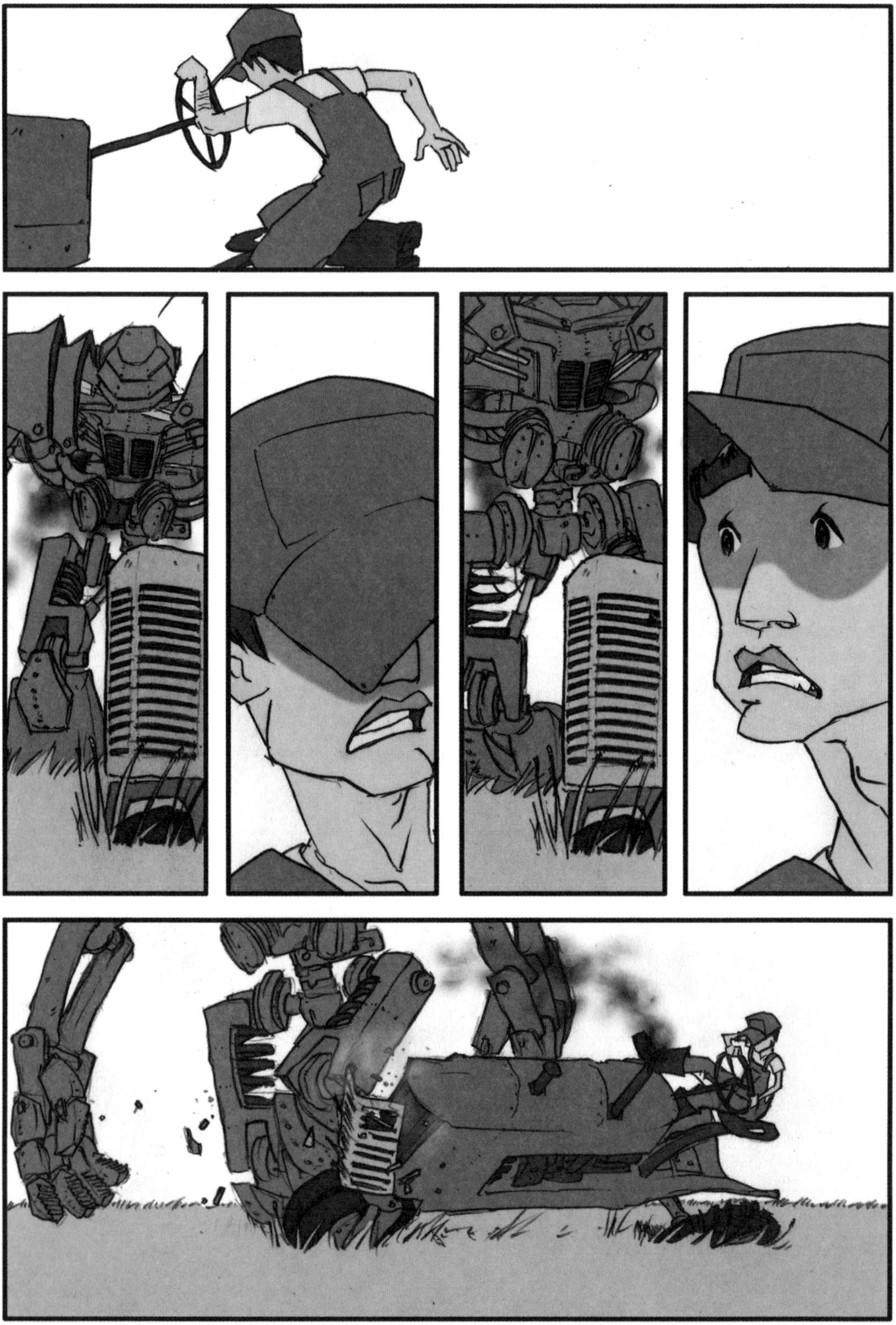

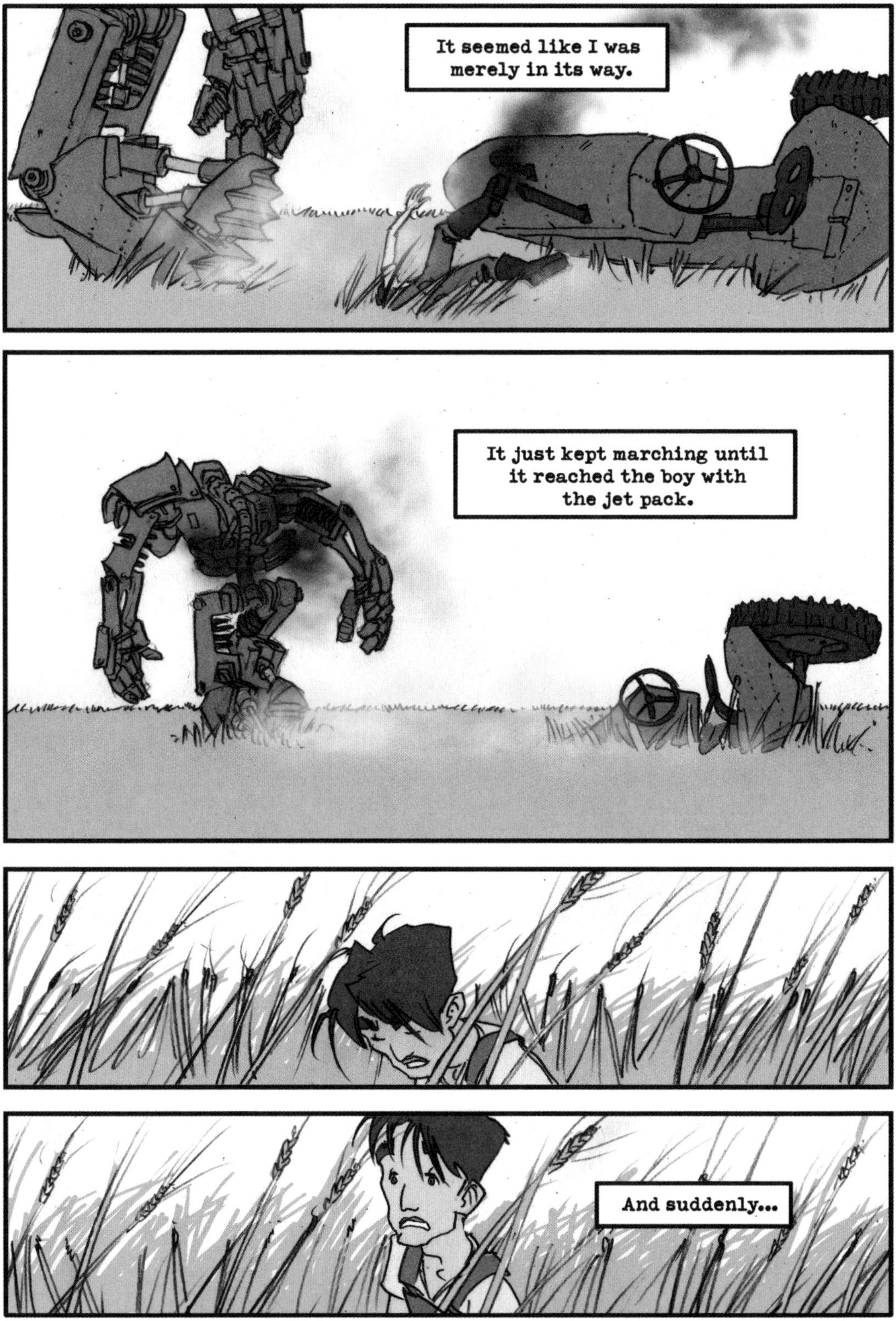
It seemed like I was merely in its way.
It just kept marching until it reached the boy with the jet pack.
And suddenly...

...the entire situation...

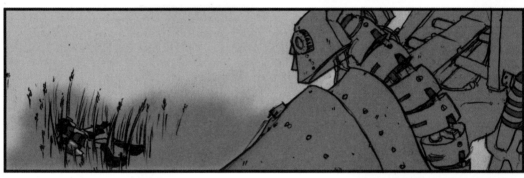

...became very clear.

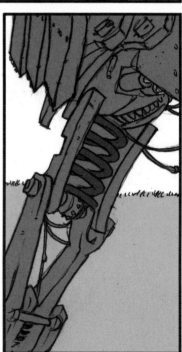

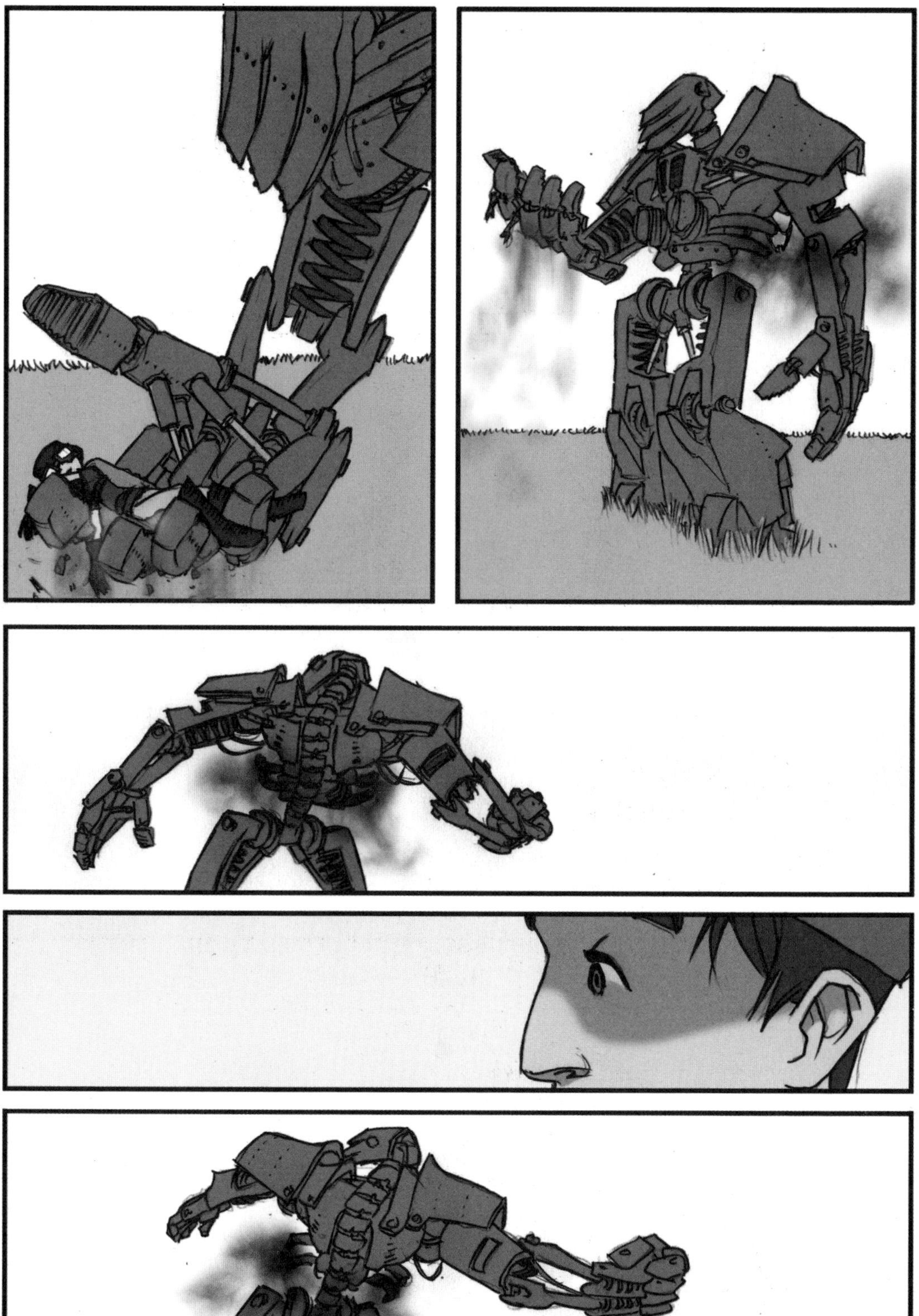

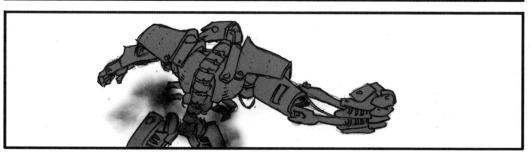

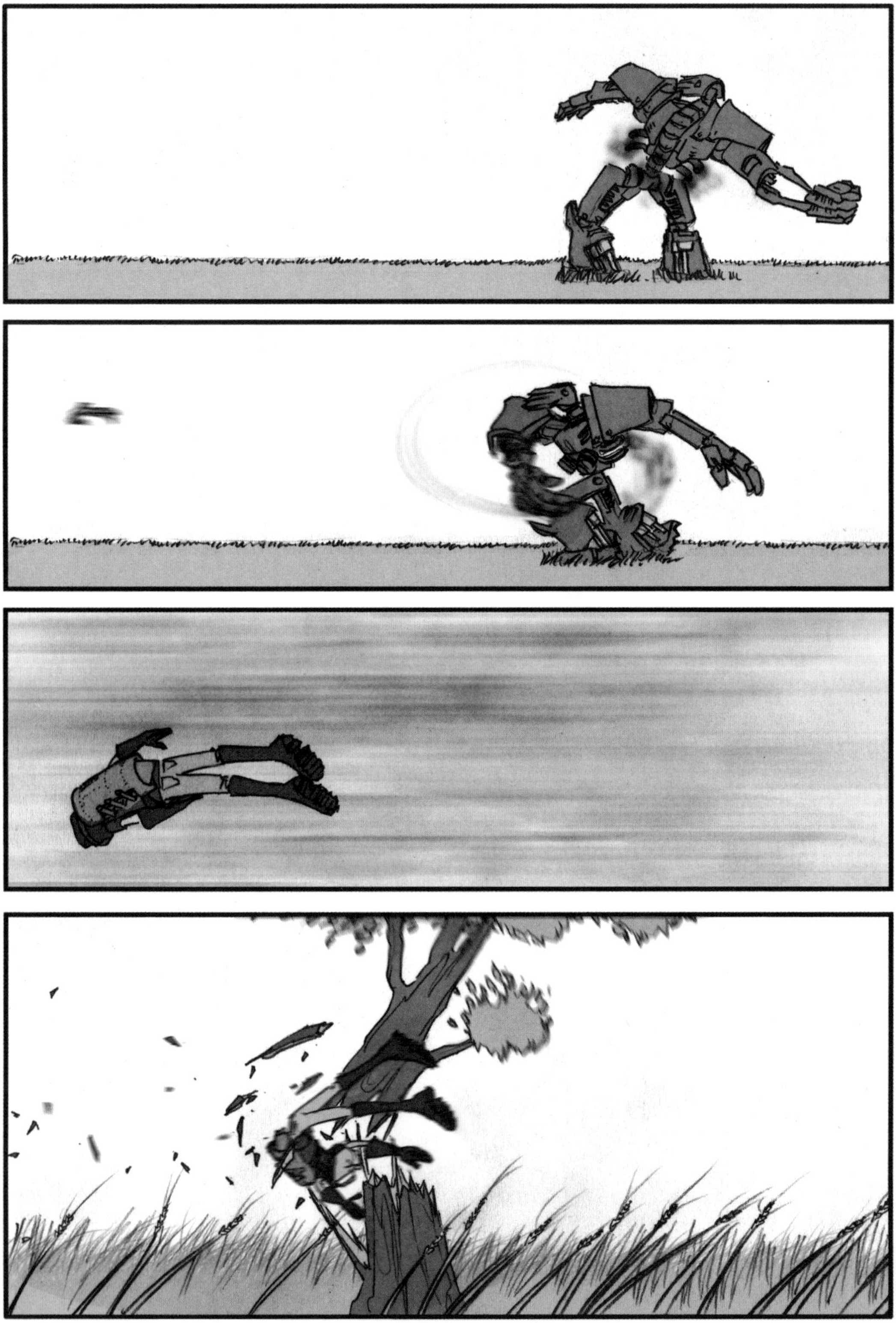

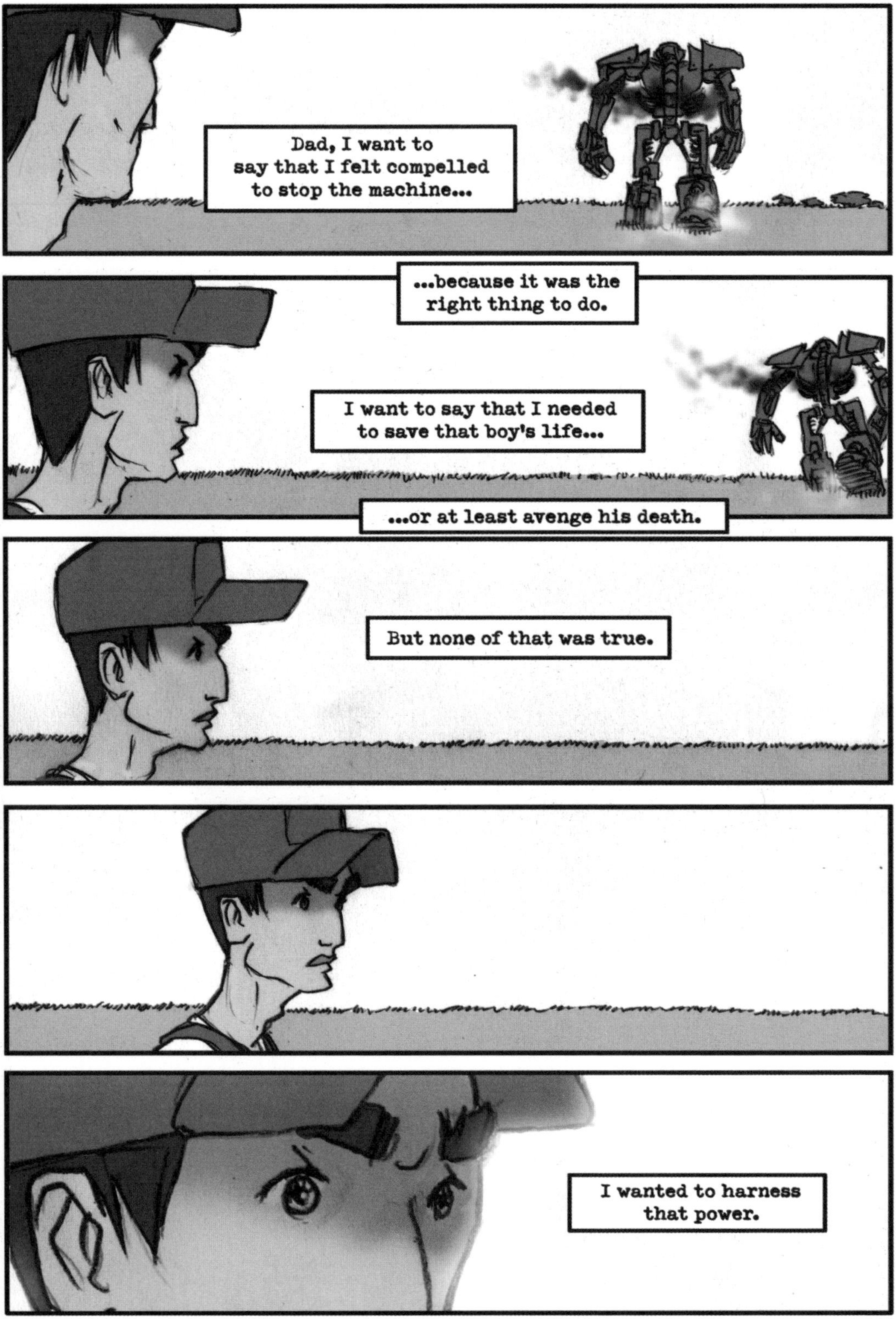
Dad, I want to say that I felt compelled to stop the machine...
...because it was the right thing to do.
I want to say that I needed to save that boy's life...
...or at least avenge his death.
But none of that was true.
I wanted to harness that power.

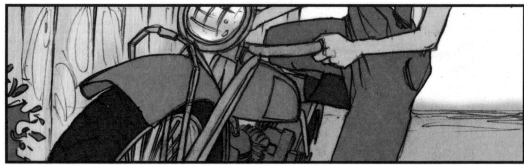

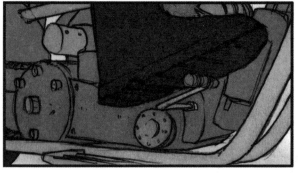

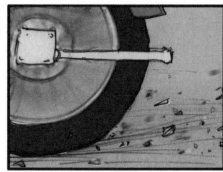

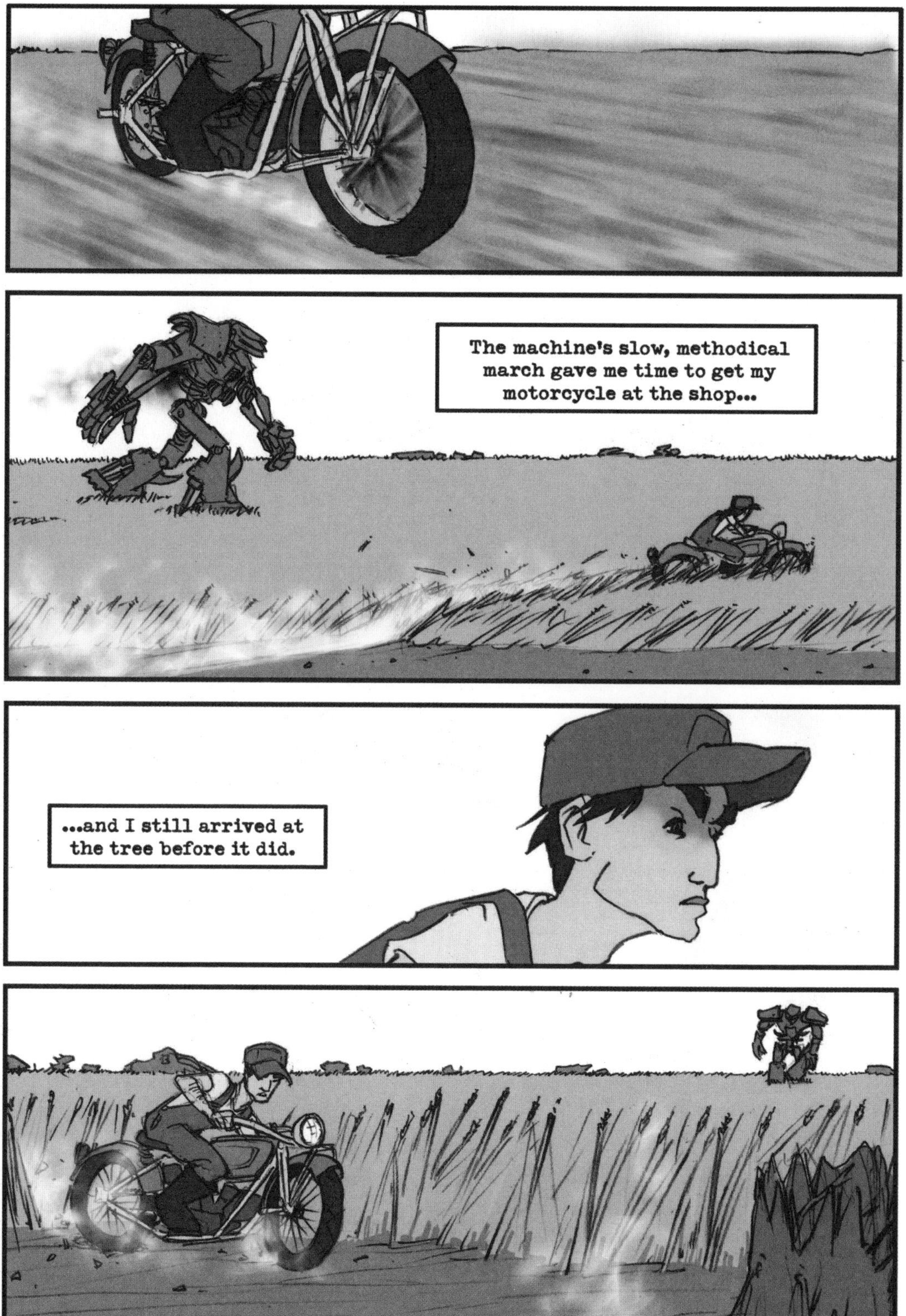
The machine's slow, methodical march gave me time to get my motorcycle at the shop...
...and I still arrived at the tree before it did.

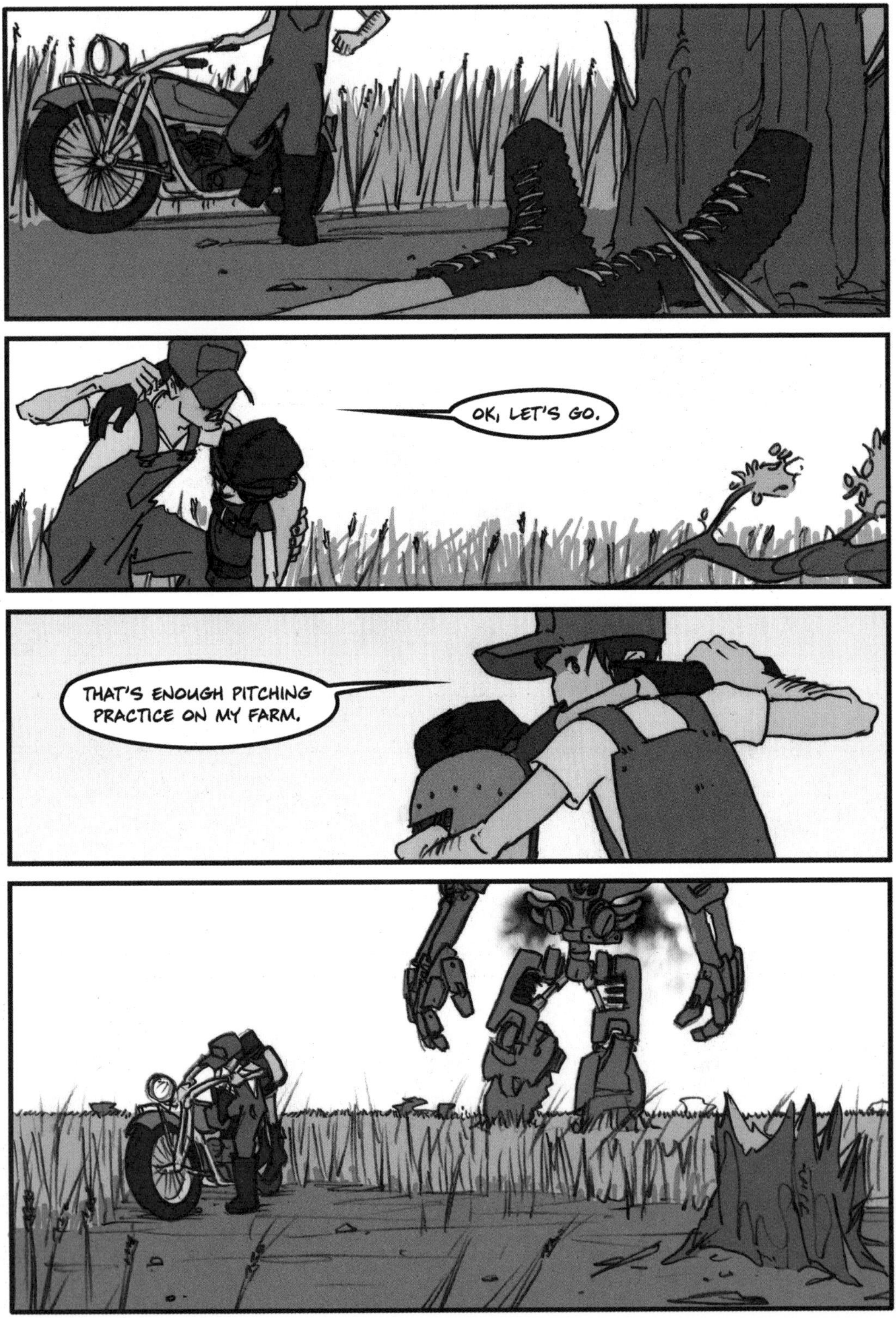
OK, LET'S GO.
THAT'S ENOUGH PITCHING PRACTICE ON MY FARM.

Before, the machine behaved as though I didn't exist.

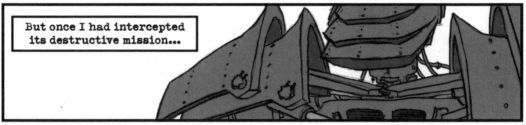

But once I had intercepted its destructive mission...

...it changed gears...

...literally.

I heard it.

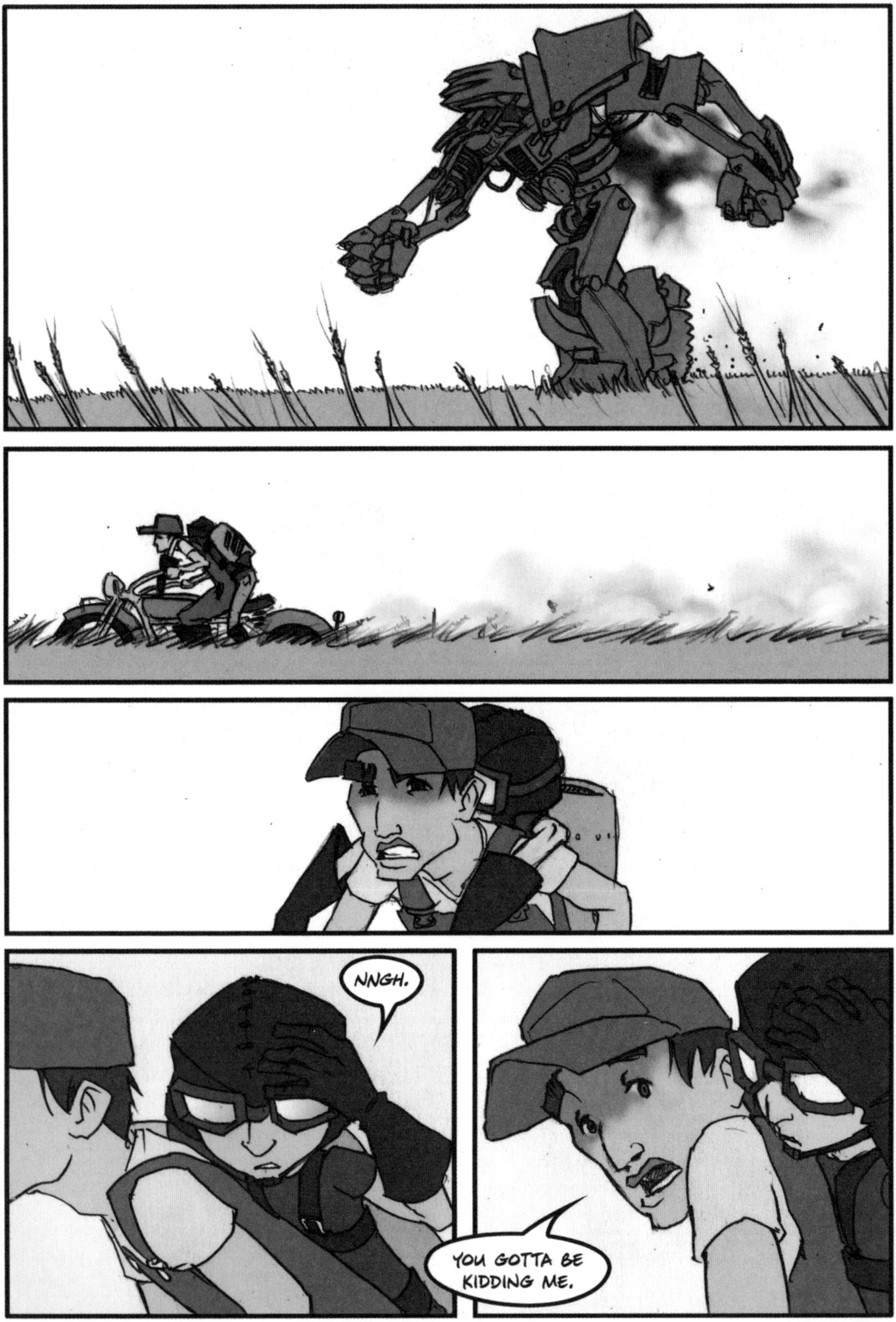
NNGH.
YOU GOTTA BE KIDDING ME.

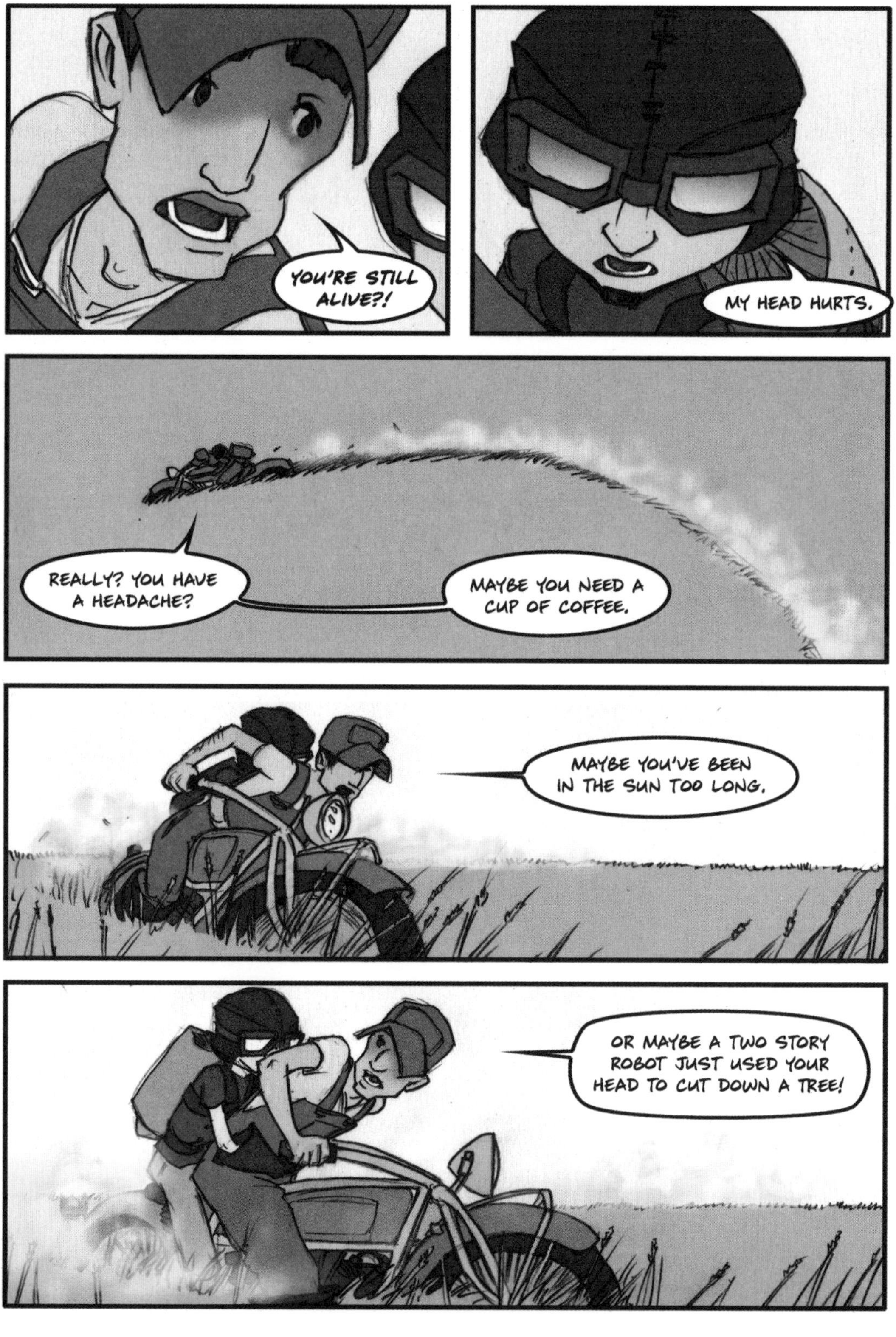
YOU'RE STILL ALIVE?!
MY HEAD HURTS.
REALLY? YOU HAVE A HEADACHE?
MAYBE YOU NEED A CUP OF COFFEE.
MAYBE YOU'VE BEEN IN THE SUN TOO LONG.
OR MAYBE A TWO STORY ROBOT JUST USED YOUR HEAD TO CUT DOWN A TREE!

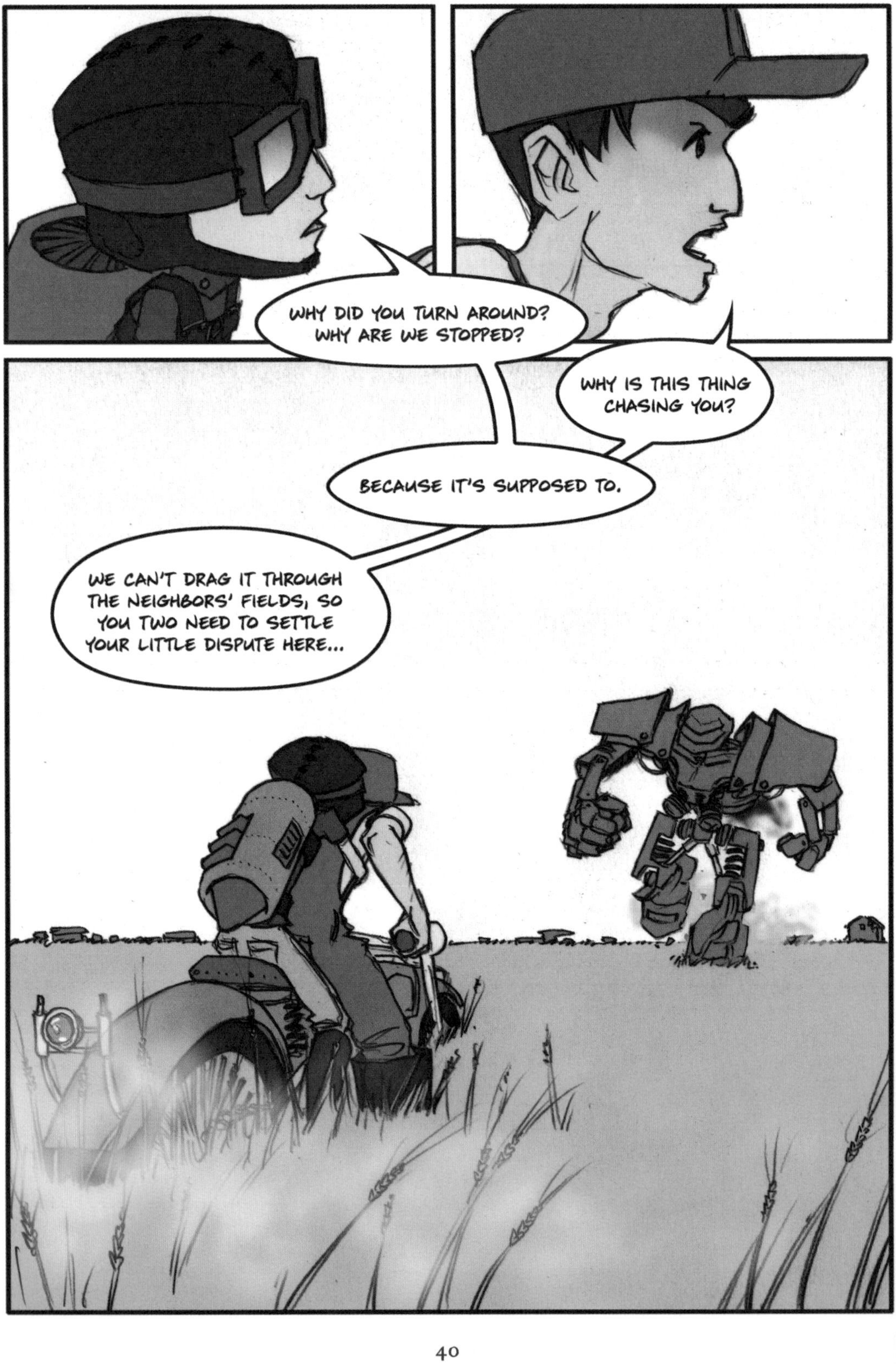
WHY DID YOU TURN AROUND? WHY ARE WE STOPPED?
WHY IS THIS THING CHASING YOU?
BECAUSE IT'S SUPPOSED TO.
WE CAN'T DRAG IT THROUGH THE NEIGHBORS' FIELDS, SO YOU TWO NEED TO SETTLE YOUR LITTLE DISPUTE HERE...

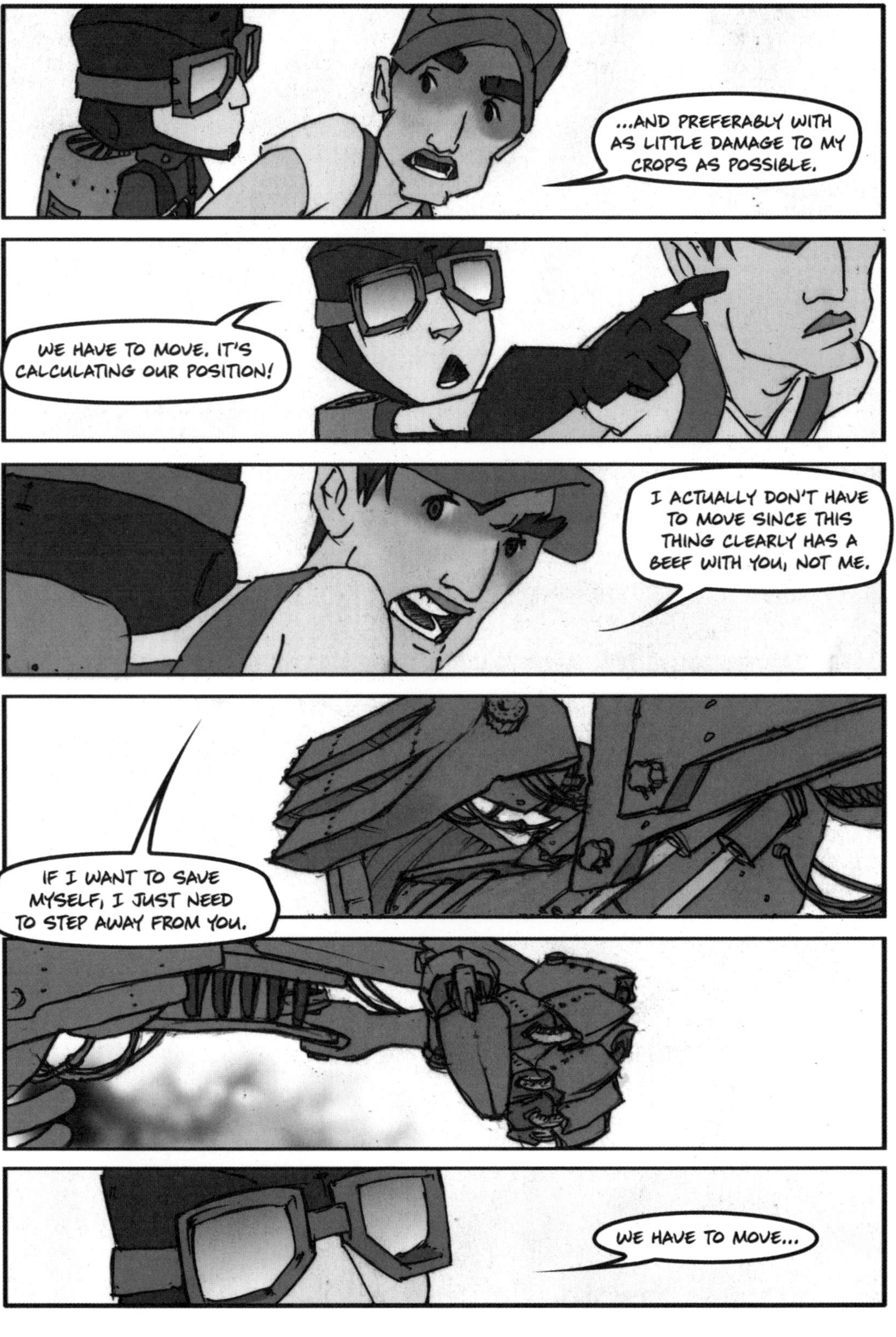
...AND PREFERABLY WITH AS LITTLE DAMAGE TO MY CROPS AS POSSIBLE.
WE HAVE TO MOVE. IT'S CALCULATING OUR POSITION!
I ACTUALLY DON'T HAVE TO MOVE SINCE THIS THING CLEARLY HAS A BEEF WITH YOU, NOT ME.
IF I WANT TO SAVE MYSELF, I JUST NEED TO STEP AWAY FROM YOU.
WE HAVE TO MOVE...

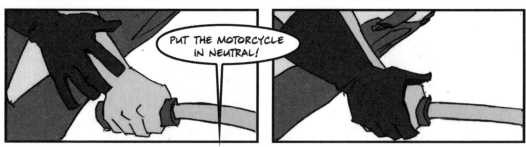

PUT THE MOTORCYCLE IN NEUTRAL!

HEY!

DO IT OR WE'LL WRECK THE TRANSMISSION!

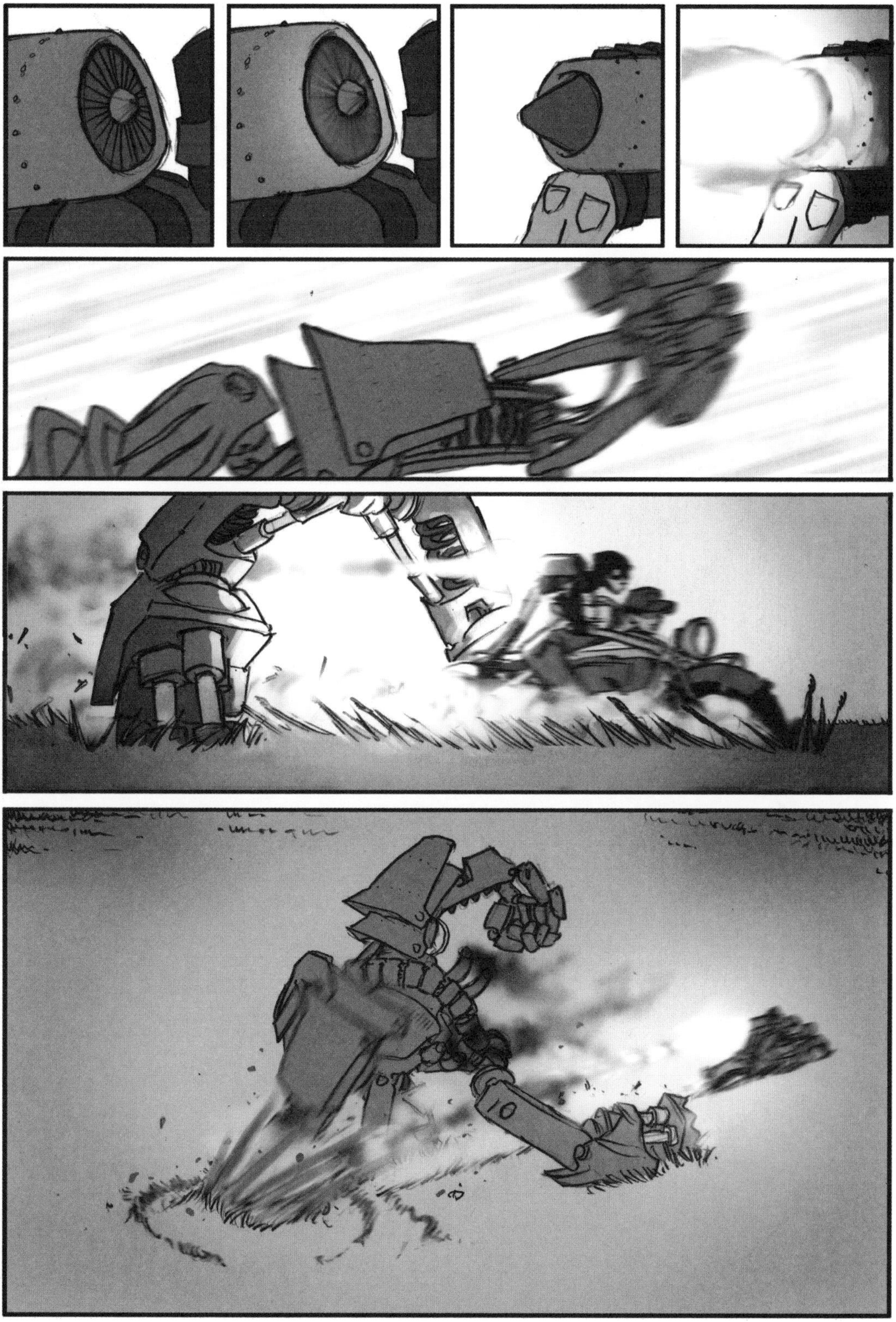

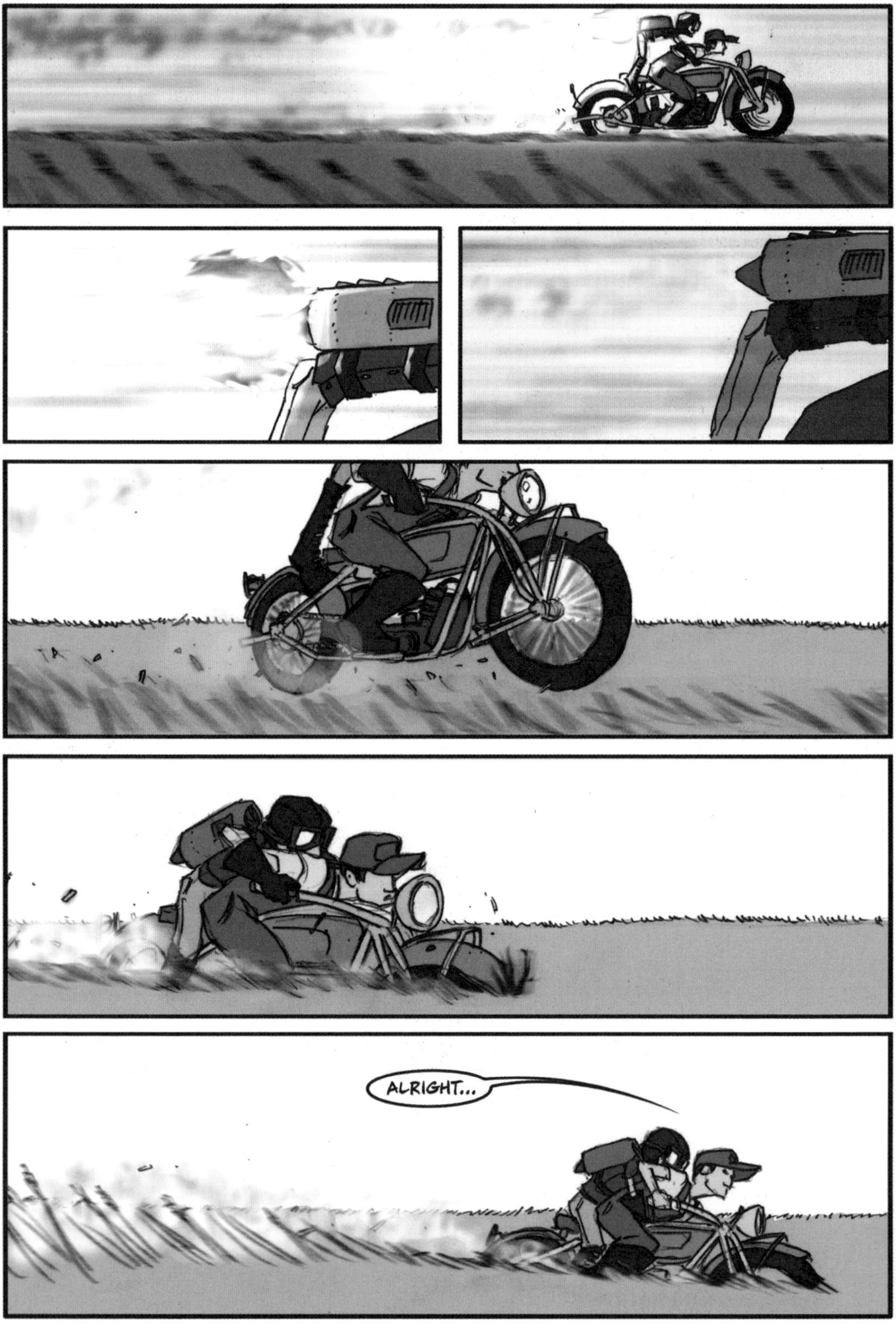
ALRIGHT...

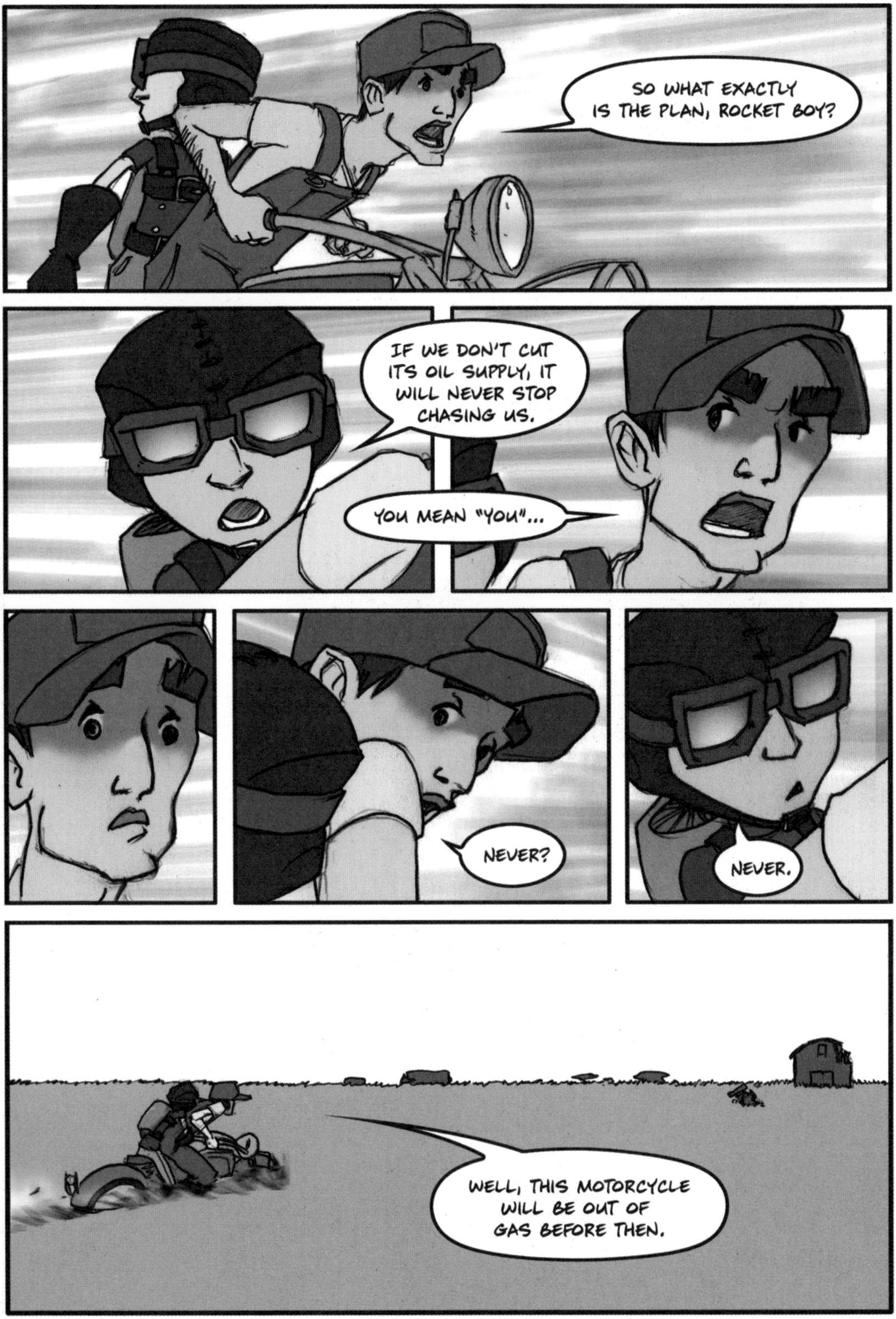
SO WHAT EXACTLY IS THE PLAN, ROCKET BOY?
IF WE DON'T CUT ITS OIL SUPPLY, IT WILL NEVER STOP CHASING US.
YOU MEAN "YOU"...
NEVER?
NEVER.
WELL, THIS MOTORCYCLE WILL BE OUT OF GAS BEFORE THEN.

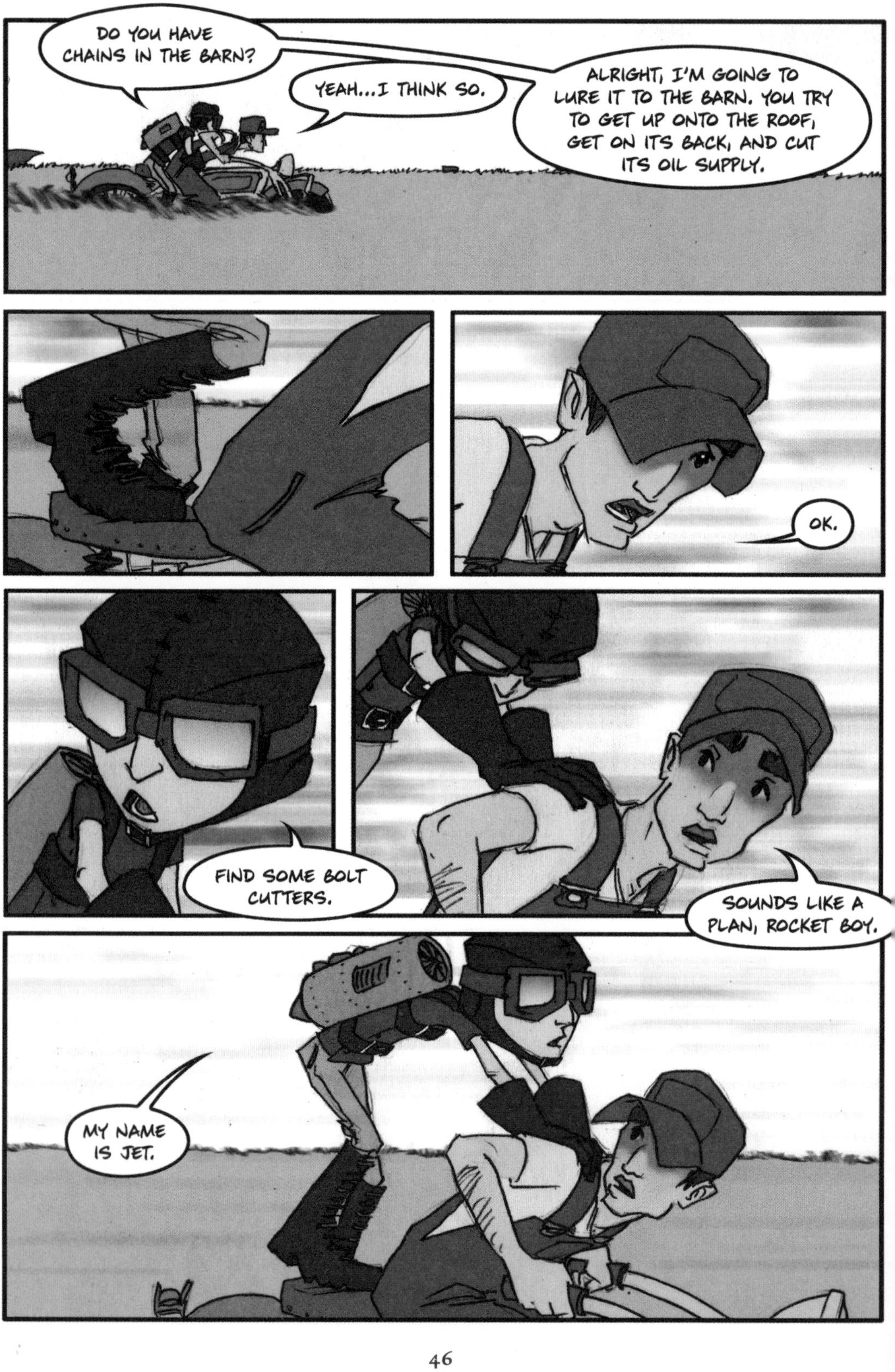
DO YOU HAVE CHAINS IN THE BARN?
YEAH...I THINK SO.
ALRIGHT, I'M GOING TO LURE IT TO THE BARN. YOU TRY TO GET UP ONTO THE ROOF, GET ON ITS BACK, AND CUT ITS OIL SUPPLY.
OK.
FIND SOME BOLT CUTTERS.
SOUNDS LIKE A PLAN, ROCKET BOY.
MY NAME IS JET.

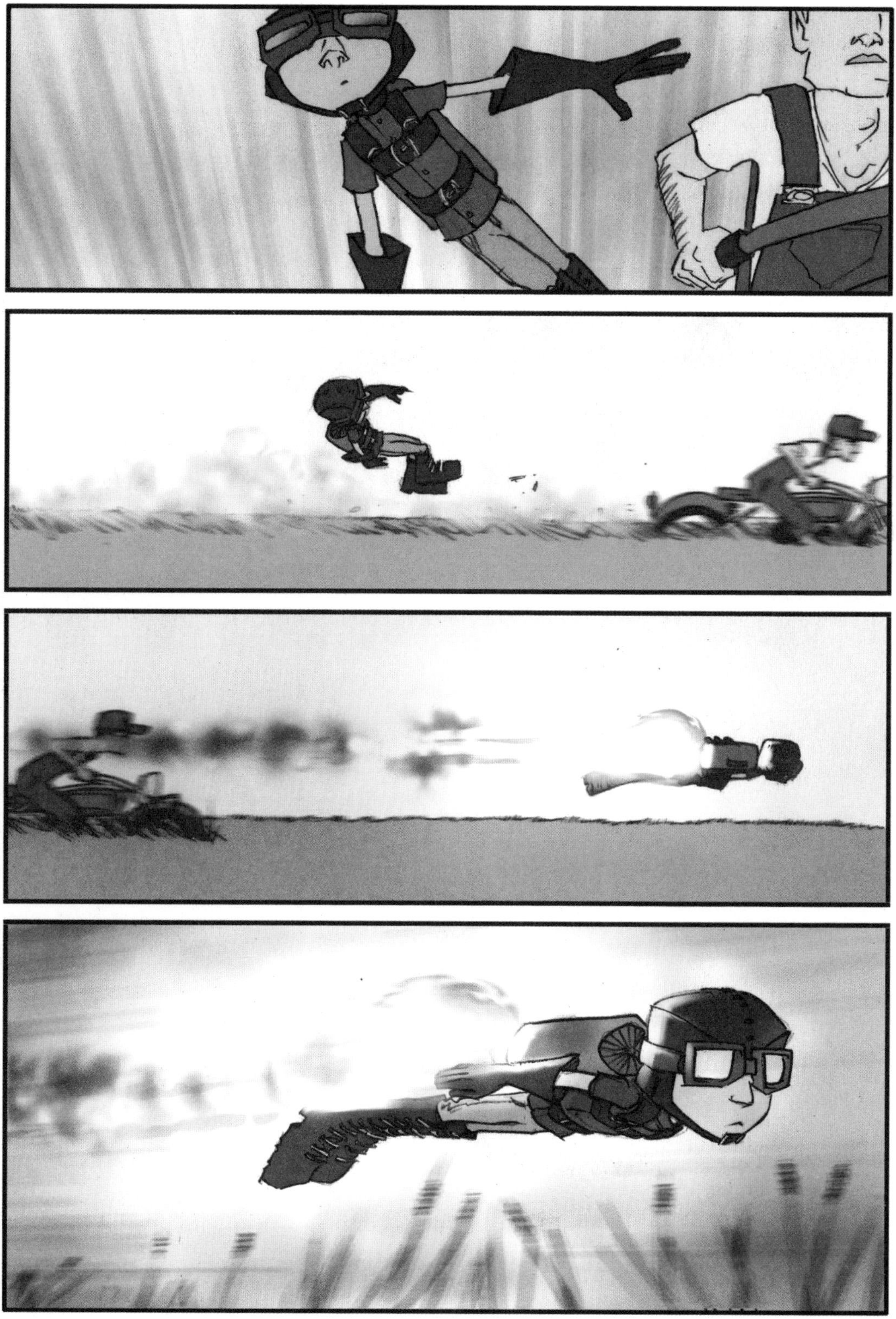

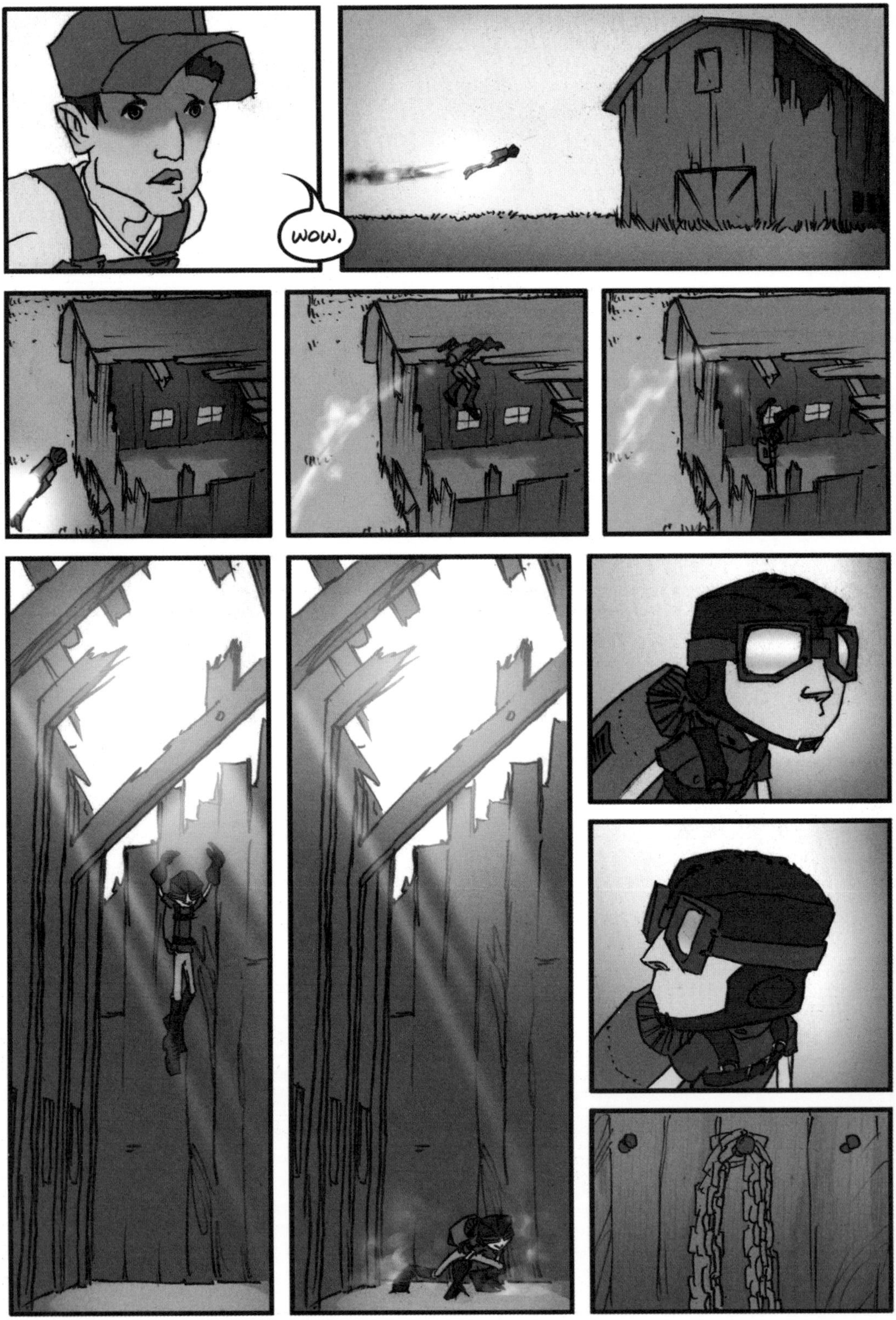
WOW.

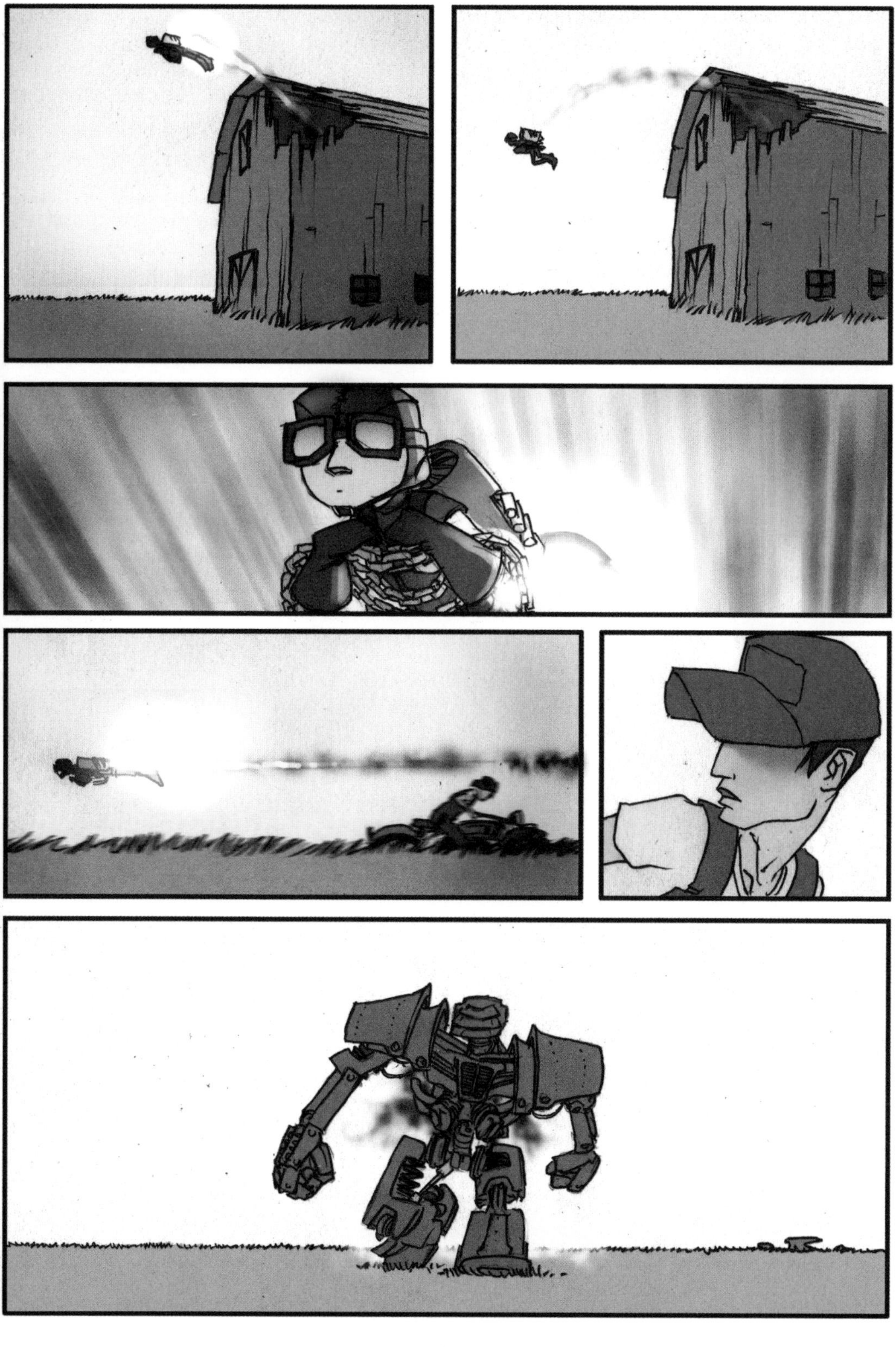

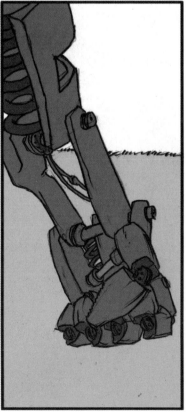

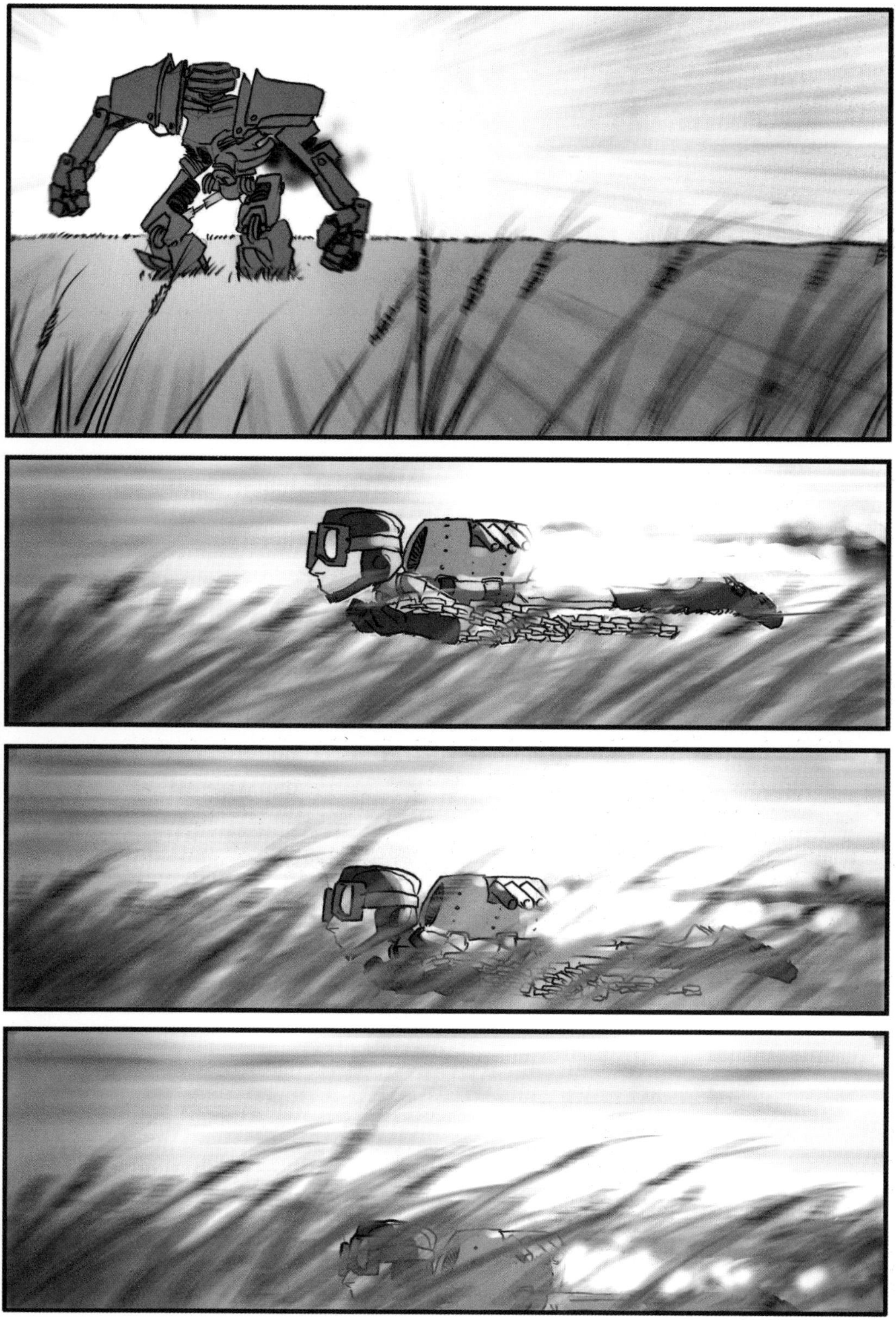

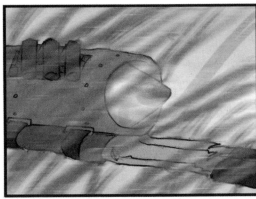
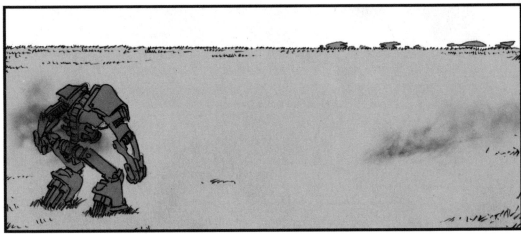

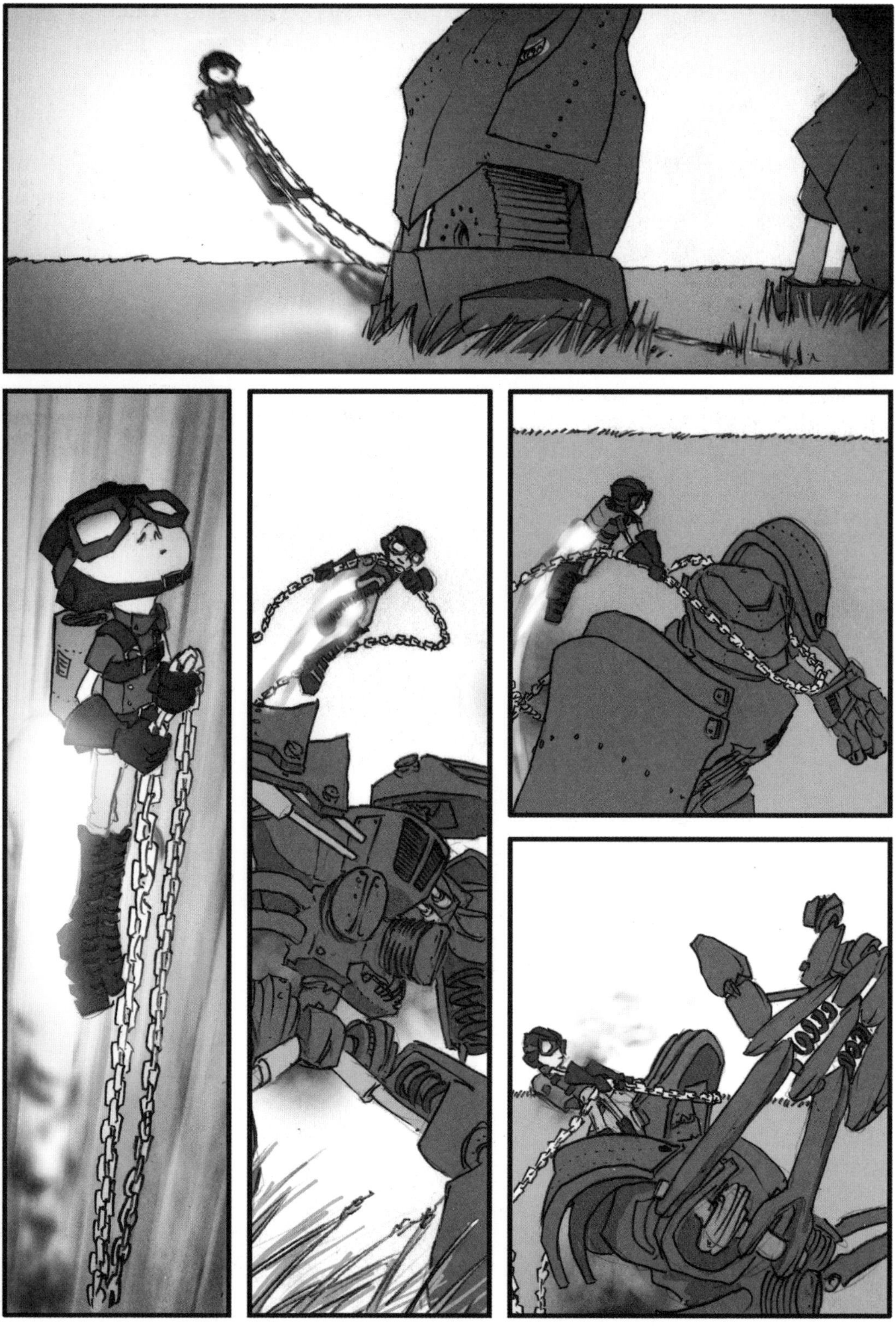

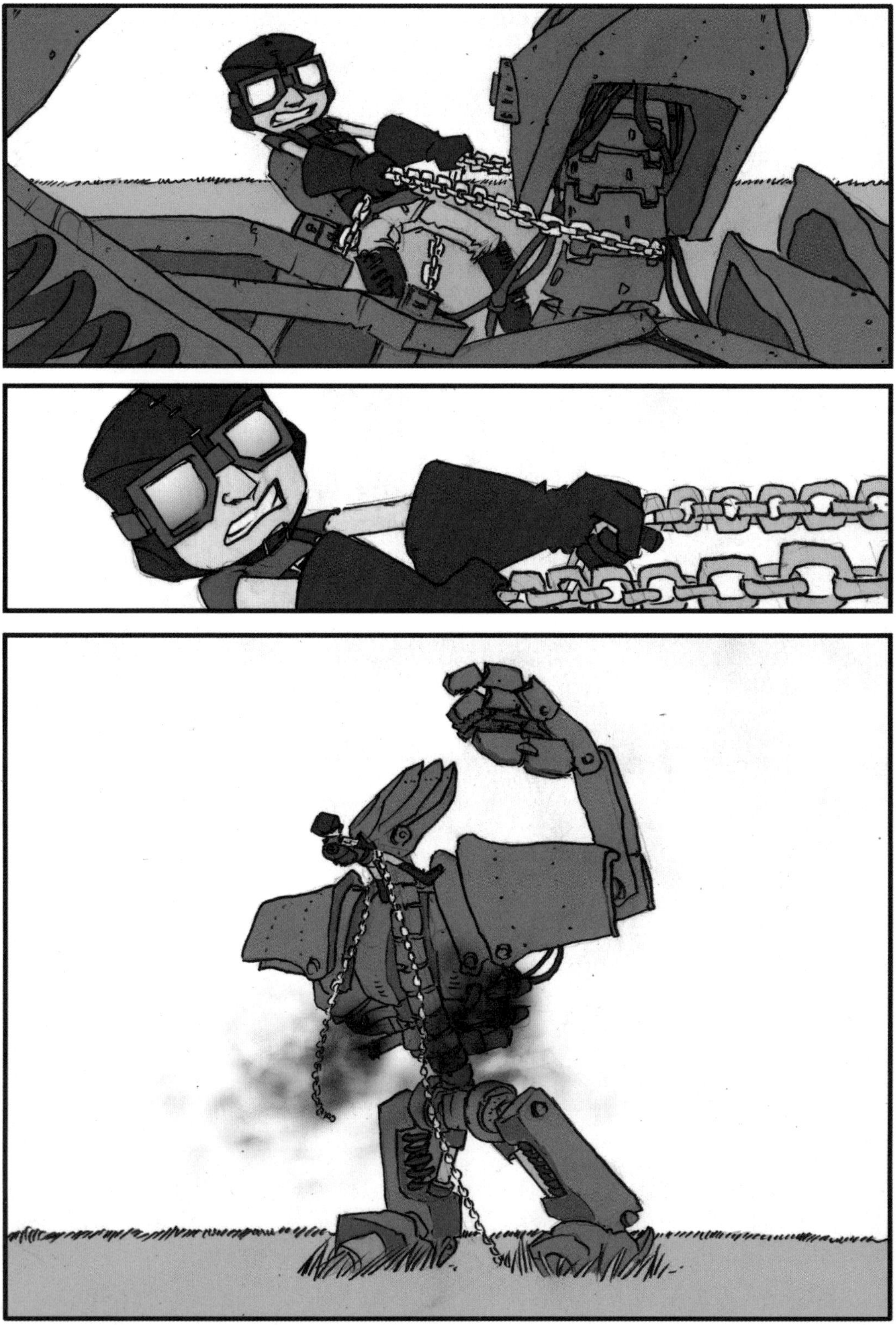

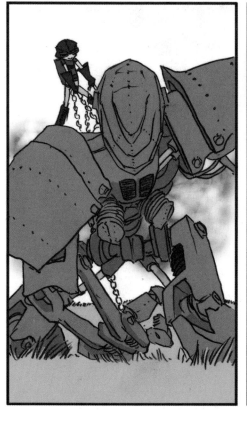

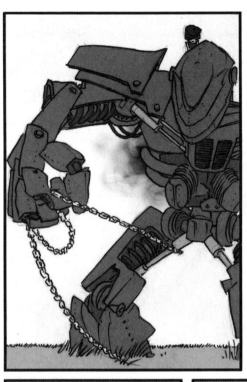

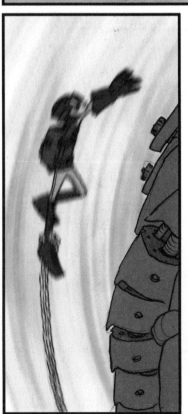

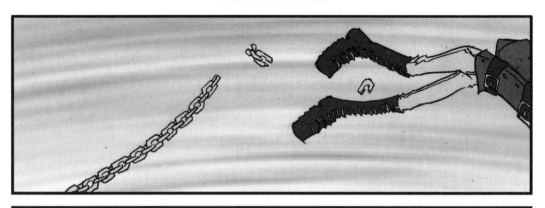

While the battle continued between Jet and the machine...

...I tried to position myself on the roof of the barn.

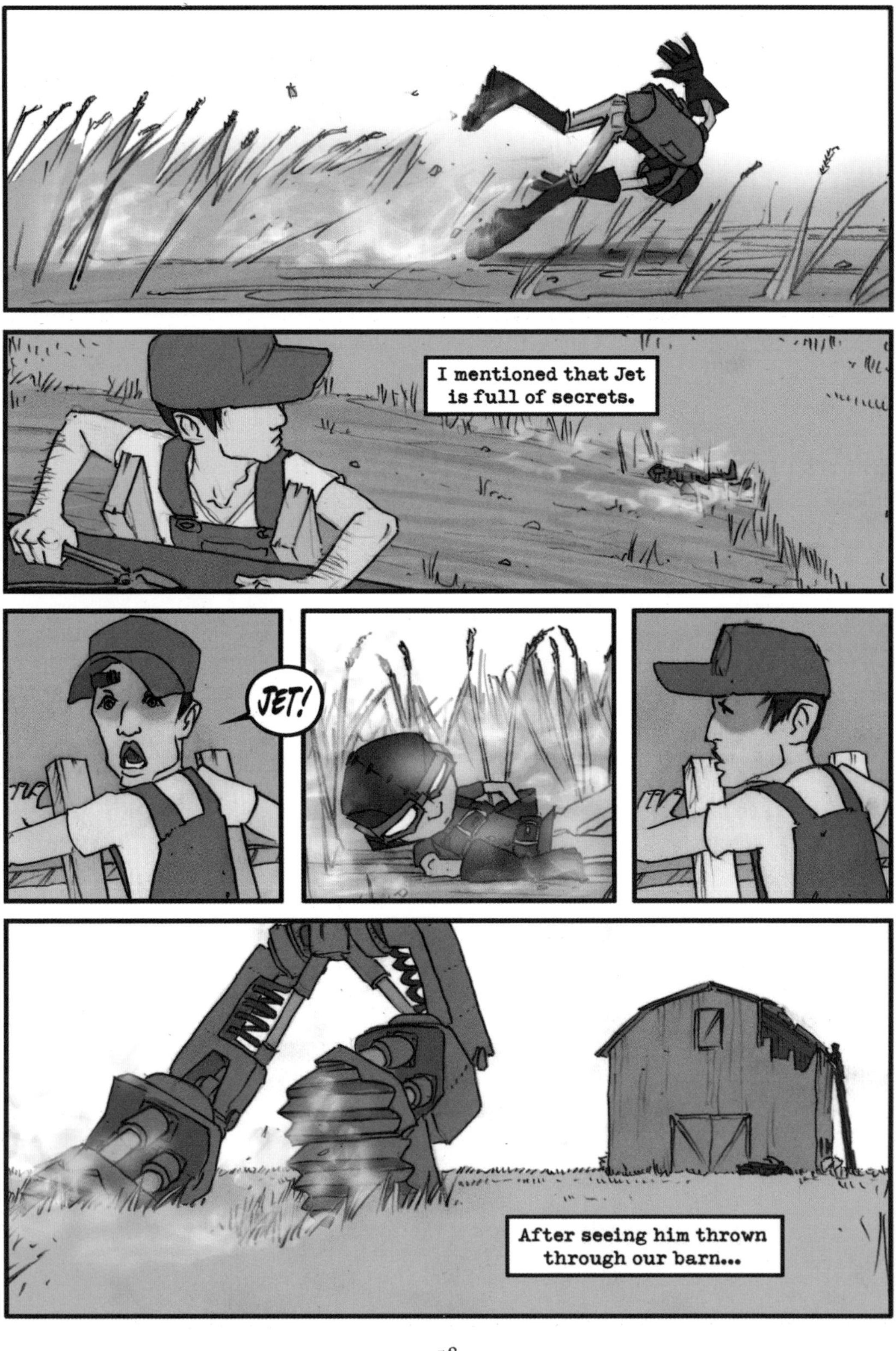
I mentioned that Jet is full of secrets.
JET!
After seeing him thrown through our barn...

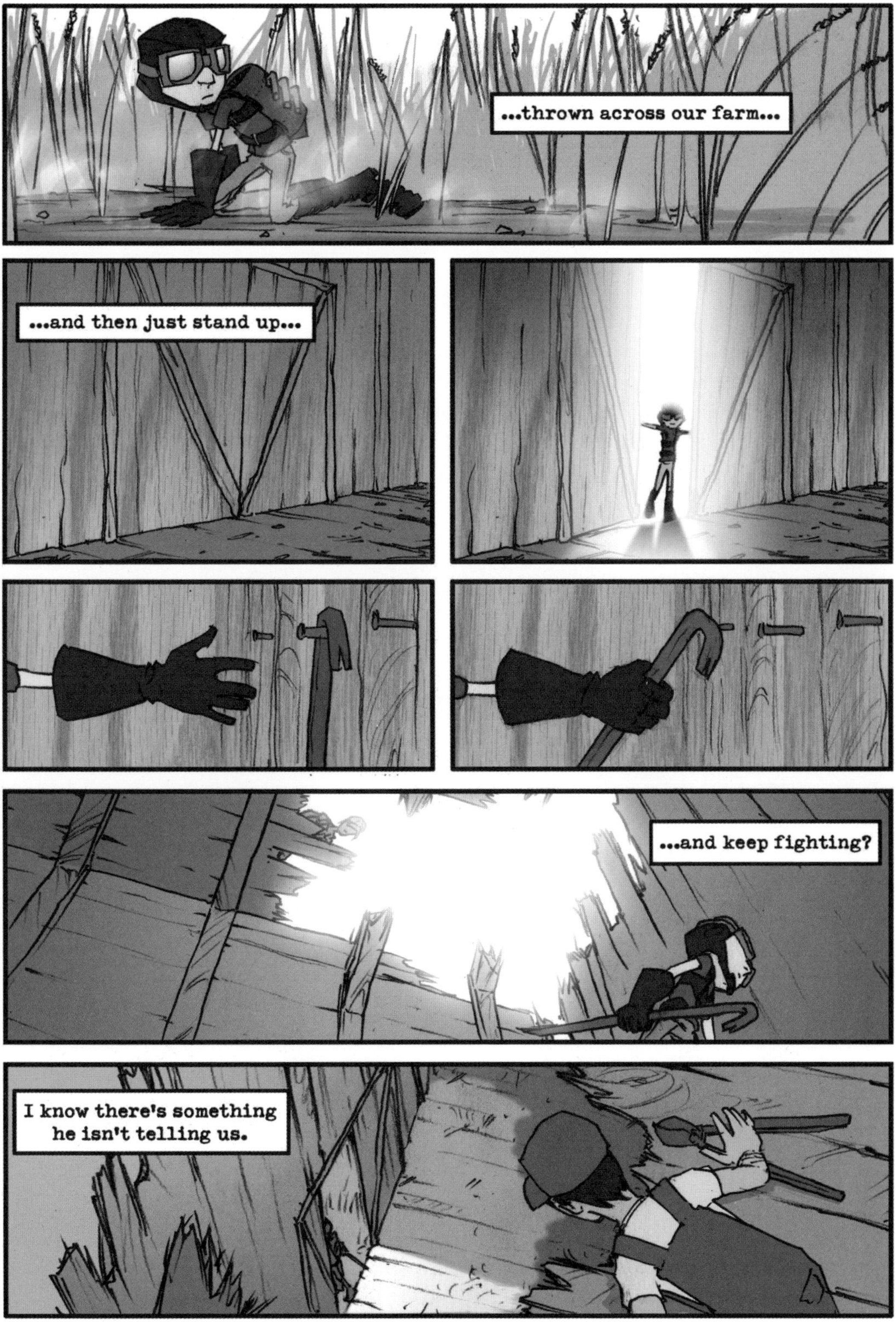
...thrown across our farm...
...and then just stand up...
...and keep fighting?
I know there's something he isn't telling us.

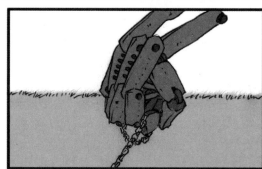

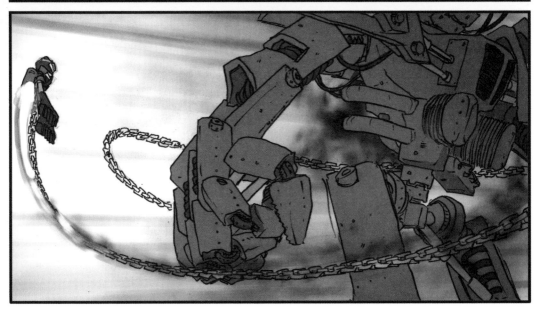

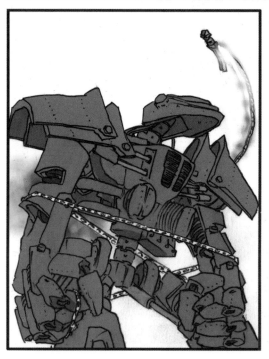

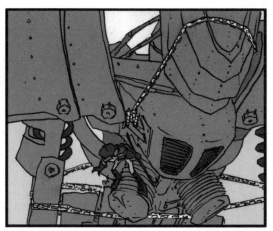

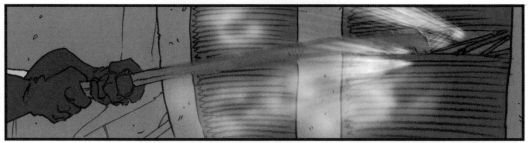

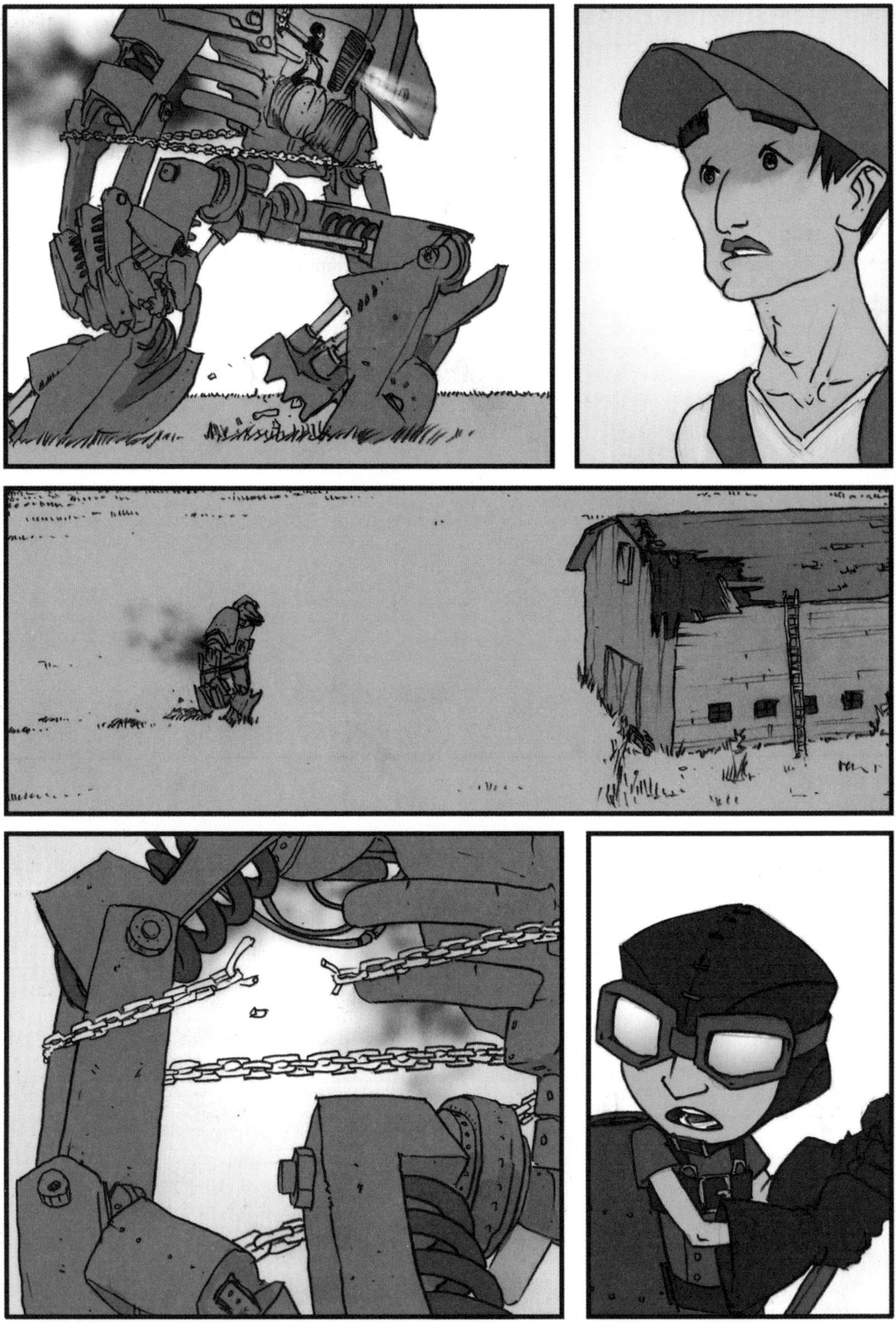

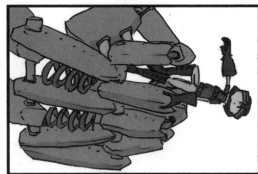

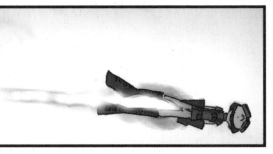

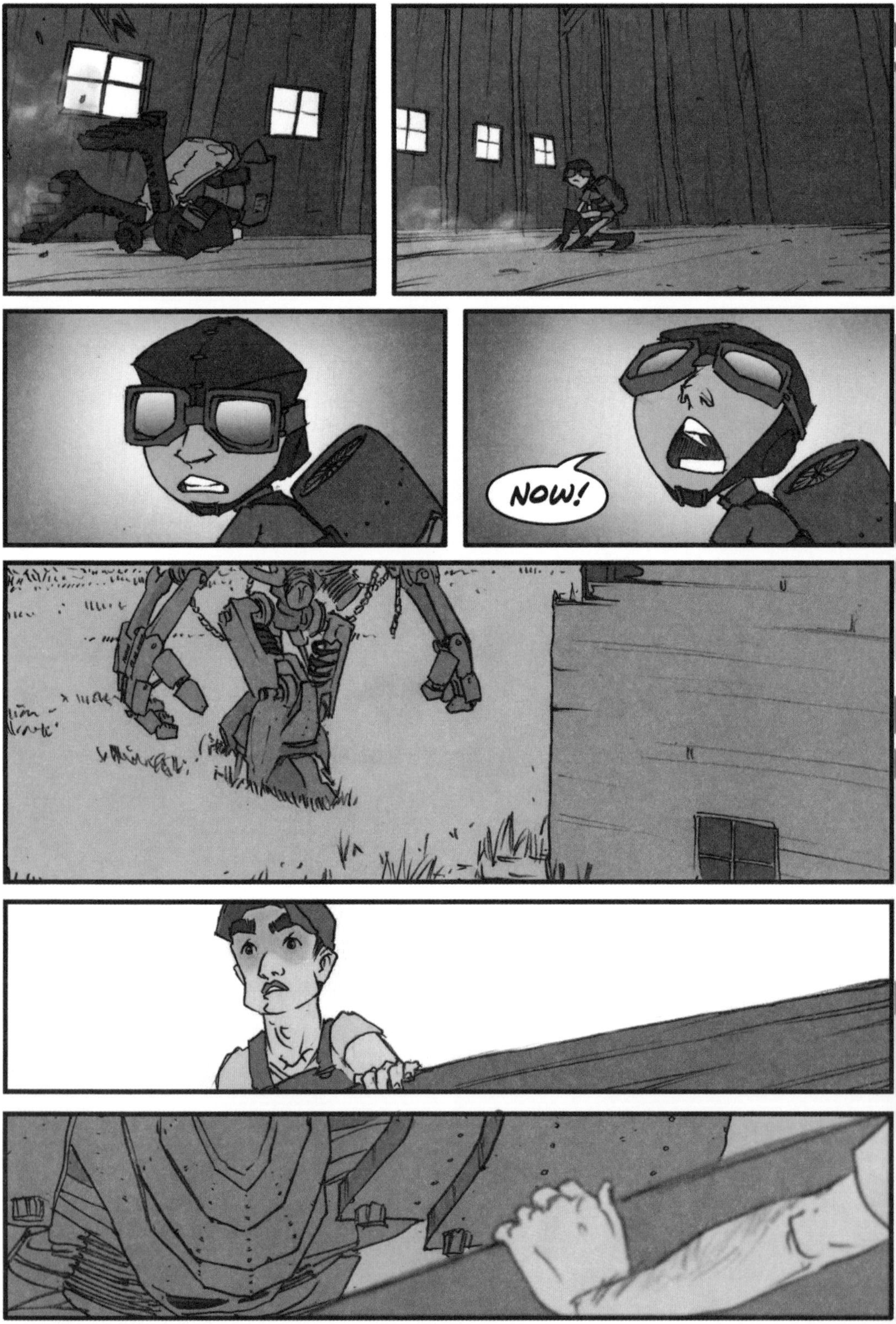
NOW!

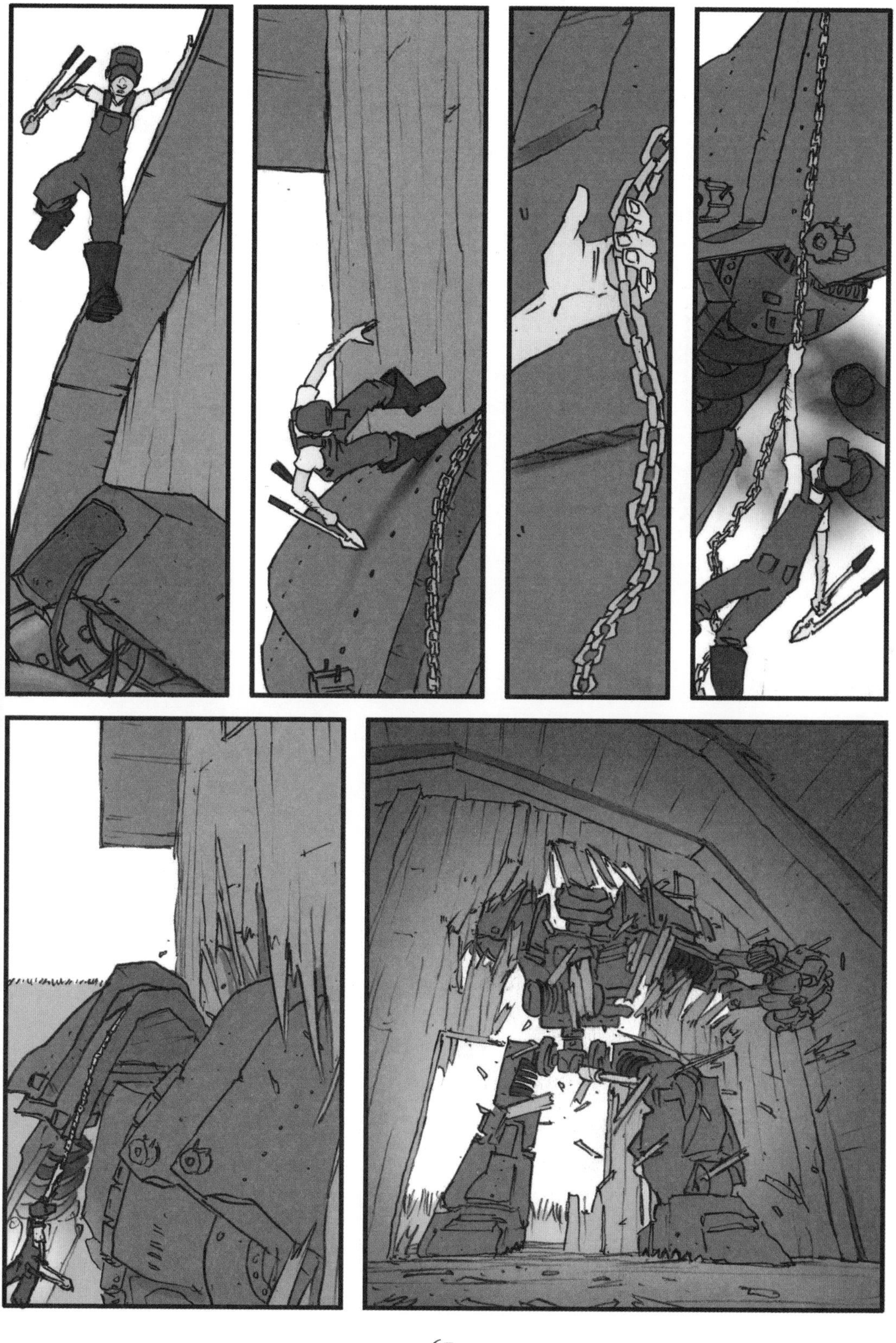

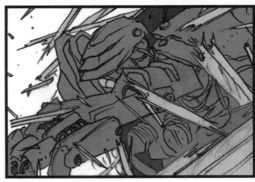

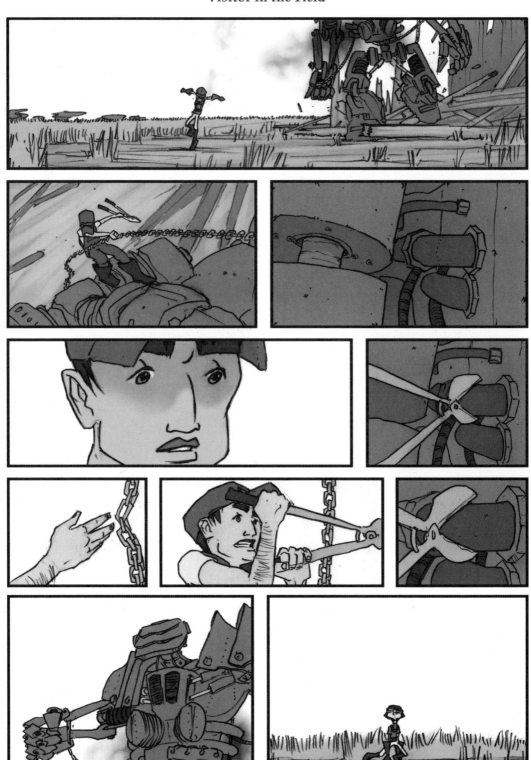

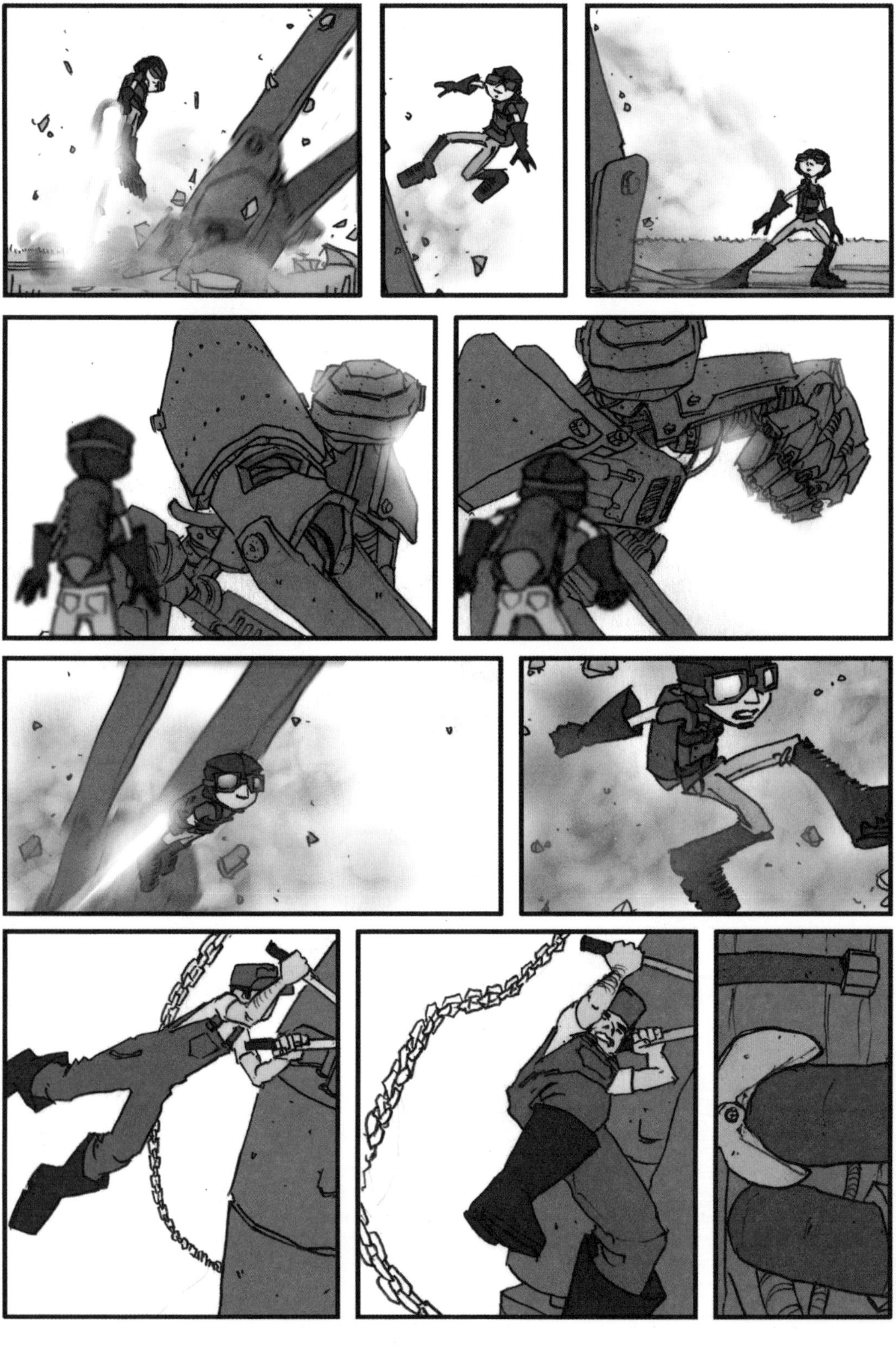

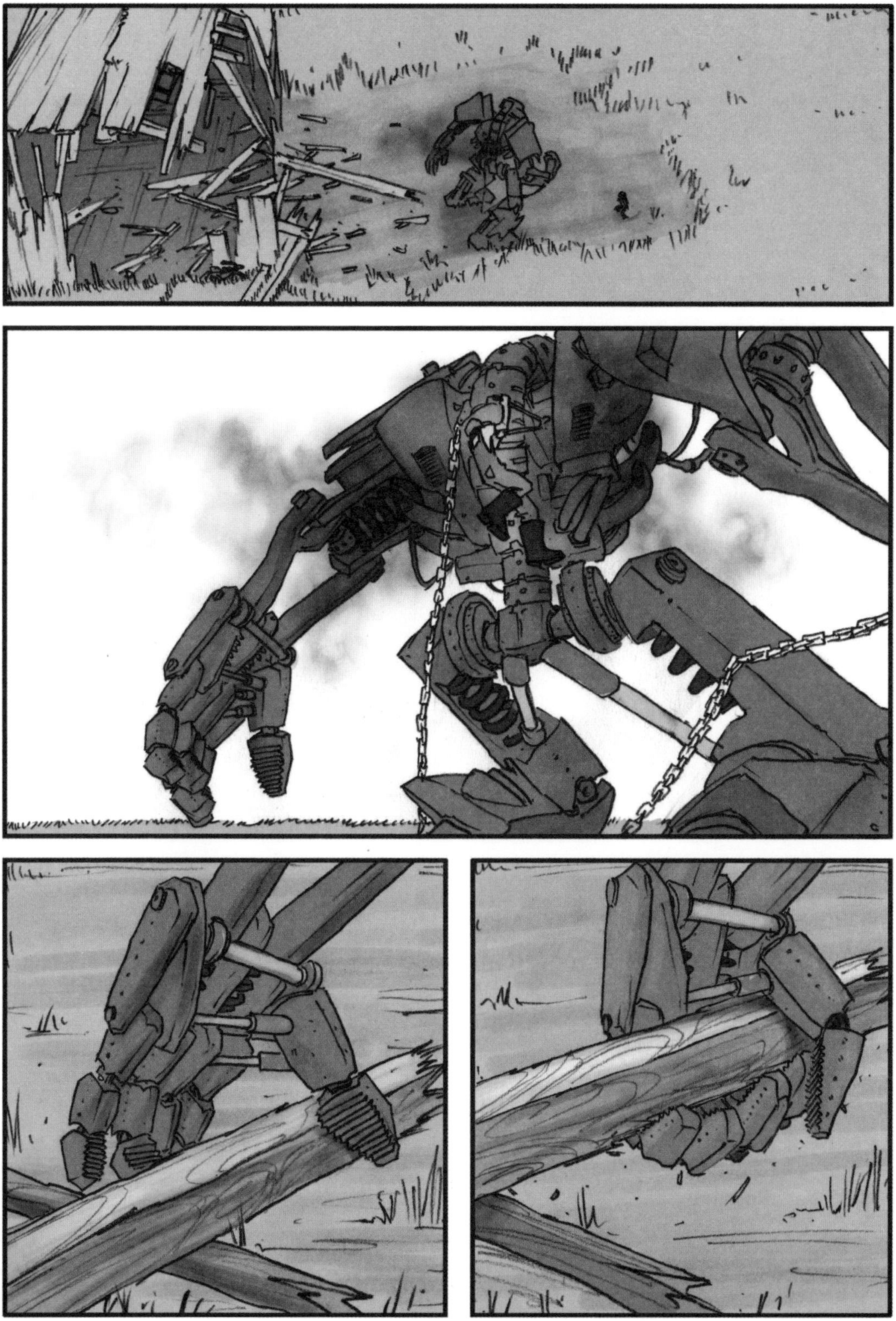

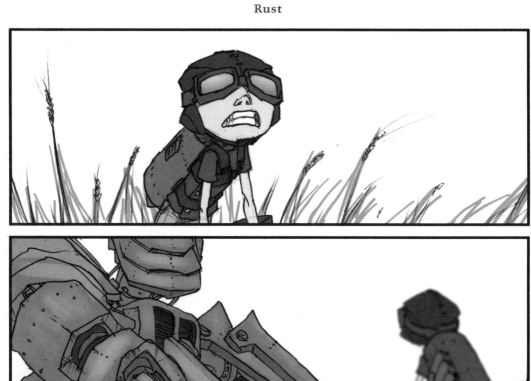

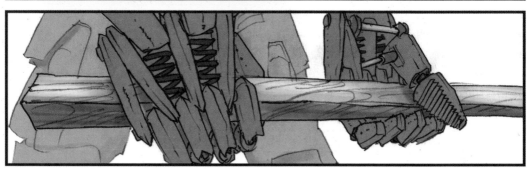

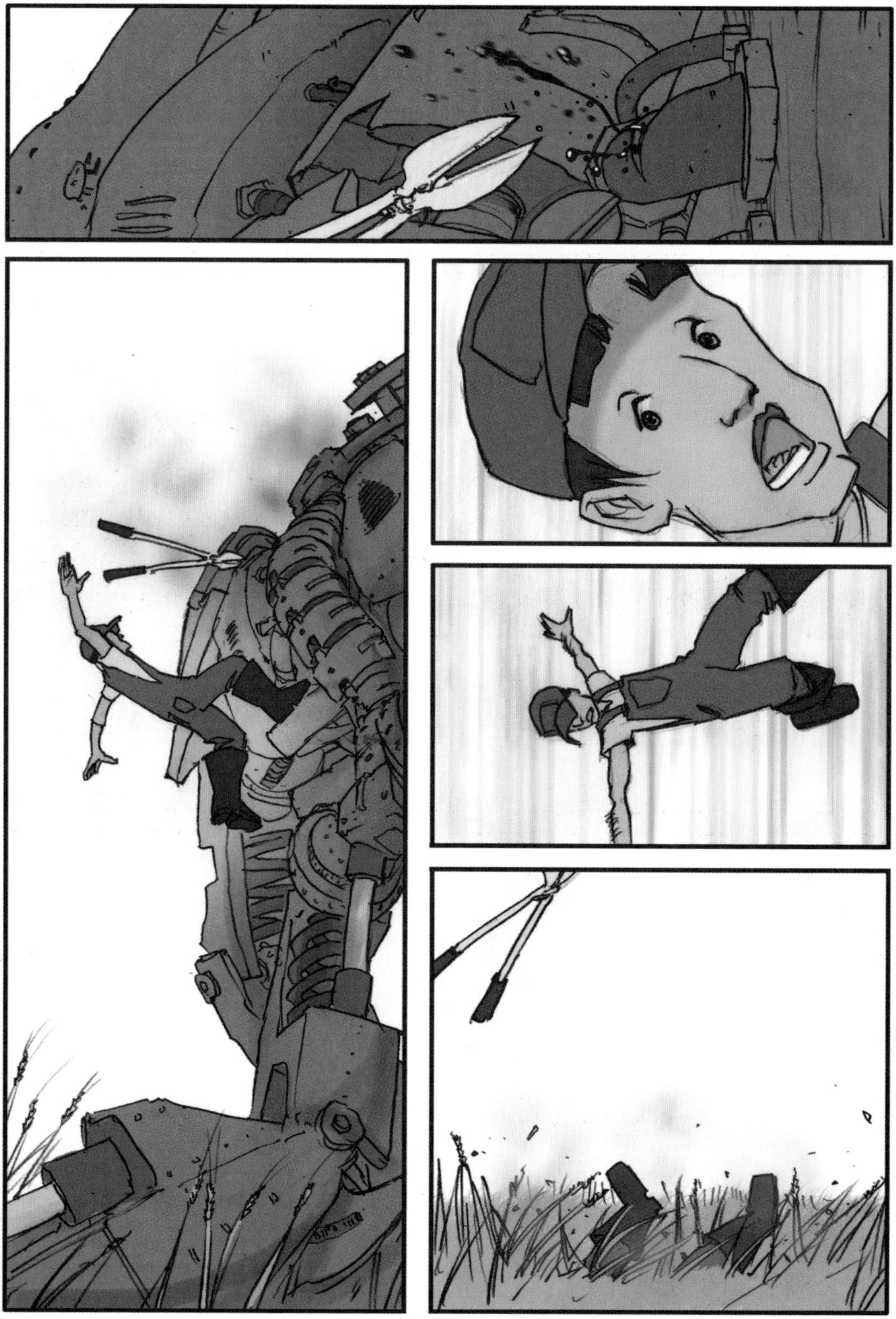

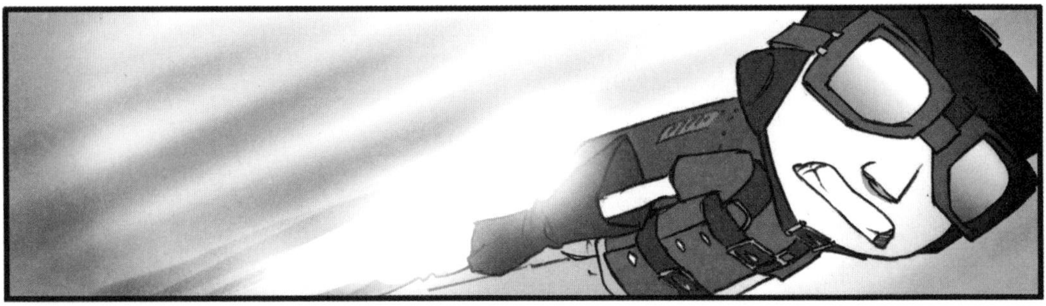

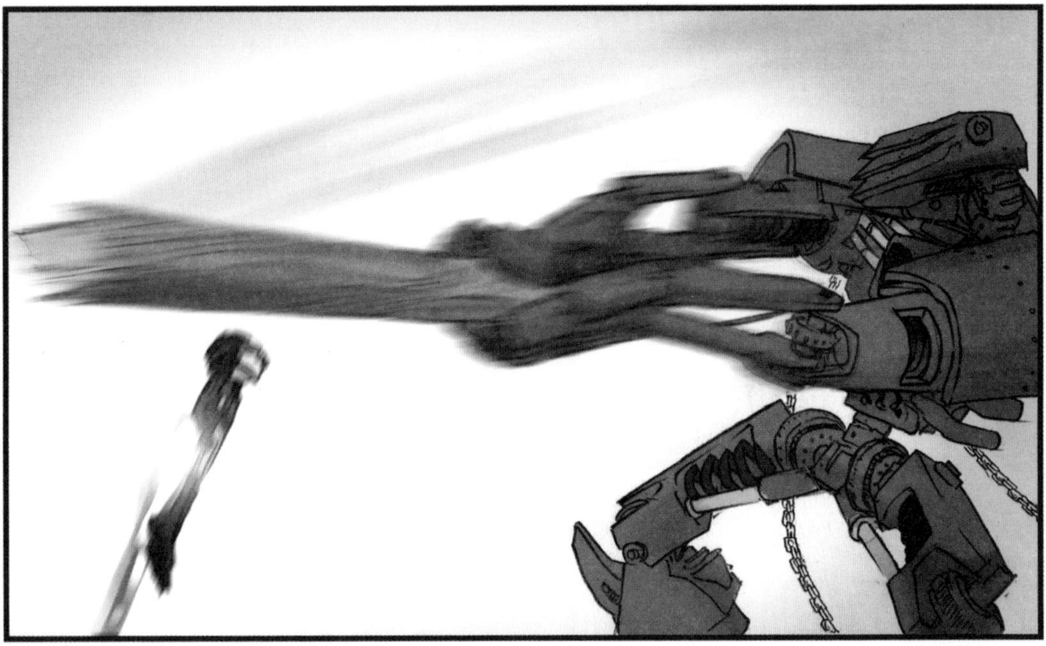

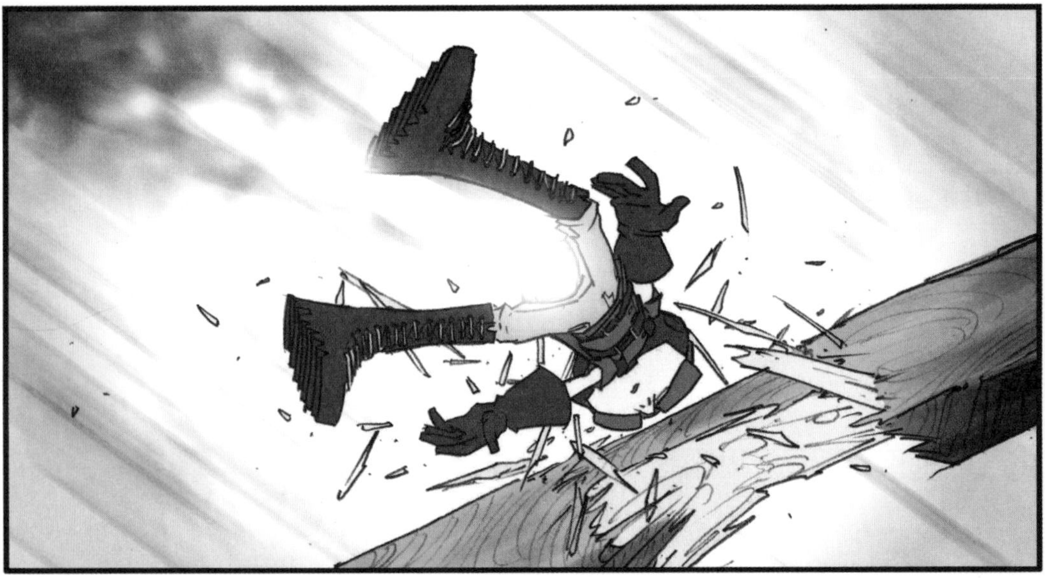

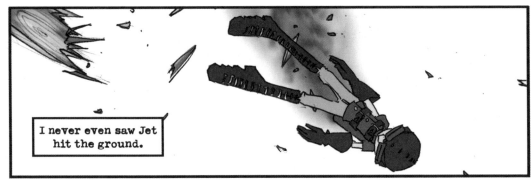

I never even saw Jet hit the ground.

When I came to...

ROMAN?

ROMAN?

HEY, OZ. WHAT DO YOU NEED?

I WAS JUST LOOKING FOR JET.

JUST ONE SEC, OZ.

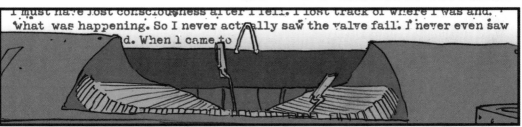

I must have lost consciousness after I fell. I lost track of where I was and what was happening. So I never actually saw the valve fail. I never even saw ...d. When I came to

When I came to, I could hear the grinding of the machine's winding springs...

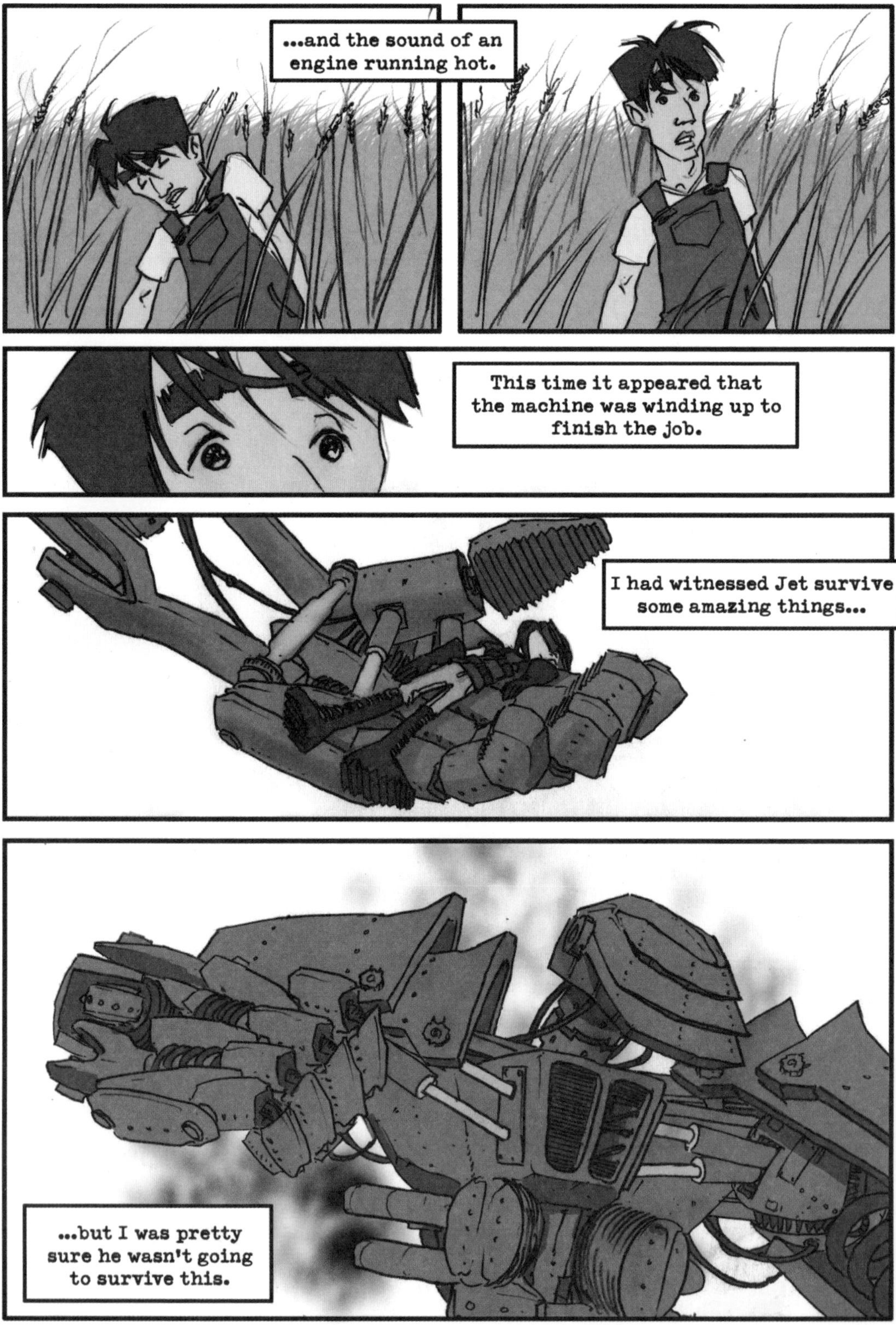
...and the sound of an engine running hot.
This time it appeared that the machine was winding up to finish the job.
I had witnessed Jet survive some amazing things...
...but I was pretty sure he wasn't going to survive this.

The oil.

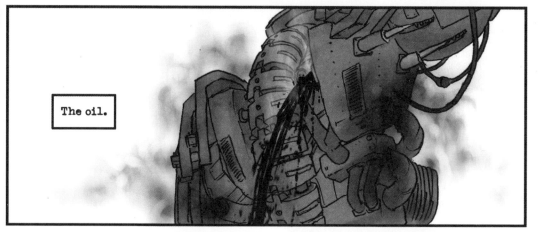

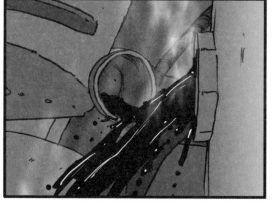

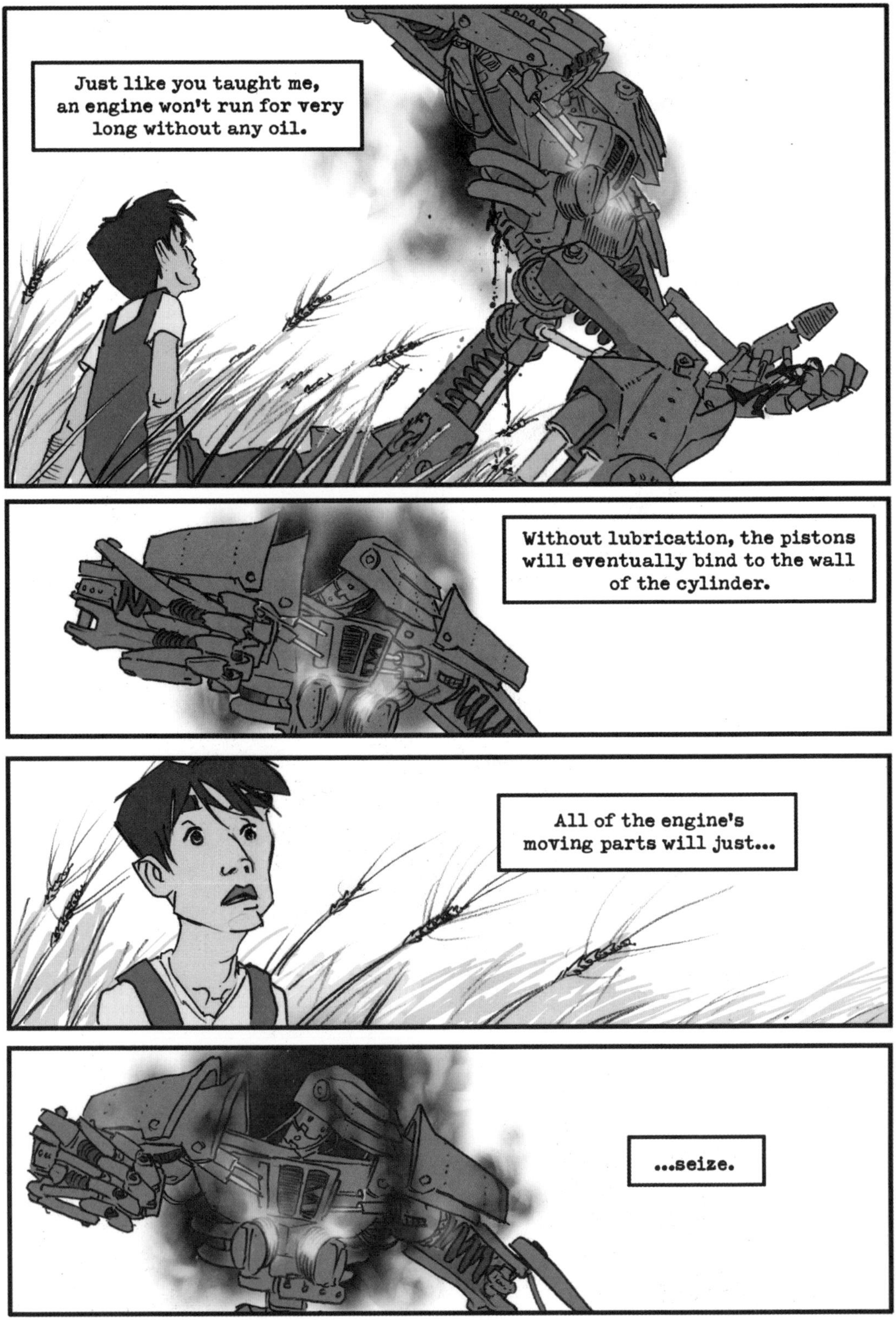
Just like you taught me, an engine won't run for very long without any oil.
Without lubrication, the pistons will eventually bind to the wall of the cylinder.
All of the engine's moving parts will just...
...seize.

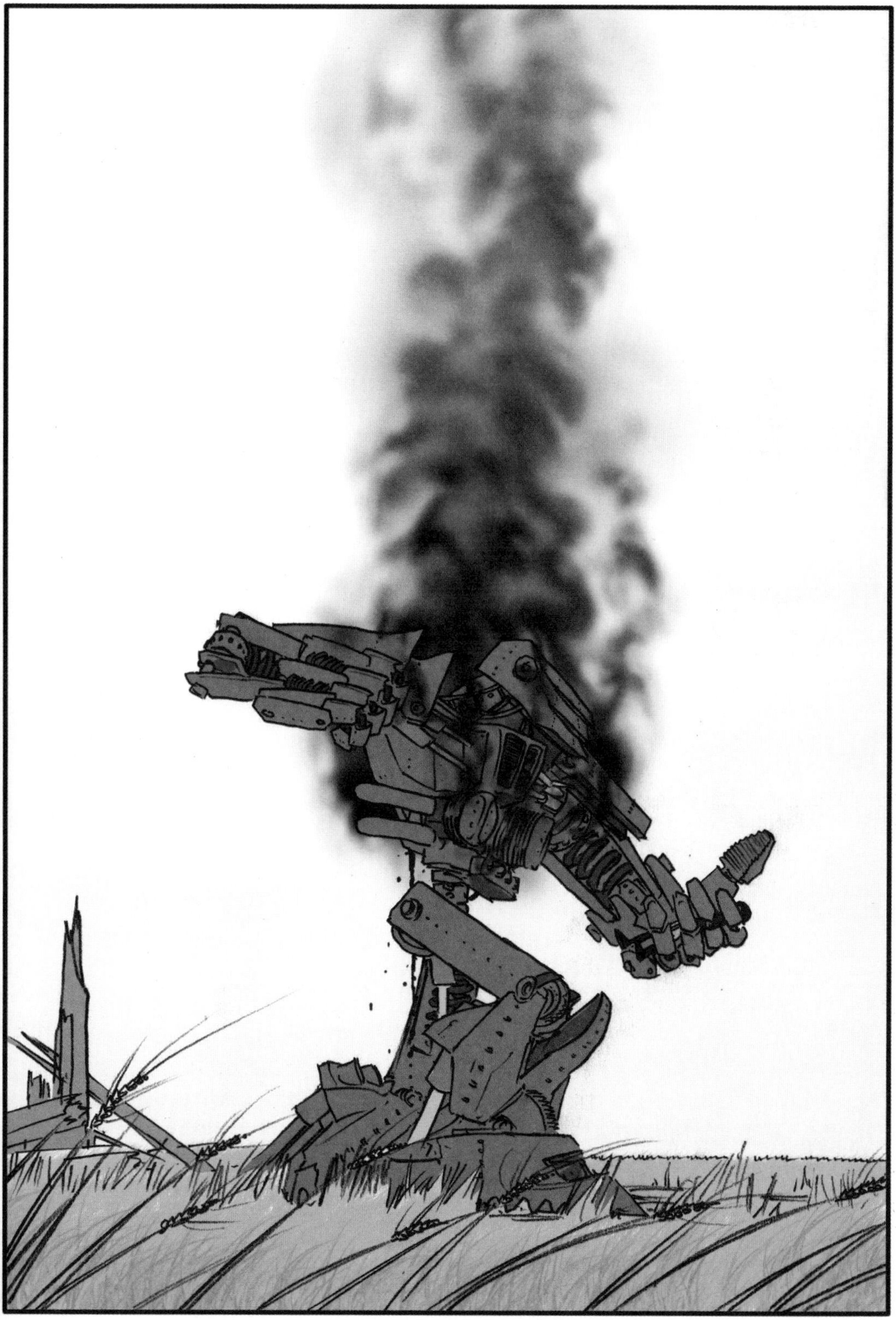

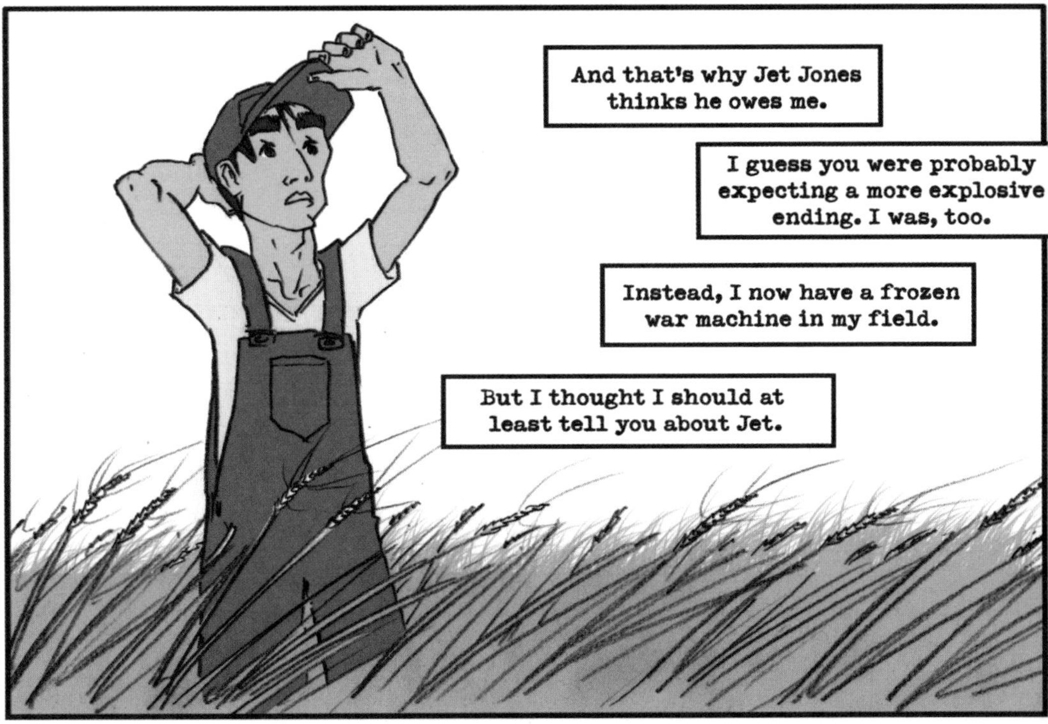
And that's why Jet Jones thinks he owes me.
I guess you were probably expecting a more explosive ending. I was, too.
Instead, I now have a frozen war machine in my field.
But I thought I should at least tell you about Jet.

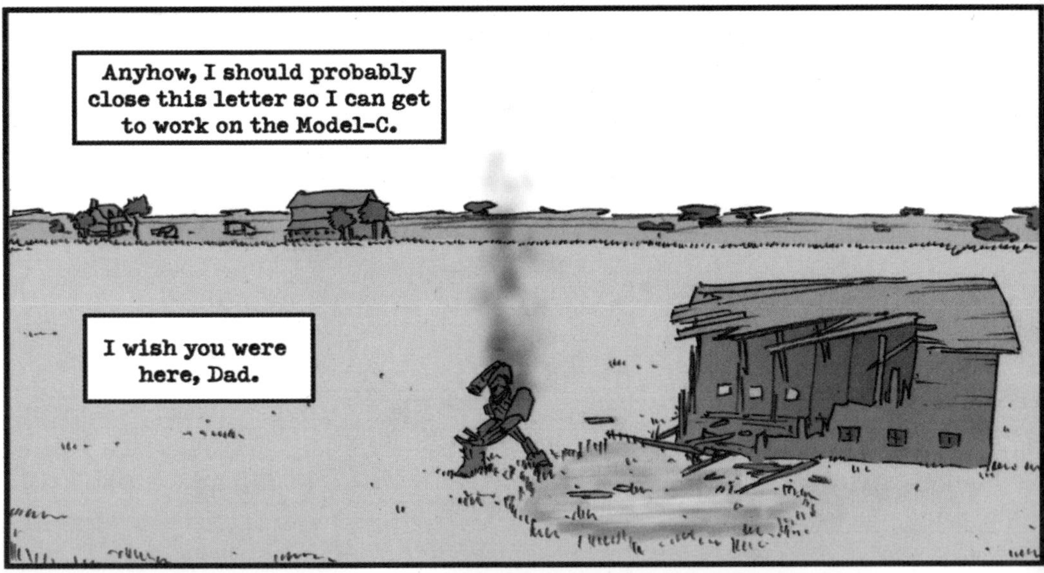
Anyhow, I should probably close this letter so I can get to work on the Model-C.
I wish you were here, Dad.

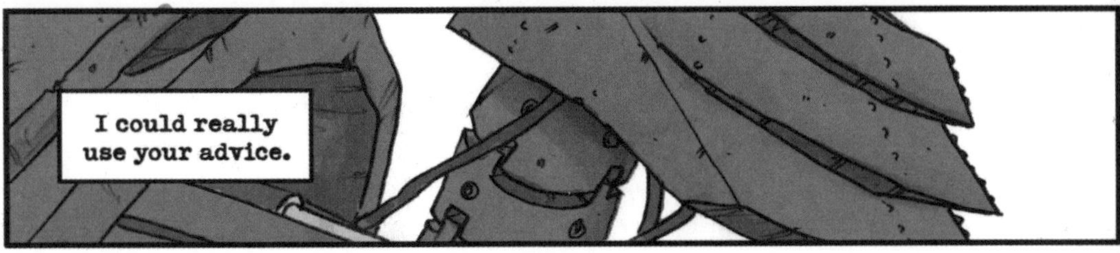
I could really use your advice.

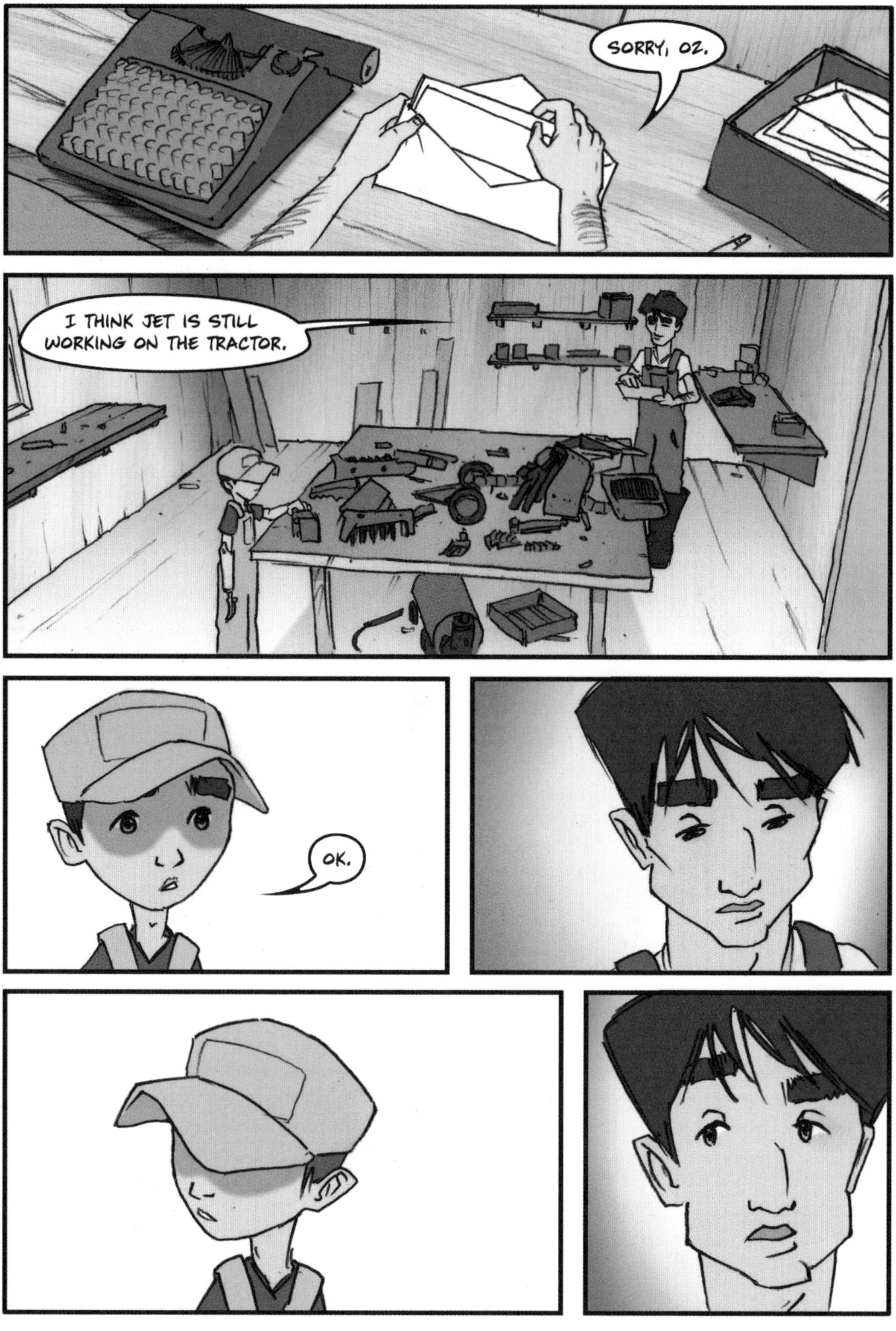
SORRY, OZ.
I THINK JET IS STILL WORKING ON THE TRACTOR.
OK.

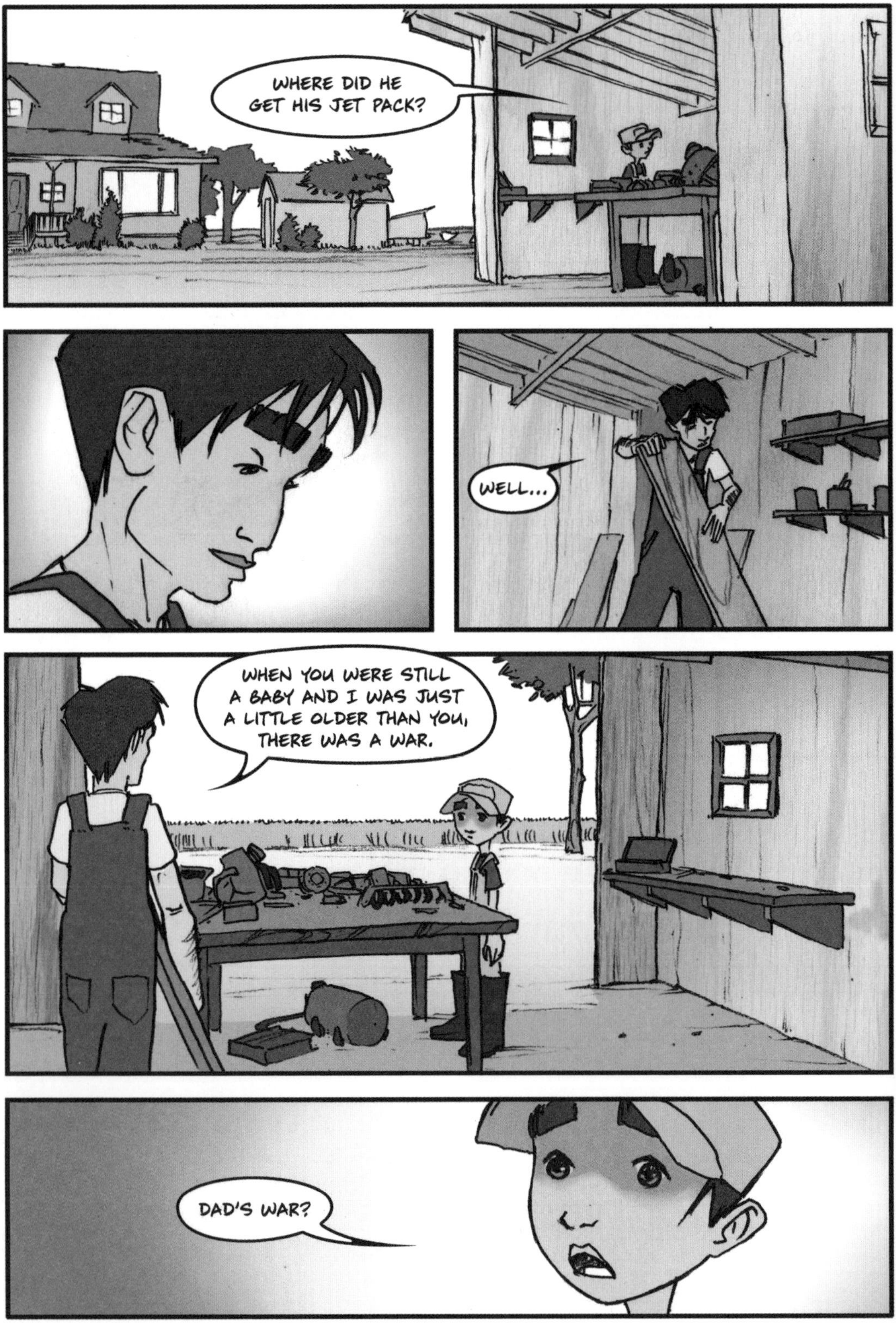
WHERE DID HE GET HIS JET PACK?
WELL...
WHEN YOU WERE STILL A BABY AND I WAS JUST A LITTLE OLDER THAN YOU, THERE WAS A WAR.
DAD'S WAR?

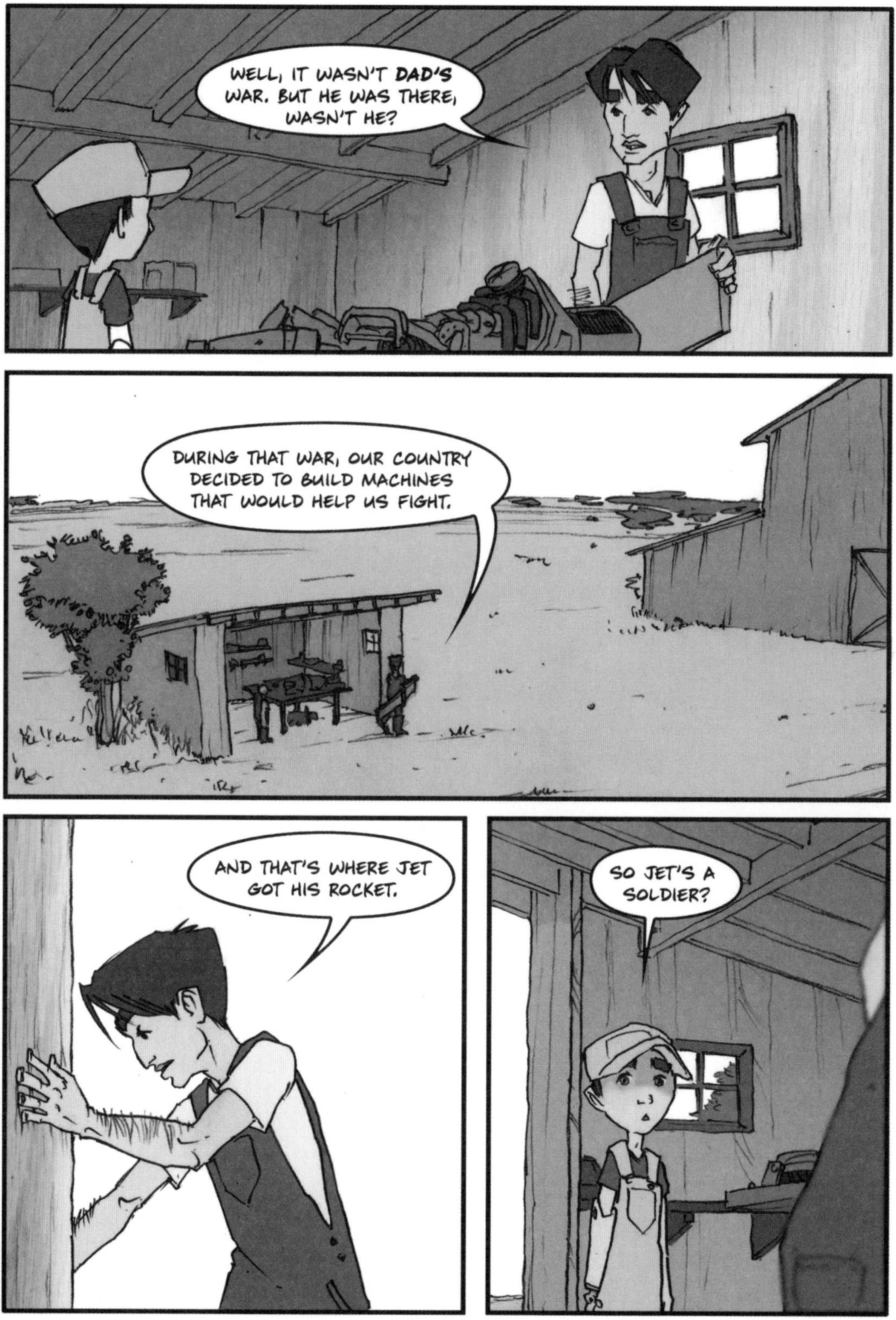
WELL, IT WASN'T DAD'S WAR. BUT HE WAS THERE, WASN'T HE?
DURING THAT WAR, OUR COUNTRY DECIDED TO BUILD MACHINES THAT WOULD HELP US FIGHT.
AND THAT'S WHERE JET GOT HIS ROCKET.
SO JET'S A SOLDIER?

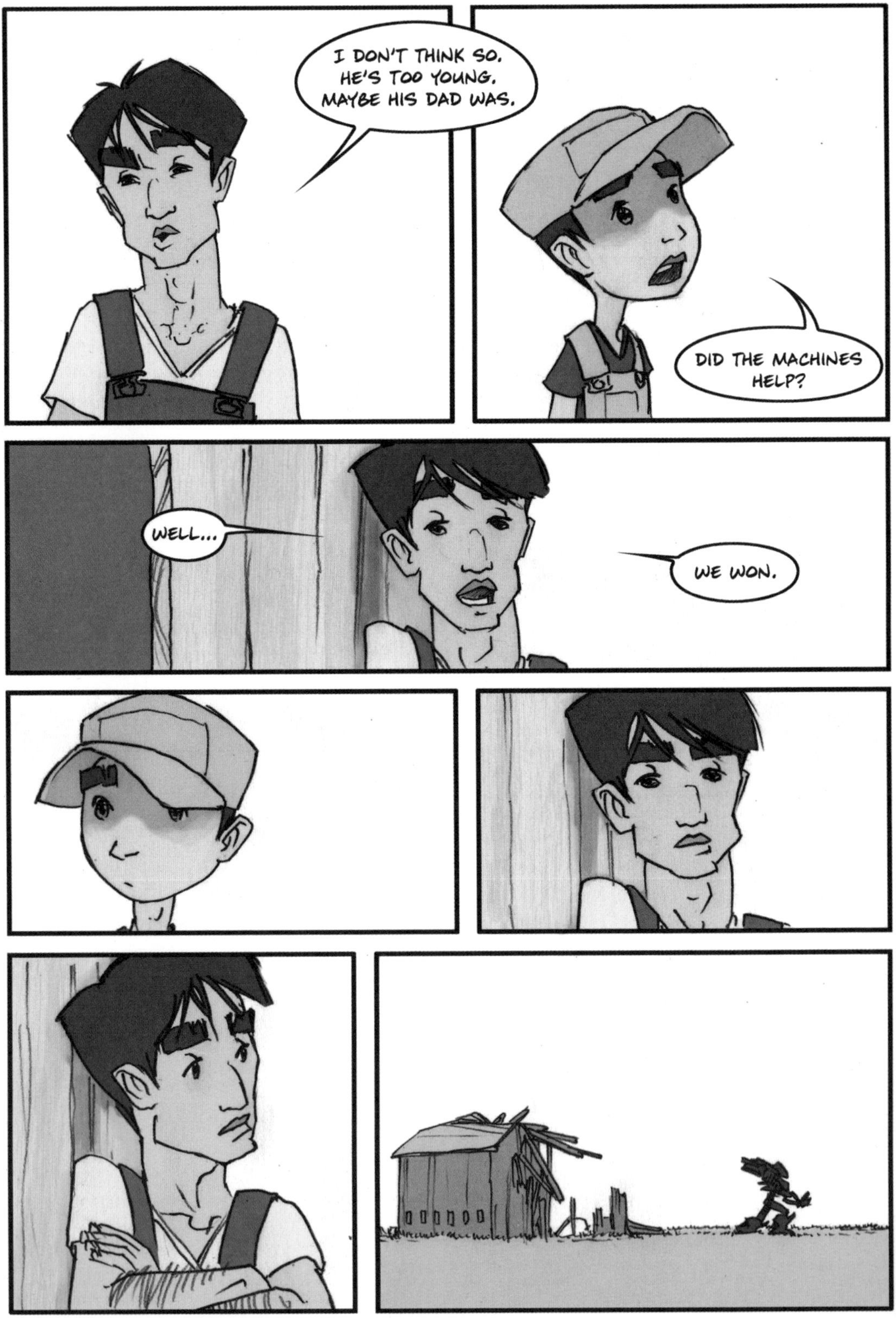
I DON'T THINK SO. HE'S TOO YOUNG. MAYBE HIS DAD WAS.
DID THE MACHINES HELP?
WELL...
WE WON.

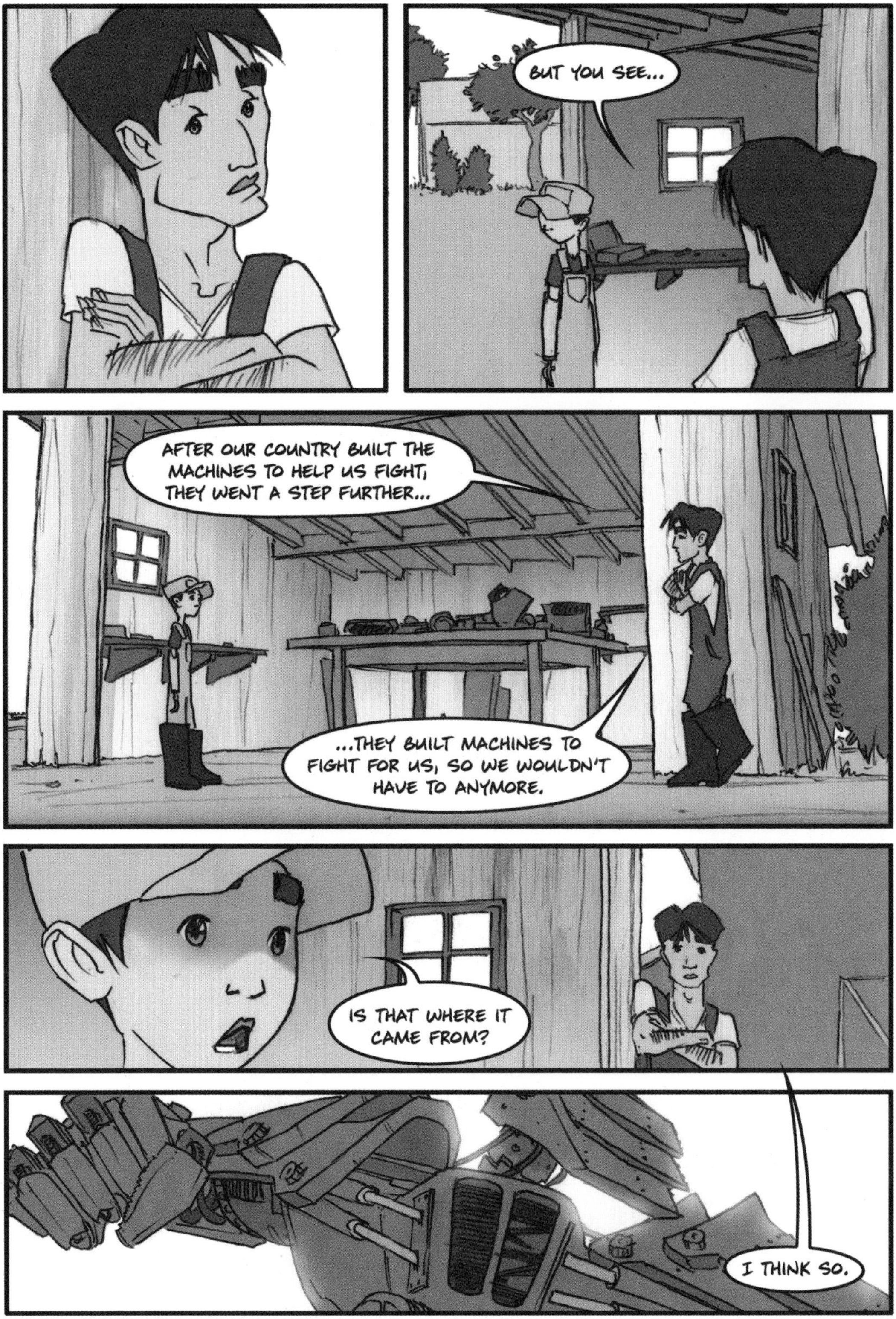
BUT YOU SEE...
AFTER OUR COUNTRY BUILT THE MACHINES TO HELP US FIGHT, THEY WENT A STEP FURTHER...
...THEY BUILT MACHINES TO FIGHT FOR US, SO WE WOULDN'T HAVE TO ANYMORE.
IS THAT WHERE IT CAME FROM?
I THINK SO.

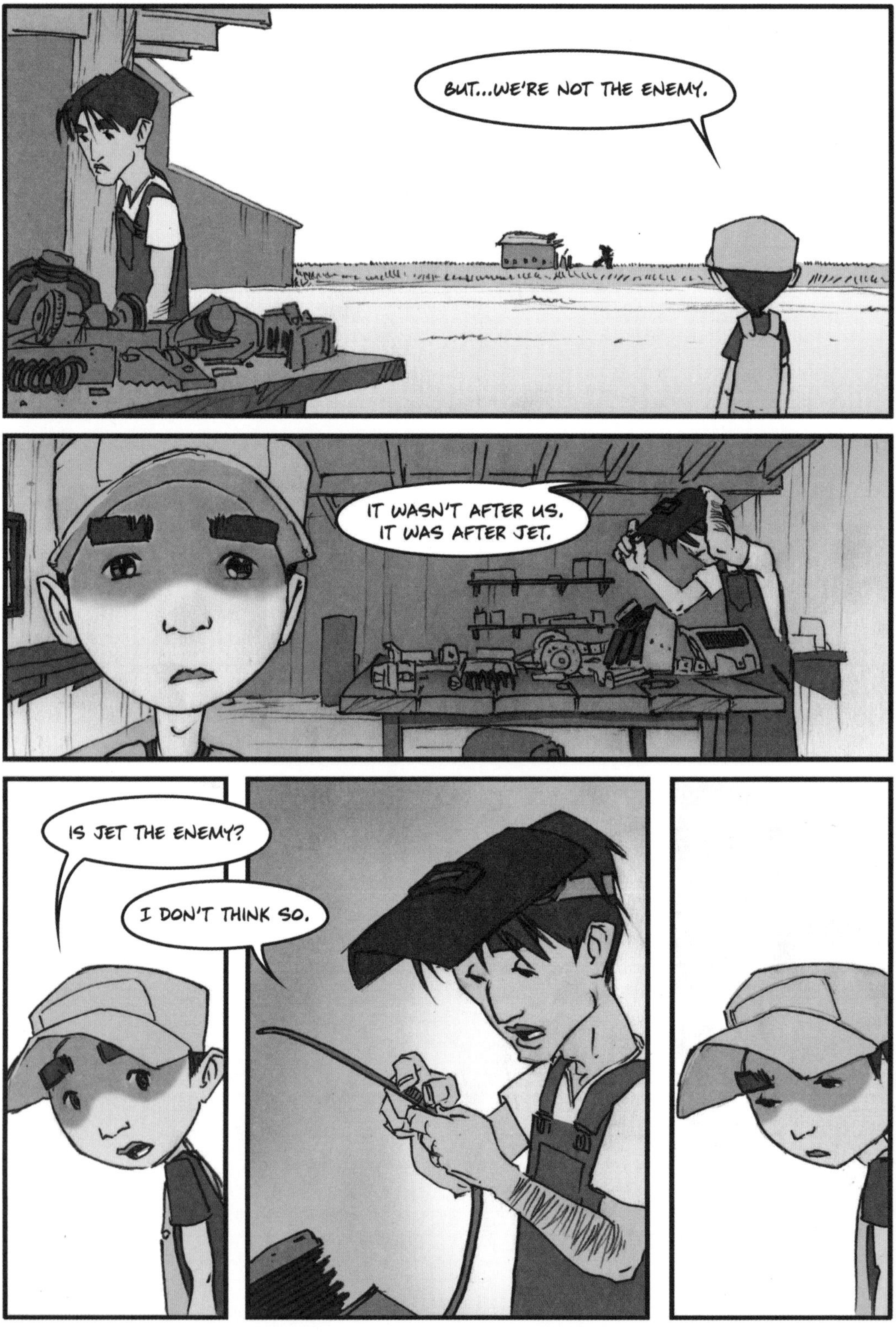
BUT...WE'RE NOT THE ENEMY.
IT WASN'T AFTER US. IT WAS AFTER JET.
IS JET THE ENEMY?
I DON'T THINK SO.

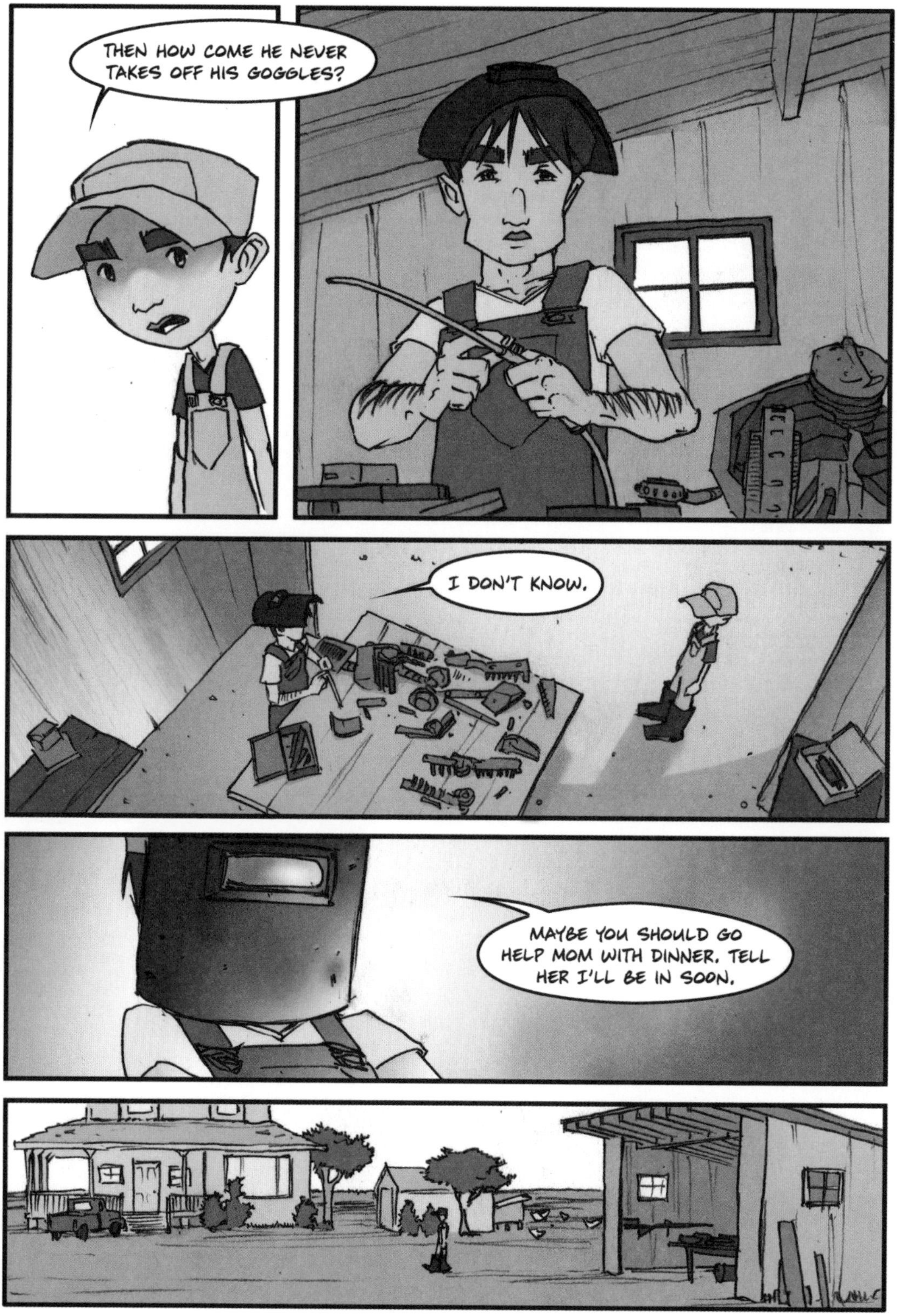
THEN HOW COME HE NEVER TAKES OFF HIS GOGGLES?
I DON'T KNOW.
MAYBE YOU SHOULD GO HELP MOM WITH DINNER. TELL HER I'LL BE IN SOON.

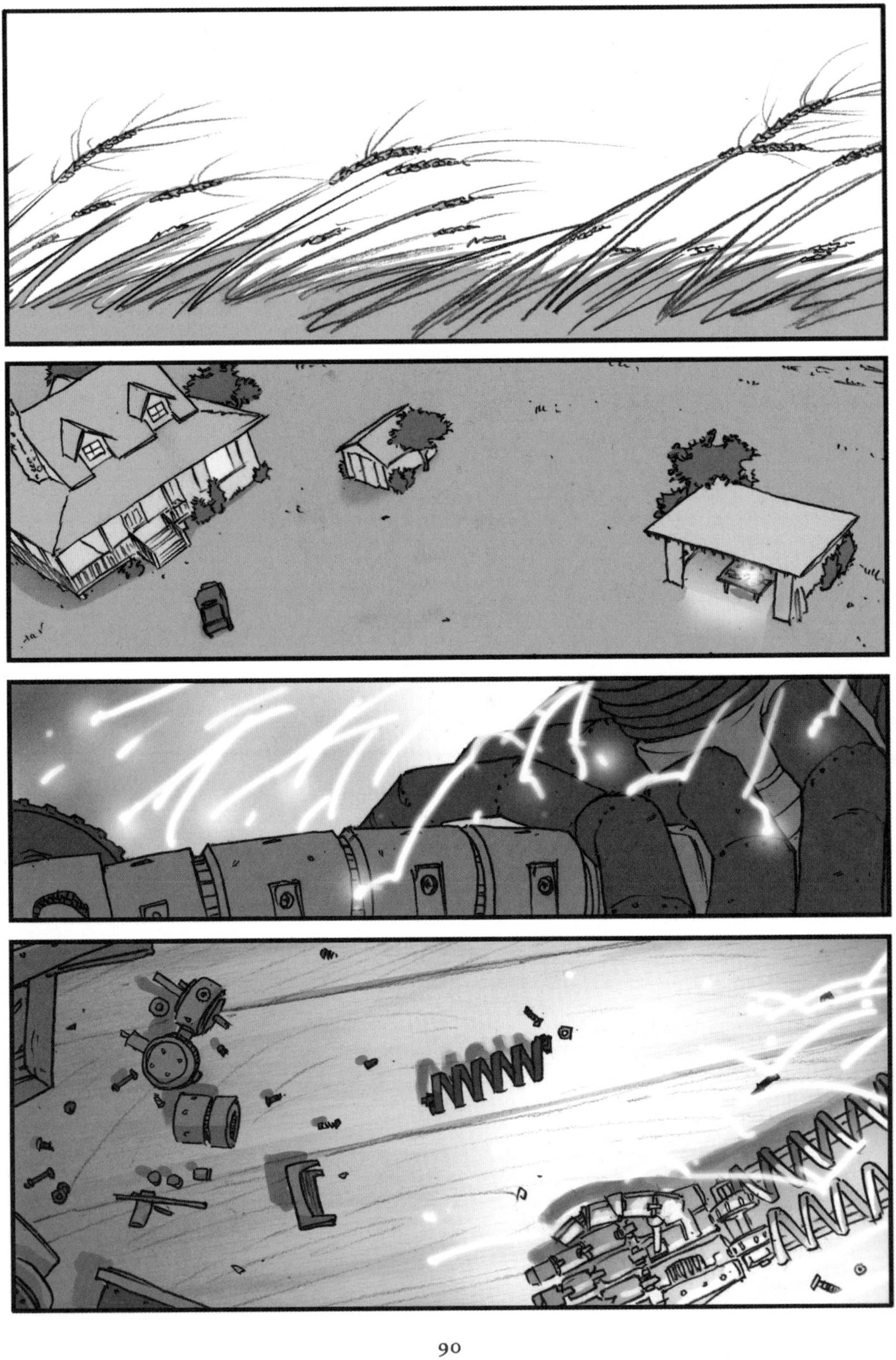

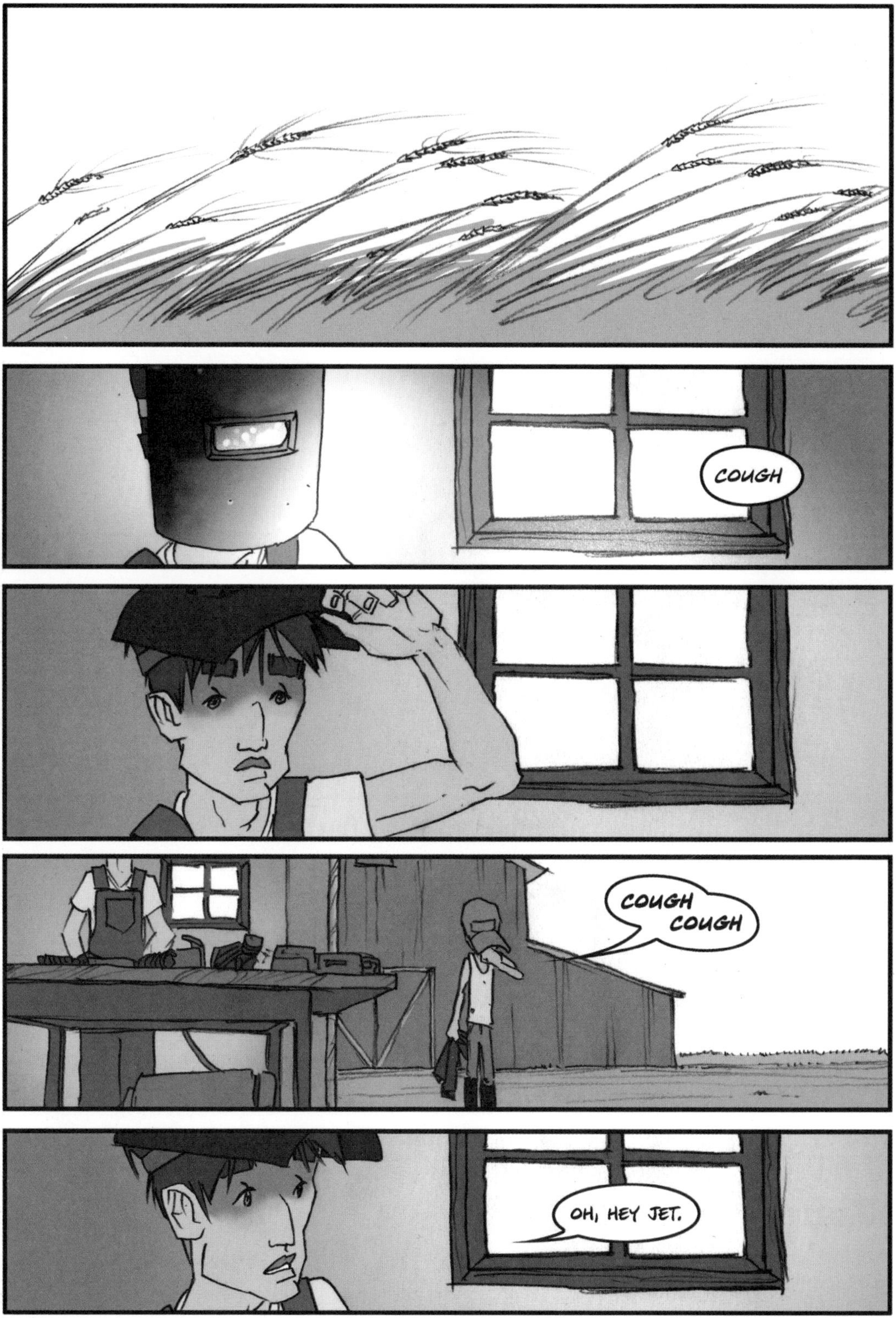
COUGH
COUGH COUGH
OH, HEY JET.

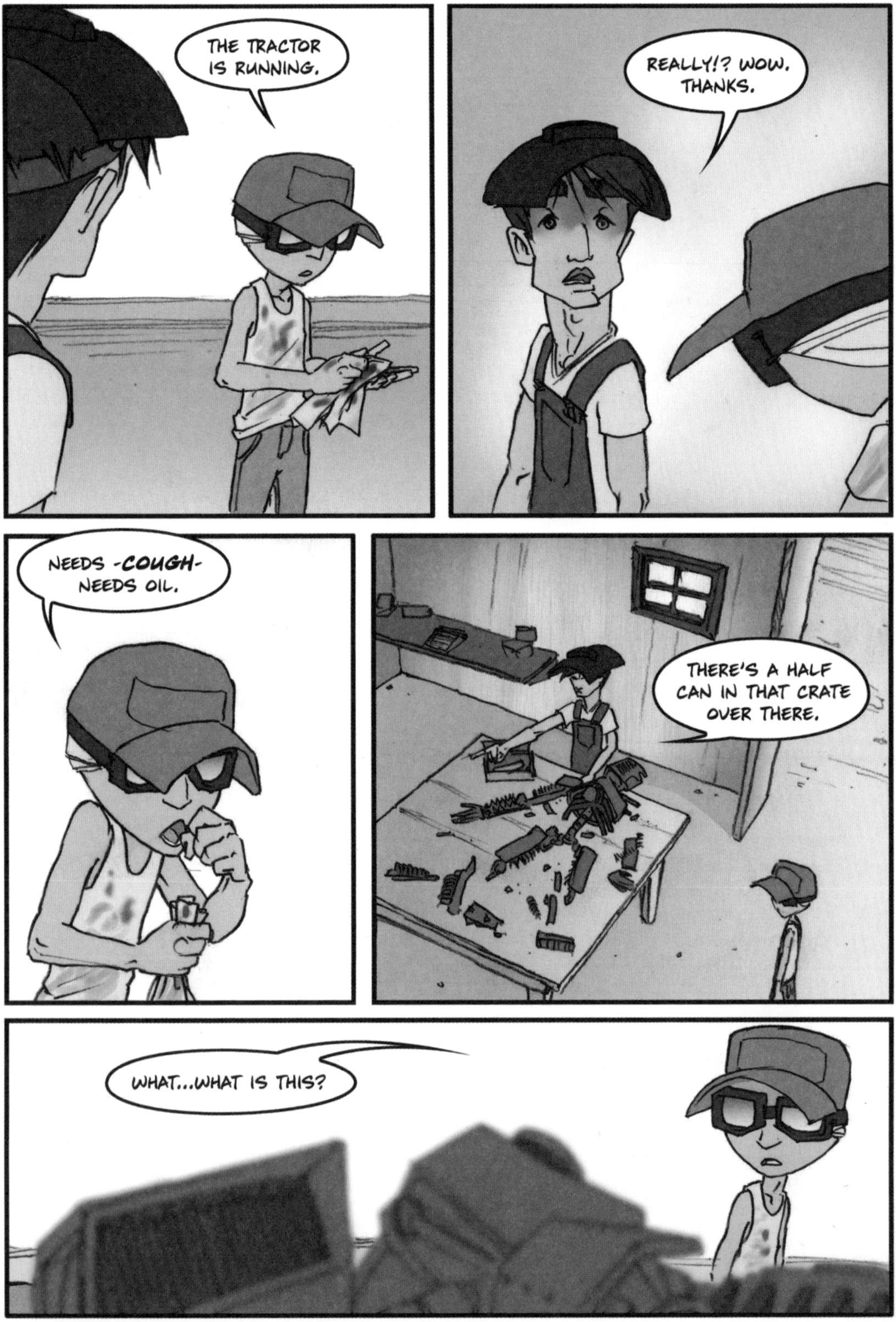
THE TRACTOR IS RUNNING.
REALLY!? WOW. THANKS.
NEEDS -COUGH- NEEDS OIL.
THERE'S A HALF CAN IN THAT CRATE OVER THERE.
WHAT...WHAT IS THIS?

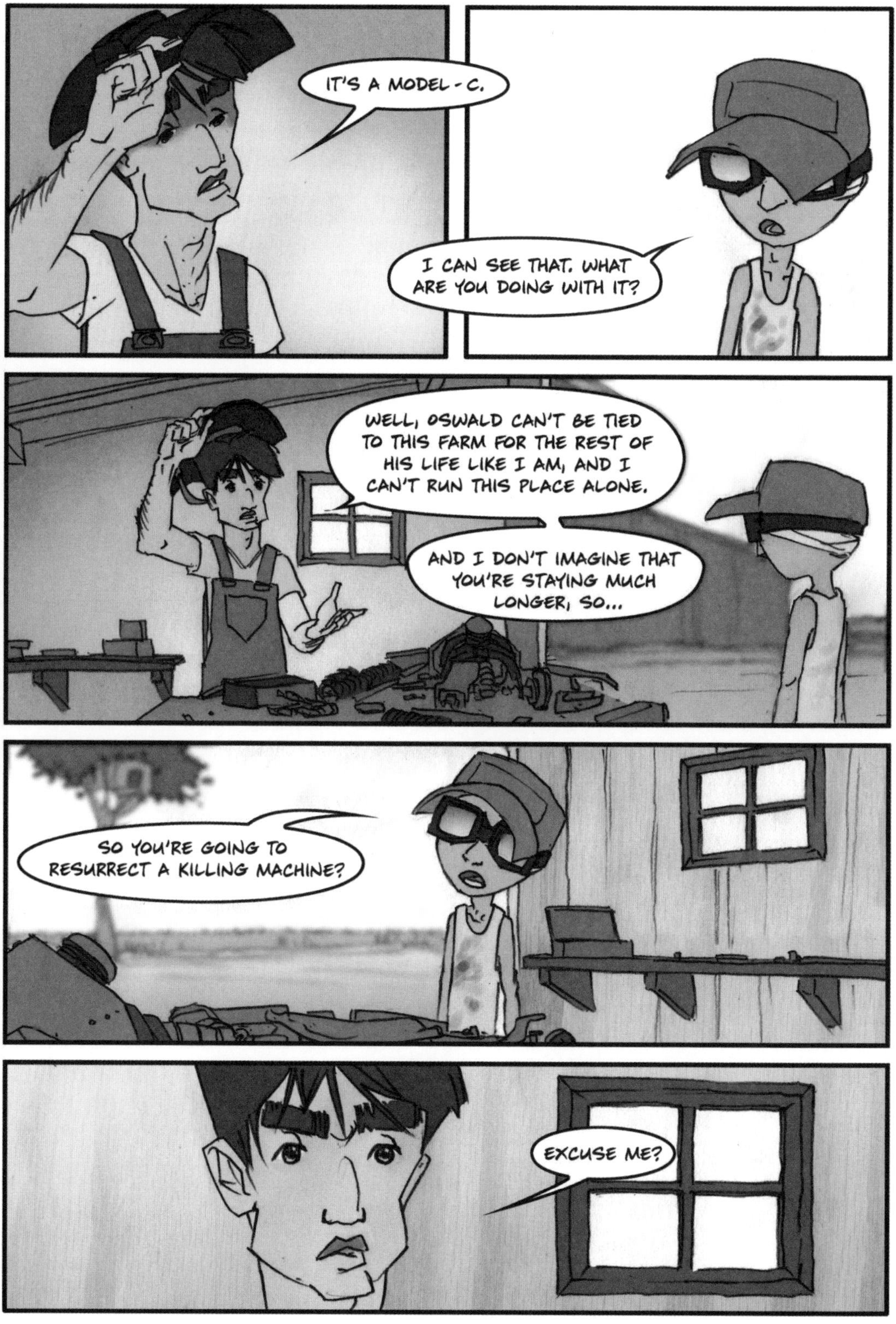
IT'S A MODEL - C.
I CAN SEE THAT. WHAT ARE YOU DOING WITH IT?
WELL, OSWALD CAN'T BE TIED TO THIS FARM FOR THE REST OF HIS LIFE LIKE I AM, AND I CAN'T RUN THIS PLACE ALONE.
AND I DON'T IMAGINE THAT YOU'RE STAYING MUCH LONGER, SO...
SO YOU'RE GOING TO RESURRECT A KILLING MACHINE?
EXCUSE ME?

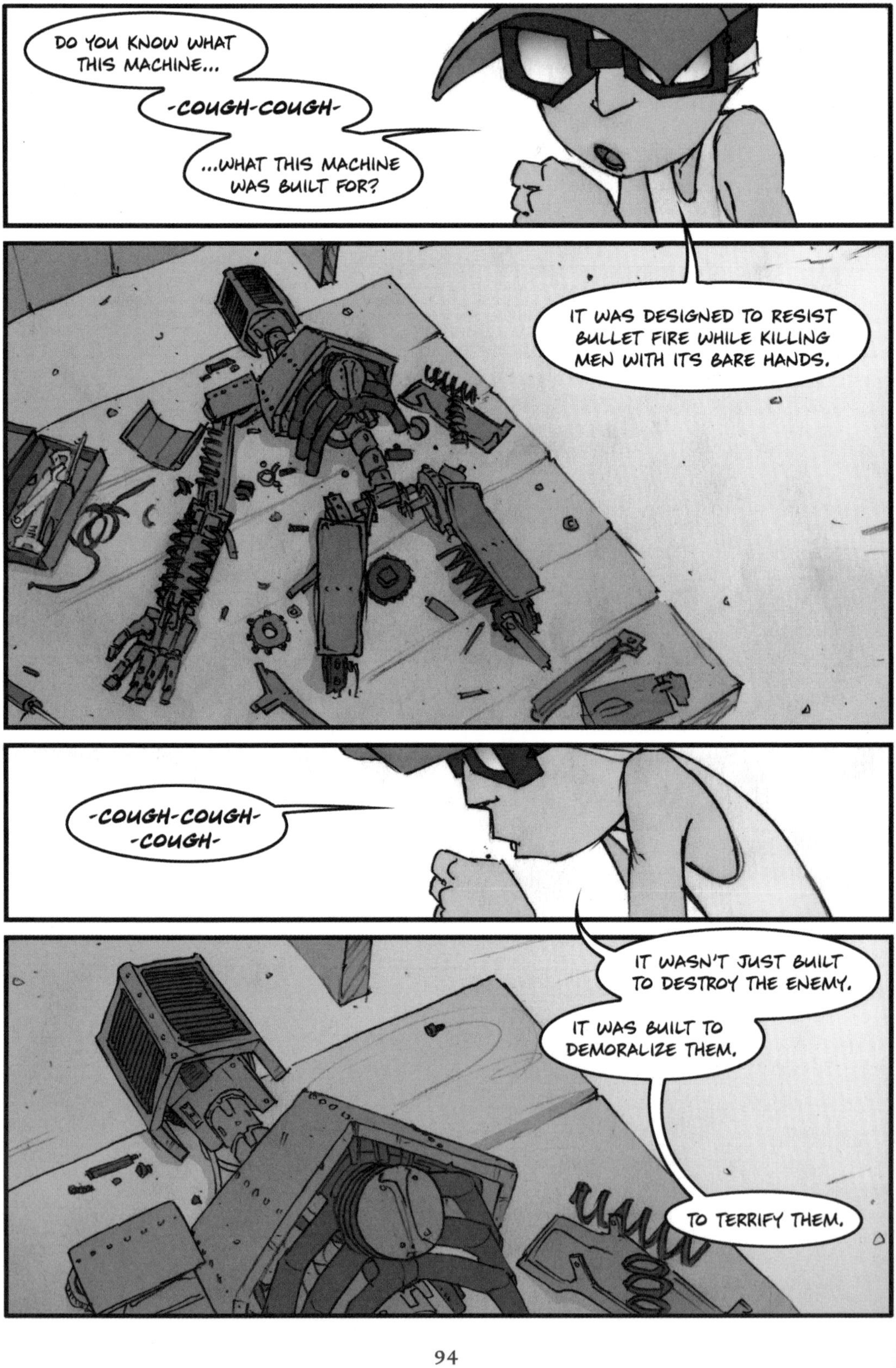
DO YOU KNOW WHAT THIS MACHINE...
-COUGH-COUGH-
...WHAT THIS MACHINE WAS BUILT FOR?
IT WAS DESIGNED TO RESIST BULLET FIRE WHILE KILLING MEN WITH ITS BARE HANDS.
-COUGH-COUGH- -COUGH-
IT WASN'T JUST BUILT TO DESTROY THE ENEMY.
IT WAS BUILT TO DEMORALIZE THEM.
TO TERRIFY THEM.

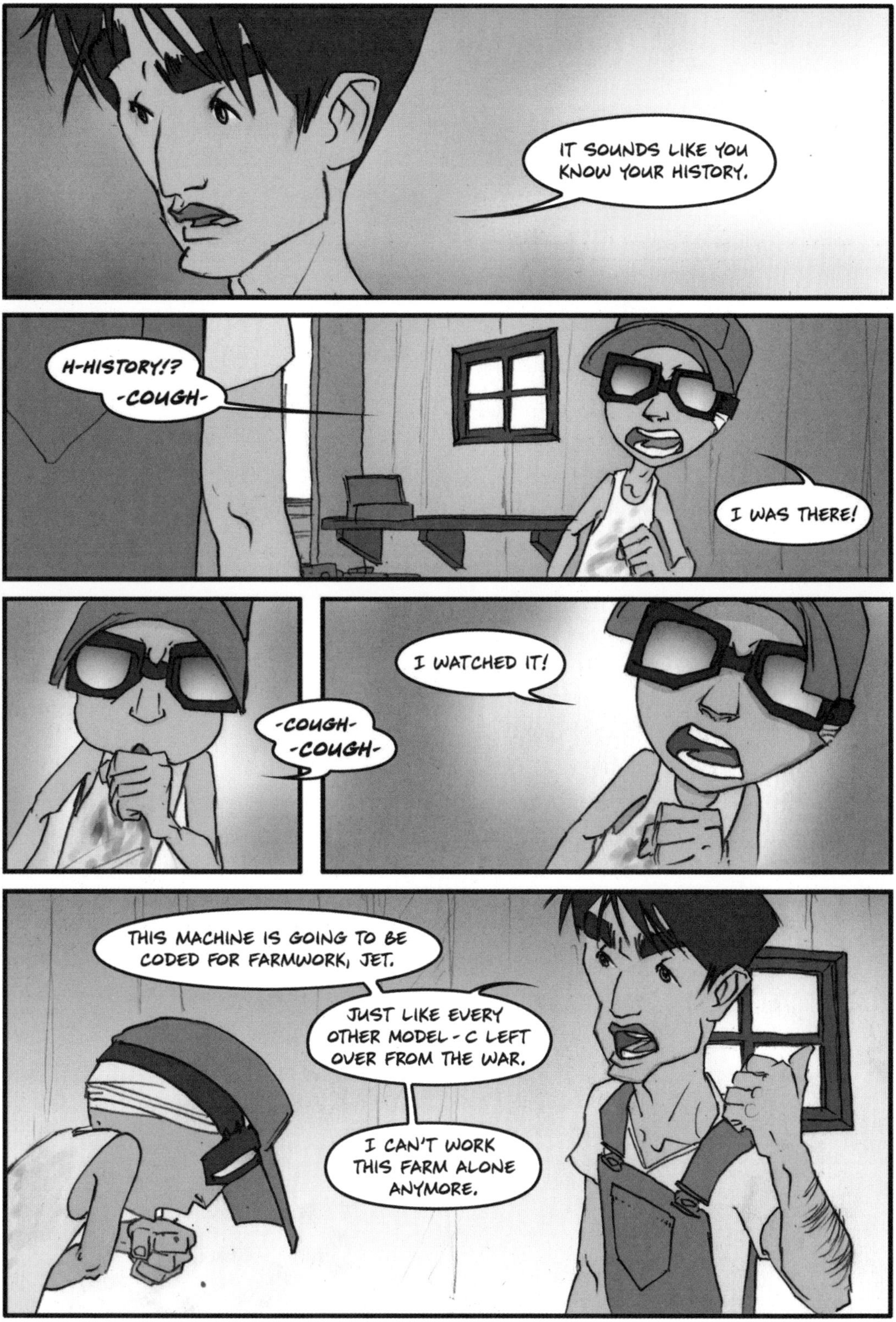
IT SOUNDS LIKE YOU KNOW YOUR HISTORY.
H-HISTORY!? -COUGH-
I WAS THERE!
-COUGH- -COUGH-
I WATCHED IT!
THIS MACHINE IS GOING TO BE CODED FOR FARMWORK, JET.
JUST LIKE EVERY OTHER MODEL - C LEFT OVER FROM THE WAR.
I CAN'T WORK THIS FARM ALONE ANYMORE.

ARE YOU OK?

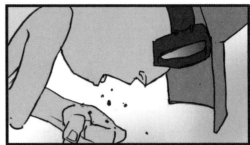

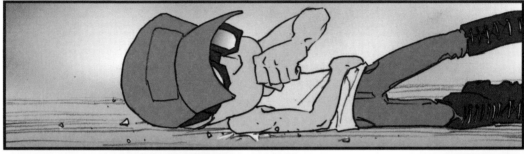

JET!

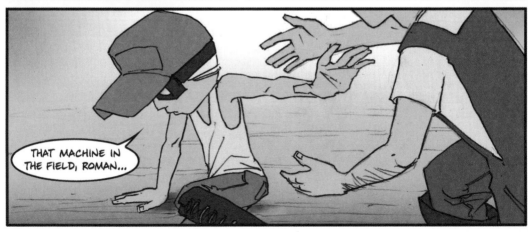

THAT MACHINE IN THE FIELD, ROMAN...

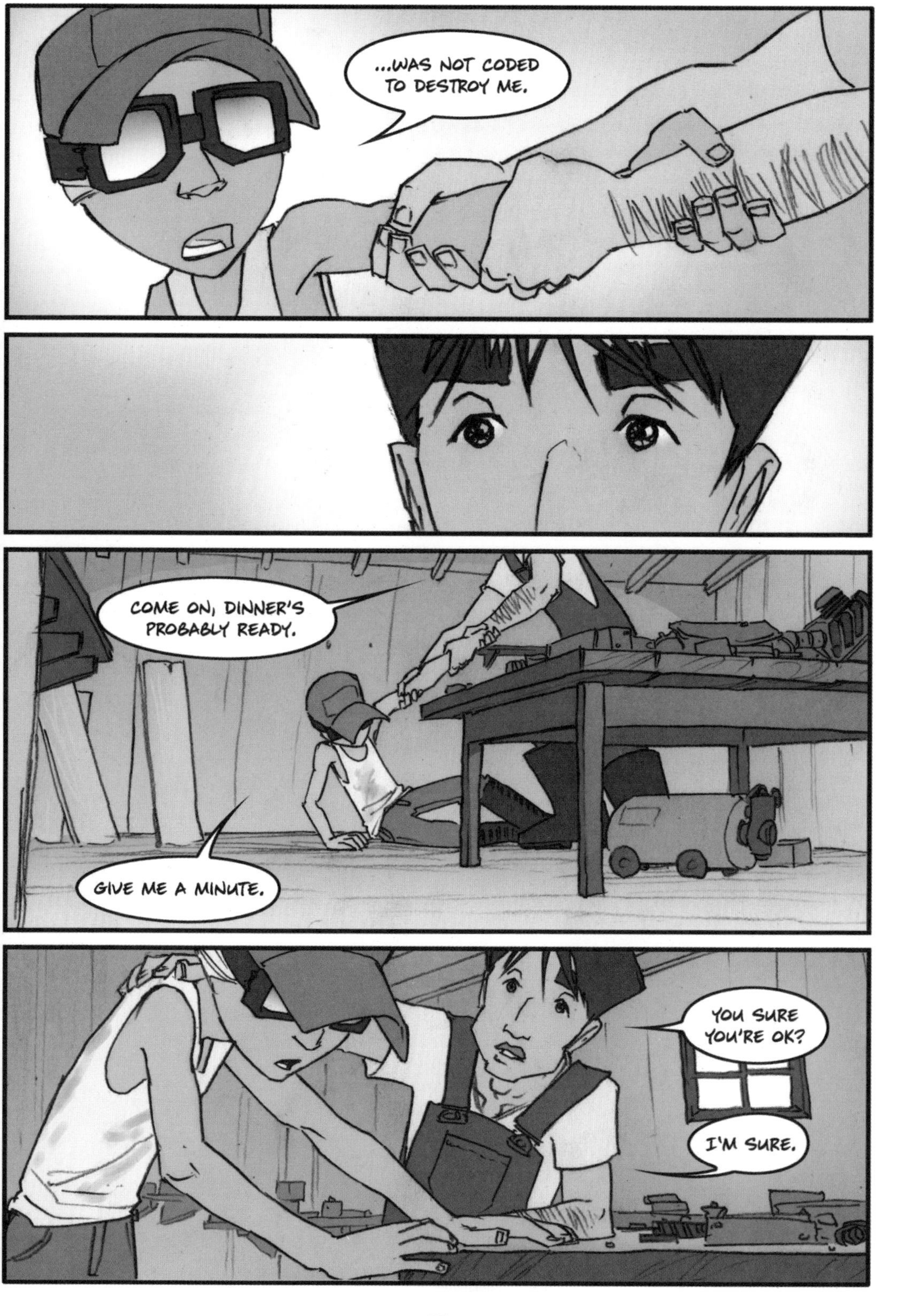
...WAS NOT CODED TO DESTROY ME.
COME ON, DINNER'S PROBABLY READY.
GIVE ME A MINUTE.
YOU SURE YOU'RE OK?
I'M SURE.

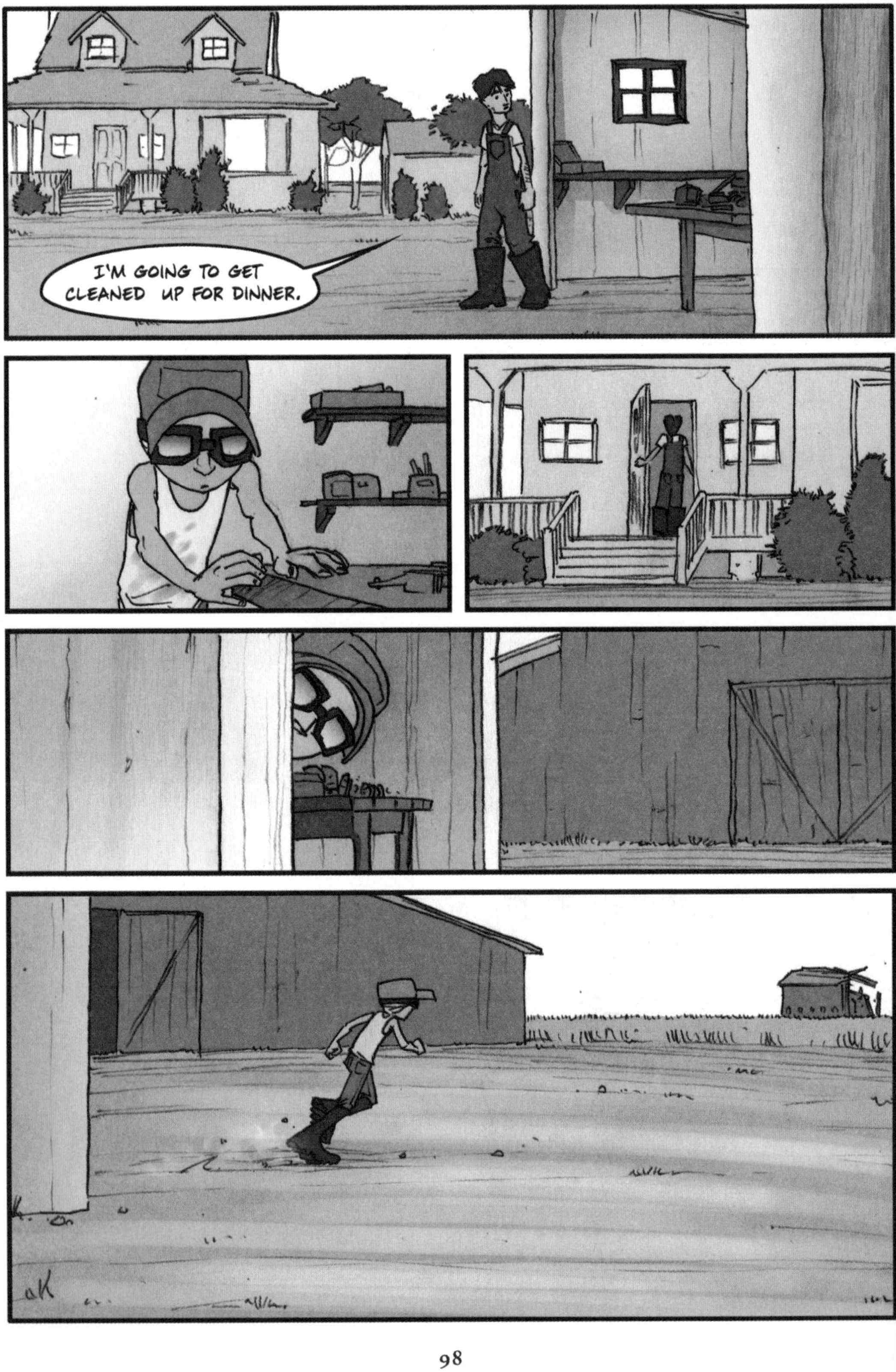
I'M GOING TO GET CLEANED UP FOR DINNER.

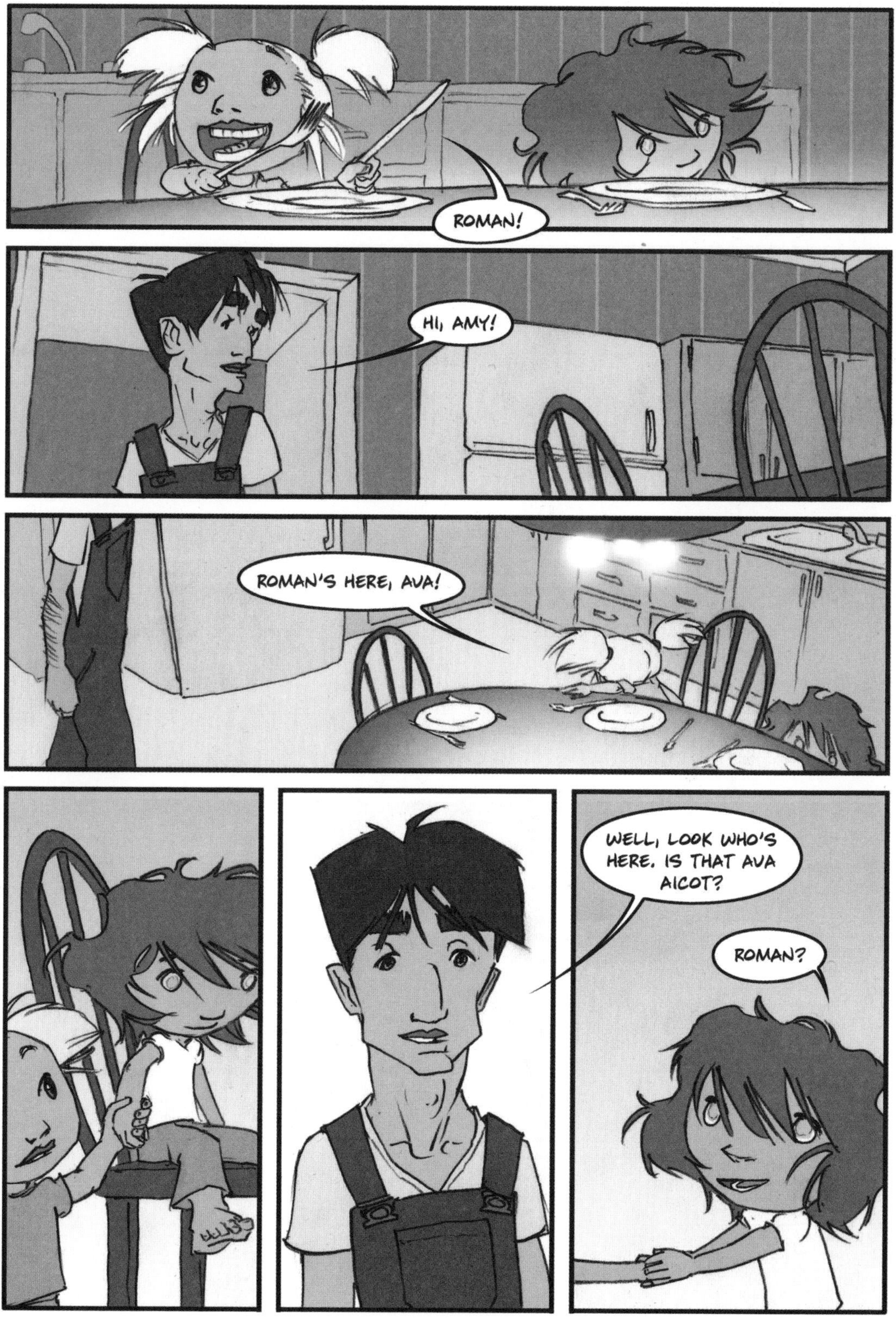
ROMAN!
HI, AMY!
ROMAN'S HERE, AVA!
WELL, LOOK WHO'S HERE. IS THAT AVA AICOT?
ROMAN?

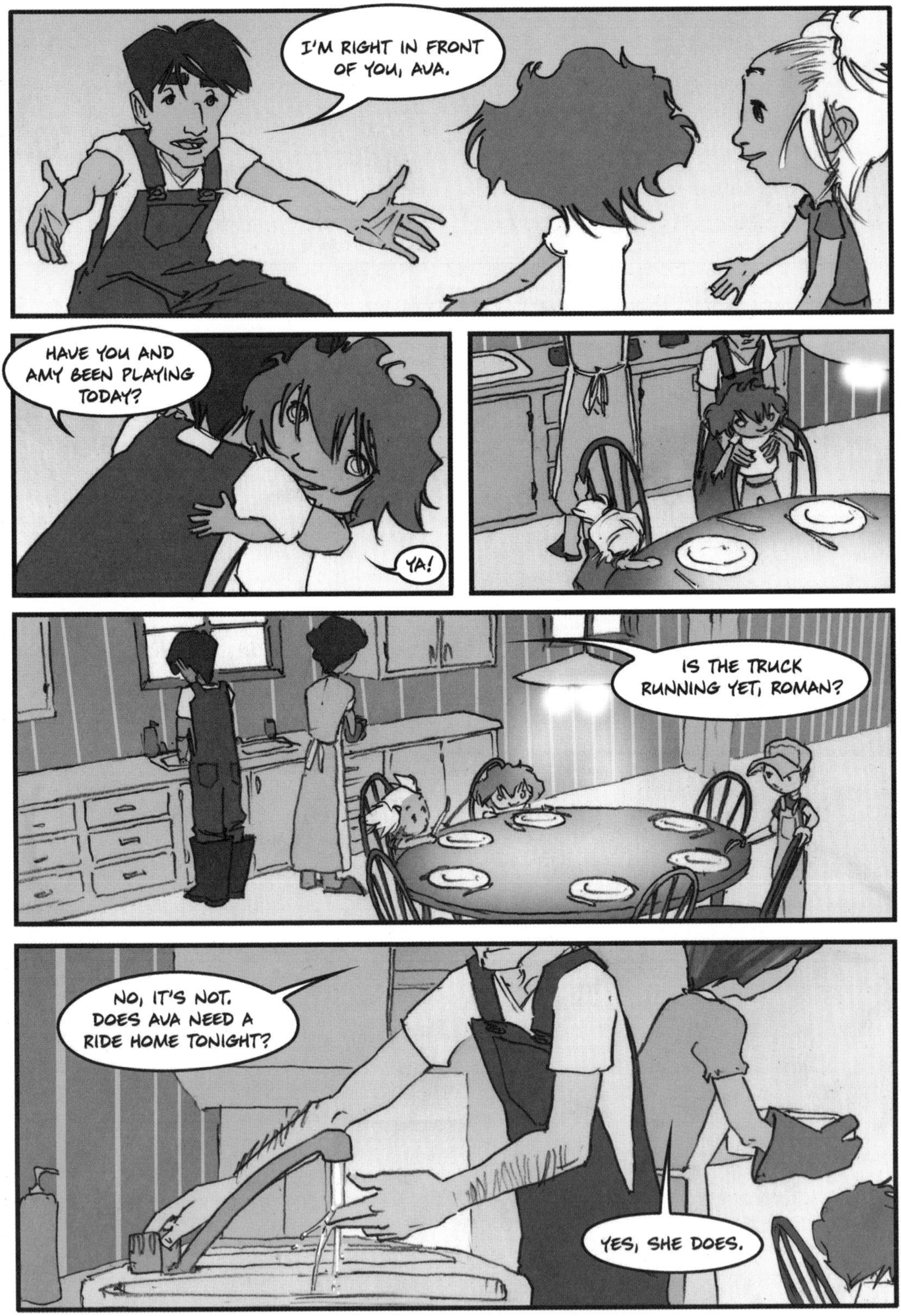
I'M RIGHT IN FRONT OF YOU, AVA.
HAVE YOU AND AMY BEEN PLAYING TODAY?
YA!
IS THE TRUCK RUNNING YET, ROMAN?
NO, IT'S NOT. DOES AVA NEED A RIDE HOME TONIGHT?
YES, SHE DOES.

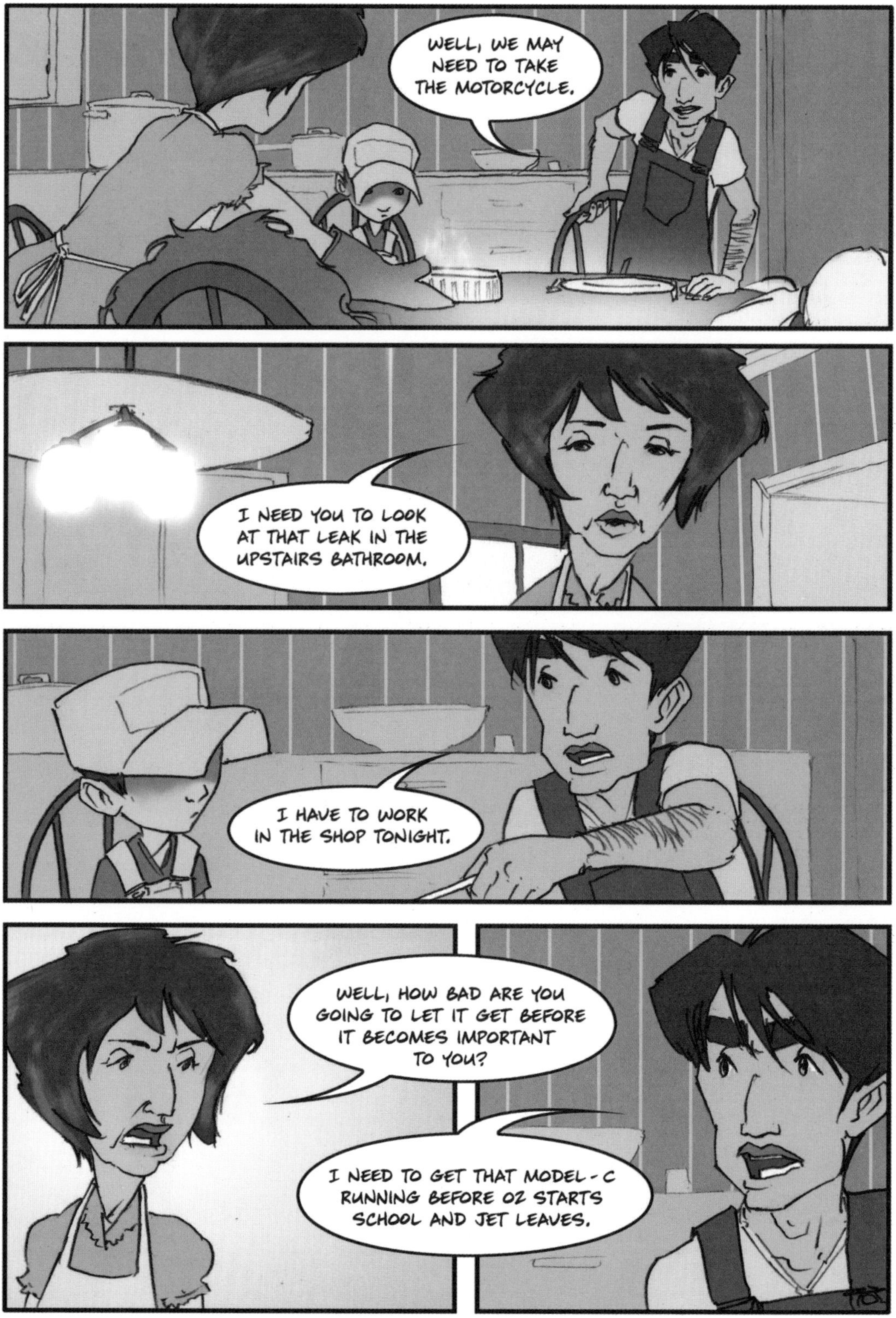
WELL, WE MAY NEED TO TAKE THE MOTORCYCLE.
I NEED YOU TO LOOK AT THAT LEAK IN THE UPSTAIRS BATHROOM.
I HAVE TO WORK IN THE SHOP TONIGHT.
WELL, HOW BAD ARE YOU GOING TO LET IT GET BEFORE IT BECOMES IMPORTANT TO YOU?
I NEED TO GET THAT MODEL - C RUNNING BEFORE OZ STARTS SCHOOL AND JET LEAVES.

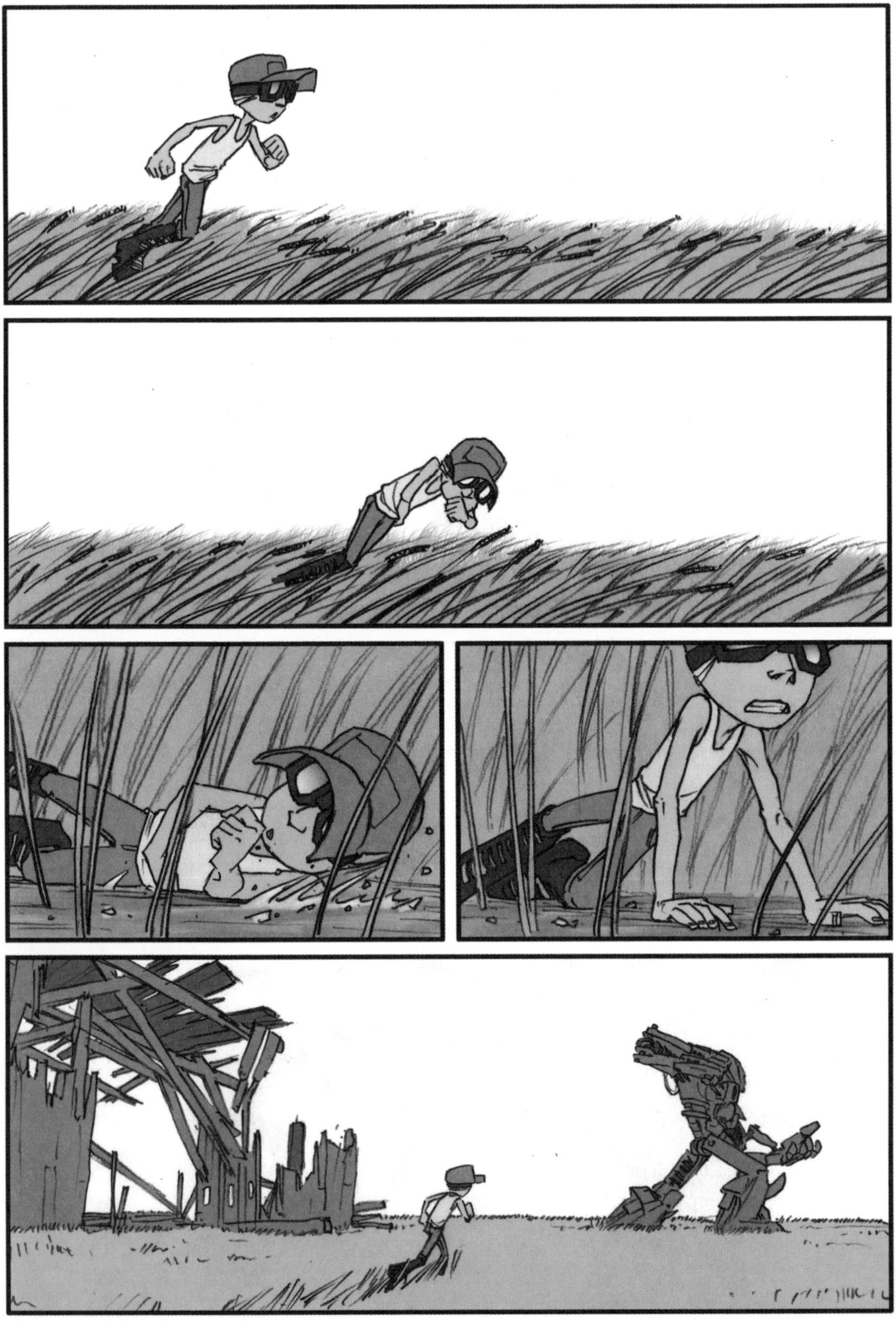

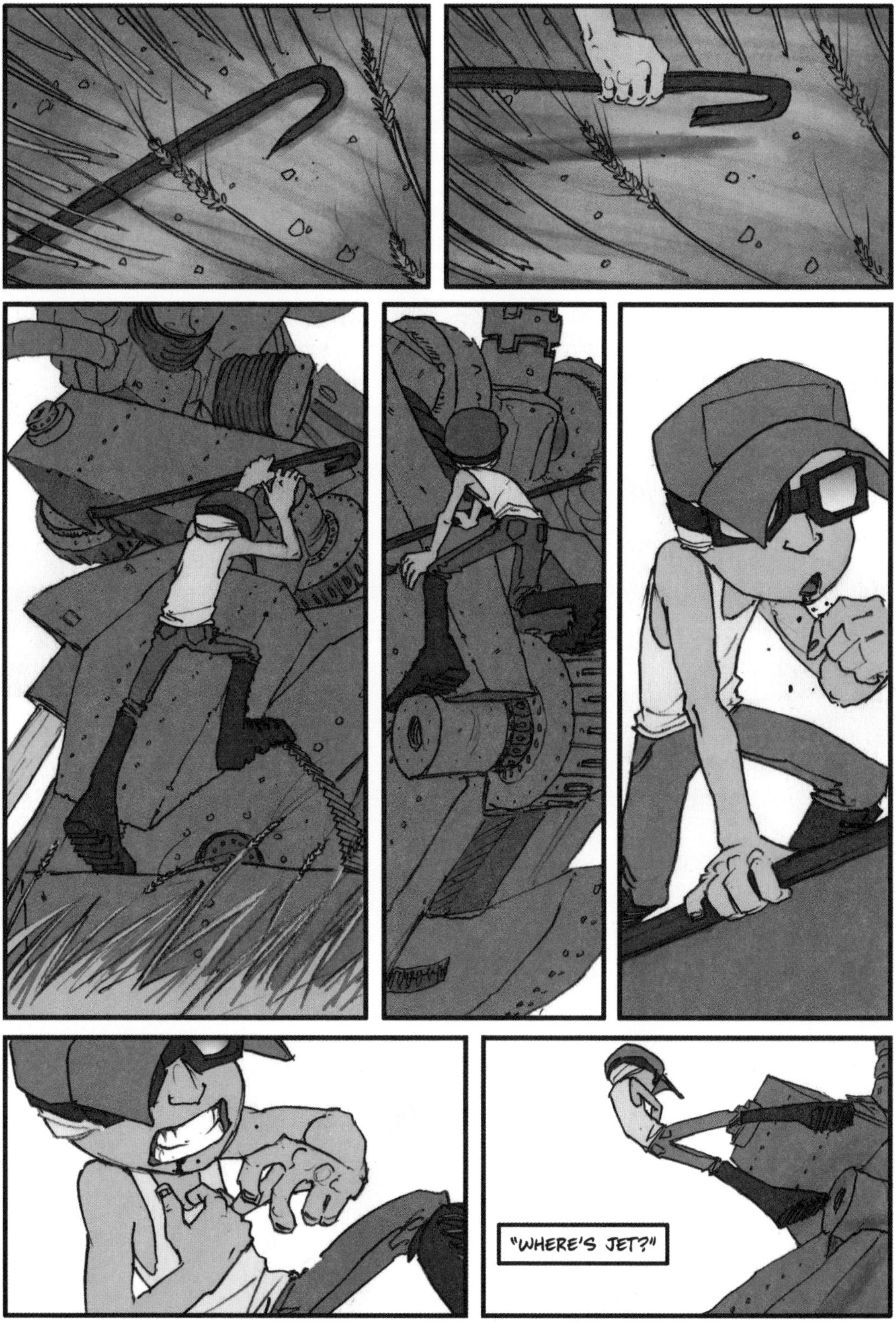
"WHERE'S JET?"

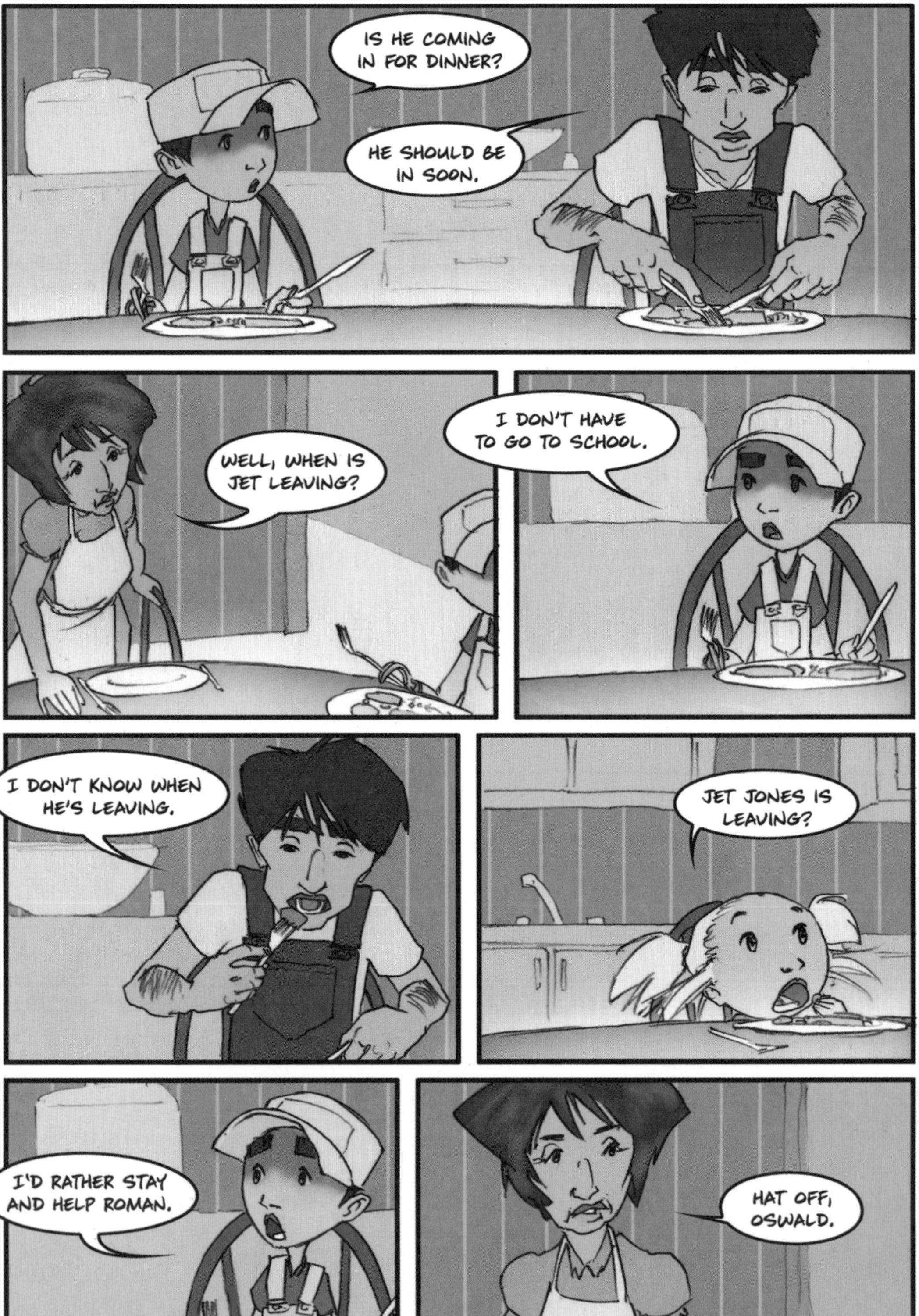
IS HE COMING IN FOR DINNER?
HE SHOULD BE IN SOON.
WELL, WHEN IS JET LEAVING?
I DON'T HAVE TO GO TO SCHOOL.
I DON'T KNOW WHEN HE'S LEAVING.
JET JONES IS LEAVING?
I'D RATHER STAY AND HELP ROMAN.
HAT OFF, OSWALD.

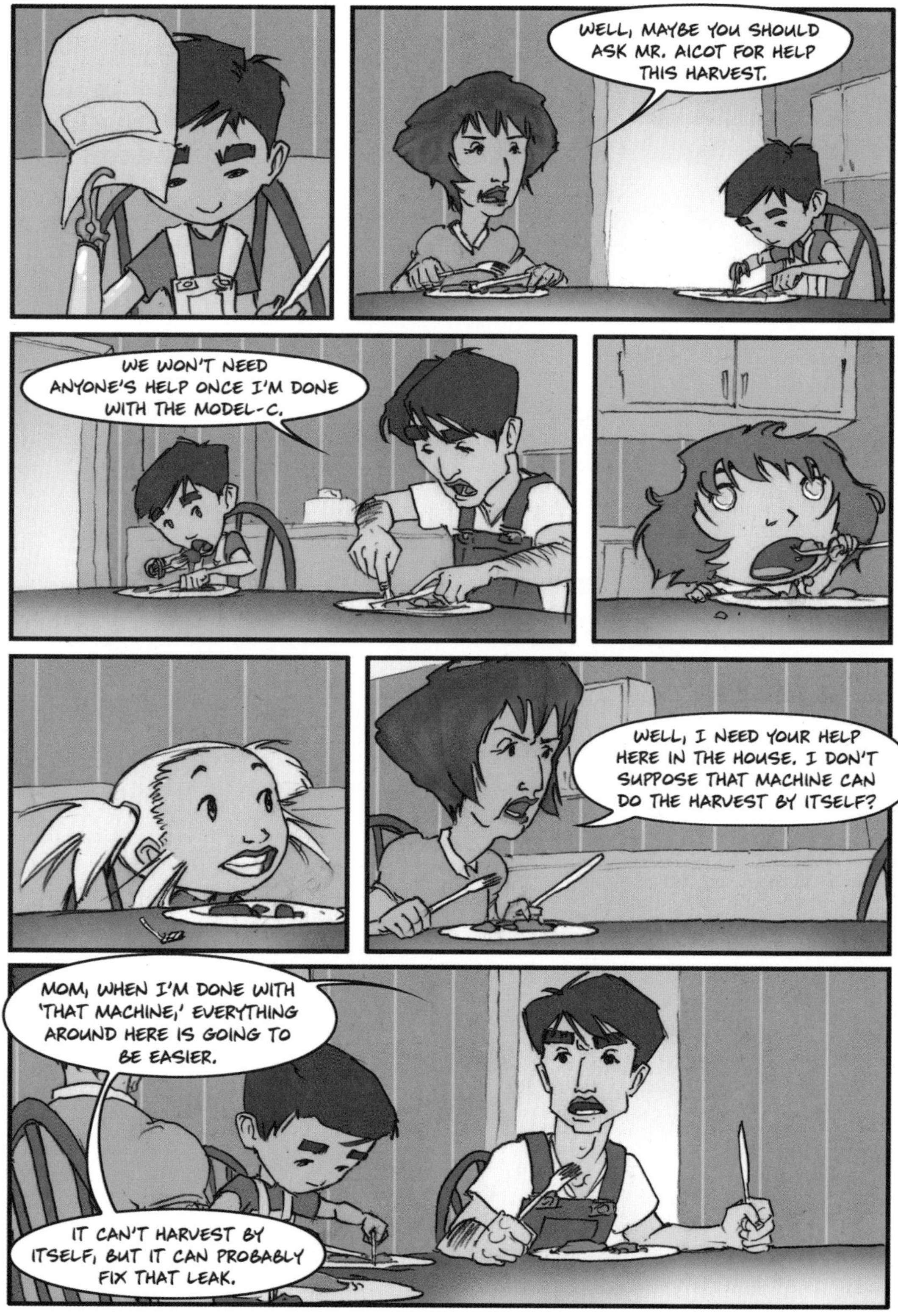
WELL, MAYBE YOU SHOULD ASK MR. AICOT FOR HELP THIS HARVEST.
WE WON'T NEED ANYONE'S HELP ONCE I'M DONE WITH THE MODEL-C.
WELL, I NEED YOUR HELP HERE IN THE HOUSE. I DON'T SUPPOSE THAT MACHINE CAN DO THE HARVEST BY ITSELF?
MOM, WHEN I'M DONE WITH 'THAT MACHINE,' EVERYTHING AROUND HERE IS GOING TO BE EASIER.
IT CAN'T HARVEST BY ITSELF, BUT IT CAN PROBABLY FIX THAT LEAK.

REALLY?

IT'S EASY...

"...IT JUST DEPENDS HOW I CODE IT."

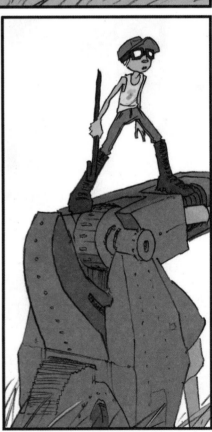

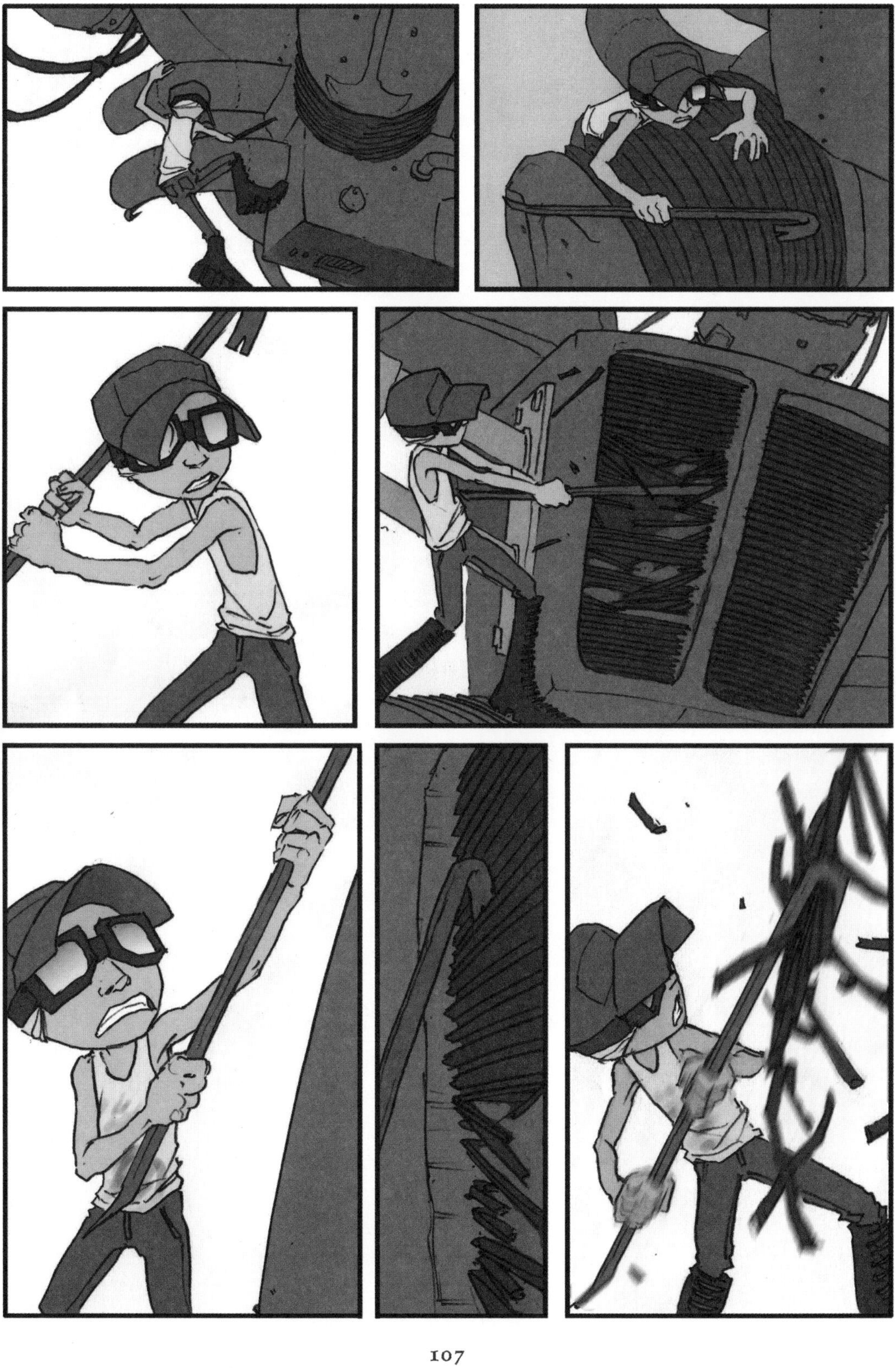

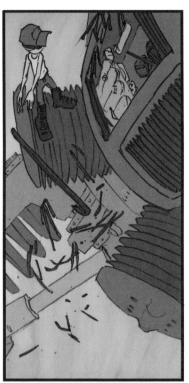

WHAT'S CODE?

I USE A CODEBOX TO DICTATE THE MODEL - C'S TASKS. MR. AICOT GAVE ME ONE.

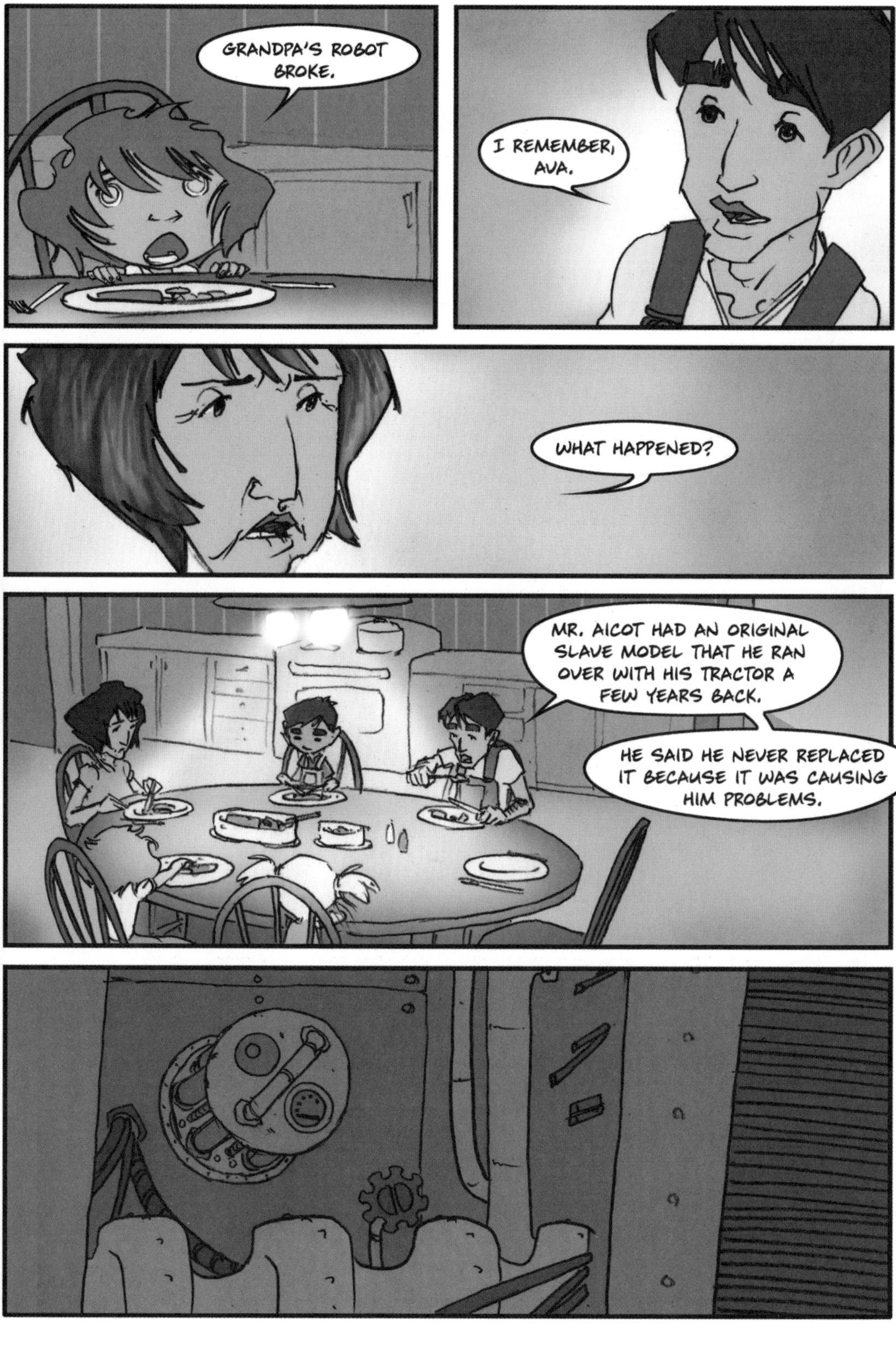
GRANDPA'S ROBOT BROKE.
I REMEMBER, AVA.
WHAT HAPPENED?
MR. AICOT HAD AN ORIGINAL SLAVE MODEL THAT HE RAN OVER WITH HIS TRACTOR A FEW YEARS BACK.
HE SAID HE NEVER REPLACED IT BECAUSE IT WAS CAUSING HIM PROBLEMS.

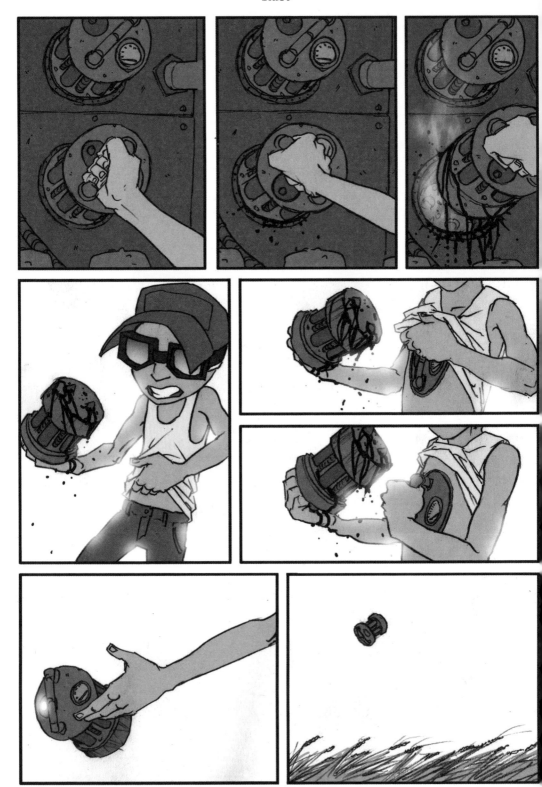

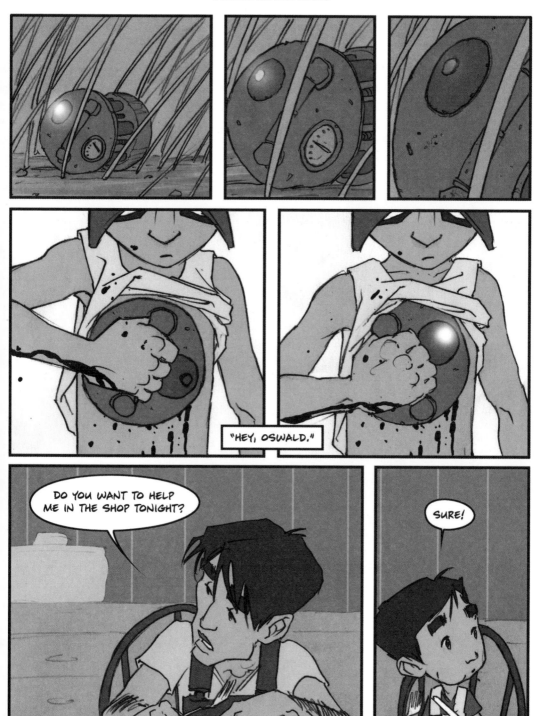

"HEY, OSWALD."

DO YOU WANT TO HELP ME IN THE SHOP TONIGHT?

SURE!

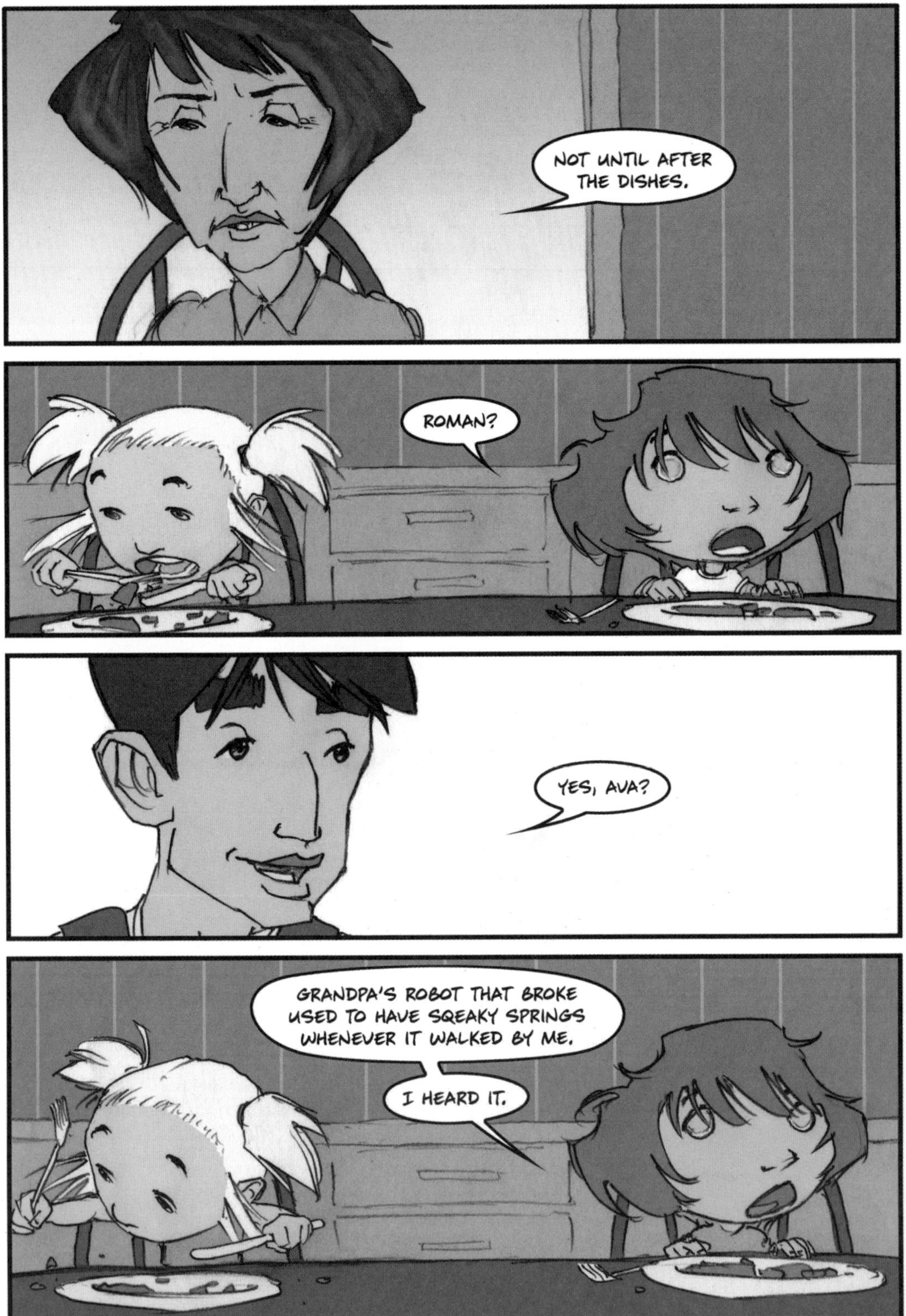
NOT UNTIL AFTER THE DISHES.
ROMAN?
YES, AVA?
GRANDPA'S ROBOT THAT BROKE USED TO HAVE SQEAKY SPRINGS WHENEVER IT WALKED BY ME.
I HEARD IT.

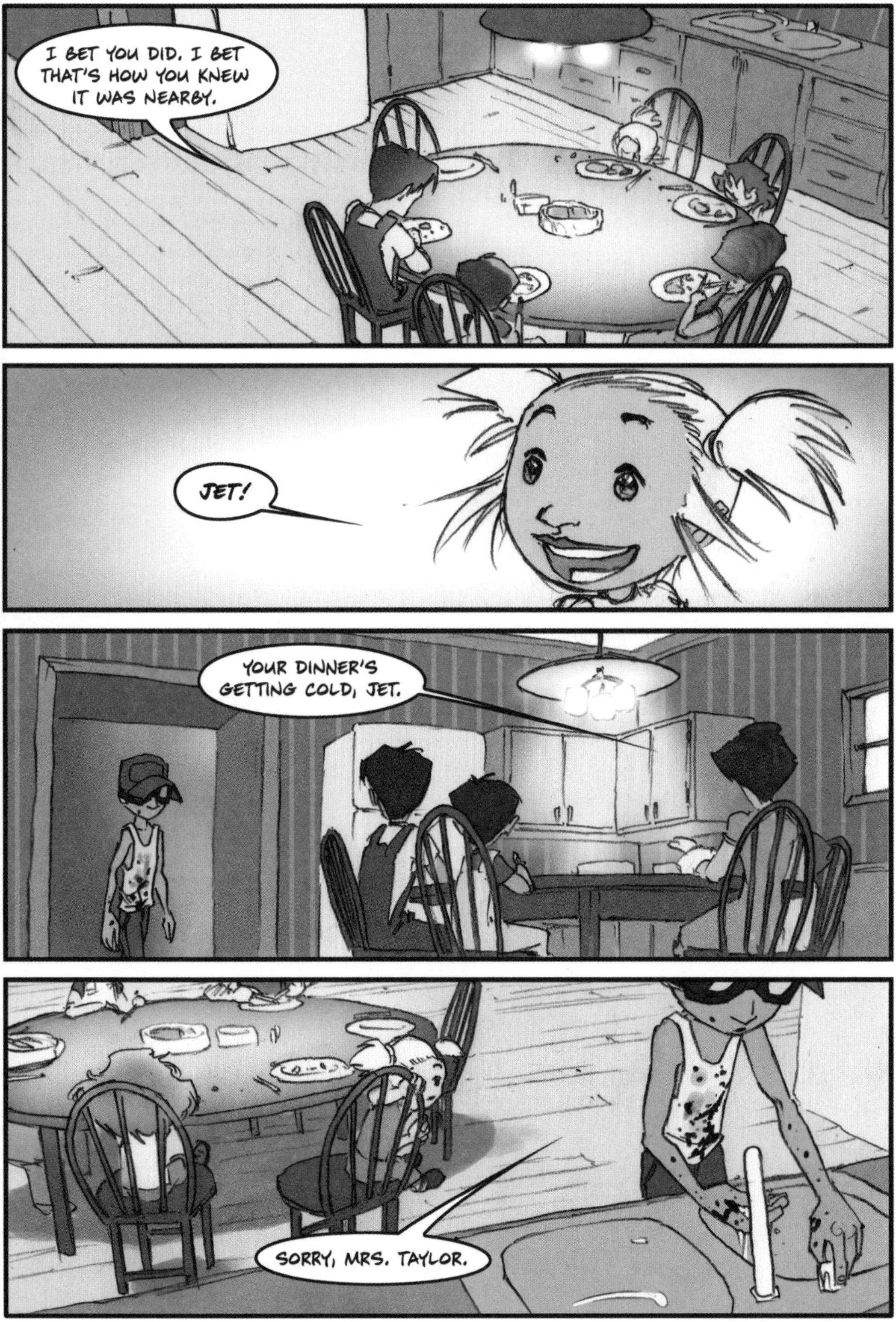
I BET YOU DID. I BET THAT'S HOW YOU KNEW IT WAS NEARBY.
JET!
YOUR DINNER'S GETTING COLD, JET.
SORRY, MRS. TAYLOR.

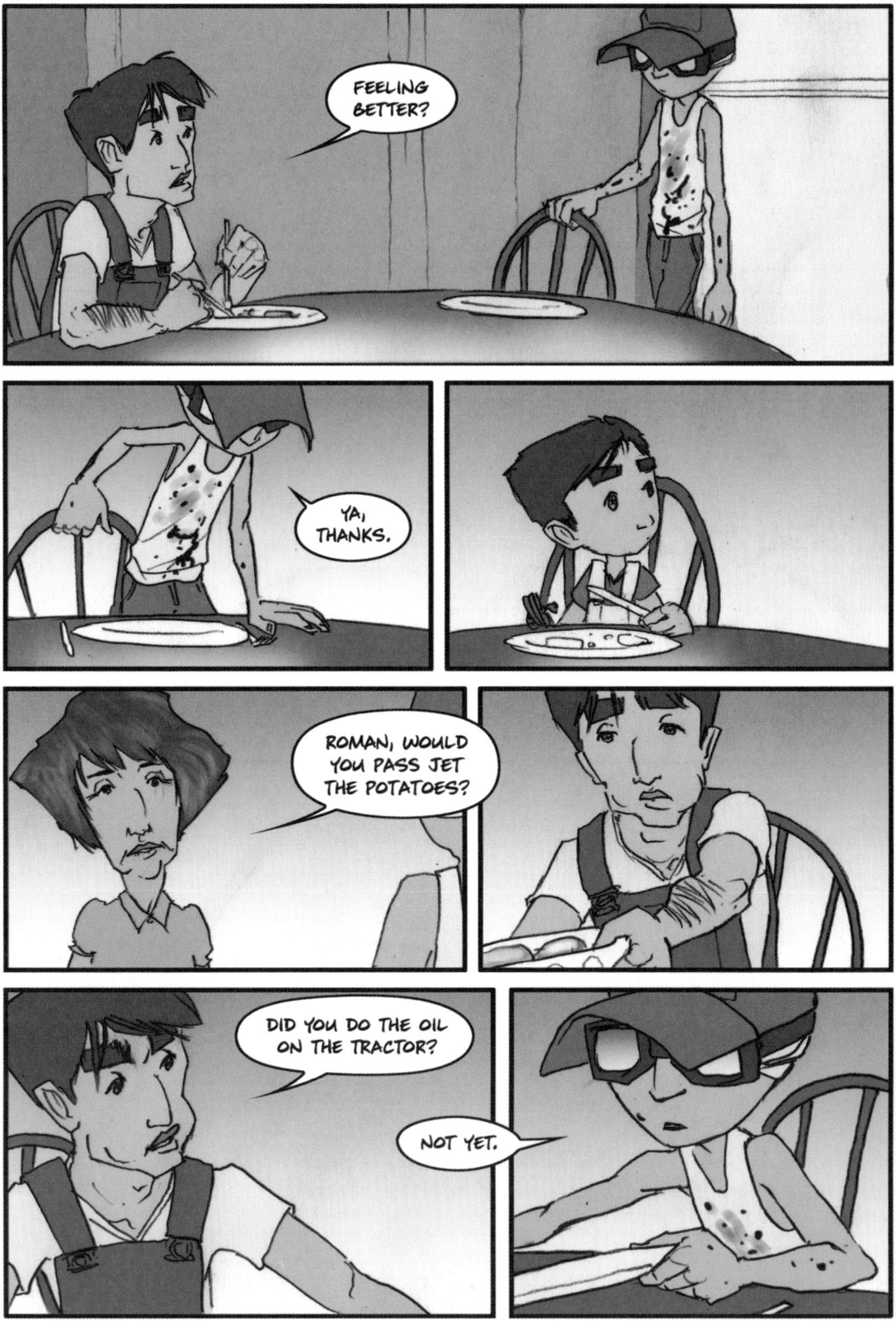
FEELING BETTER?
YA, THANKS.
ROMAN, WOULD YOU PASS JET THE POTATOES?
DID YOU DO THE OIL ON THE TRACTOR?
NOT YET.

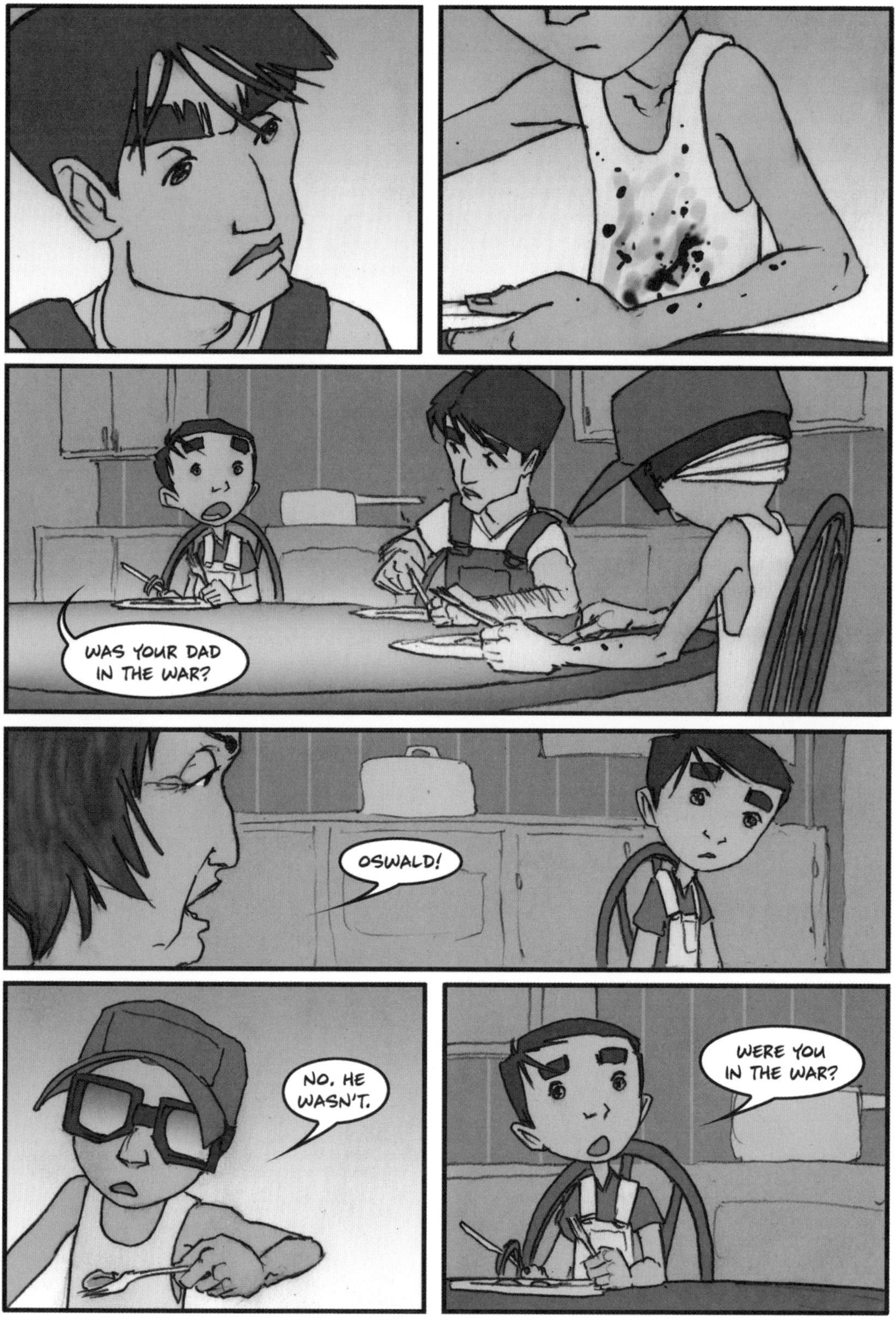
WAS YOUR DAD IN THE WAR?
OSWALD!
NO. HE WASN'T.
WERE YOU IN THE WAR?

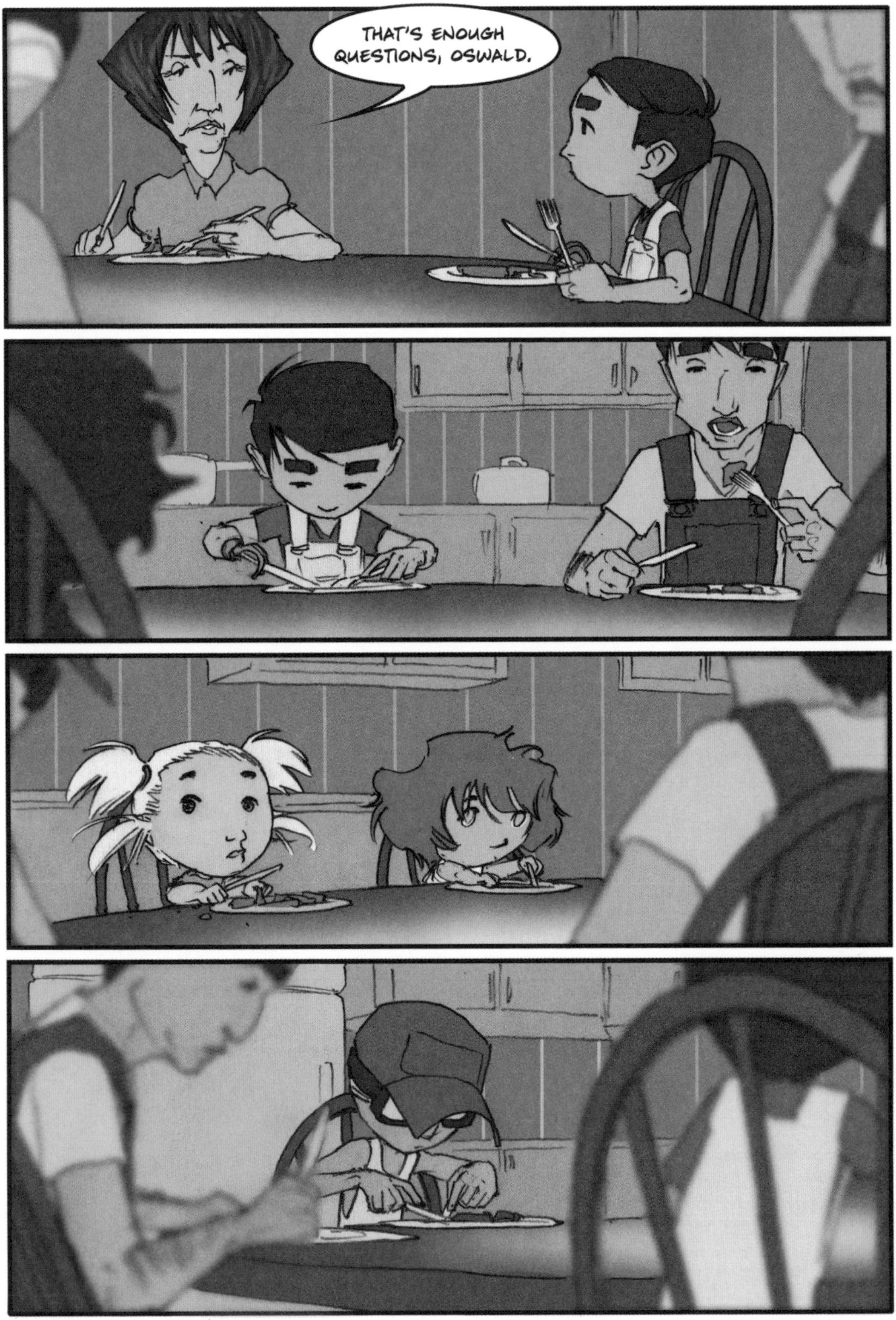
THAT'S ENOUGH QUESTIONS, OSWALD.

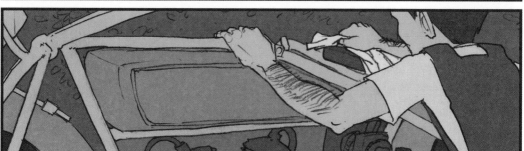

THERE SHE IS.

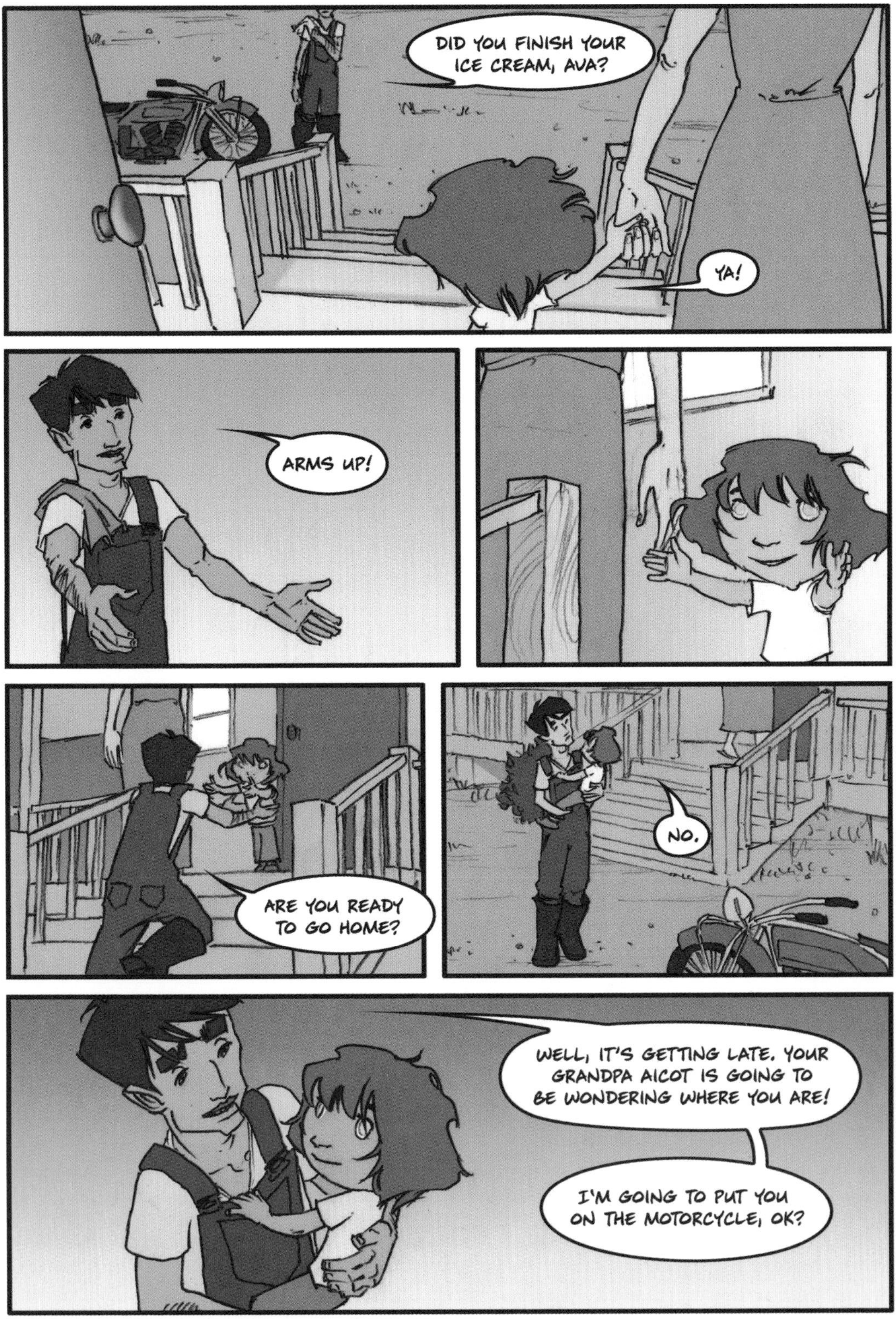
DID YOU FINISH YOUR ICE CREAM, AVA?
YA!
ARMS UP!
ARE YOU READY TO GO HOME?
NO.
WELL, IT'S GETTING LATE. YOUR GRANDPA AICOT IS GOING TO BE WONDERING WHERE YOU ARE!
I'M GOING TO PUT YOU ON THE MOTORCYCLE, OK?

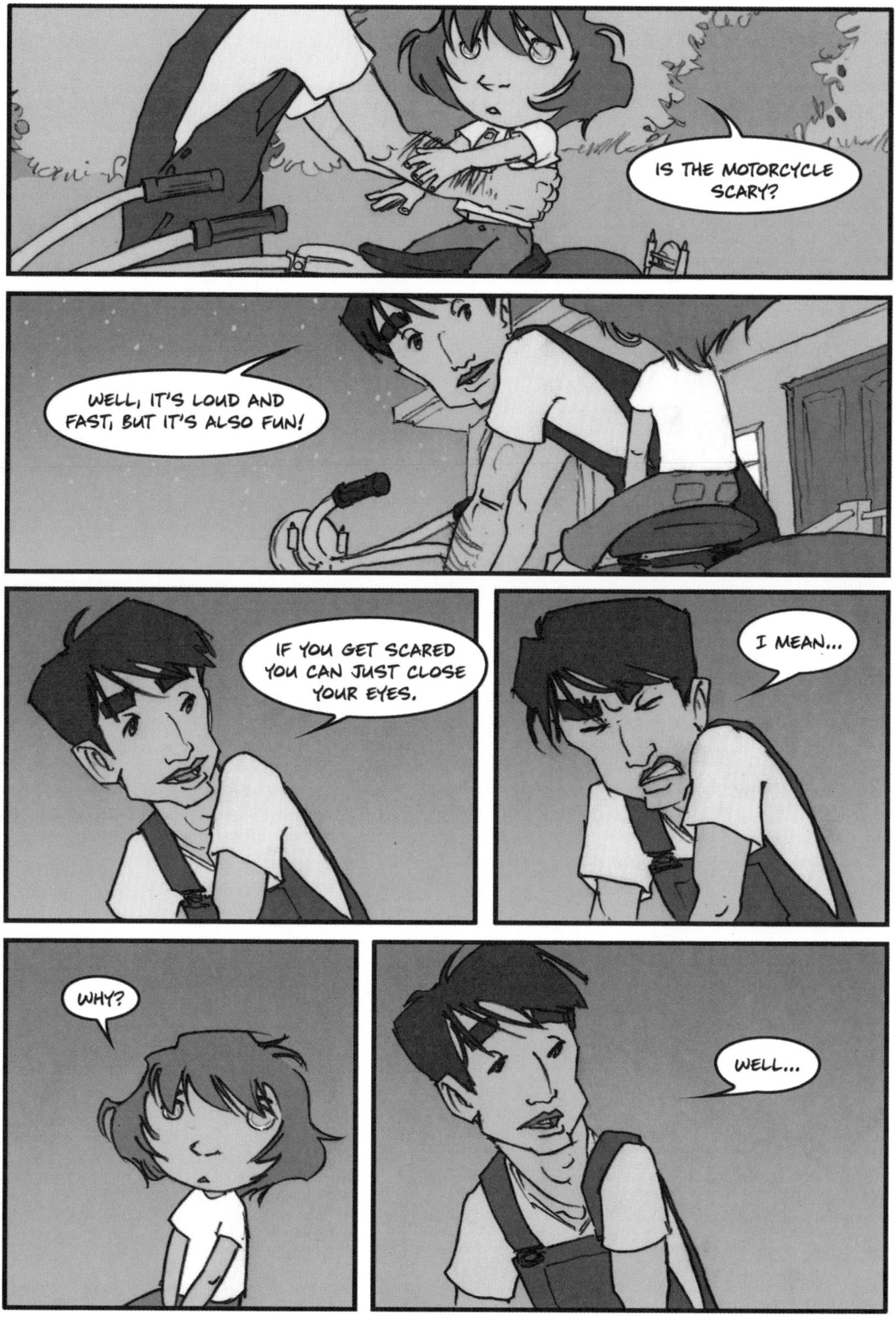
IS THE MOTORCYCLE SCARY?
WELL, IT'S LOUD AND FAST, BUT IT'S ALSO FUN!
IF YOU GET SCARED YOU CAN JUST CLOSE YOUR EYES.
I MEAN...
WHY?
WELL...

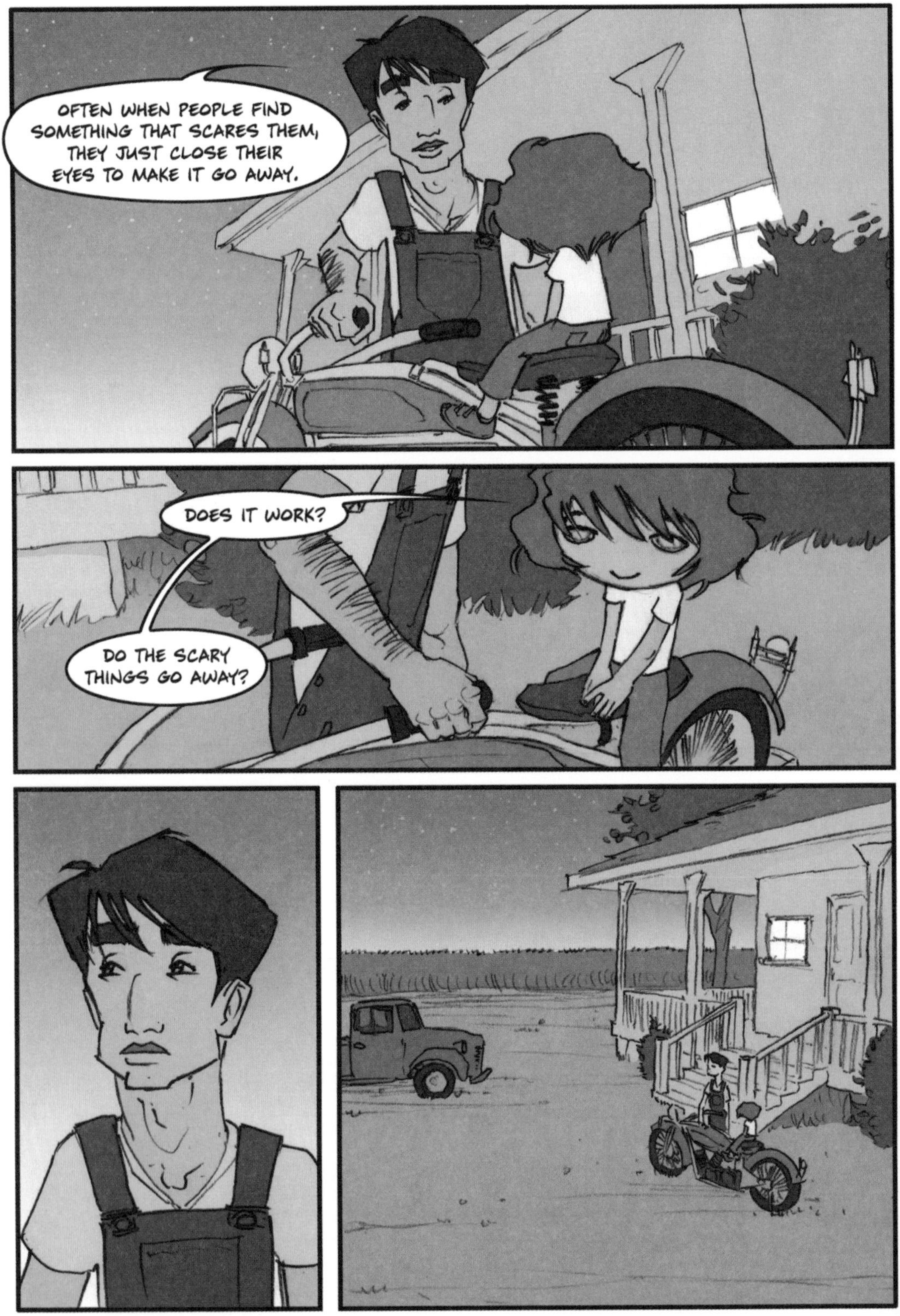
OFTEN WHEN PEOPLE FIND SOMETHING THAT SCARES THEM, THEY JUST CLOSE THEIR EYES TO MAKE IT GO AWAY.
DOES IT WORK?
DO THE SCARY THINGS GO AWAY?

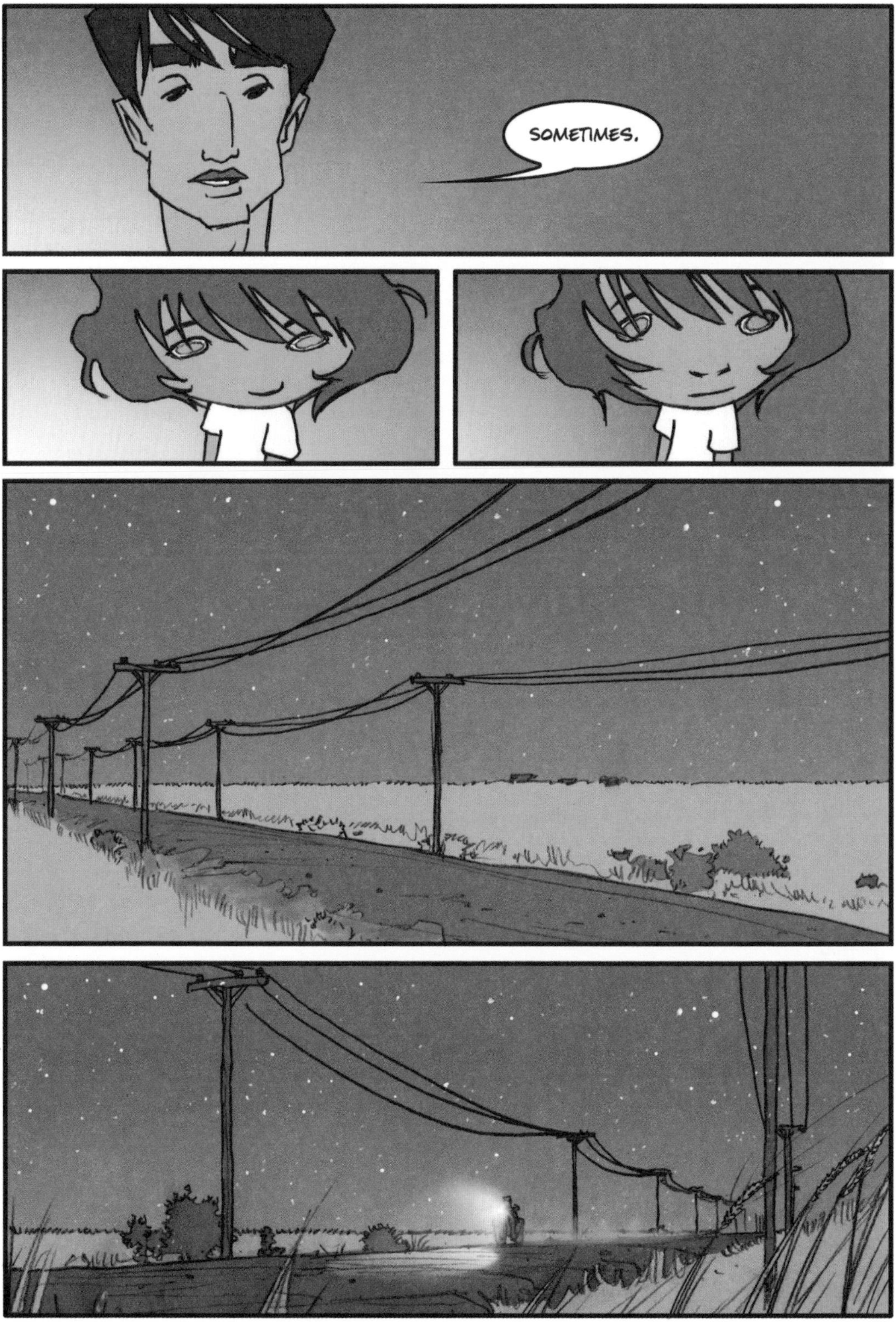
SOMETIMES.

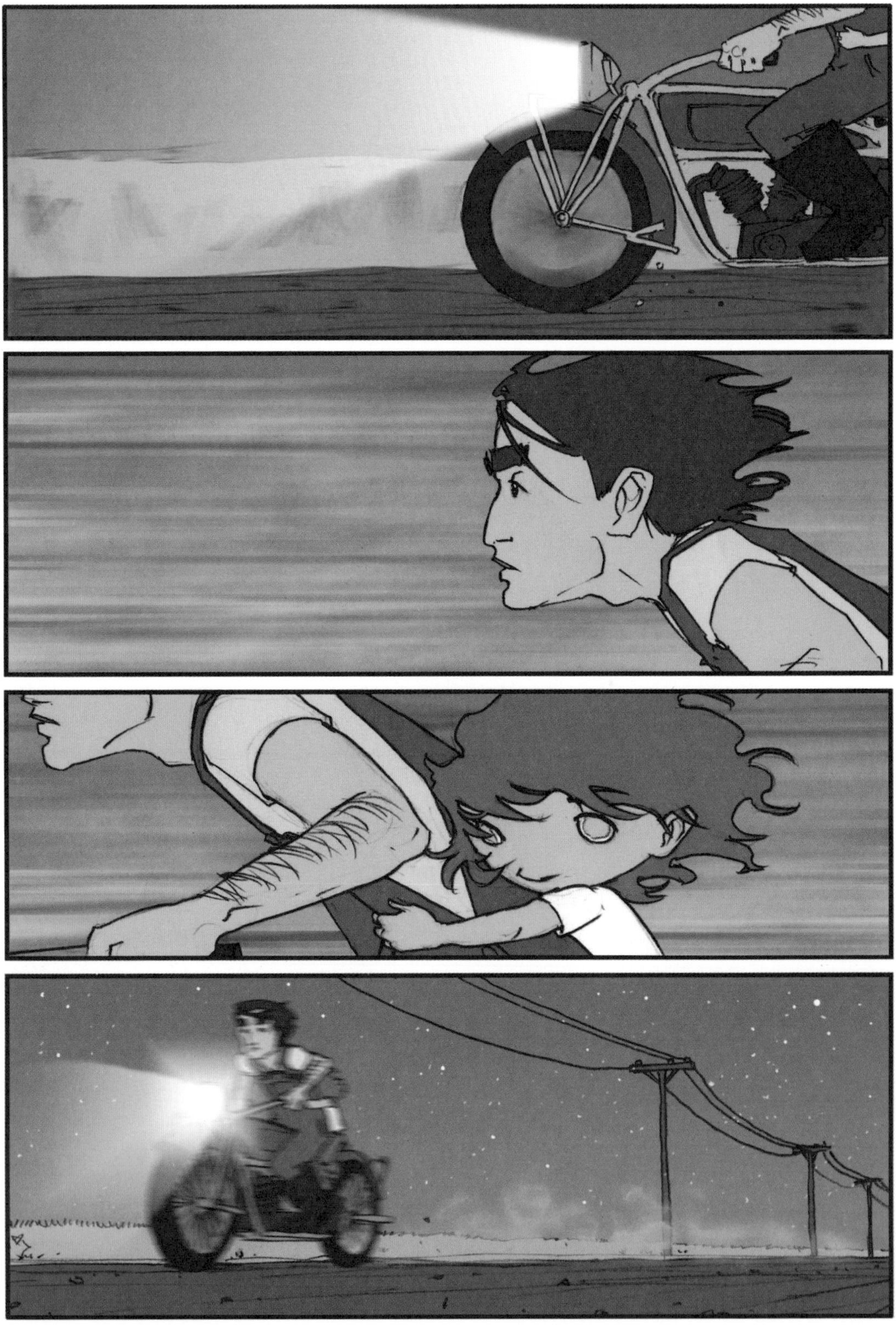

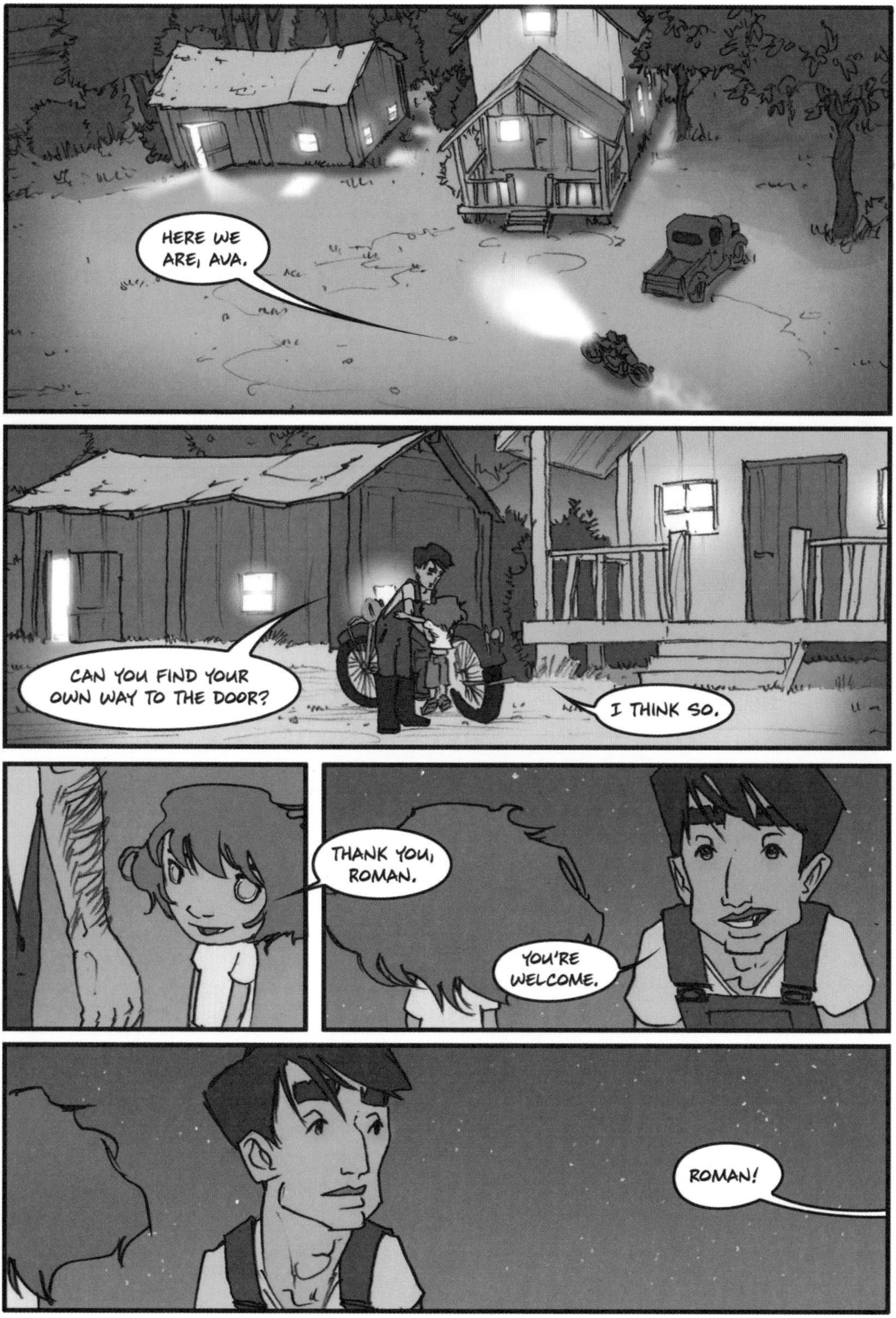
HERE WE ARE, AVA.
CAN YOU FIND YOUR OWN WAY TO THE DOOR?
I THINK SO.
THANK YOU, ROMAN.
YOU'RE WELCOME.
ROMAN!

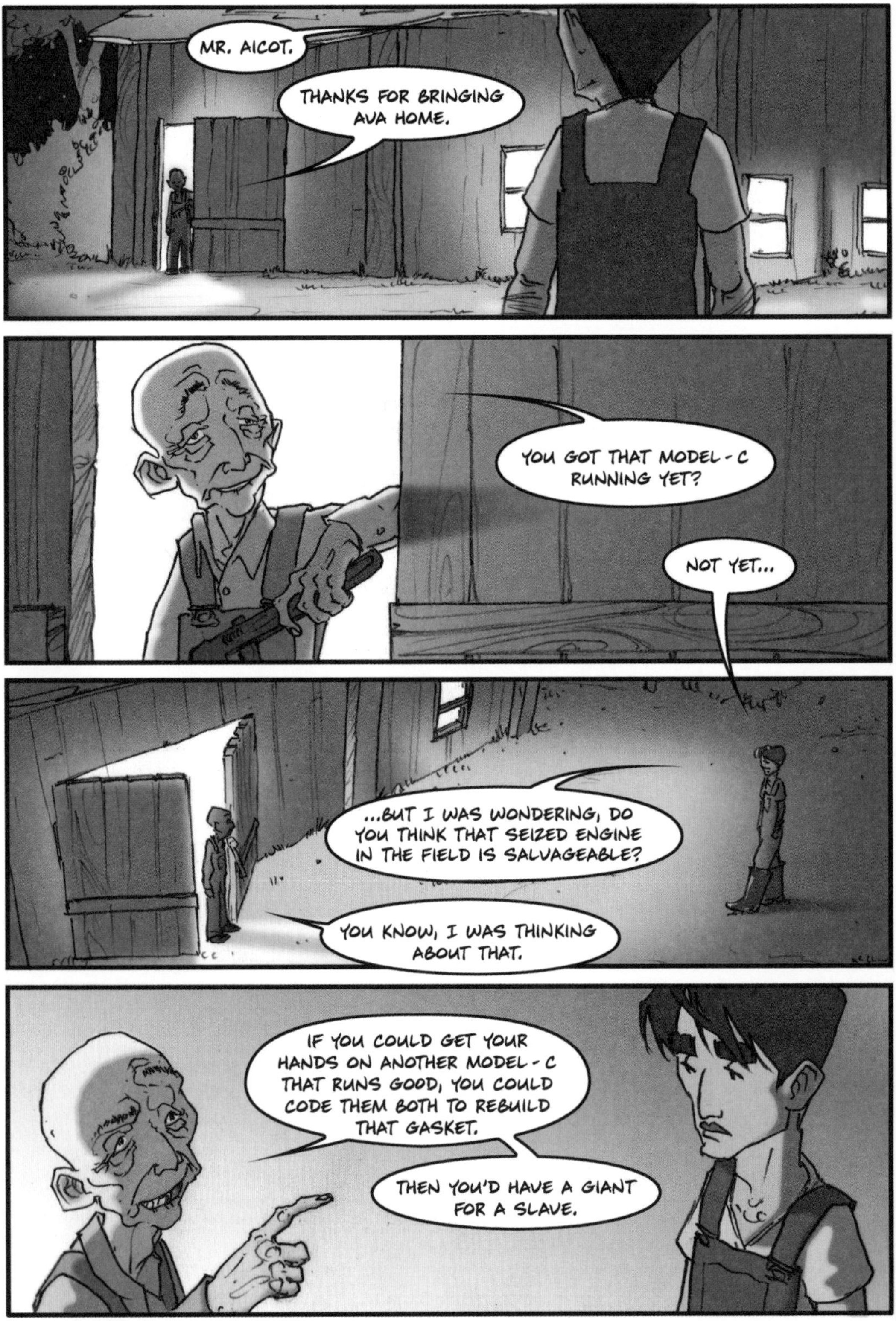
MR. AICOT.
THANKS FOR BRINGING AVA HOME.
YOU GOT THAT MODEL - C RUNNING YET?
NOT YET...
...BUT I WAS WONDERING, DO YOU THINK THAT SEIZED ENGINE IN THE FIELD IS SALVAGEABLE?
YOU KNOW, I WAS THINKING ABOUT THAT.
IF YOU COULD GET YOUR HANDS ON ANOTHER MODEL - C THAT RUNS GOOD, YOU COULD CODE THEM BOTH TO REBUILD THAT GASKET.
THEN YOU'D HAVE A GIANT FOR A SLAVE.

JET IS STILL WITH YOU?

WOW. THEN I WOULDN'T NEED OZ OR JET.

YA, BUT I THINK HE'LL BE LEAVING SOON.

THE SOONER THE BETTER, ROMAN. THAT KID'S GOT HISTORY.

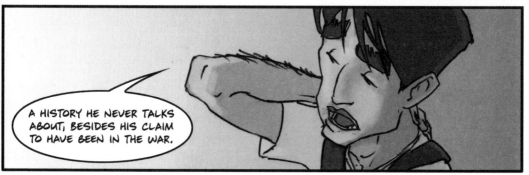

A HISTORY HE NEVER TALKS ABOUT, BESIDES HIS CLAIM TO HAVE BEEN IN THE WAR.

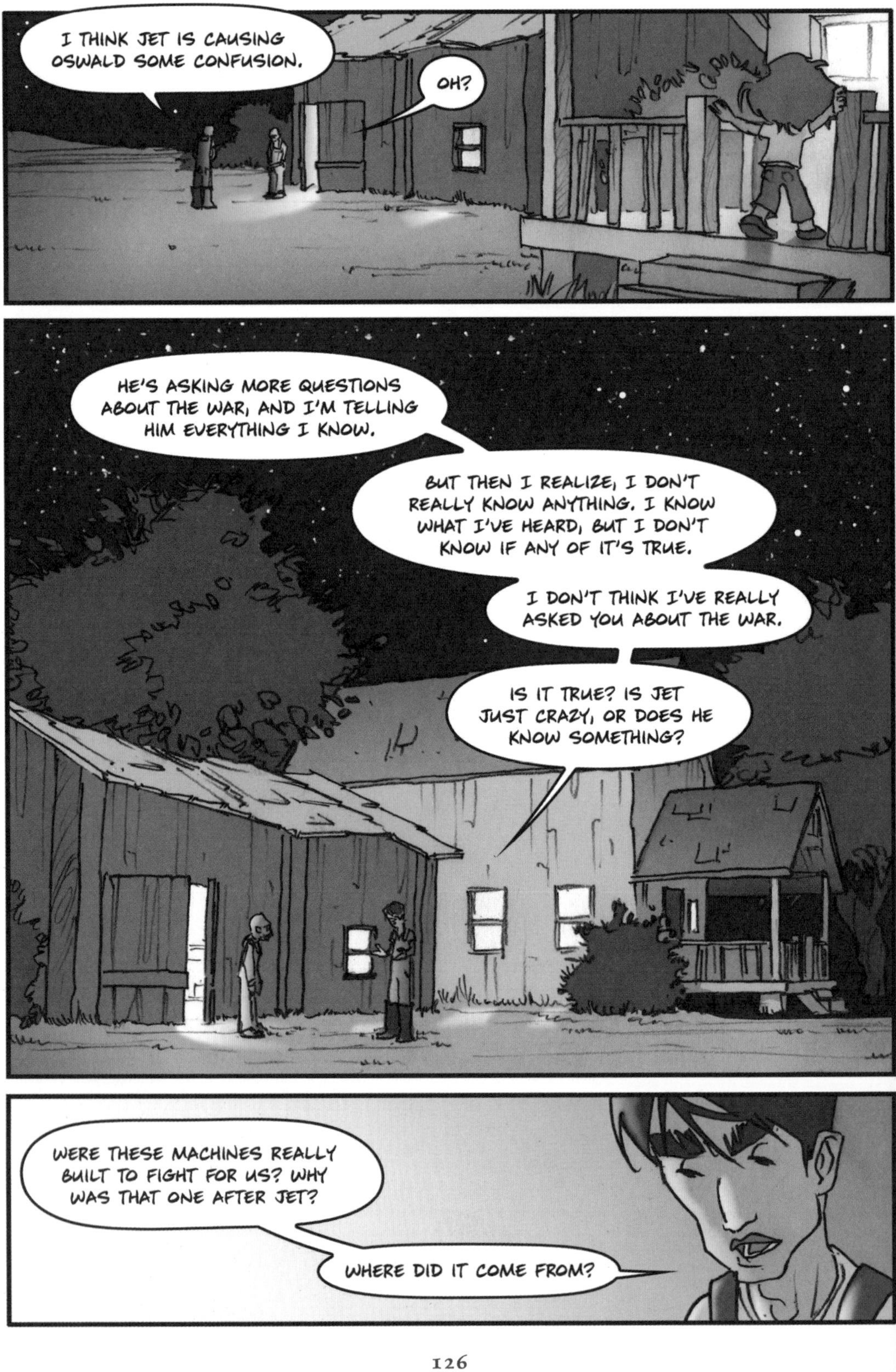
I THINK JET IS CAUSING OSWALD SOME CONFUSION.
OH?
HE'S ASKING MORE QUESTIONS ABOUT THE WAR, AND I'M TELLING HIM EVERYTHING I KNOW.
BUT THEN I REALIZE, I DON'T REALLY KNOW ANYTHING. I KNOW WHAT I'VE HEARD, BUT I DON'T KNOW IF ANY OF IT'S TRUE.
I DON'T THINK I'VE REALLY ASKED YOU ABOUT THE WAR.
IS IT TRUE? IS JET JUST CRAZY, OR DOES HE KNOW SOMETHING?
WERE THESE MACHINES REALLY BUILT TO FIGHT FOR US? WHY WAS THAT ONE AFTER JET?
WHERE DID IT COME FROM?

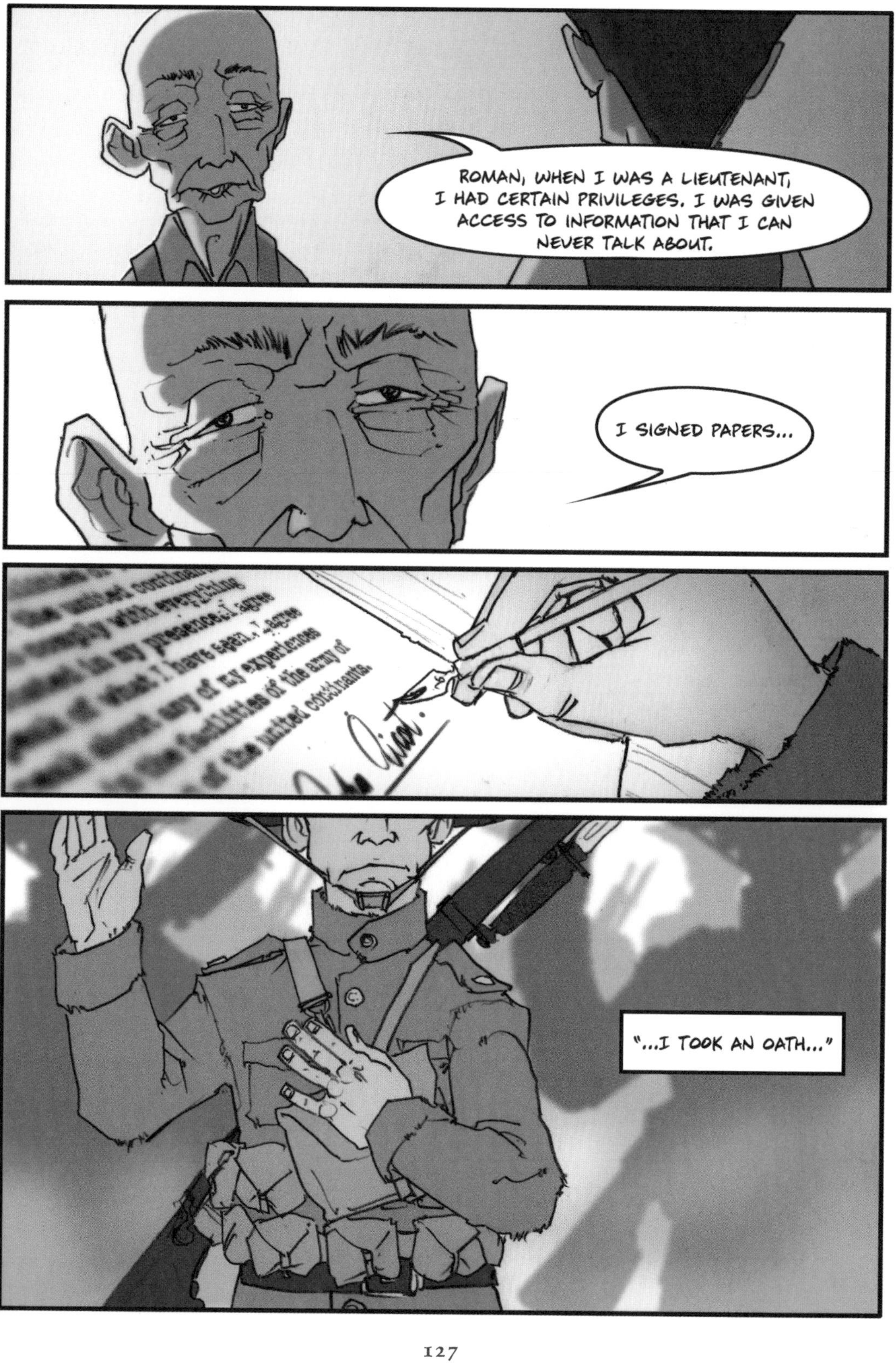
ROMAN, WHEN I WAS A LIEUTENANT, I HAD CERTAIN PRIVILEGES. I WAS GIVEN ACCESS TO INFORMATION THAT I CAN NEVER TALK ABOUT.
I SIGNED PAPERS...
"...I TOOK AN OATH..."

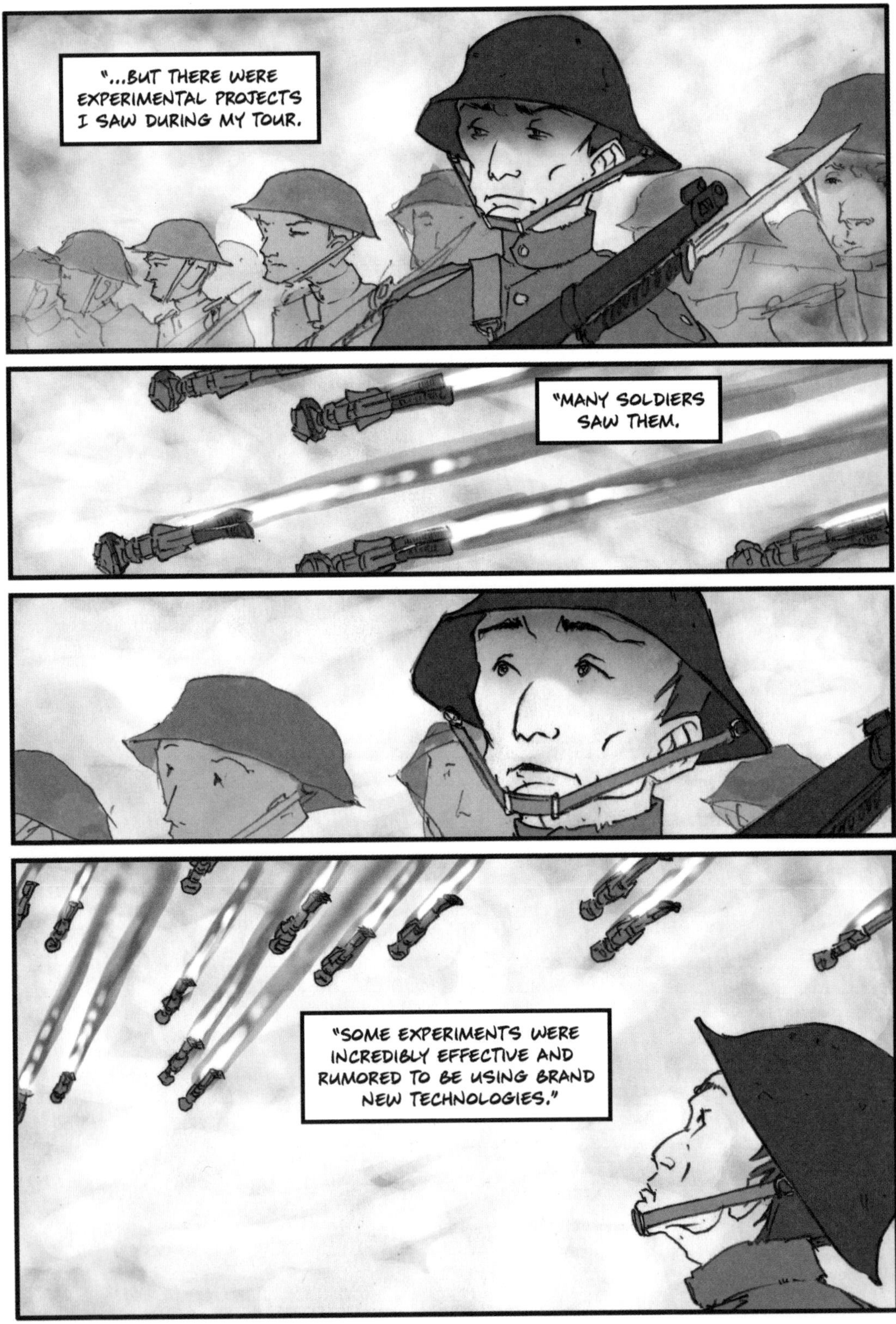
"...BUT THERE WERE EXPERIMENTAL PROJECTS I SAW DURING MY TOUR.
"MANY SOLDIERS SAW THEM.
"SOME EXPERIMENTS WERE INCREDIBLY EFFECTIVE AND RUMORED TO BE USING BRAND NEW TECHNOLOGIES."

"THE MACHINES WERE DEFINITELY BUILT TO REPLACE US.

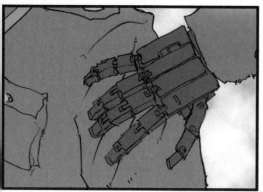

"THEY MARCHED PAST IN SILENCE."

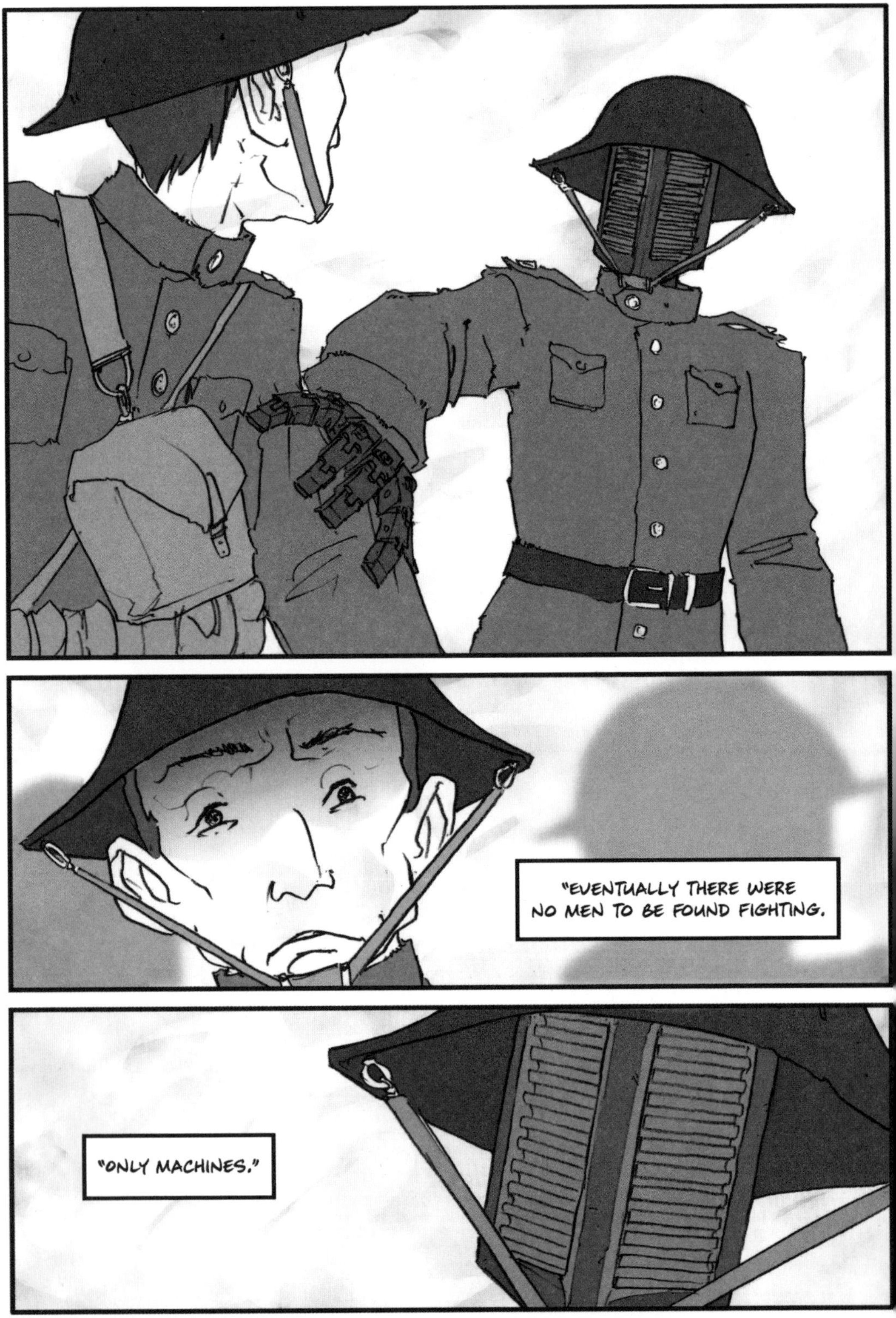
"EVENTUALLY THERE WERE NO MEN TO BE FOUND FIGHTING.
"ONLY MACHINES."

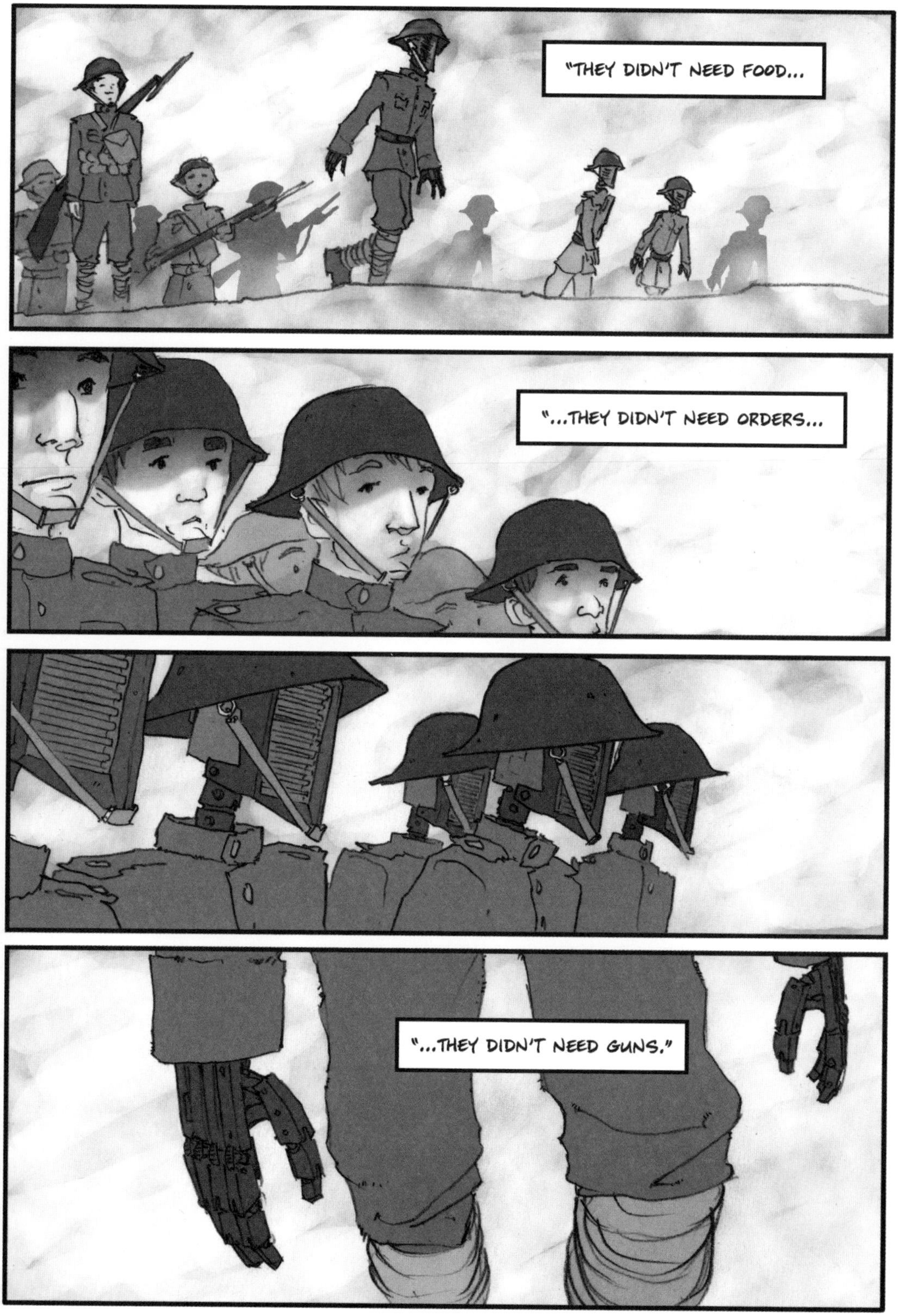
"THEY DIDN'T NEED FOOD...
"...THEY DIDN'T NEED ORDERS...
"...THEY DIDN'T NEED GUNS."

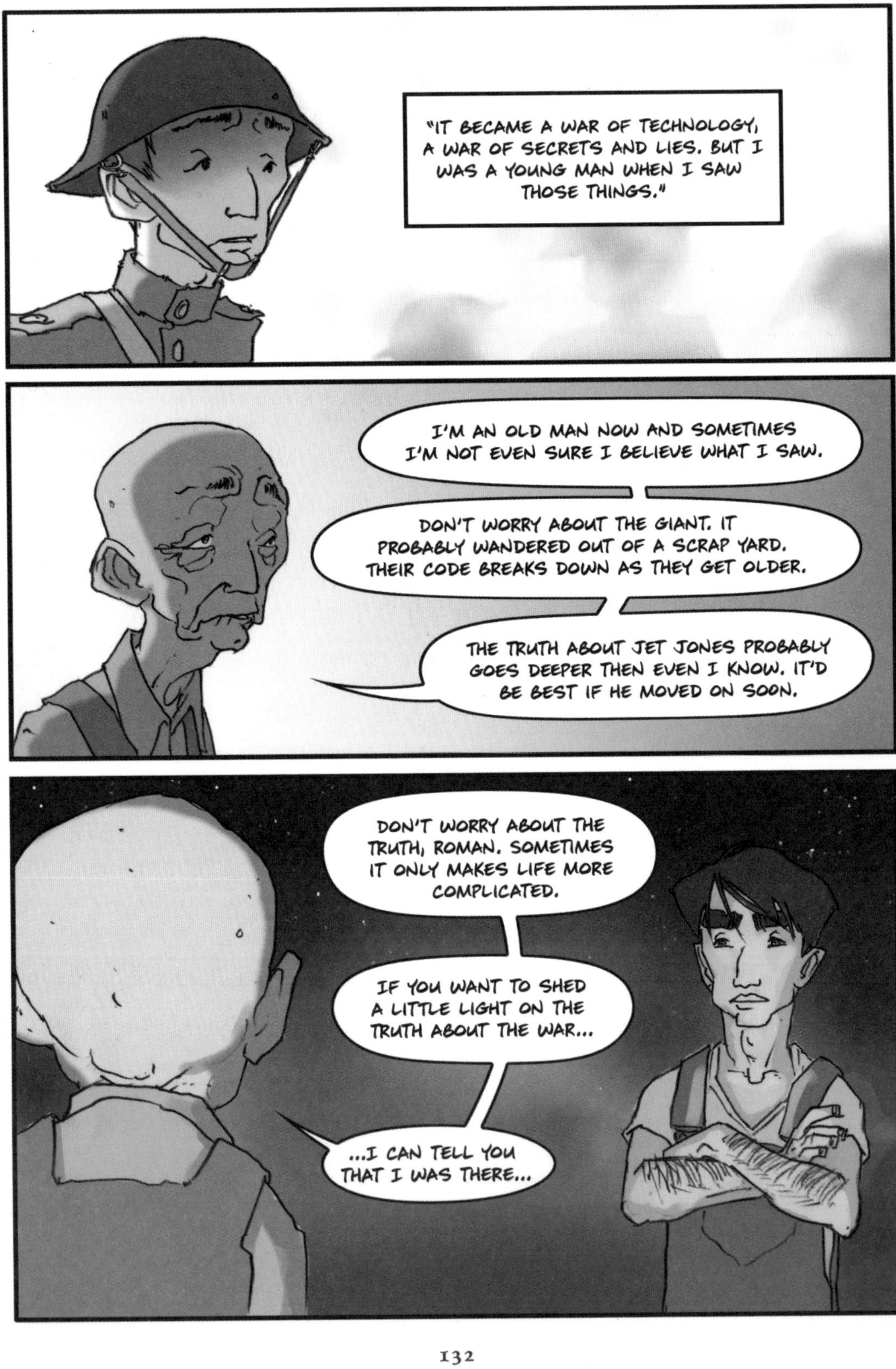
"IT BECAME A WAR OF TECHNOLOGY, A WAR OF SECRETS AND LIES. BUT I WAS A YOUNG MAN WHEN I SAW THOSE THINGS."
I'M AN OLD MAN NOW AND SOMETIMES I'M NOT EVEN SURE I BELIEVE WHAT I SAW.
DON'T WORRY ABOUT THE GIANT. IT PROBABLY WANDERED OUT OF A SCRAP YARD. THEIR CODE BREAKS DOWN AS THEY GET OLDER.
THE TRUTH ABOUT JET JONES PROBABLY GOES DEEPER THEN EVEN I KNOW. IT'D BE BEST IF HE MOVED ON SOON.
DON'T WORRY ABOUT THE TRUTH, ROMAN. SOMETIMES IT ONLY MAKES LIFE MORE COMPLICATED.
IF YOU WANT TO SHED A LITTLE LIGHT ON THE TRUTH ABOUT THE WAR...
...I CAN TELL YOU THAT I WAS THERE...

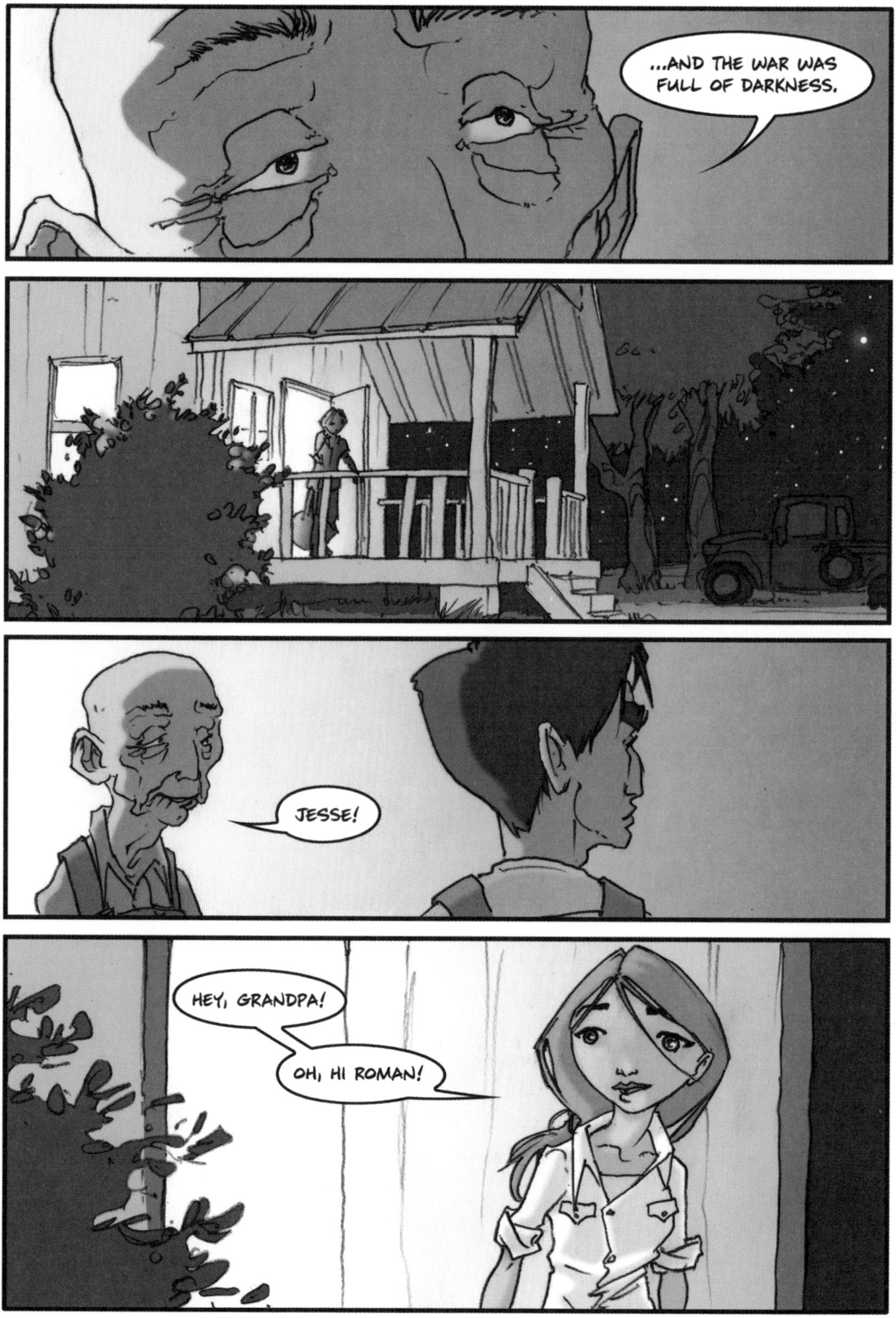
...AND THE WAR WAS FULL OF DARKNESS.
JESSE!
HEY, GRANDPA!
OH, HI ROMAN!

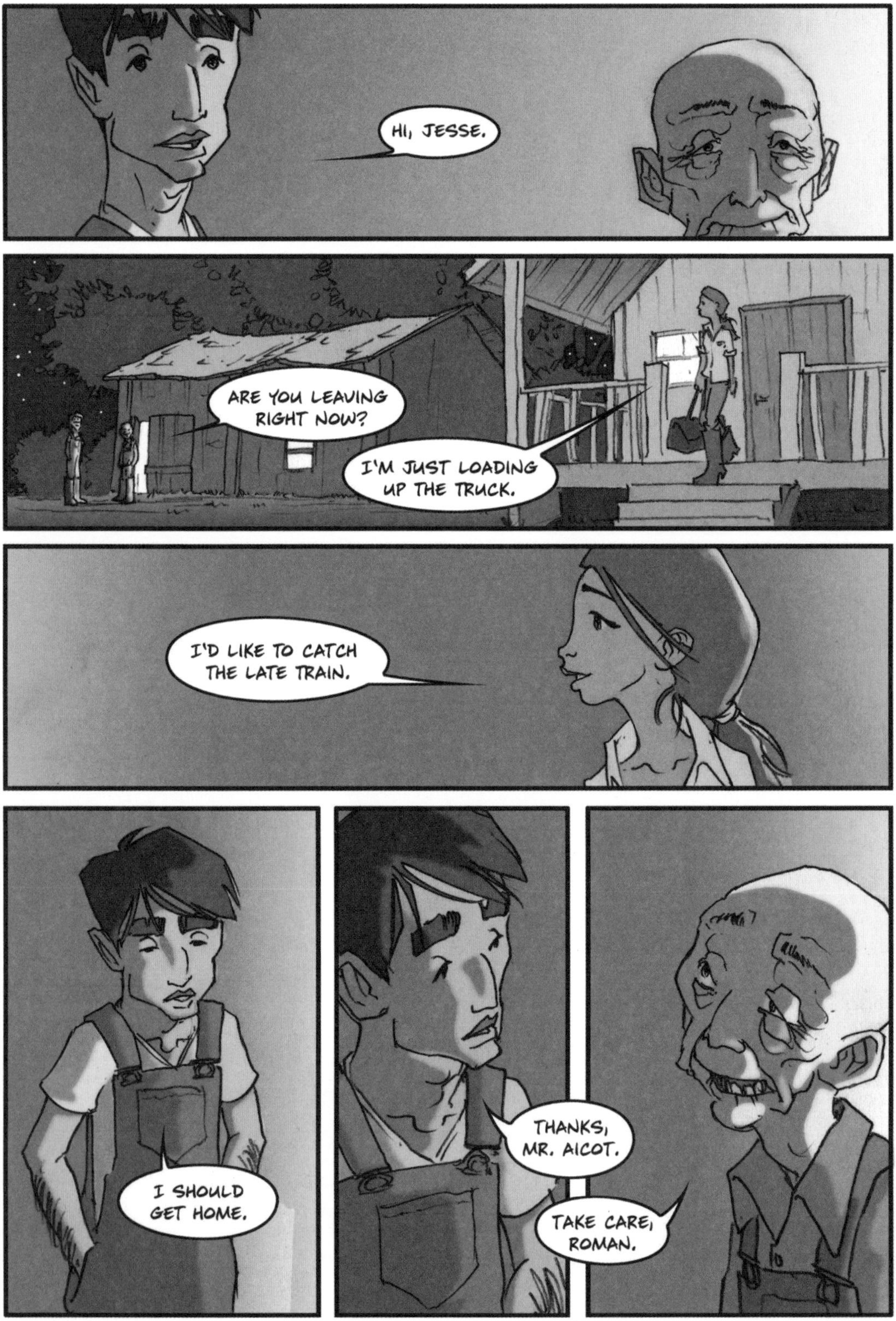
HI, JESSE.
ARE YOU LEAVING RIGHT NOW?
I'M JUST LOADING UP THE TRUCK.
I'D LIKE TO CATCH THE LATE TRAIN.
I SHOULD GET HOME.
THANKS, MR. AICOT.
TAKE CARE, ROMAN.

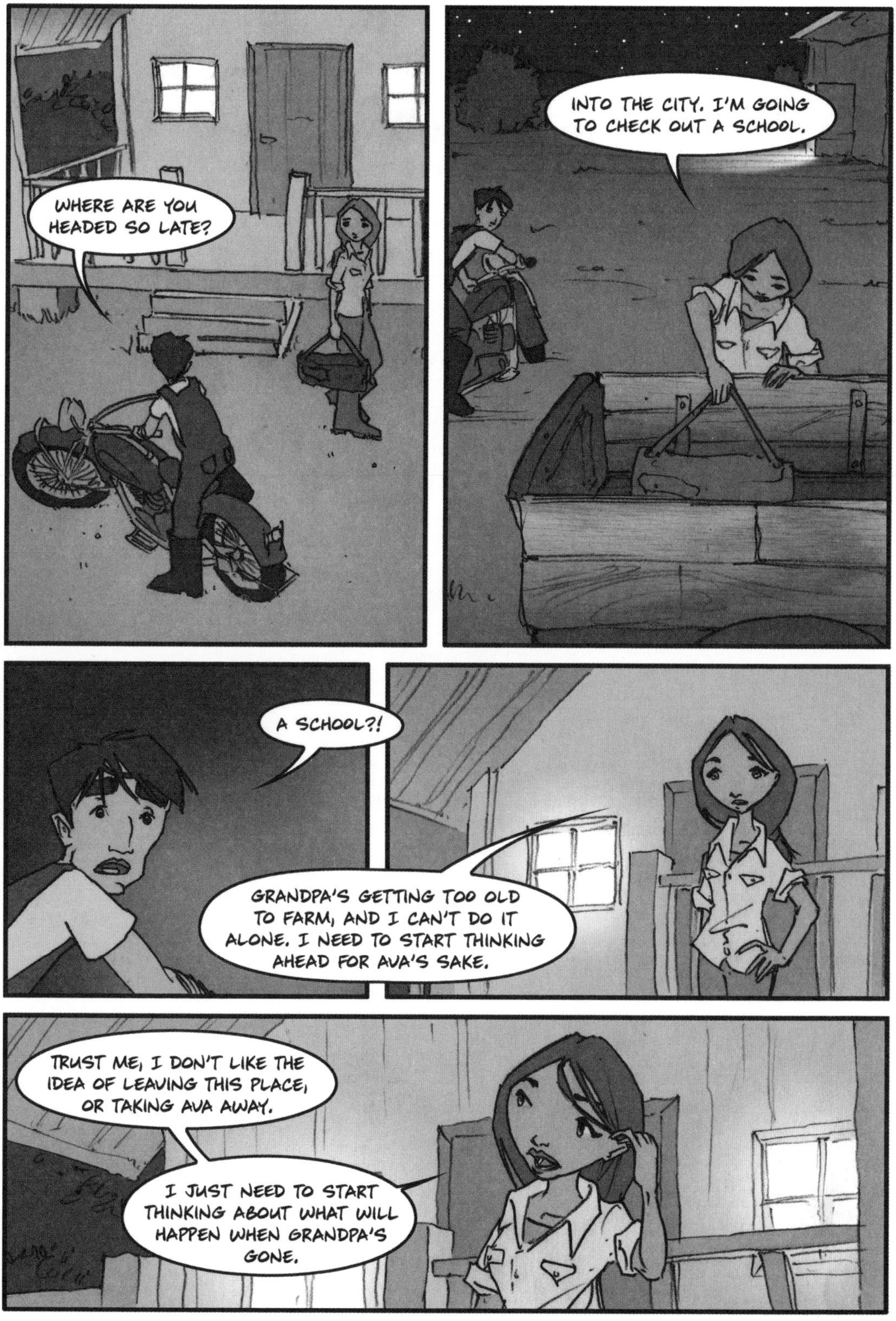
WHERE ARE YOU HEADED SO LATE?
INTO THE CITY. I'M GOING TO CHECK OUT A SCHOOL.
A SCHOOL?!
GRANDPA'S GETTING TOO OLD TO FARM, AND I CAN'T DO IT ALONE. I NEED TO START THINKING AHEAD FOR AVA'S SAKE.
TRUST ME, I DON'T LIKE THE IDEA OF LEAVING THIS PLACE, OR TAKING AVA AWAY.
I JUST NEED TO START THINKING ABOUT WHAT WILL HAPPEN WHEN GRANDPA'S GONE.

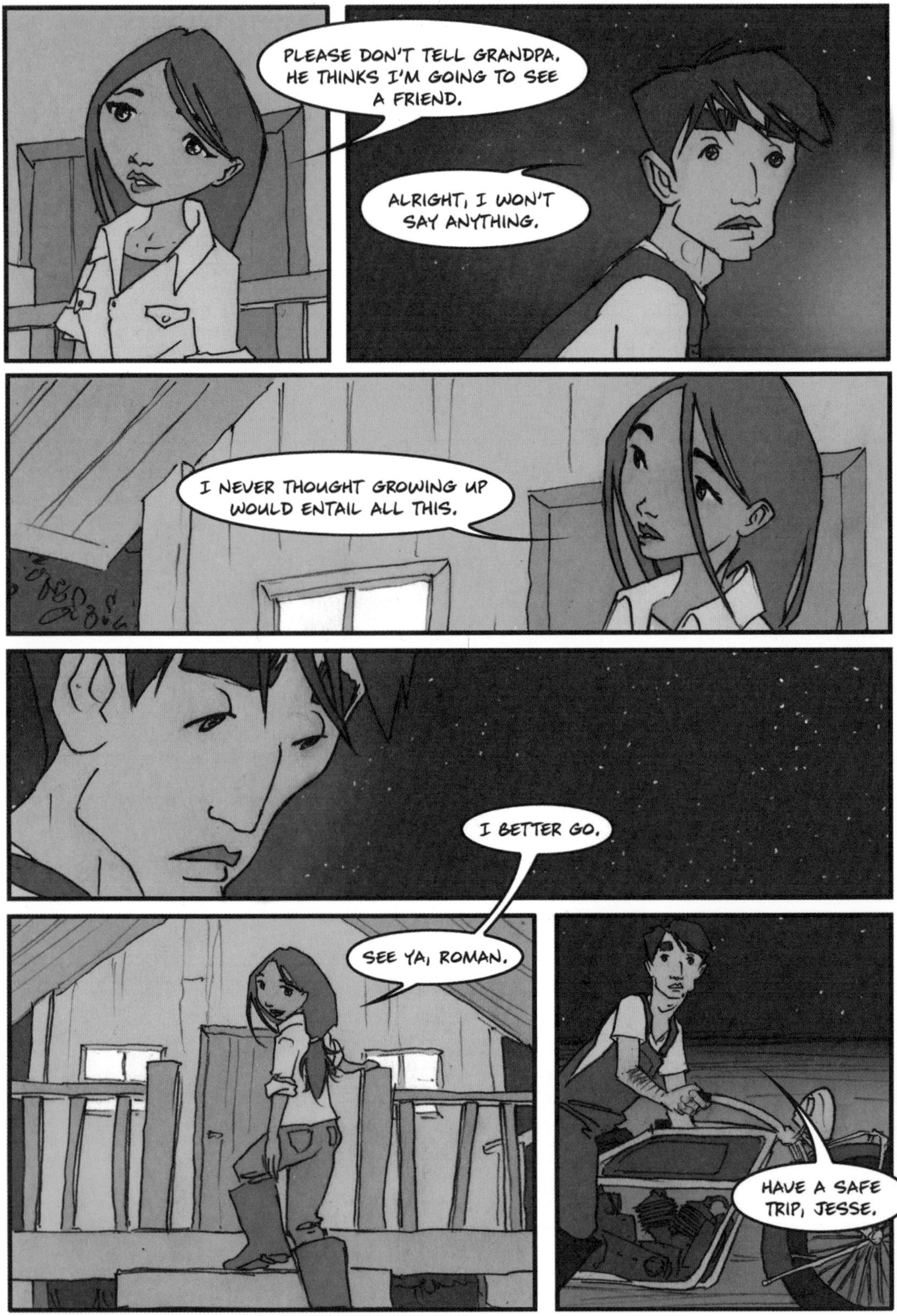
PLEASE DON'T TELL GRANDPA. HE THINKS I'M GOING TO SEE A FRIEND.
ALRIGHT, I WON'T SAY ANYTHING.
I NEVER THOUGHT GROWING UP WOULD ENTAIL ALL THIS.
I BETTER GO.
SEE YA, ROMAN.
HAVE A SAFE TRIP, JESSE.

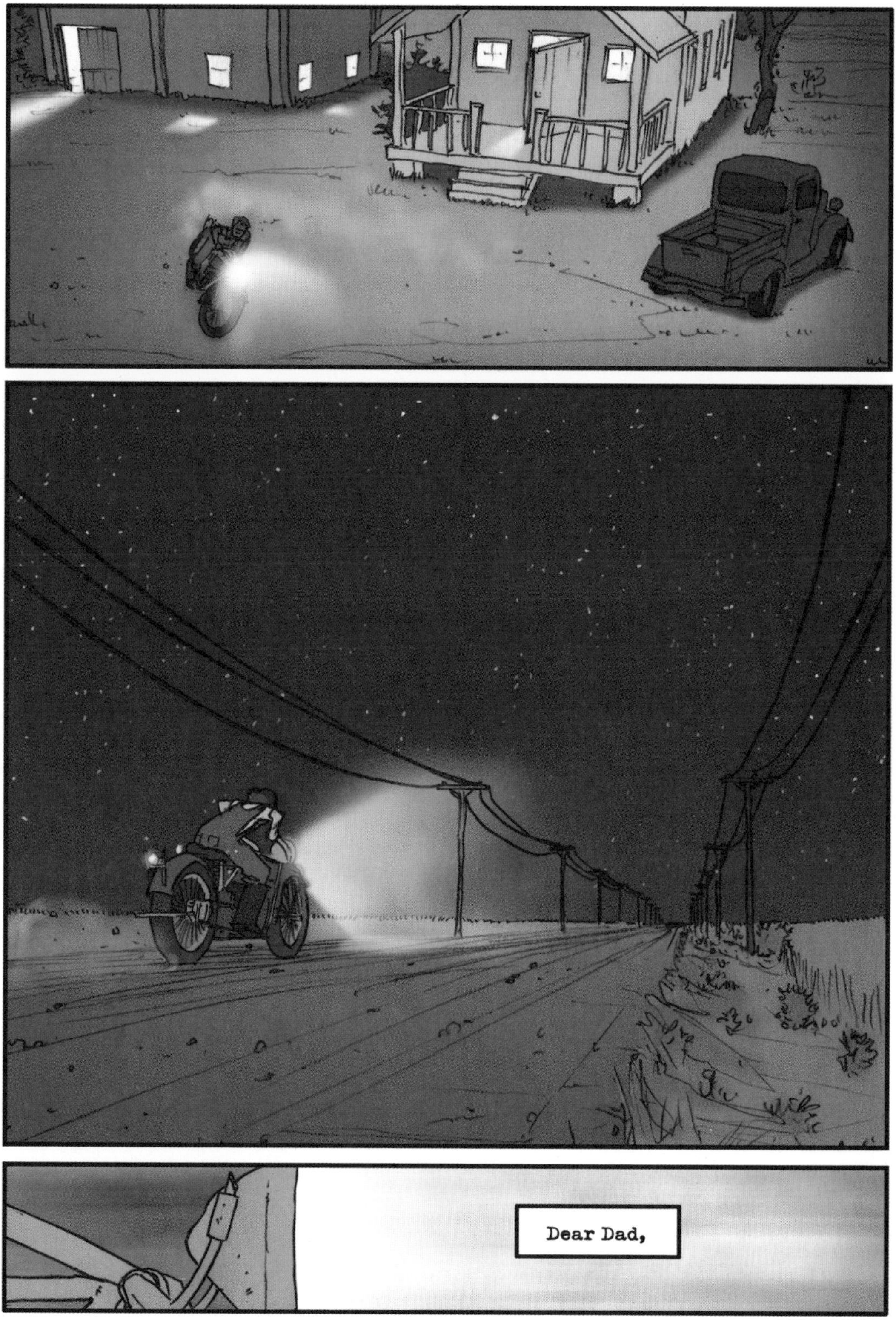
Dear Dad,

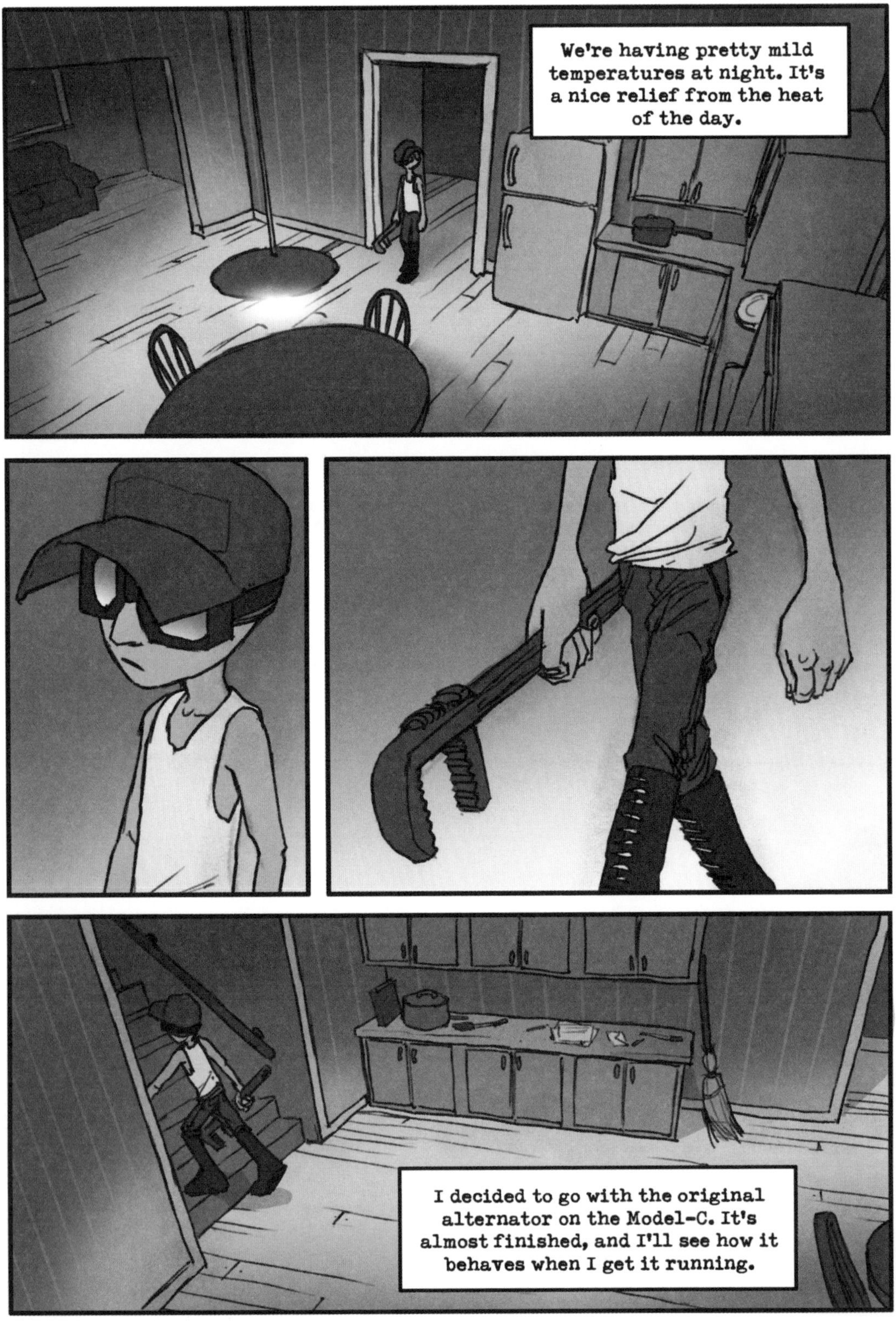
We're having pretty mild temperatures at night. It's a nice relief from the heat of the day.
I decided to go with the original alternator on the Model-C. It's almost finished, and I'll see how it behaves when I get it running.

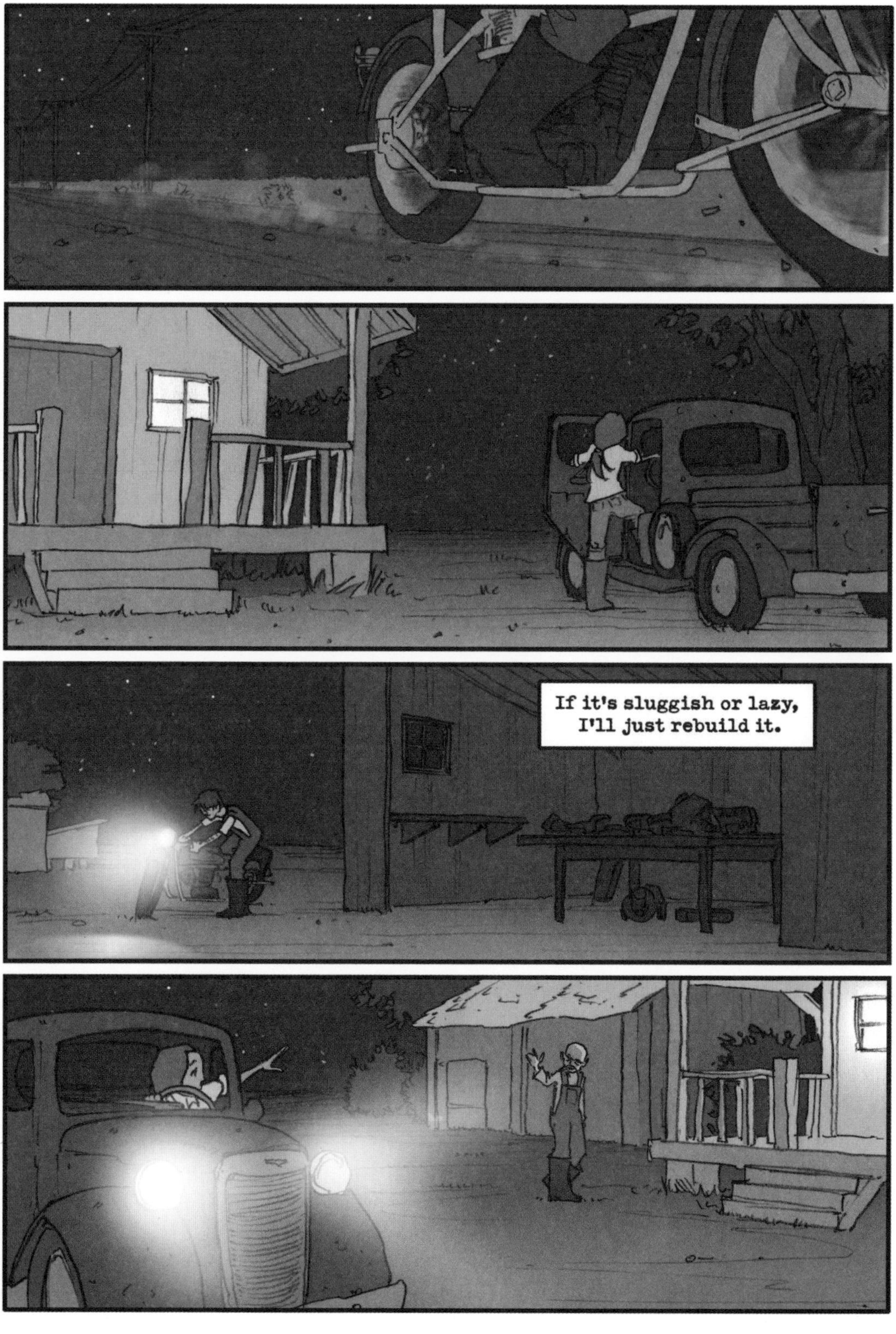
If it's sluggish or lazy, I'll just rebuild it.

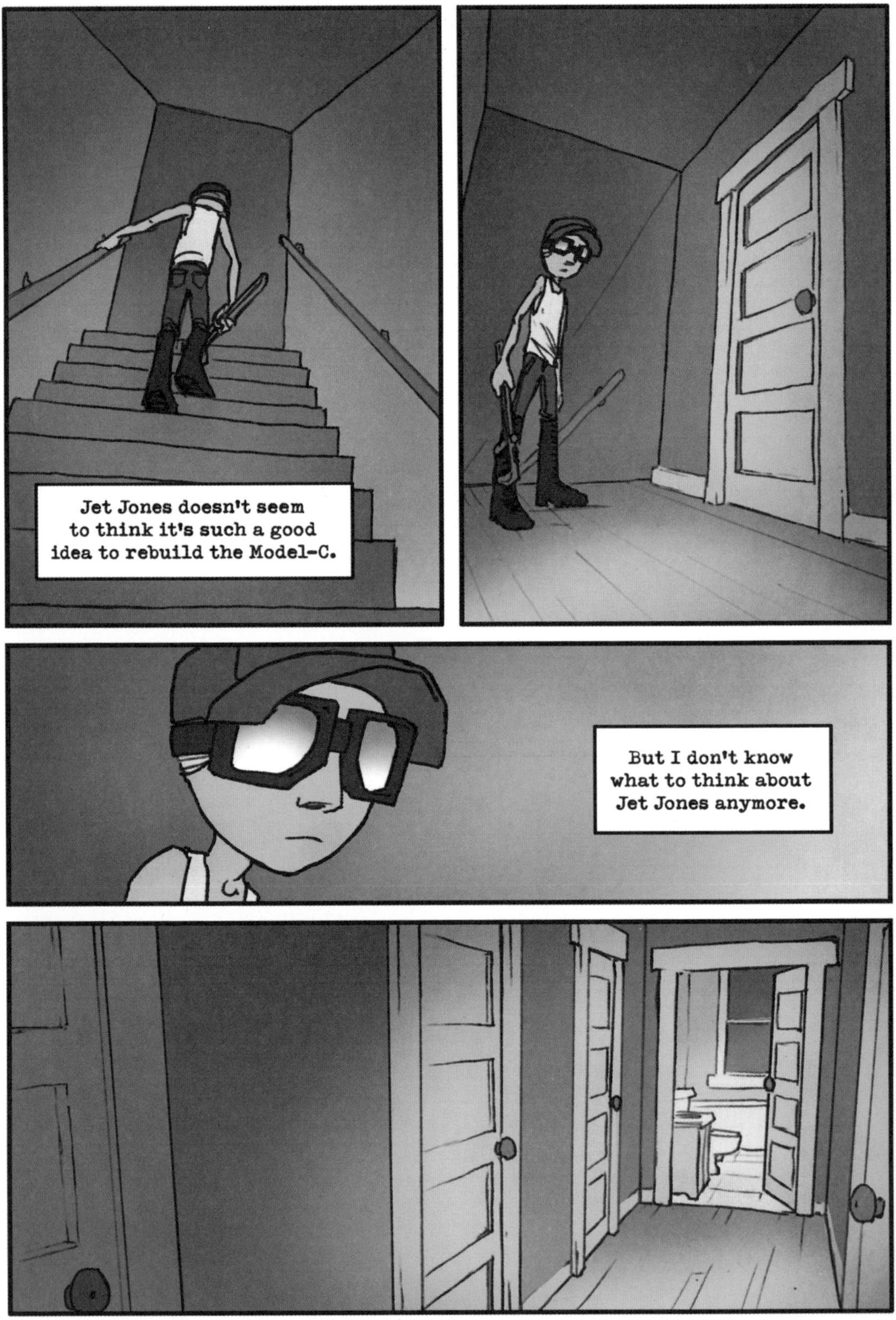
Jet Jones doesn't seem to think it's such a good idea to rebuild the Model-C.
But I don't know what to think about Jet Jones anymore.

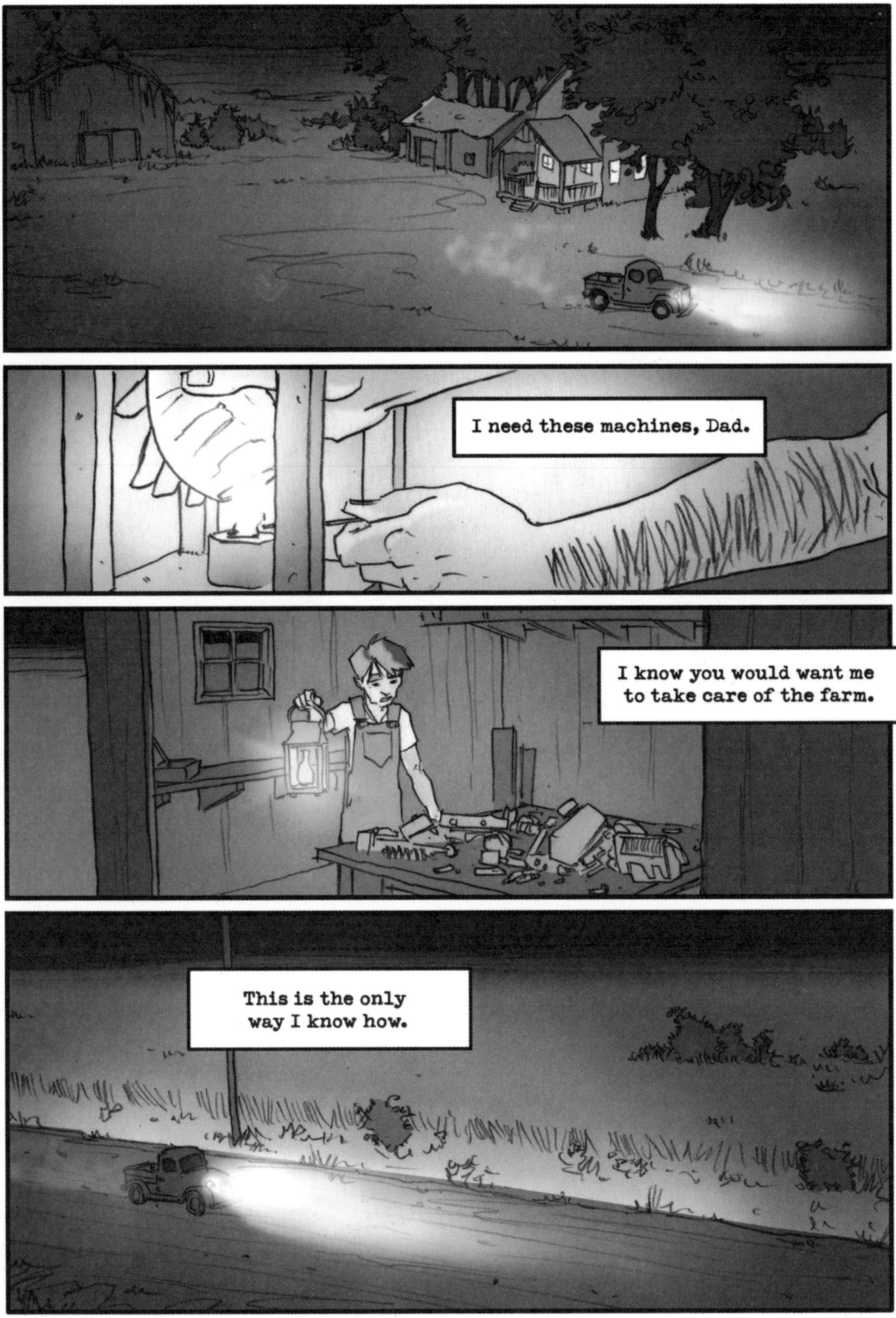
I need these machines, Dad.
I know you would want me to take care of the farm.
This is the only way I know how.

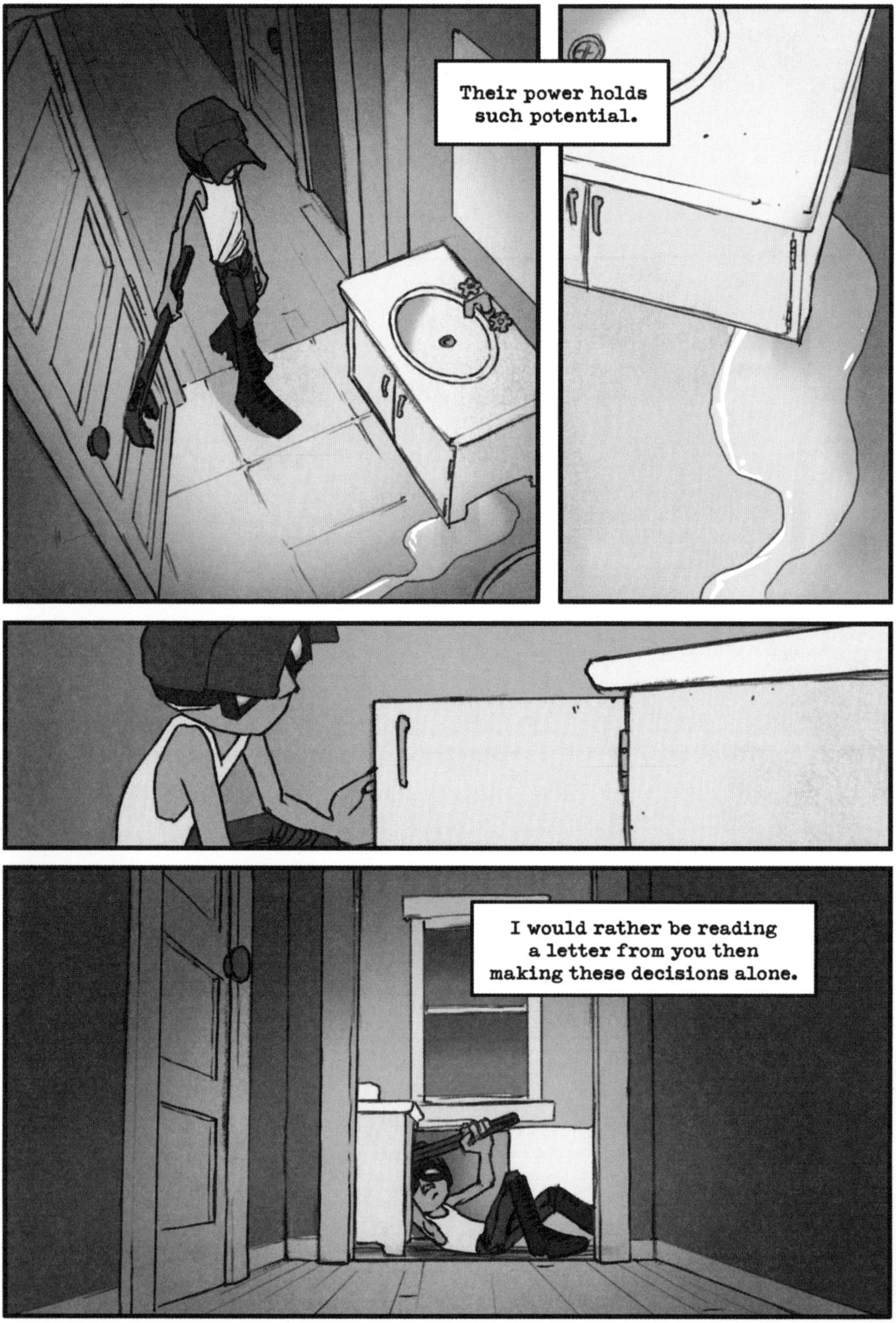
Their power holds such potential.
I would rather be reading a letter from you then making these decisions alone.

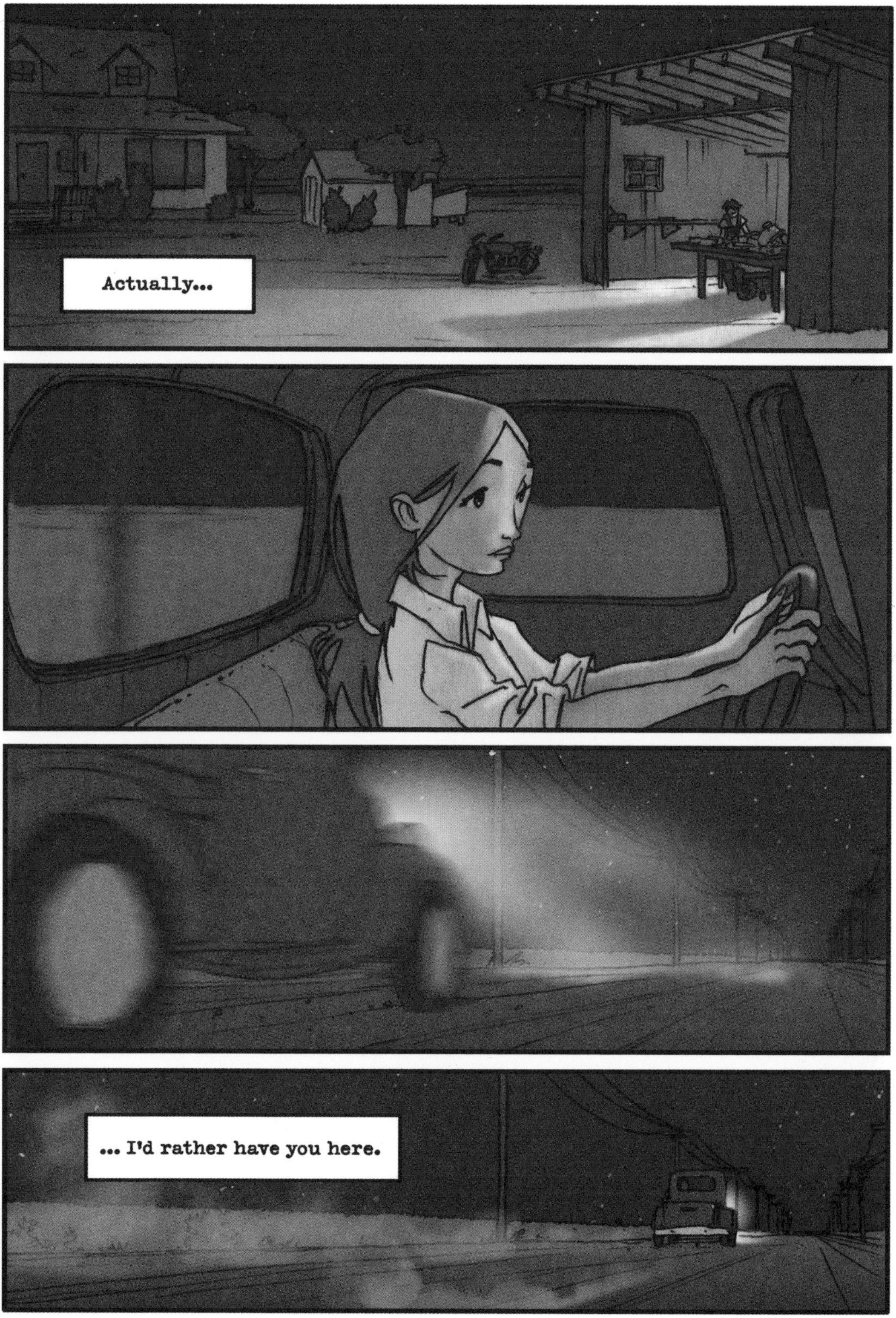
Actually...
... I'd rather have you here.

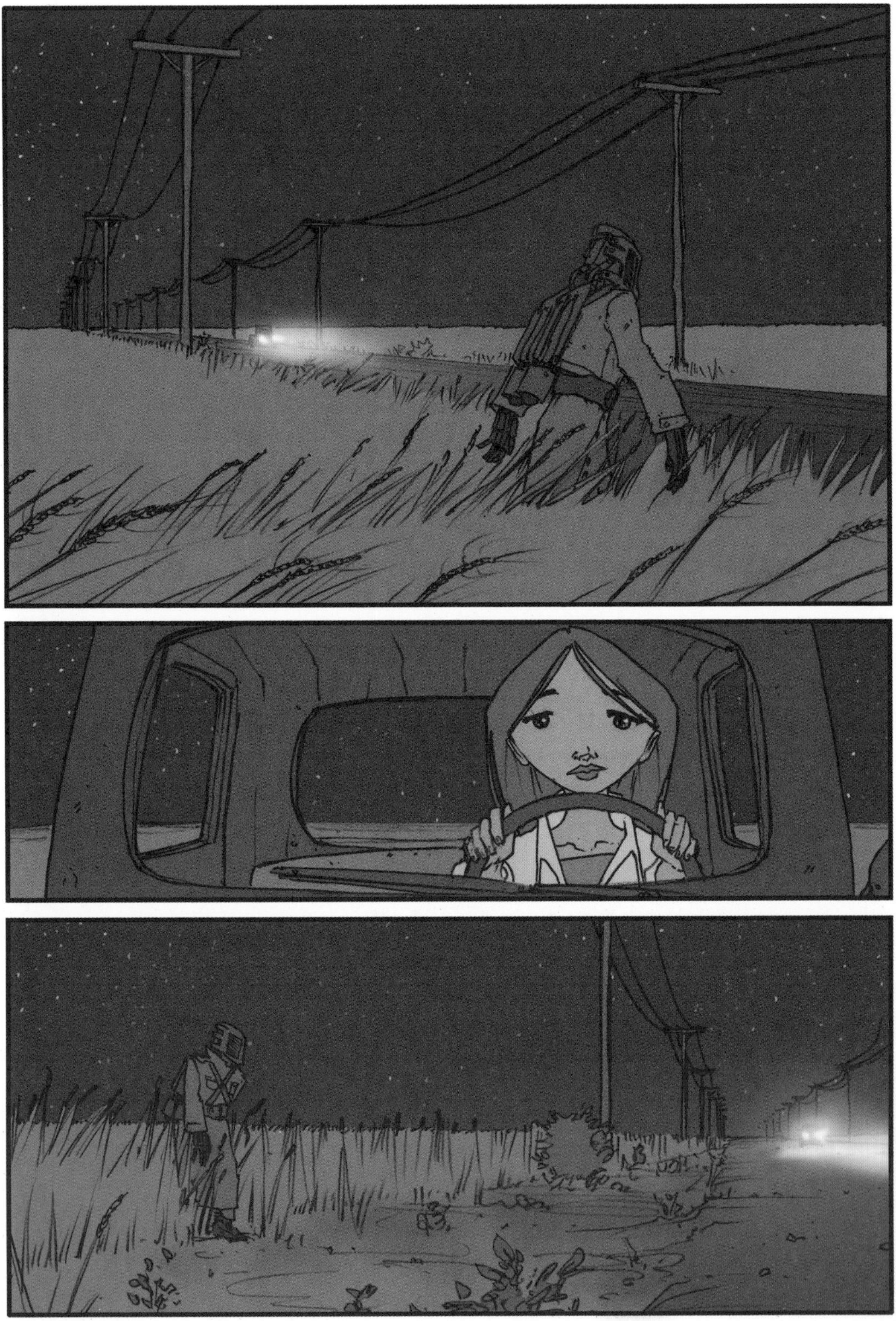

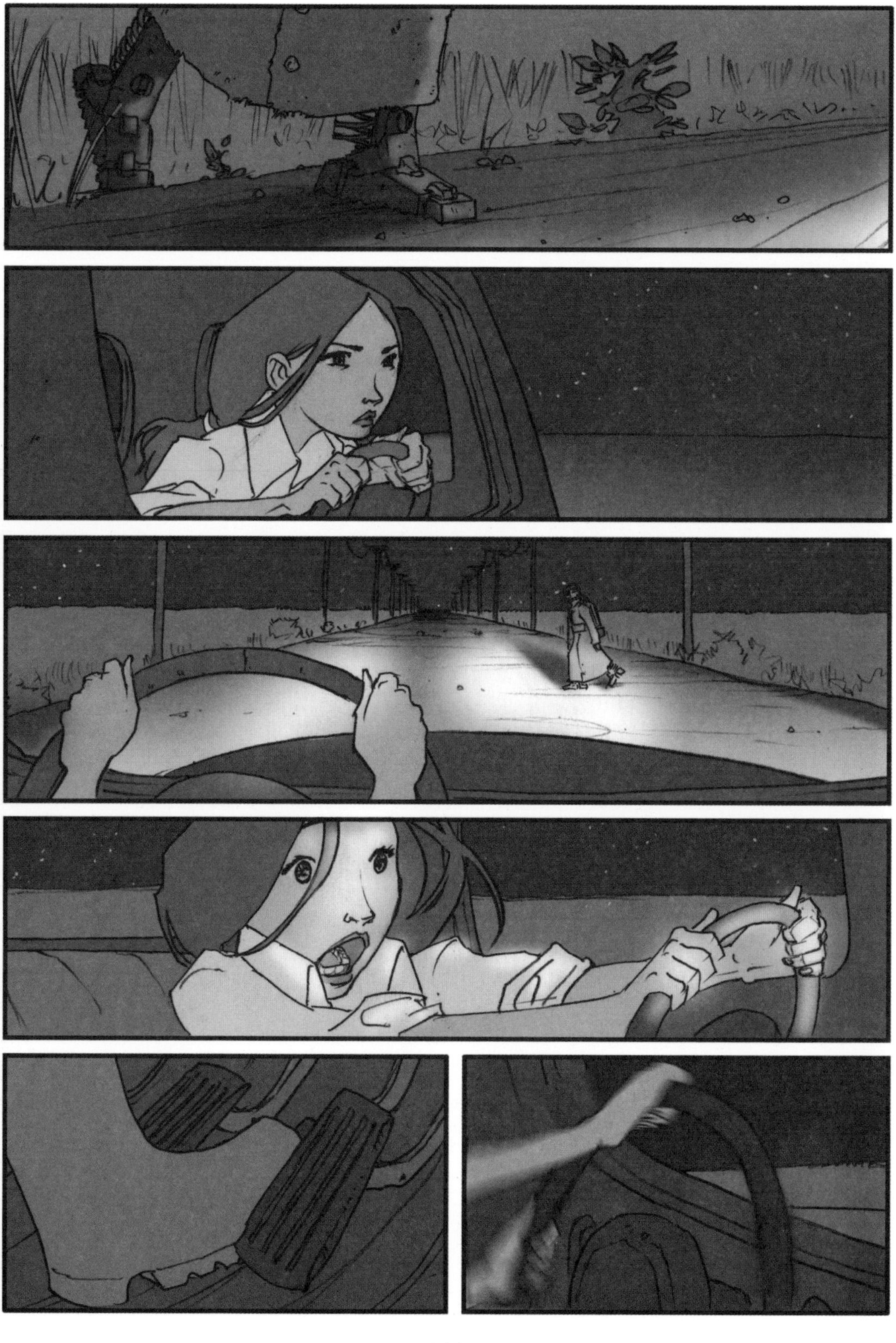

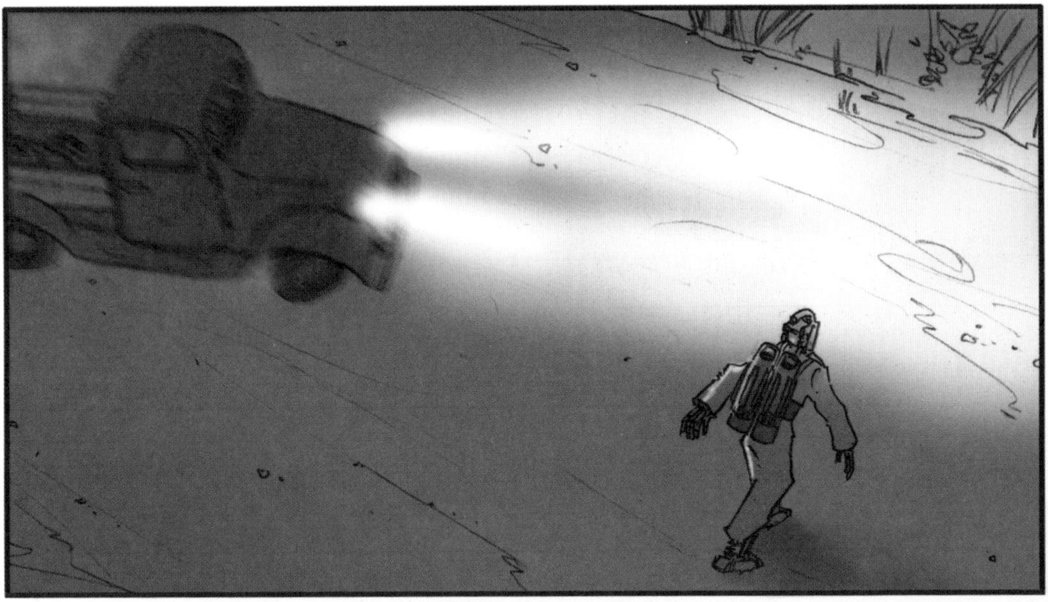

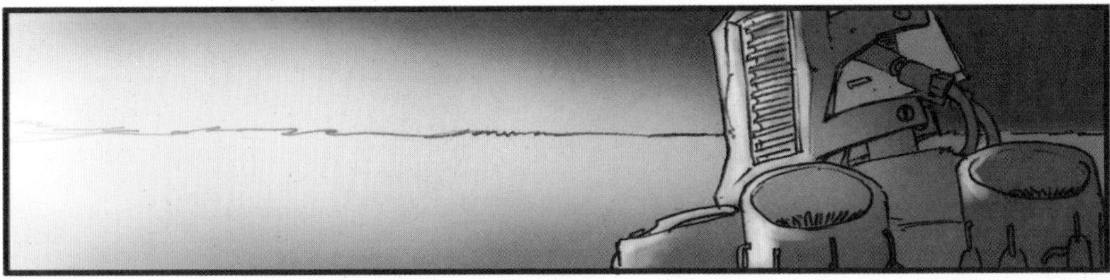

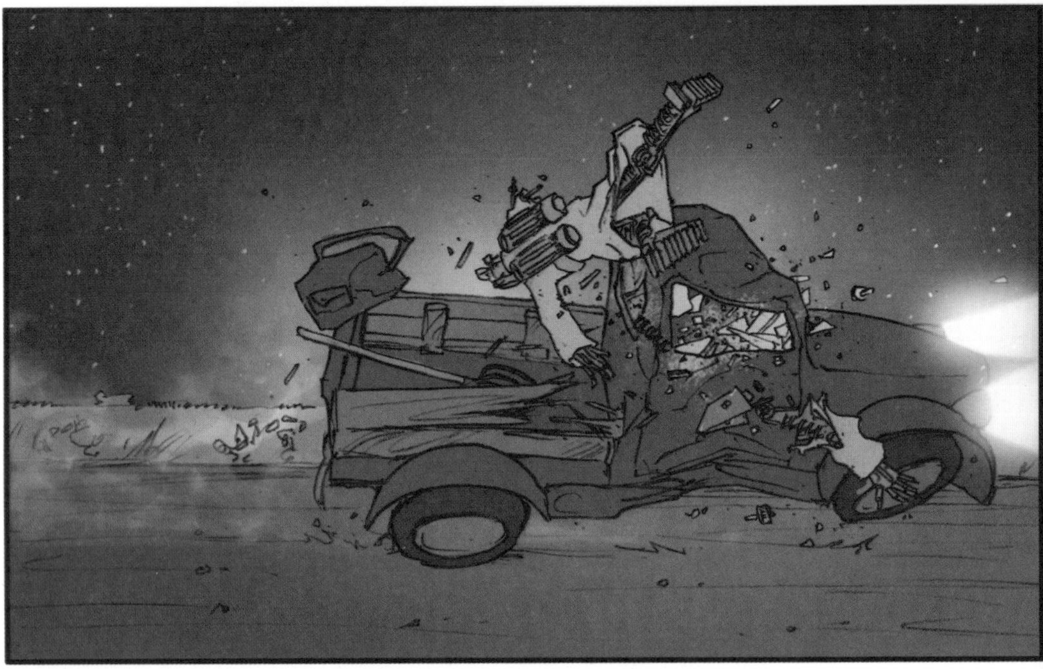

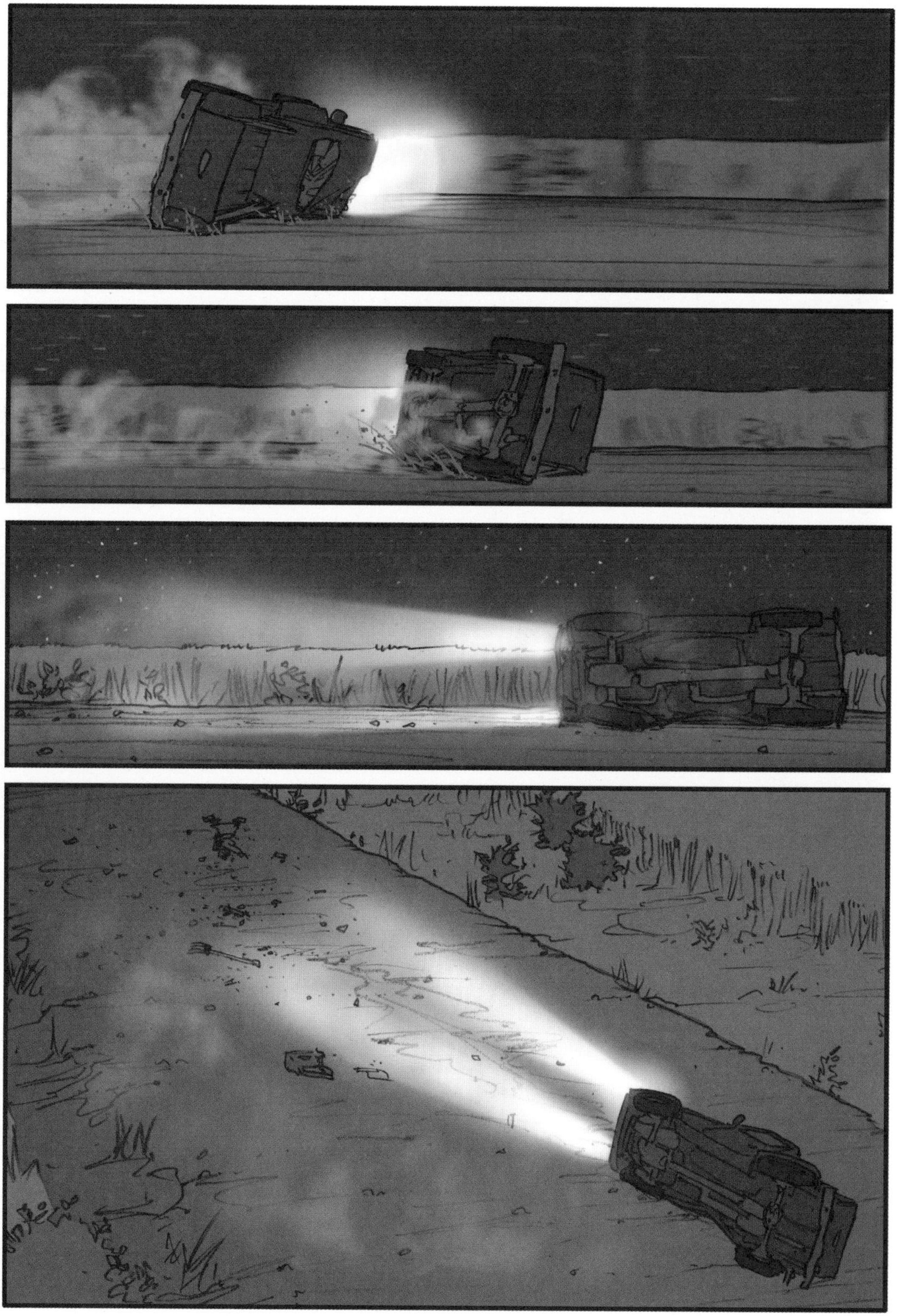

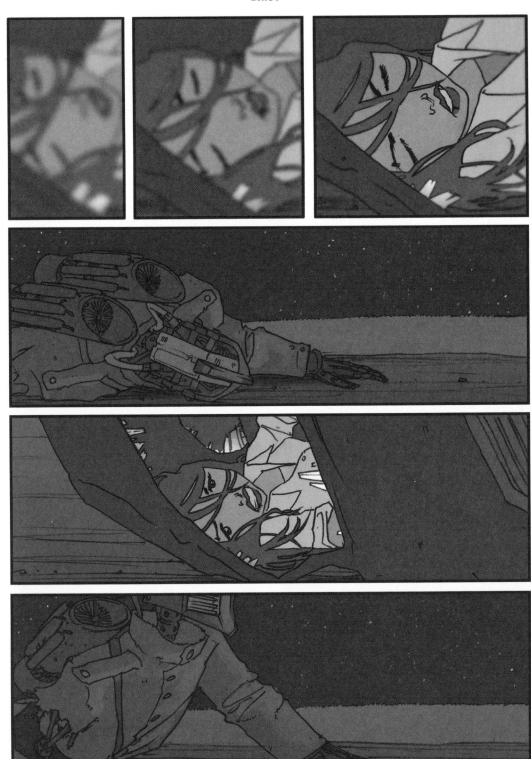

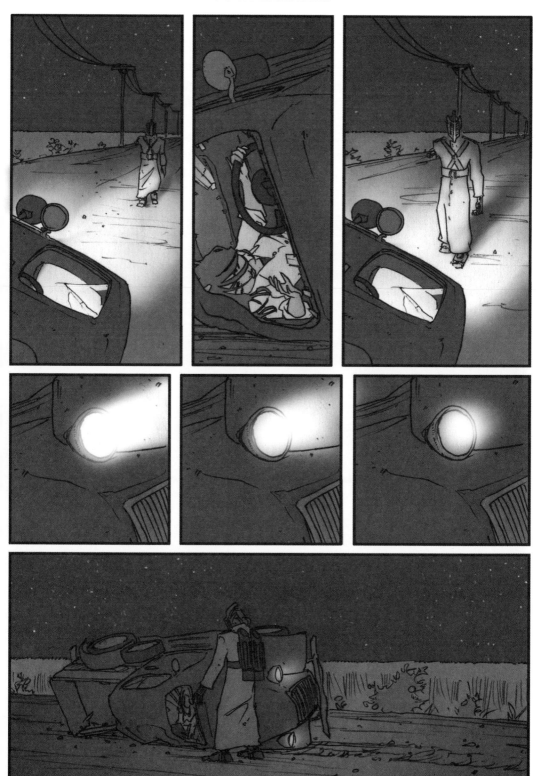

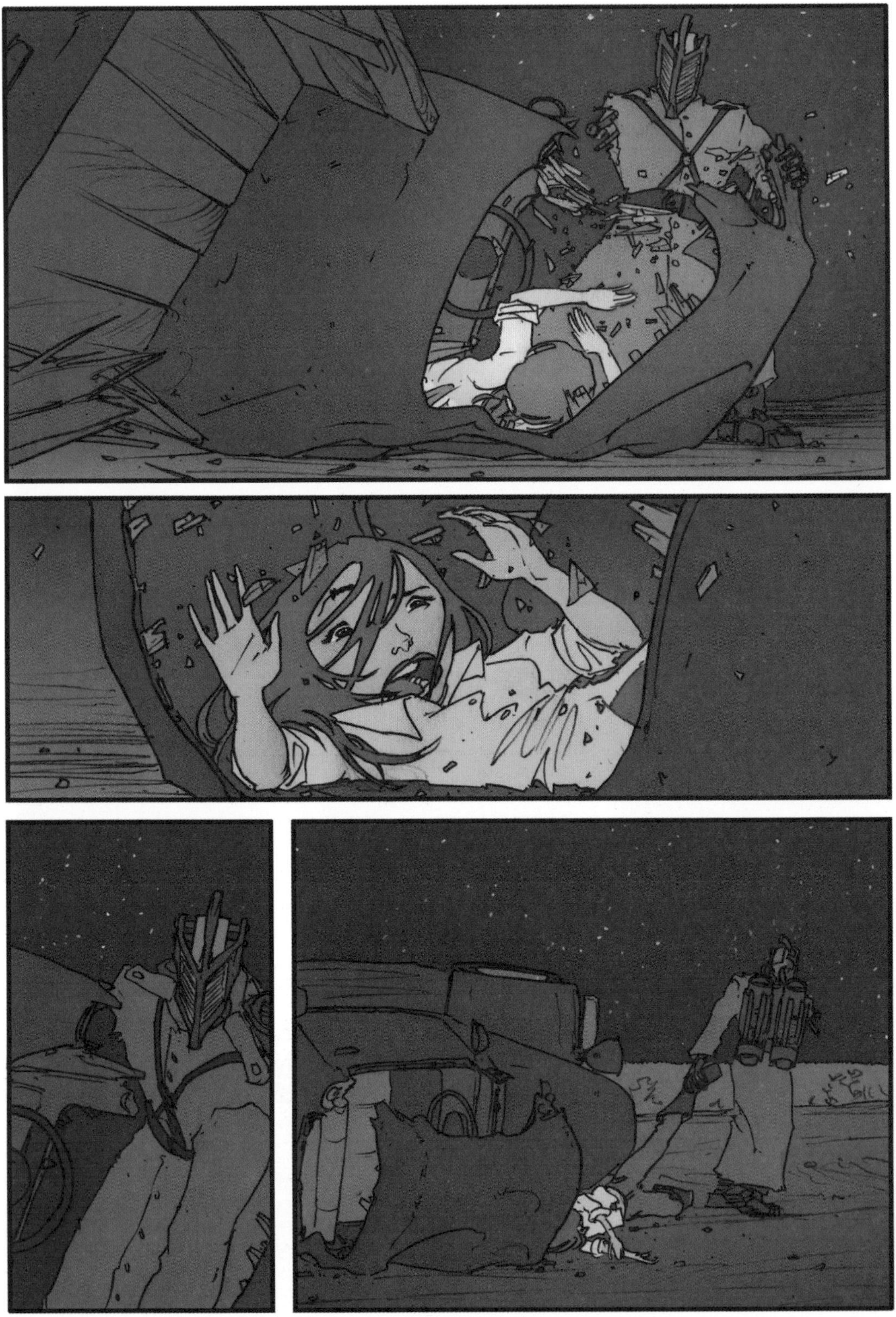

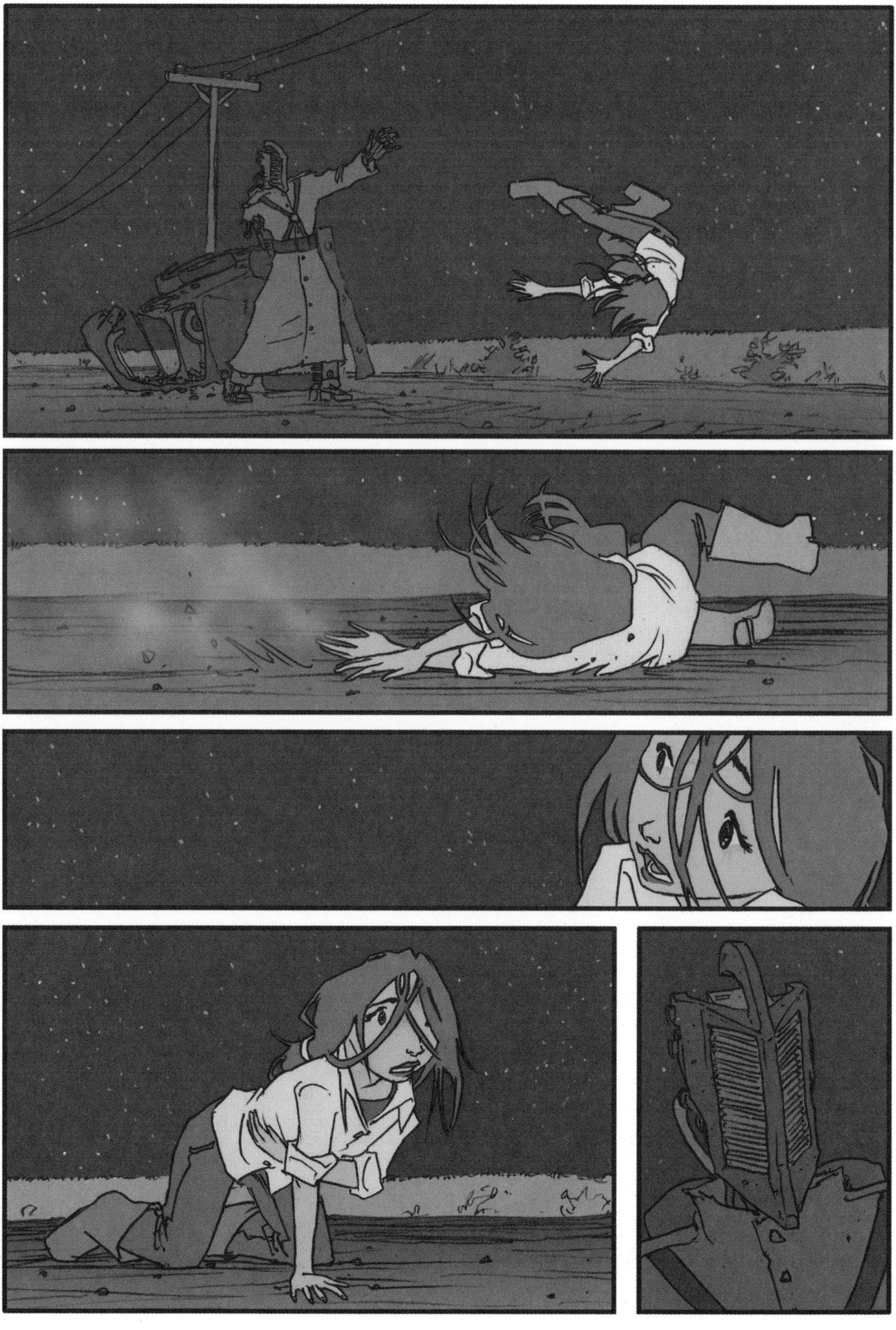

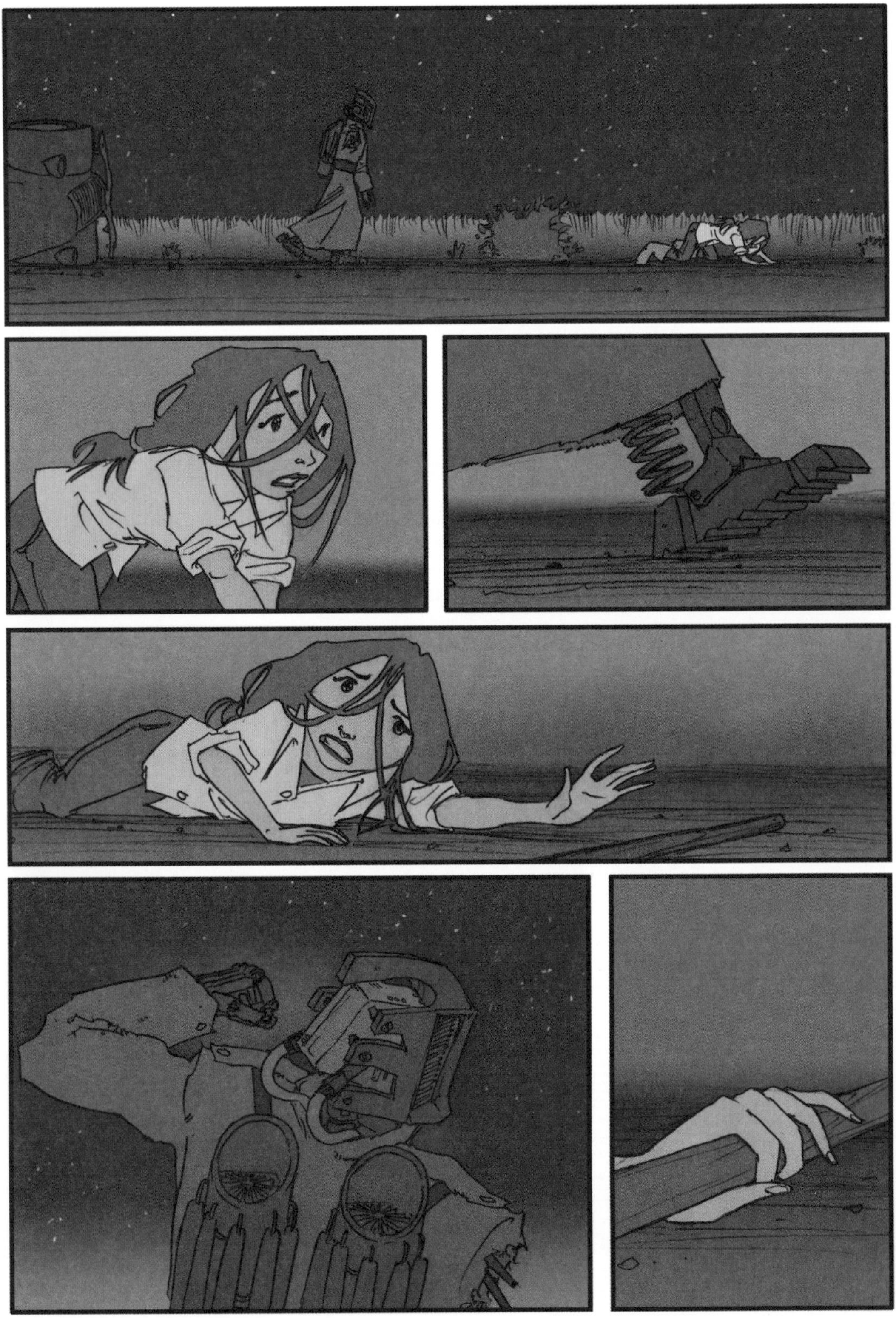

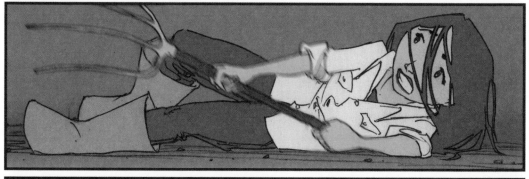

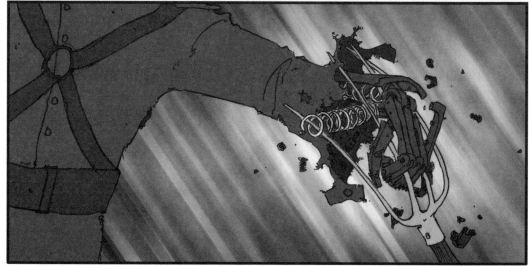

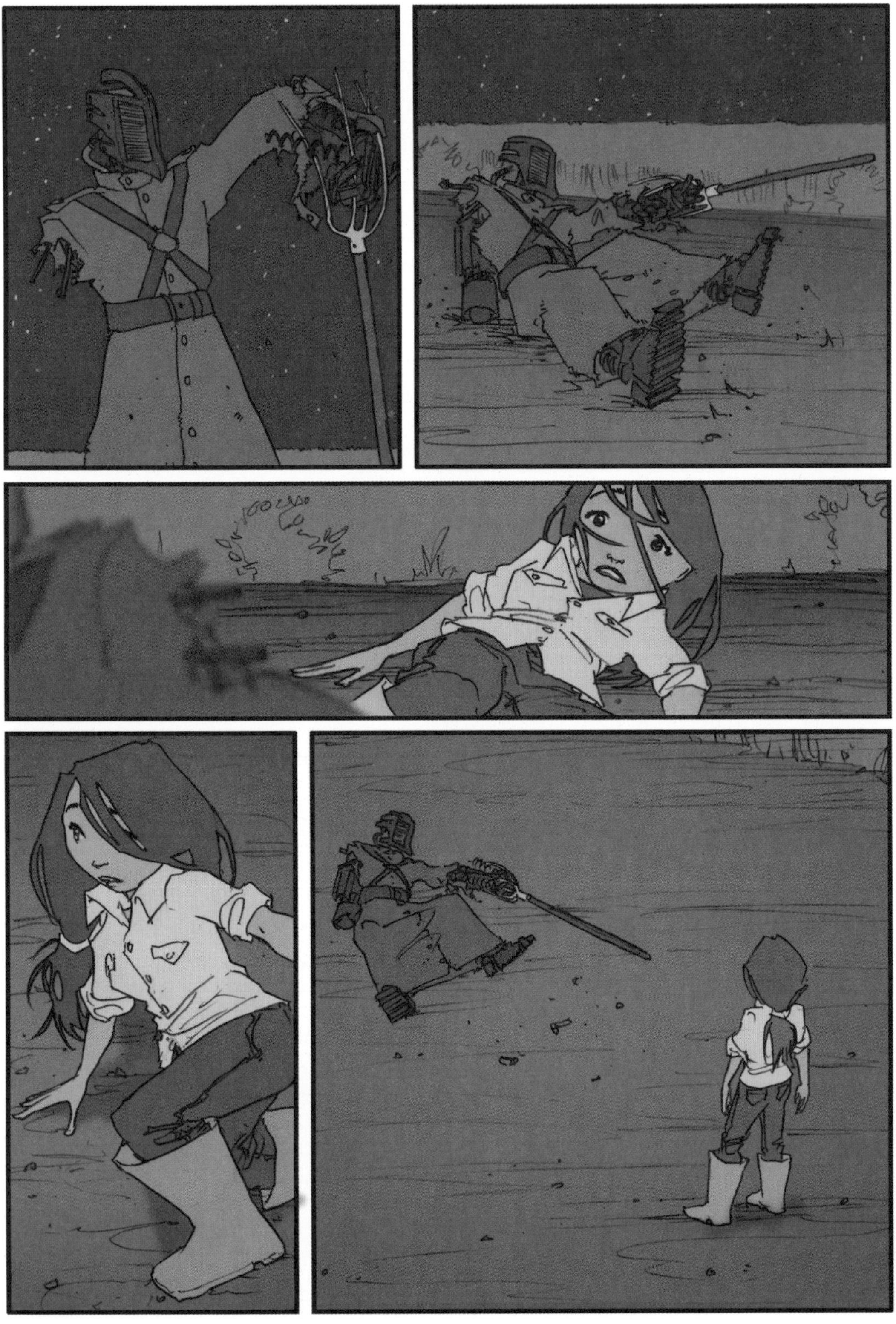

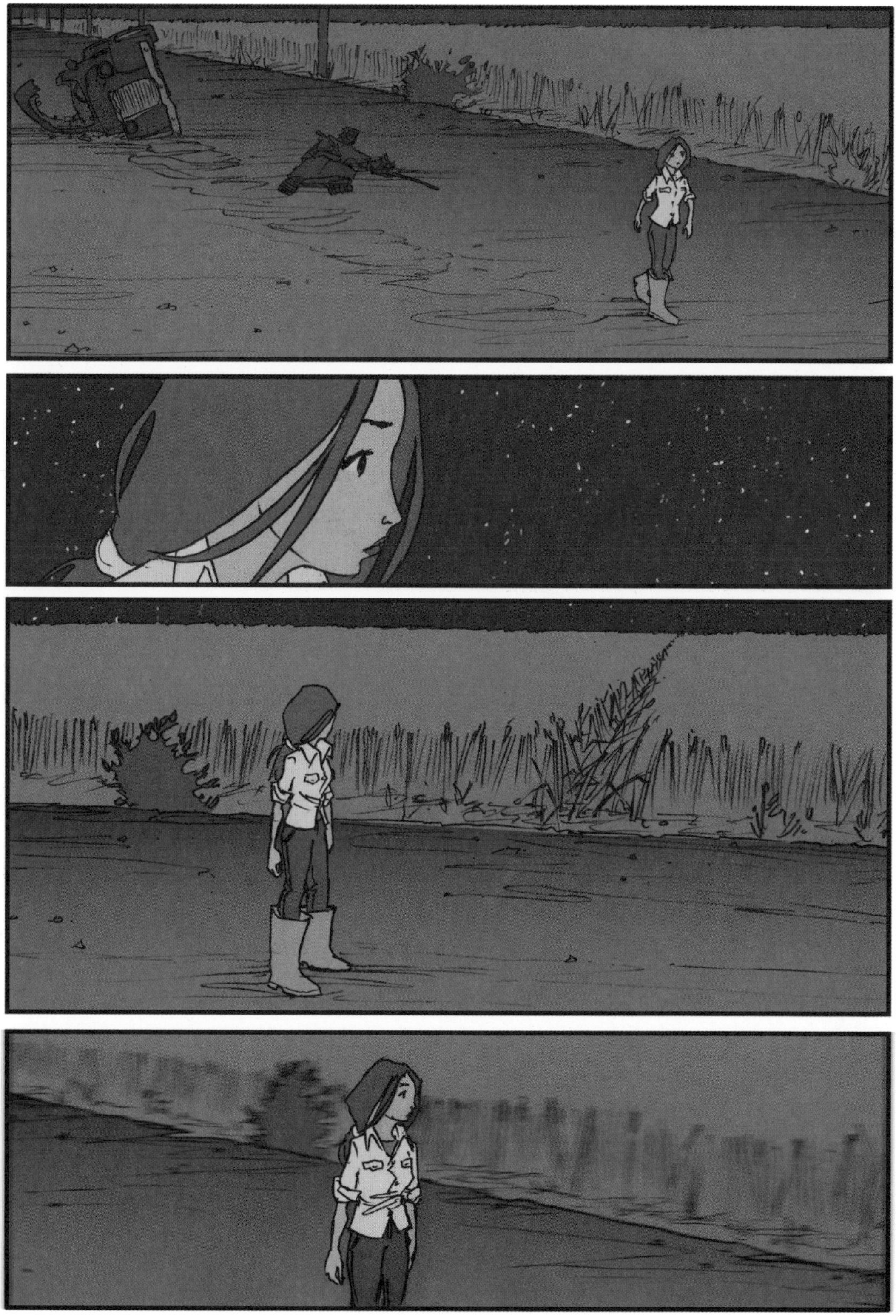

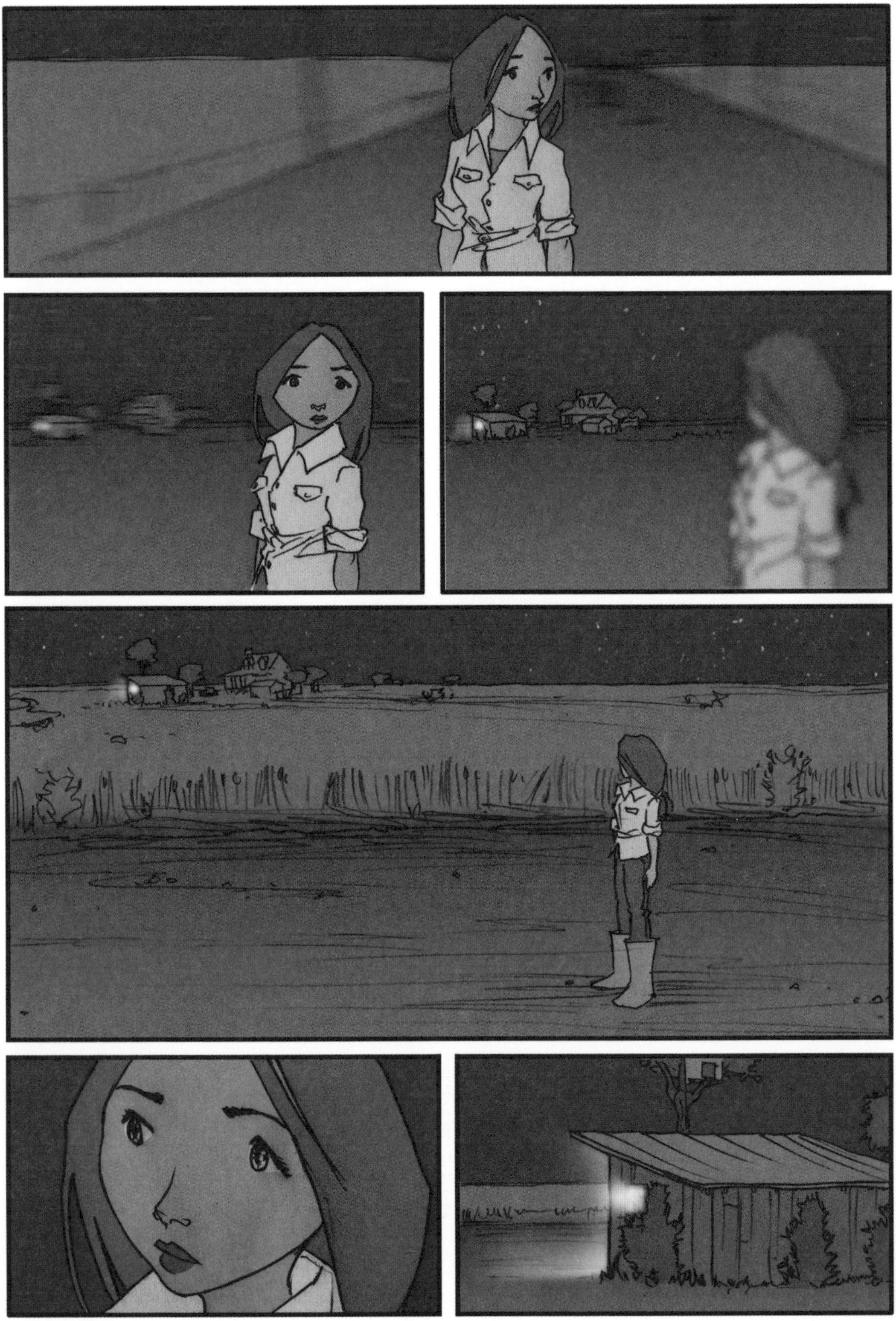

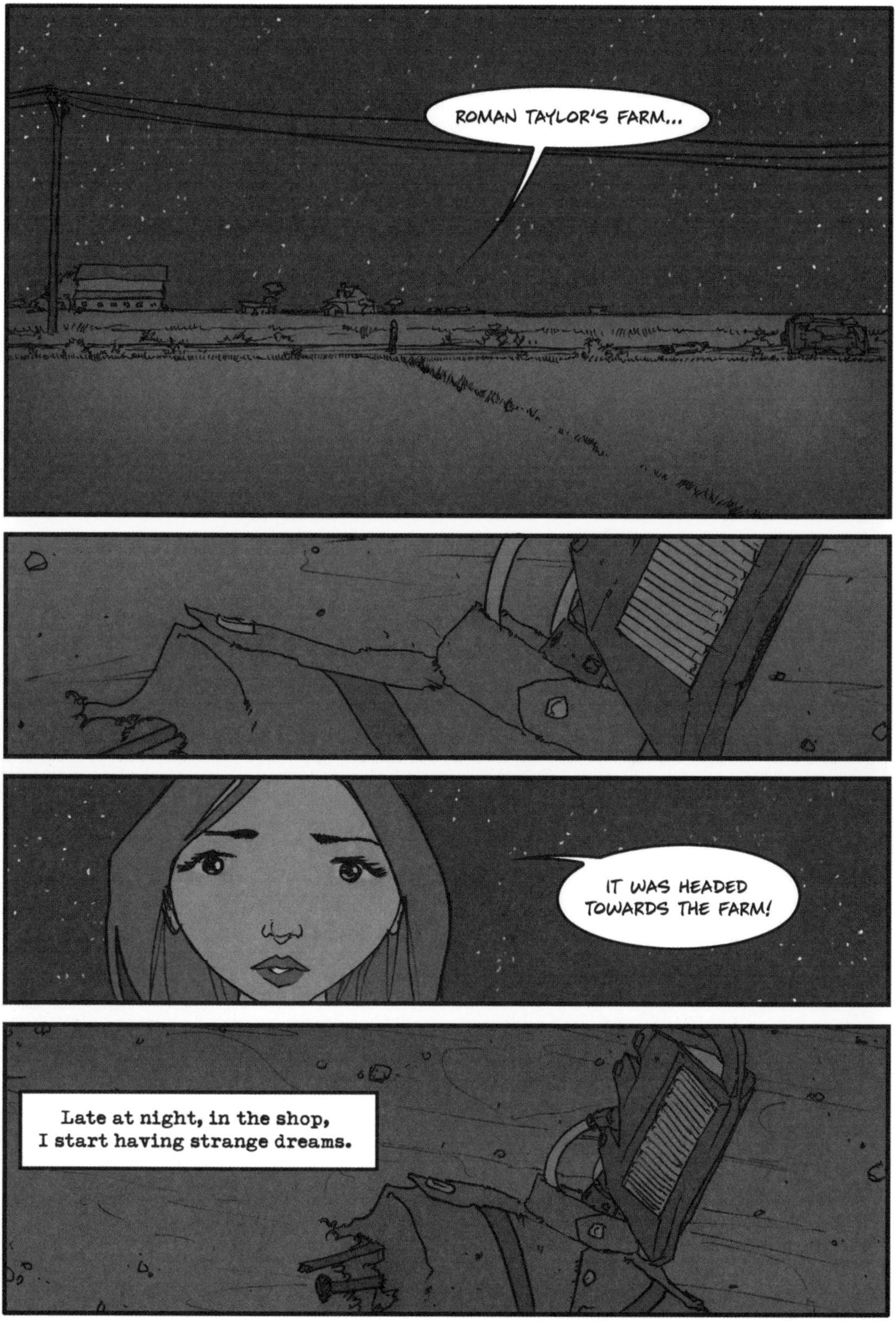
ROMAN TAYLOR'S FARM...
IT WAS HEADED TOWARDS THE FARM!
Late at night, in the shop,
I start having strange dreams.

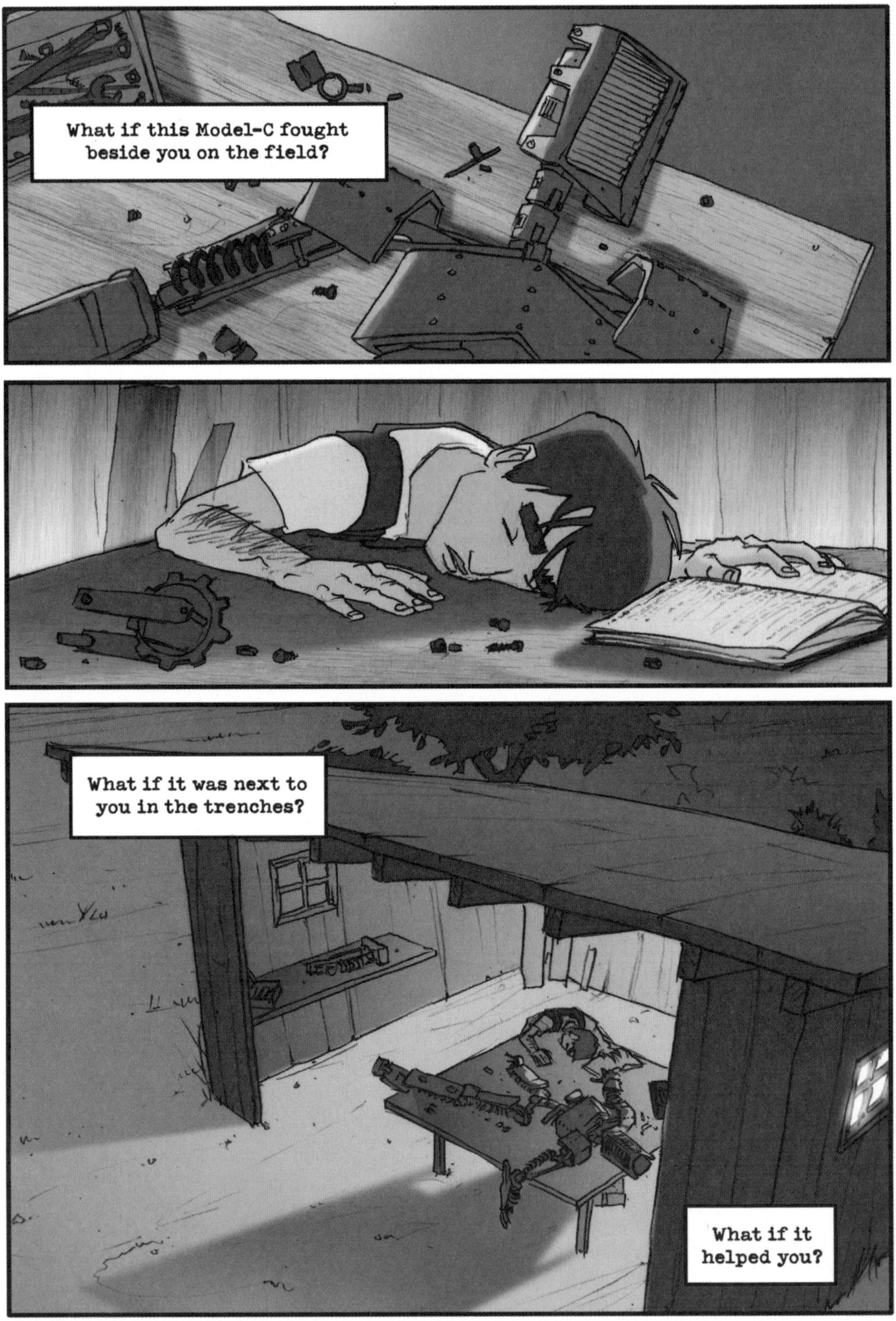
What if this Model-C fought beside you on the field?
What if it was next to you in the trenches?
What if it helped you?

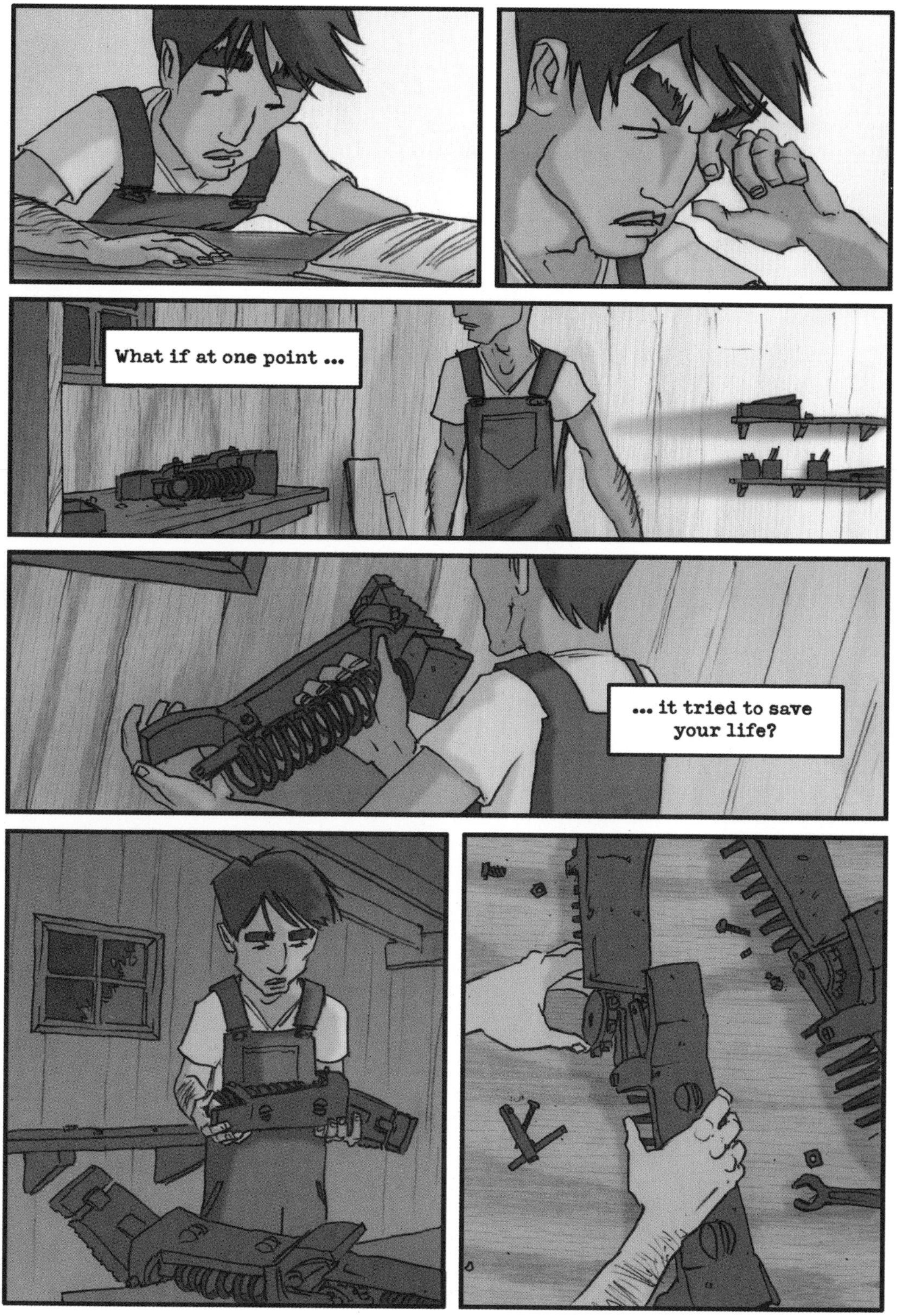
What if at one point ...
... it tried to save your life?

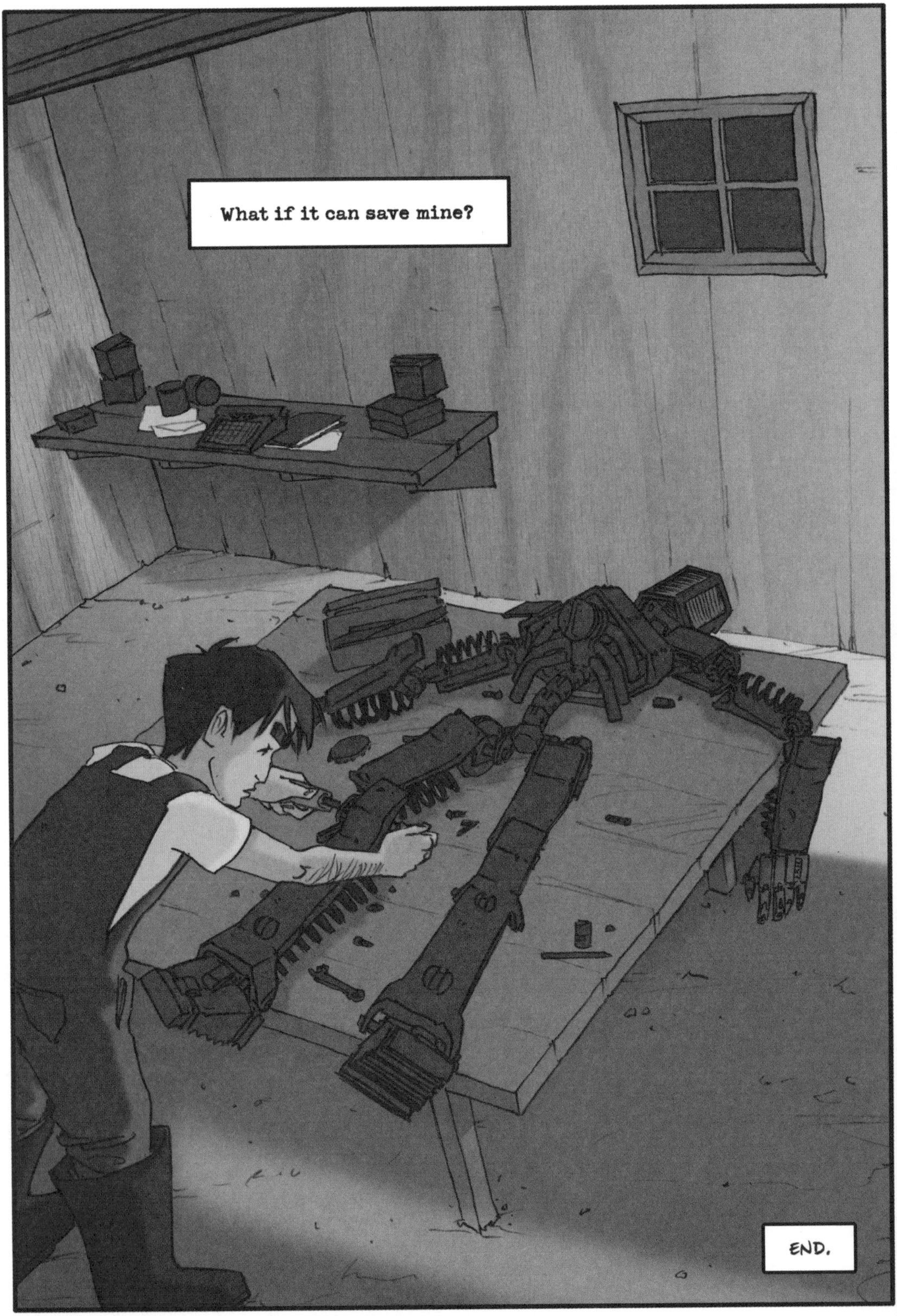
What if it can save mine?
END.

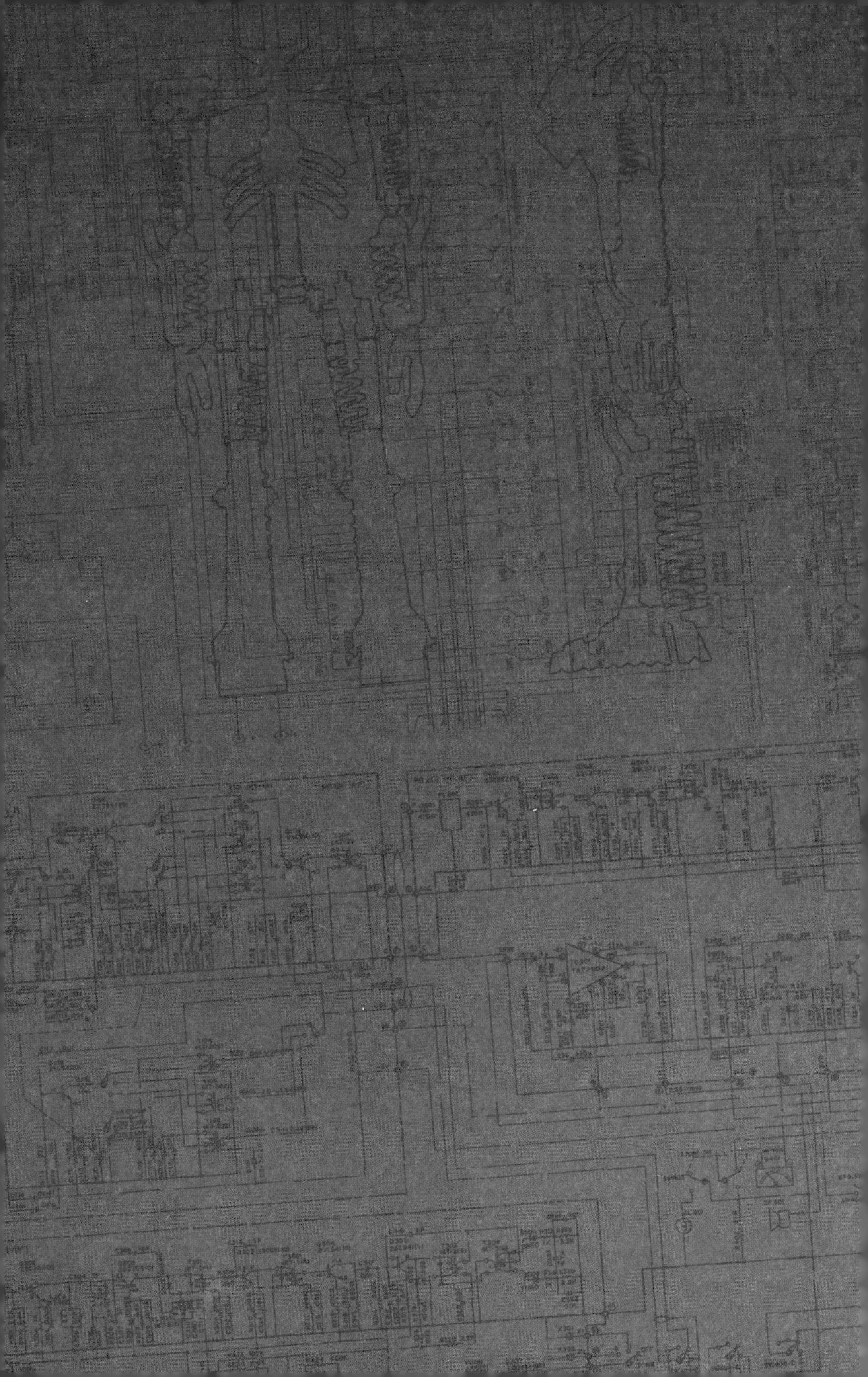

Photos from the
World of Rust

In 2005, my wife gave me a digital SLR camera for my birthday and that began my passionate affair with the shutter and photography. Comics had become my side project to my day job. Eventually photography became my side project to comics. By 2011, I'd been published in several magazines for my wildlife photography and my camera became another tool next to my pencil.

I know there's supposed to be a story behind every photograph but I've taken a lot of photos and that always seems to be more true about the photos I've taken for Rust. They've always involved talking with strangers, sometimes handing them a copy of the book and asking if I can wander around their farm. Each photo represents many other photos and many hours of searching and exploring to find the world of Rust inside our own.

The first shoot was done one evening in my neighbor's backyard, but it was preceded with many weeks spent on Craigslist, meeting people in parking lots selling old typewriters, letters, and stamps from World War II. I scoured eBay for old rusty tools, springs, and tools kits but everything looked too new and shiny. That's where our elderly neighbors Dot and Cliff came in.

Dot had a typewriter from her days working at a bank that was ten times better than the one I'd bought on Craigslist, and Cliff's monkey wrench looked like it was brand new…maybe fifty years ago. Those, along with the vintage envelope collection I borrowed from one of the nicest guys I've ever met on the internet, and a handful of black and white photos of my Dad and my Grandpa on the farm, were plenty to shoot.

Another photo shoot opportunity came when my father-in-law was at a motorcycle swap meet in Canada and saw an old Indian motorcycle. An eight hour drive later, I was pushing a several hundred pound antique Indian into a wheat field with the bike's owner behind me saying, "whatever you do, don't drop it."

My wife, Ruth, always seemed to have the photos in mind. On a drive from our hometown in Canada to Seattle, we passed by an old antique car museum that we'd passed a million times before but she thought that maybe we'd find something interesting inside. We stopped and there were a lot of really cool old antiques. But in the back of the yard was an old truck that had been wrecked. It was away from the "show floor" but not hidden enough. It was rusted and had a shattered windshield. It was beautiful. It reminded me of Jesse hitting the robot on the road outside the Taylor farm. I took so many photos at that museum but the one of the wrecked truck with the broken windshield is still one of my favorites.

The photo shoots have become my way of ending the journey of each volume, by going on a little physical journey out into the country as I look for Roman's barn or his tractor. I look for the steps that lead up into the Taylor's house or the stacks of hay in the yard barn. I still see old motorcycles and locomotives, and sometimes in the stillness of the appendages of a modern day excavator, I see the frozen giant robot in the Taylor field. But without any prodding from Ruth, there is one thing that will always get me to pull over and get out of the car even if I don't have my camera with me, even if I don't really need the photo: a field of tall golden wheat, blowing and bending in the late summer wind.

Royden Lepp

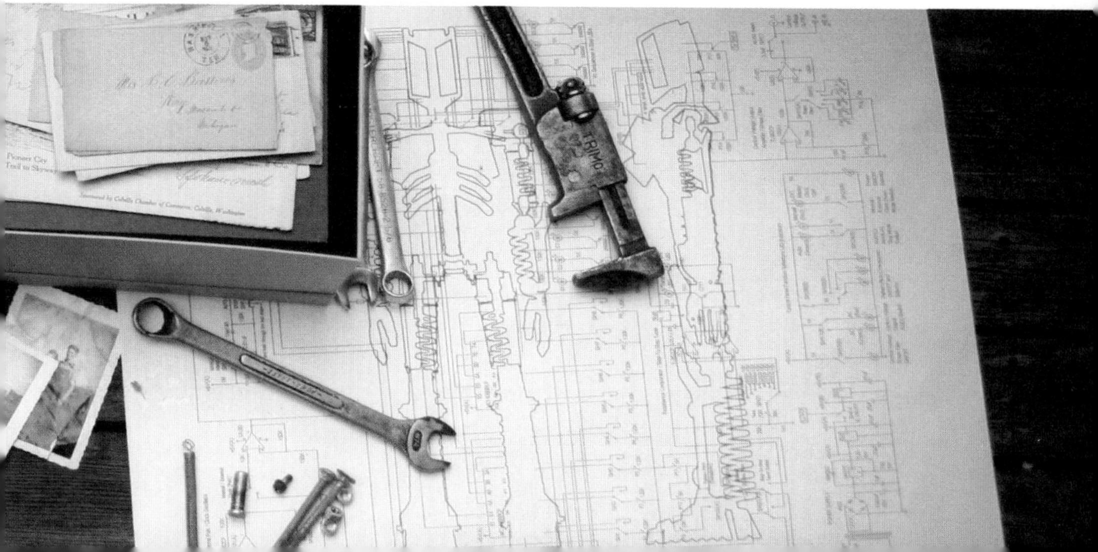
TRIMO

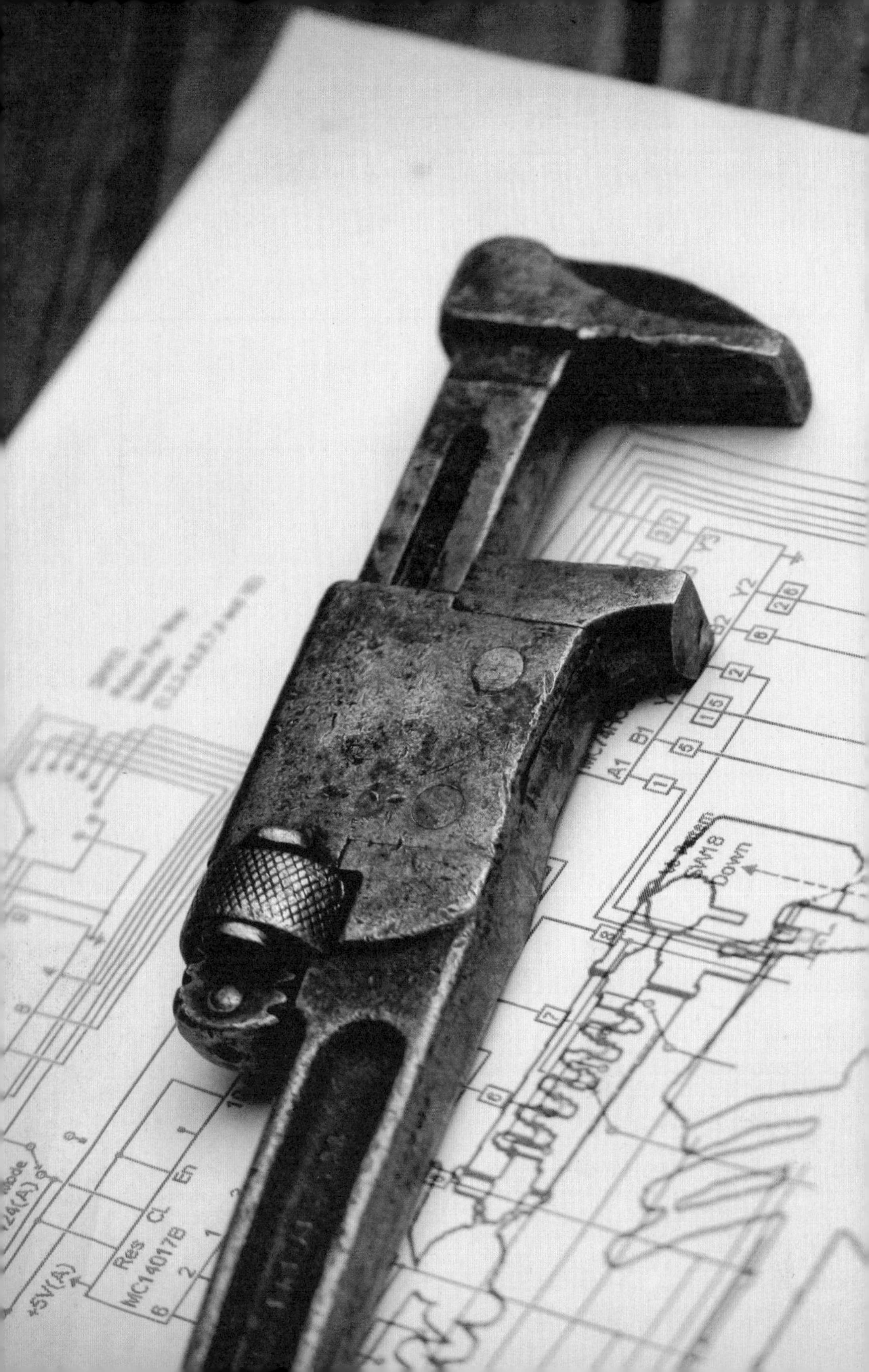

+5V(A)
MC14017B
Res
CL
En
A1
B1
B2
Y2
SW18
Down

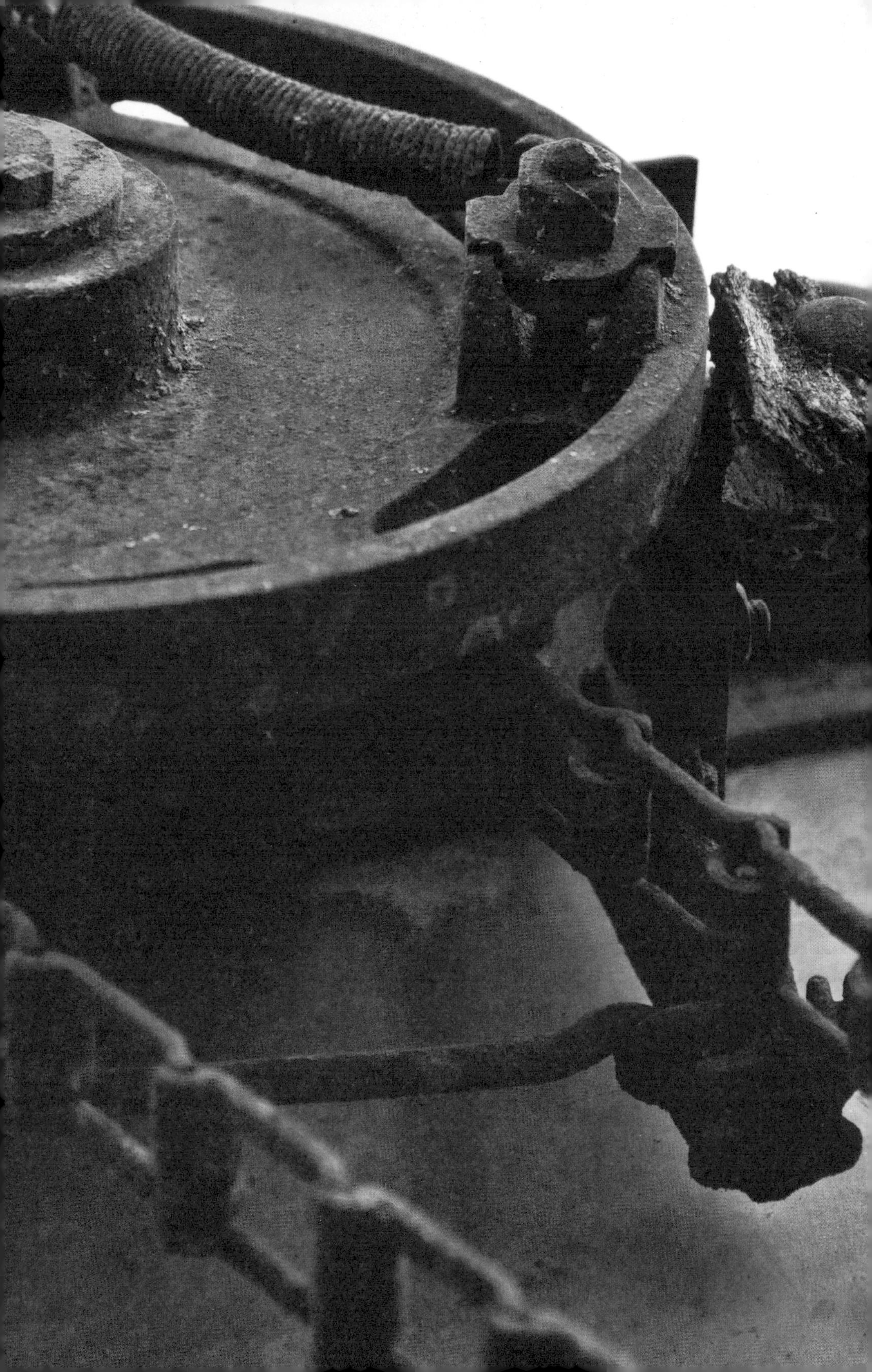

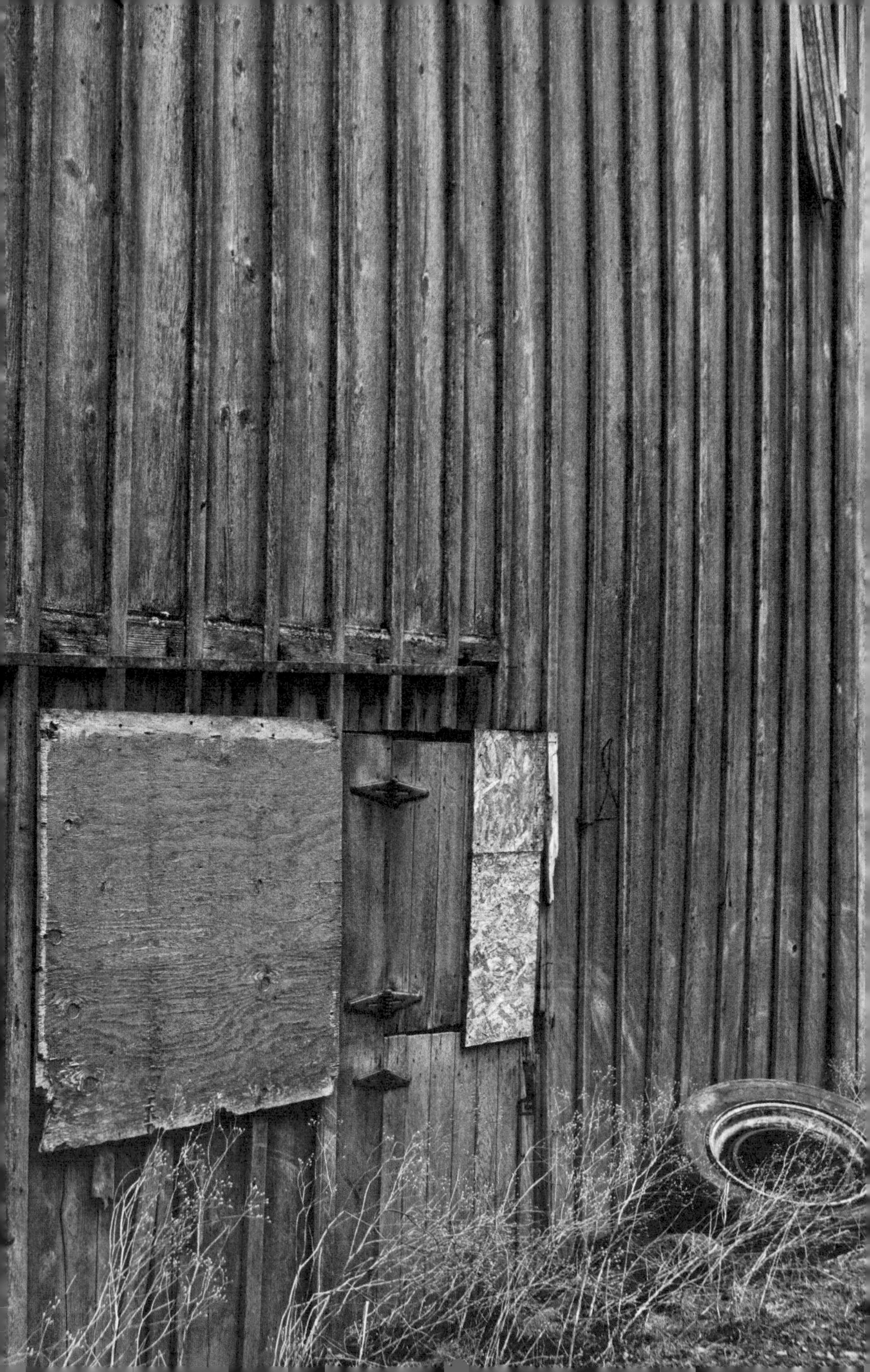

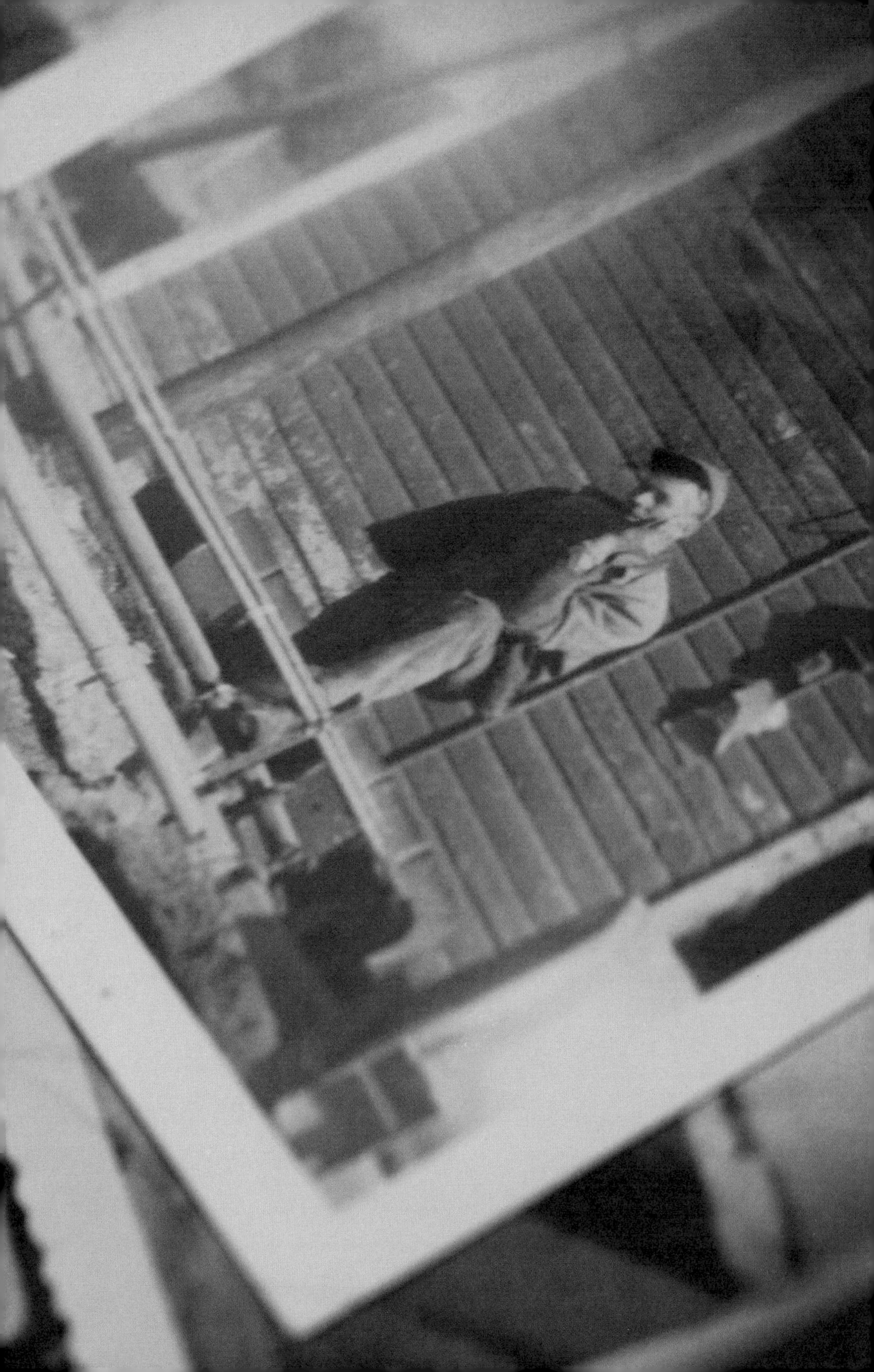

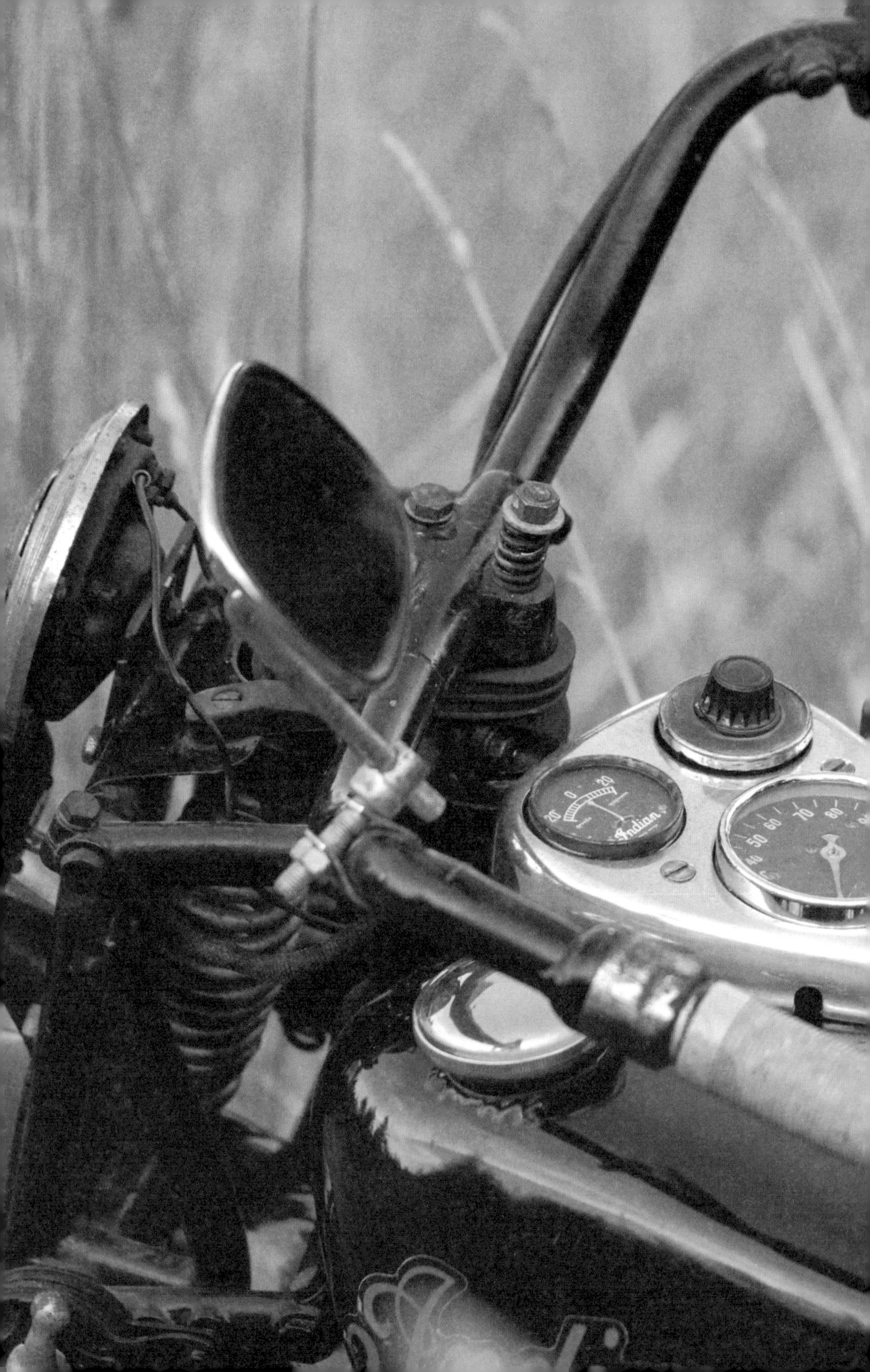
20 0 20
Indian
40 50 60 70 80

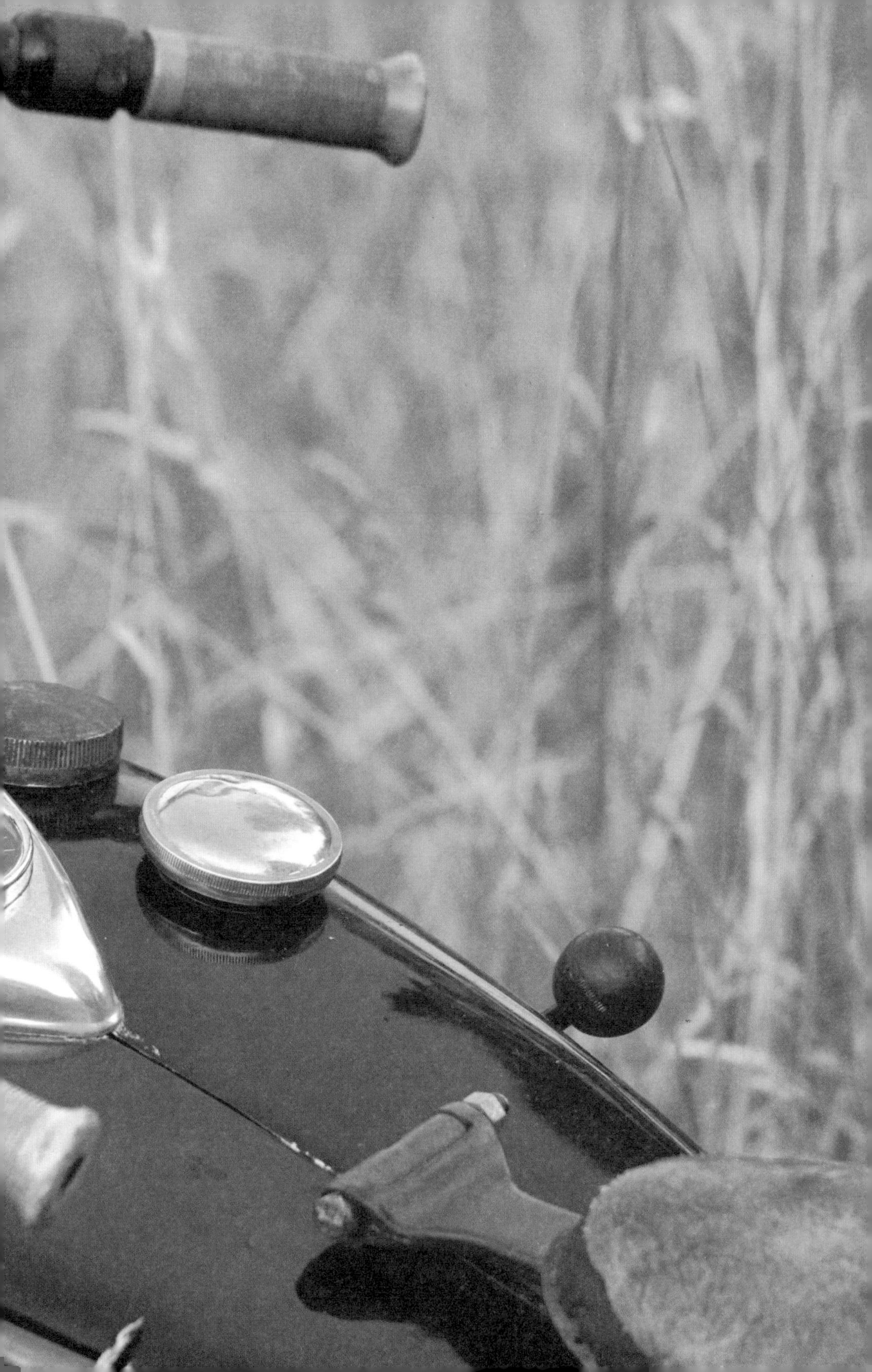

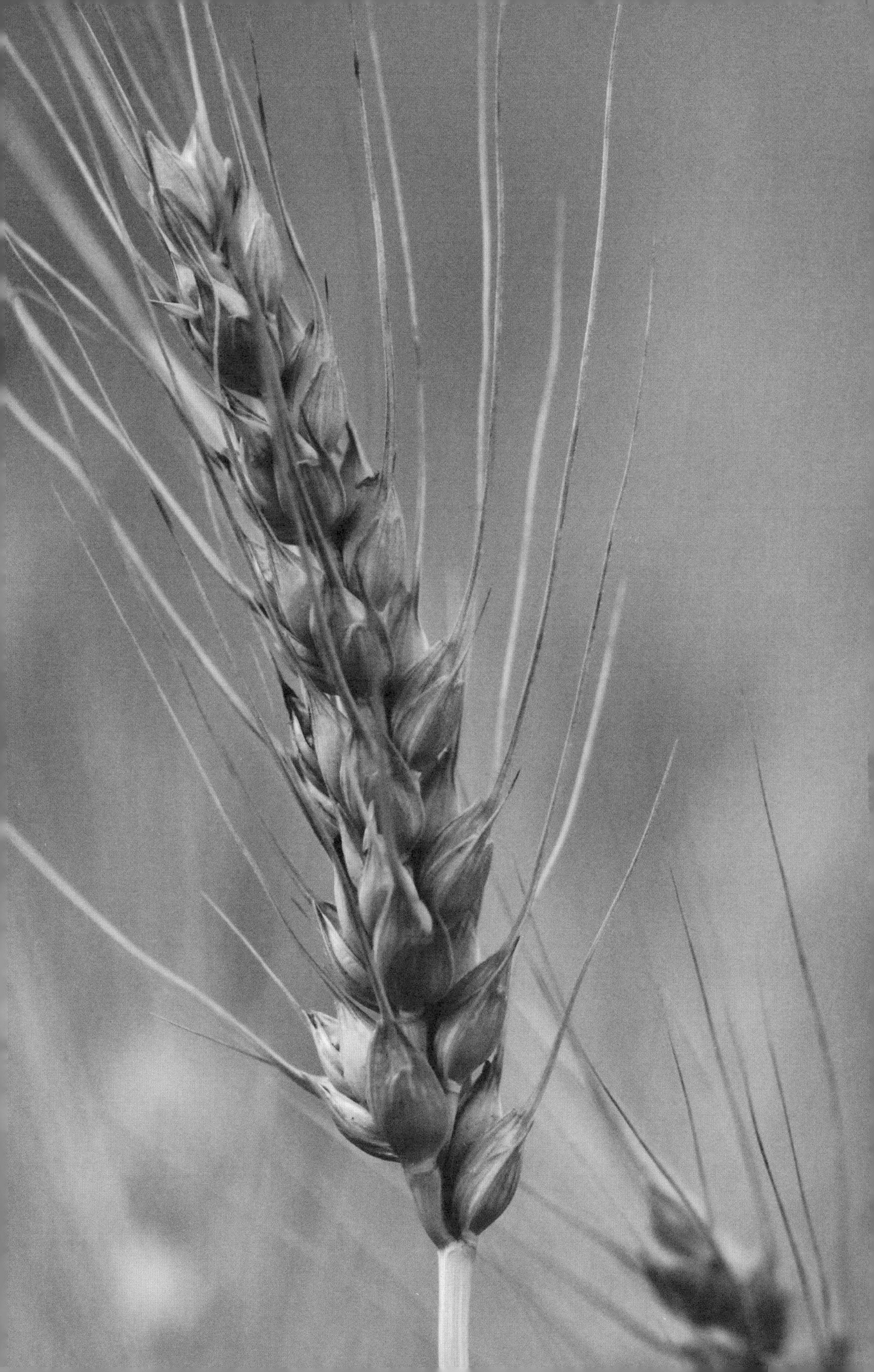

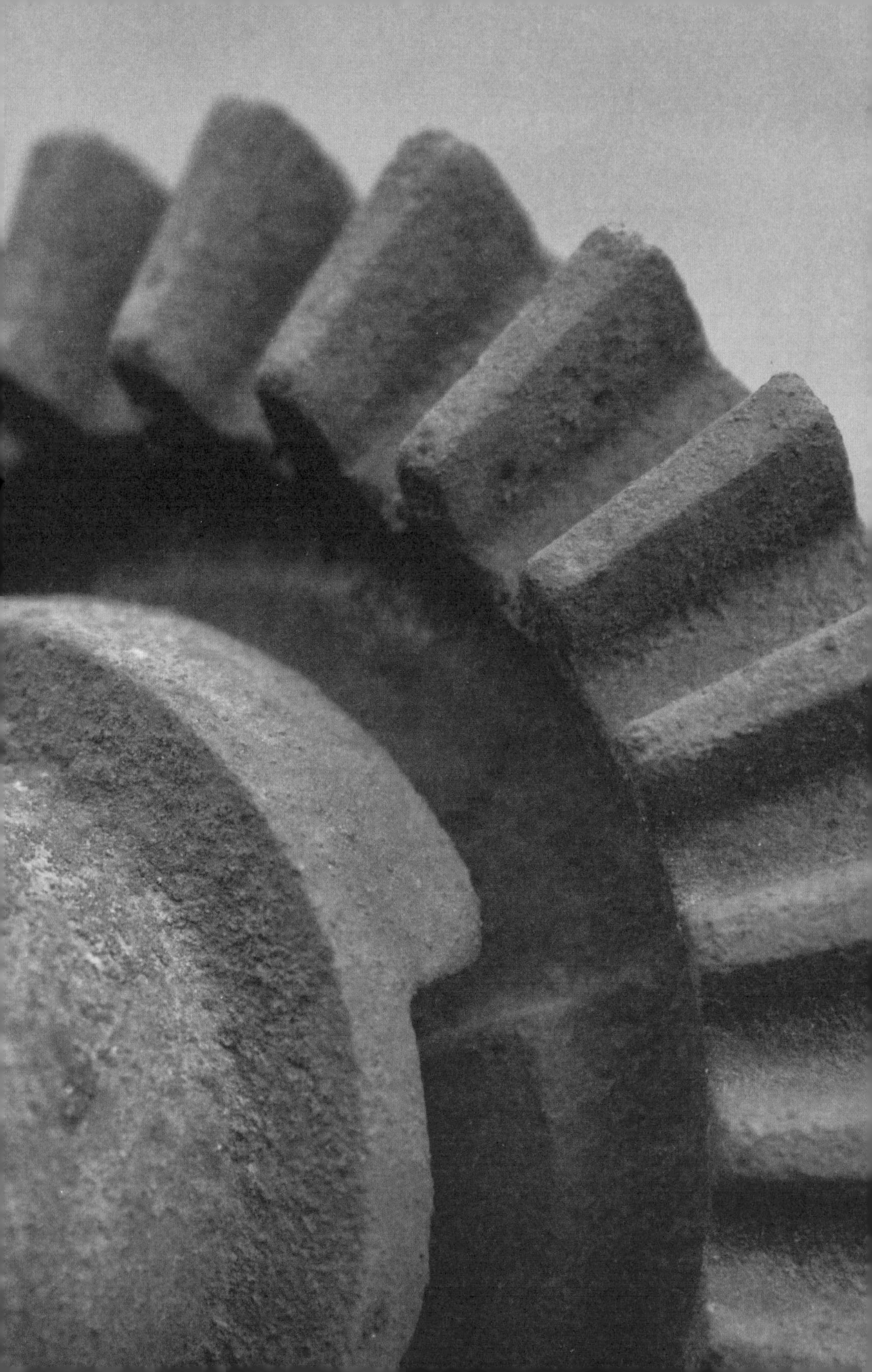

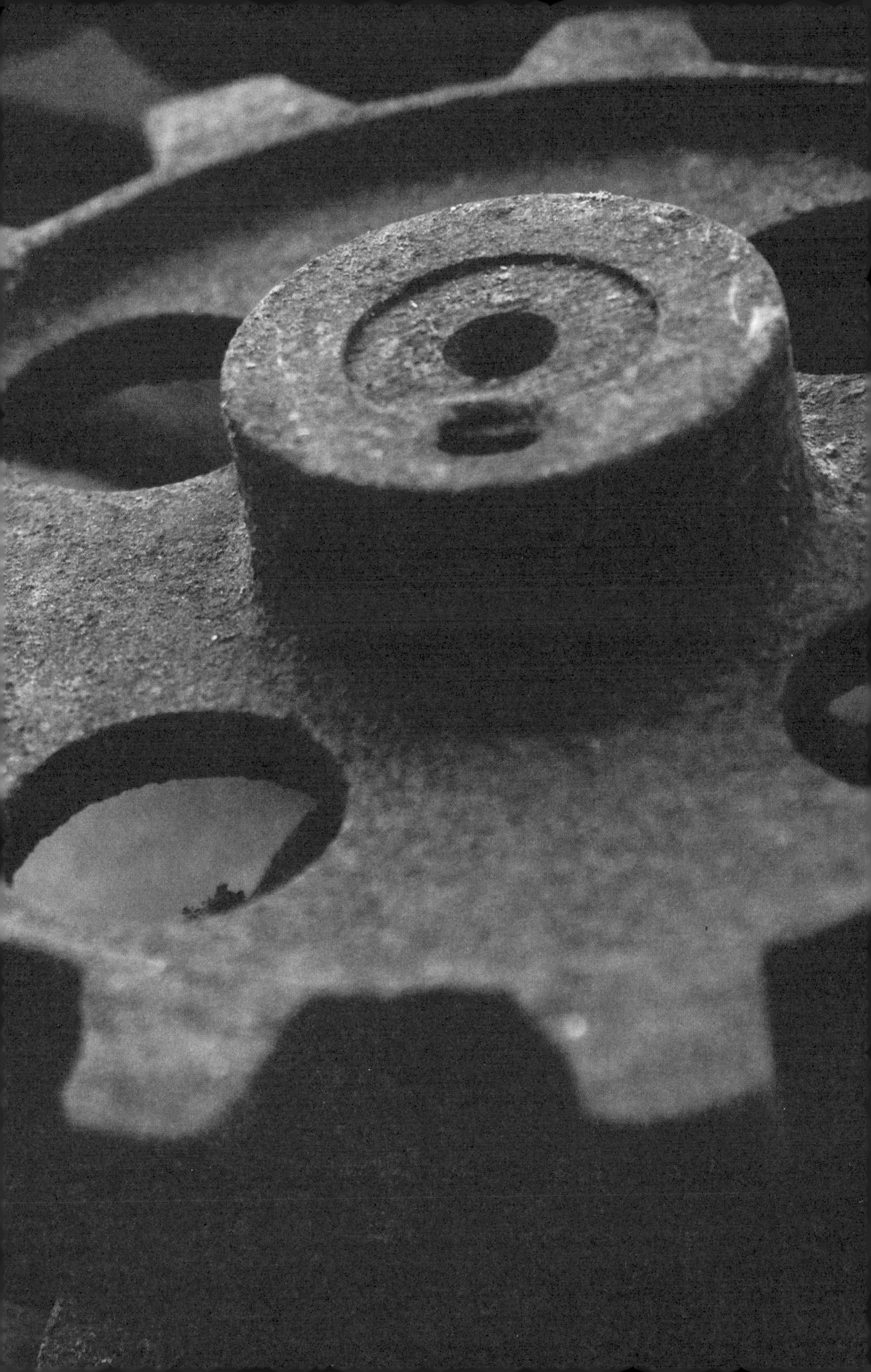

Dear Dad,

How are you? It's

to end. I'm writing

up from a local

whether it wa

start rewri